DINA YAFASOVA

DON'T CALL ME A VICTIM!

I0742412

Published with the support of the Inge
Genefke and Bent Sørensen Anti Torture
Support Foundation

GLAGOSLAV PUBLICATIONS

DON'T CALL ME A VICTIM!

by Dina Yafasova

First published in the Danish language under the title
Kald mig ikke offer! by Gyldendal publishing house

© 2009, Dina Yafasova

Translated from the Russian by Melanie Moore and Clare Kitson

© 2014, Glagoslav Publications, United Kingdom

Glagoslav Publications Ltd
88-90 Hatton Garden
EC1N 8PN London
United Kingdom

www.glagoslav.com

ISBN: 978-1-78437-907-0

CONTENTS

To Inge Genefke and Bent Sørensen,
whom I esteem no less than my own parents,
and whom I consider to be among the greatest humanitarians
of our time — the equals of Mahatma Gandhi and Mother Teresa.

To Inge and Bent, founders of the RCT and IRCT, the first
centres in the world for the treatment and rehabilitation of
torture victims. They chose the heaviest stone, the heaviest among
the very heaviest, and have carried it for thirty-five years.
This book is dedicated to them, to all those
into whom they have breathed
a second life — and those
into whom they
could
not.

"And the heart does not die when one thinks it should."

— *Czeslaw Milosz. Elegy for N.N.*

PROLOGUE

This story stepped straight out of life and into my heart. The events and heroes are drawn from life as far as the fog of the intervening years allowed. If, in order to create a consistent whole, I have had recourse to imagination or, rather, to intuition and logical assumptions based on the available facts, then these were only as much as a pinch of saffron in a pot of pilau big enough to feed a family of ten. I give due credit to real life in this story because, to my immense regret, in this instance real life is richer than any fiction and, indeed, provides the rough draft for literature itself.

And I do mean literature because, although this story was written from eyewitness accounts, I wanted to get away from the documentary form, to escape the shackles of my profession, and do more than merely rehash reality.

There are some lives which cannot be recounted without emotion, without straining every nerve, without engaging every fibre of your being. That would be tantamount to theft. And I don't want to rob anyone of anything, not myself, not the reader, and not the life being recounted. Just as I don't want to avoid the moral, ethical, and philosophical questions that have to be asked and given due consideration. Not to mention that there is one issue in this story, of which to say nothing would be to play dangerous games not just with my own conscience but with society and humanity at large.

It is precisely because I refuse to play these games that I opted for the role of a writer of literature. By doing so, I have retained the storyteller's freedom, her treasured right not just to emotions and intuition, sympathy and antipathy, but also to her own understanding, opinion, and position.

Lastly, I have reserved the right to the artist's gaze, the right to choose my own range of colours and the brushes that helped fill in an outline drawn by the omniscient hand of Him who once upon a time determined that in this life everything — heaven and hell and the bridge between — is possible.

Even when I had couched this story in my own words, often marvelling at the unpredictability, at the twists and turns of human fate, often grieving over the weaknesses and mean-spiritedness of a particular character or thrilling at another's inner fortitude, even when I had ended the story with the long-awaited full stop, which would have been better as dot-dot-dot, I was still mystified as to why I had been the one my heroine trusted with the story of her life and in doing so told me her secret. Her most important secret. Her elixir of life.

It is the sort of secret that more than one generation of engineers of human souls has pursued and will continue to pursue, over which more than one generation of engineers of human thought has racked and will continue to rack its brains. It is easy to understand these hard-working, passionate researchers, whether practitioners or theoreticians. The secret is worth it. It appears to be what keeps our troubled, fragile world going, for *the heart does not die when one thinks it should.*

But why doesn't the heart die? Why not when something akin to death afflicts us? When the circumstances of our life are capable of cutting off our air supply and blocking out the light? When all at once life becomes a series of tribulations? When we enter what seems to be a spell of never-ending bad luck? After all, anything can happen in life. Fate always finds a pretext for showing us not its fine and lovely face but a dreadful, twisted grimace. It also finds a pretext for turning us into victims. But that's not the issue, there's another question. When a day comes that is darker than night, where do we find the strength not to choke on our own pain? Where do we find the strength to rise from the ashes? To live with what has happened? To go on living? To live at all?

The world's greatest minds cannot answer this question and yet my heroine, an ordinary woman of the people, can. She knows the answer. She has demonstrated its truth throughout her life. It is for the sake of that answer that this book has been written.

Even before I began to write, however, the world had heard my heroine's story in brief, in summary, thanks to journalists from Denmark, India, Germany, Japan, the USA, and Britain.

Journalists surrounded her, especially in those troubled years, the 1980s and 90s, at the height of her turbulent fame. A dense ring of journalists surrounded her day after day, year after year, blocking her path, preventing any escape from the prism of public opinion each time this small, shy, modest woman, who was fighting like an Amazon and refusing to surrender even an ounce of her dignity to the powers that be, to her abusers, left court, the human court in which she was naively seeking justice. Journalists, the public, states, relatives, friends, and those who waited in agony to see her fall or even die, all watched to see who would prevail in the age-old struggle, the battle between good and evil that her life had come to embody.

Later on, those journalists came to her one by one for an interview, to write an article or the script for a play to be performed on the amateur stage. To the best of their ability, they each moulded her into either a heroine or a victim. Each of them shaped a legend, using the words, "the first in the world". Because there really are things in which, however pretentious it might sound, she *was* the first in the world. There are enough newspaper and magazine articles about her to fill an encyclopaedia. I spent months reading them. But however much I read, I couldn't find an answer to my question. The heart does not die when one thinks it should. But why not? Why not?

It may be that at the time, in the thick of things, my heroine didn't know the answer or hadn't thought about it. You can see more from a distance. And distance is time as well, if, of course, time can be measured in steps.

I saw her for the first time in 2003 when, weary of all the commotion and the journalists (and keeping out of their way), she was dividing her time quietly and unassumingly between Calcutta and Copenhagen. For three years I observed her from the sidelines since our paths used to cross and my social circle had been boosted by people from hers. Sometimes we met by chance at social events, allowing ourselves to exchange greetings but nothing more. For her, I was just one of many, as she was for me, but then I discovered that in a way experience had made us sisters because at one time the same rope of tragedy had almost strangled us both. As for the rest... The more I learnt about her from the newspaper archives and from friends, the more I was drawn to this person who became no less of an enigma over the years. A life like that deserved a book, not just articles. Perhaps even more than one. I made my decision.

In 2006, I rang her up. I said, "I know, if not all the legend, then most of it and we don't need any more. I'm not interested in the image, in the media chorus, but in the *person*. Only a real person can give me a real answer to the issue that interests me more than anything else."

"Do you think there's any point stirring up the past?" she asked, thoughtfully, over the phone as she mulled over my proposal.

"Yes, yes, I do," I replied. "Because there are other people who've been through the same thing. And their number is growing rather than falling as the years go by. Time passes but these people carry on living a past they never asked for. They can't break out ... into the light... They need... not instructions, perhaps... but guidelines."

"Alright then, if only for their sake," she said.

We met in the café at Copenhagen University Hospital. She suggested it herself. It was easy for her to get there.

It was June. She arrived, wearing a sari the colour of the light summer sky, the colour of periwinkles. She trod lightly and slowly, limping slightly. She spoke little and softly, her smile broad, and listened, and listened.

Trays in hand, we stood in a long queue at the counter, taking one another's measure, mentally putting out feelers, getting used to one another. Without prior agreement, we went for the same thing — an open sandwich, topped with cheese and rings of sweet red pepper. She politely declined my offer to pay for us both. We sat down at a table and ate our lunch without knives and forks, without ceremony, drinking our tea through lumps of sugar. Then she stirred milk into hers, pouring it in a stream from its little cardboard tub while I, with her permission, signed a copy of my first book, *Sandholm Diary*. Sipping her milky tea, she turned the pages, quickly and impassively, lingering perhaps on the two-line epigraph to the first chapter and my photo on the cover which — and for this, thank the photographer — was far better than the original.

"Yes," she said. "Inge and Bent told me. You and I are like family. Which means we'll be talking about *that* as well... I believe you'll understand. I really need to tell someone about it ... about everything. Especially as this will be the last time. There are things the journalists don't know about."

And this was the signal that I could open my new notebook, to which I had, as usual, stuck a four-leafed clover so that at least there was some sign of life on the thick, black cover. Then and there, in front of her, I wrote down the date, time and place of the first entry. Watching the movement of my pen, she asked once more:

"Do you really want to hear all this? Even just listening isn't so easy..."

I said I did.

"Alright, but on one condition. Once I've got it all out, I don't want any interviews or photos in the papers."

I agreed, saying nothing, just nodding, although how could I promise? There are lives that become public property whether we like it or not. Her life was one of those.

And so this story began.

When our conversations came to an end six months later, I set about transcribing the recordings and going through my notebook, or rather notebooks, of which there were seven by then, all densely covered in writing. On one page, I found the answer to the question that interested me most of all.

I read it over and over many times. Each time the intonation was different and new aspects emerged, but its meaning and significance remained the same. I was now even more certain that I could not keep knowledge of this kind to myself or hide it away in a drawer. My heroine agreed. I am therefore passing this knowledge on to you. Please pass it on again to those who need it most. There is no shortage of them…

Yours faithfully,
   Dina Yafasova

PART ONE

Punishment Without a Crime

You who are weary, downcast and bruised, you who fall, who think perhaps that you are defeated, hear the voice of a friend. He knows your sorrows, he has shared them, he has suffered like you from the ills of the earth; like you he has crossed many deserts under the burden of the day, he has known thirst and hunger, solitude, and abandonment, and the cruellest of all wants, the destitution of the heart. Alas! he has known too the hours of doubt, the errors, the faults, the failings, every weakness. But he tells you: Courage! Hearken to the lesson that the rising sun brings to the earth with its first rays each morning. It is a lesson of hope, a message of solace."

The Mother

Chapter I
The Triangle

Archana. Her name is Archana. Three syllables, seven letters. The stress is on the first "A" but it's pronounced "O". Archana. Orchana. Or-cha-na.

But she had other names too.

She was Sonali in her barefoot childhood, which sped past in ringing laughter on the ancient banks of the Ganges. She was Sona in her diligent years at school, her loose fringe exposing a moist, stubborn forehead. To her loving mother, she was always Sunu and her little brother, tenderly, called her Sezdi. To her little sister she was the strict Sundi. Her colleagues at work used the sisterly Archana-ji. Her pupils respectfully called her didi. On the deep blue of official forms she was Archana Guha. To the rest of the world she was Arkana, a "k" there by mistake, breaking the flow of the word, rather than a melodious "ch", and the stress moved a syllable forward.

To me she is just Archana. Ar. Cha. Na. The initial "A" surprisingly long, like the note of a song. Like a mantra. Like an incantation. Like a mystery to be solved. Like the woman herself, who never ceases to amaze me. How on earth did she do what she did?

Runu. His name is Runu. Two syllables, four letters, and the stress on the final "u". The pronunciation cold like that final "u".

Runu. Ru-nu. Ru. Nu.

Although he had other names too.

To his loving mother he was "khoka". He was "master" to his wife and "Babu" to his son and daughter. He was "Mister" or

"Sir" to his subordinates. His birth certificate in 1935 recorded him as Ranajit Guha Niyogi. To the rest of the world he was simply Runu. Police Officer Runu. As broad as a barn door, he was quite a sight. I wish I'd never laid eyes on him.

And there was a third person too. Someone else. Or rather two others who acted as one.

For that reason, I'm not giving the name. Not just yet. I'm getting bogged down in these riddles myself — which of these two... Anyway, you'll work it all out for yourself as the story unfolds.

And there you have it, our triangle. If we abide by the rules of the genre, one party has to suffer, another to inflict suffering, and the third to come to the rescue. We won't rush to allocate the roles, however. It's really not important to us even if it seems all too obvious. After all, this isn't the theatre. This is the human jungle where black and white are part of the same continuum. Everything could go any way...

Does the story have other heroes too? Of course, it does. As many as you like. It couldn't be otherwise. Without some of them, there would be no story. Without others, there would be no life.

So, let's begin.

Roll up, roll up, visitors to the fairground of human life! What spectacles we have in store for you! Life itself is quite a spectacle and if, in addition, it tries to communicate with the person who lives it in the only language it knows, there is good reason to believe that their passage through life on earth will not have been a waste of time.

Chapter 2
The Tilak Mark

Archana was born in 1941 at the time of the June monsoons and the height of the rainy season, when Nature was amusing itself in its own unique fashion, effortlessly blending the three worlds of the earth, its inner depths, and the sky into one explosive mixture, and orchestrating an encounter between light and dark.

Her great-grandfather, a man of Bengali descent and Hindu faith, was a prominent landowner in Faridpur District, in what was then eastern Bengal, later to become East Bengal, then East Pakistan, and is now Bangladesh. At that time, however, many moons ago, the borders were different and all points on the map were India — British India.

As the eldest son, Archana's grandfather, Lalit Chandra Guha, stood to inherit his father's land. He would inherit and would also maintain his family's traditions in order to increase its wealth year by year, or at least not to lose it. As it turned out, however, farming was the least of his interests. This newly-minted Bangladeshi disposed of his inheritance like a lord, taking no thought for the future as he made his fortune over to relatives. They too treated his gift with indifference. What's more, when this became apparent, Lalit Chandra Guha was far away, or rather high up, up in the eastern Himalayas, and not just in any old place but in Darjeeling, the most peaceful part of India, where even the human pulse kept time with the silence. He had enlisted with the British, securing a position as a clerk in the forestry department where he worked until he took his pension and never regretted his choice. He lived well but without luxury. Bengalis would say he always had enough salt in his food. He didn't accumulate possessions. He was content in rented accommodation and from its threshold would contemplate the world beneath his feet and eternity above his head. What more was there to do?

His wife, a wilful woman with hints of the major-general in her voice, took children and husband in hand and taught them always to walk on eggshells. She had one particular characteristic: she idolized everything European. Lychee juice came in delicately worked glasses, tea with sugar and always at five o'clock. Her hairstyle was layered like a society lady's, her chats with a friend sprinkled with foreign words: "This is the life, my dear," "Oh, how shocking!" "Don't you agree?" "Certainly, certainly."

With the enviable doggedness of a woman who could remake the world to match a new sari, she nagged her husband for not having learnt to wear European clothes in all his years of work in a British office. Even when he did, it wasn't with real style but purely for work reasons. Deep in her power-hungry soul, she dreamt of her husband looking, even on his days off, like the gentlemen-sahibs who smelt of mists, damp tweed, and tobacco, of their standing in society, and a perfumed prosperity unknown to them as Bengalis, and were able to sit on benches with "No Indians Allowed" signs.

Archana's father, Nalini Ranjan Guha, grew up in Darjeeling. His parents took care to see that his manners, clothes, and university degree, everything about him, spoke of a nice young man. At twenty-six, Nalini Ranjan married fourteen-year-old Sudharani. His bride's eyes were the colour of northern nights, her skin the colour of southern days. A native of east Bengal, she was from the same clan — the Kayastha Kshatriya caste. She even grew up in his aunt's family.

It just so happened that his aunt, who was widowed shortly after her wedding, before she had time to produce children, undertook to bring up her sister's little girl. She devised this wedding between her nephew and niece, who were not related by blood, to suit herself in her haste to cushion the onset of old age. Nalini Ranjan's parents objected to their son's choice. They could not understand why he was suddenly and so quickly in cahoots with his aunt. The Guha family thought themselves terribly clever. Their future daughter-in-law was their equal in terms of caste but she lacked education. The would-be groom, however, had the strength to stick to his guns and his parents gave in, albeit not immediately.

It was a marriage in every sense, with the added bonus of money by way of a dowry and a youthful bride. It was an arranged marriage not a love match. Although, tell me, what is love? Can it really not shed its gentle, meditative light on hands joined together by quick-thinking relatives?

After the wedding, Nalini Ranjan and Sudharani settled first in Calcutta and then on its outskirts in Howrah. They didn't neglect their relatives, occasionally travelling to Darjeeling or the eastern part of Bengal. It was on one of these trips, in the east, in the hamlet of Chadpatti that Archana was born. Before collapsing unconscious from loss of blood, her mother anxiously counted the baby's tiny fingers and toes, and cautiously ran a finger from her nose to her chin, feeling the neat little folds around the greedy button of a mouth. Finding no physical defects, no cleft palate or hare lip, she was content to hand the infant over to the care of a relative.

The baby was taken back to Howrah even before she could support her own head. No horoscope was drawn up although many Bengali families were crazy about the practice. But no, it wasn't a Guha tradition. Archana's father didn't believe in a fate foretold in the stars or perhaps simply couldn't bring himself to look into the future for he knew what lay in store. "Life is not a bed of roses," was a favourite, time-soured adage that he loved to repeat. Her father believed in something else, neither superstition nor the gods.

Meanwhile, time moved fatefully on. Far away, beyond the seven seas and thirty rivers, as Bengalis say, a world war raged and gathered pace. Germany had conquered Eastern Europe and was storming towards the Soviet Union. Japan had not yet attacked the United States (that was still six months away) but was steadily pressing its advance on South-East Asia. At the same time, Gandhi's pacifist speeches were encouraging non-violent resistance to evil. Even in the event of a Japanese attack on India, Gandhi would have preached the same thing in order to avoid millions of casualties. The world order could no longer be what it had been before the war. India remained a British colony but had woken up and realized that freedom could come at any time. There was a premonition of bloodshed. Politicians began to talk of partitioning the country because of the different religions.

And yes, all in all, these disasters did catch up with Archana. Soon after she was born, her family lost its chance to go home: Bengal was split into East and West. In 1947 India itself achieved independence and partition with Pakistan. It came with wholesale slaughter. The exchange of millions of people (as Hindus headed for an India they had never seen and the Muslim minority tried to leave for Pakistan) plunged India, now two countries, into chaos and destitution. Interesting times for historians, terrible times for humanity.

The descendants of the unsuccessful farmer led a middle-class existence. Archana's father was a teacher. He taught maths, physics, and chemistry in a college in Howrah but, as the years went by, he preferred to give private lessons, and ultimately confined himself to a group of students that he taught in his own home. He was one of the most popular teachers in town. People asked for him, sought him out. There was enormous respect for him and his family, although it never made them wealthy. He had a time-worn wooden trunk that contained two simple dhotis — in white and saffron cotton. He had no need of more.

Archana's mother, from the time her husband applied red

sindoor to the parting in her hair, had been a selfless recluse and housewife. She gave birth to seven children, at intervals of two to three years — her seven living diamonds to be protected from illness and taught to love virtue and fear sin. She never once left the house on her own, never took the bus, or rode in a rickshaw. She never once walked through the bazaar although the Guhas rented a house on a very lively street with a huddle of stalls right outside. But no, and not just because it was still rare for a woman to be abroad in the streets of Howrah without a brother, father, or husband. It was not something Sudharani wanted. Her home was her whole world and all that lay outside its walls seemed to her as remote as the Andaman Islands.

If you think, however, that this marriage of a scholar and a housewife was not happy, you understand nothing about Indian practices. These are precisely the type of marriages set out in the veda verses: "He is right, She is duty … He is sun, she is glory … He is wind, She is motion … He is lamp, She is light, He is song, she is note …"

And I dare say that, yes, her main note was respect for her husband. Everything her husband suggested, came up with, or actually did, Archana's mother accepted with a trust and deference not every woman would understand. She accepted and was happy with that. Her placid, unassuming nature sometimes astounded even her female friends, who couldn't understand why Sudharani was so unnaturally indifferent to all the celebrated objects — muslin saris, silk cholis, gold trinkets — of which many Bengali women were so enamoured that they became skilled in the millennium-old art of pestering and befuddling their beloved husbands. Was she overly pious? It seems not. She was not seen to have any particular ties to religion. The entire collection of Sudharani's sins was limited to keeping some of the children's naughtiness and misbehaviour from her husband. Add to that a few outbursts of anger and a single conversation with her husband in an uncharacteristically raised and impatient voice, with tears in her eyes and fire in her words so that it seemed the earth had turned upside down. But let's not get ahead of ourselves.

As well as Archana, who was the fifth child, there were three other girls in the family — Monobina, Smriti and Anjali — and three boys — Sibendra, Ramendra, and Saumen.

It is worth noting that Bengali parents rarely call a child by its name. Names on official forms are intended for the outside world. Within the family, children and, indeed, adults are showered with nicknames — they are their constant companions. I am not going to use them, however, to avoid confusion and panic over this polyphony among non-Bengali readers. The only exception will be Smriti whom everyone knew as Emmy, so that's what I'll call her too.

Apart from the oldest sister, Monobina — who married when she was only just fifteen and went to live with her husband — brothers and sisters, mother and father, all eight of them, lived together as one organism, cramped and sweltering, but harmonious. The older children were responsible for the ones in the middle, and the ones in the middle for the little ones. When the little ones grew up, it would be their duty to follow in their elder siblings' footsteps and provide for their parents in their old age. Many families will recognize themselves if they take a careful look at this verbal portrait (and there were no others at the time) of the Guha family.

* * *

The house the Guhas rented on the busy Kashundia Road, where they spent their best 24 years, consisted of two bedrooms, a kitchen that was the first room entered from the street, and a small extension to the kitchen, screened off with plywood, and converted into their father's study. He effectively lived there, sitting up late at night, in the liquid light of an oil lamp, devoting himself to his main love — to learning, to studying books and commentaries in Sanskrit and English.

Their mother lived in the old way in the women's part of the house, which consisted of just one room — the bedroom she shared with Emmy, Archana, and Anjali. In the middle, a vast bed stood on carved elephant legs. They slept together, one beside the other, deciding in advance who would lie next to their mother. They went to bed at ten and were up at five. During the day, the bed was covered in a hand-embroidered bedspread of heavy cotton. It was where they sat, legs stretched out or crossed in a half-lotus, where they studied, read, and talked.

The men's half of the house also consisted of a single room, inhabited by the three brothers, Sibendra, Ramendra, and Saumen. The bed was just as big but there were books along the wall from floor to ceiling — their father's books. On week days the boys' bedroom became the students' classroom. The students, five to eight boys, arrived after breakfast and took their seats on padded mattresses. Then Father came in. They all folded their hands in front of their chests and humbly bowed their heads as they muttered their greeting, "Namaskar," and the lesson began.

The thin shingle roof bowed almost low enough to touch the family's heads and was not always able to protect the house from the devilry of the natural world. There were times during the rainy season when a trickle of water would snake its way into the room and, by night-time, would be a fountain, gushing rudely in. At these times, their father would rise from his textbooks, stretch his hands to the roof, and wait until they overflowed with water. Then, with a "donnobat" (thank you), he would wash his face, chest, and shoulders in the heavenly bounty that had been cast unbidden on the house.

Their mother was less hospitable towards these seasonal adversities. She stayed up, enlisting the help of her simple household utensils. When the water in one pan threatened to overflow, she made a sprightly run for the kitchen, although "run" is overdoing it: it took only three strides to be out of one room and into the other. On the earth floor and in the dark (there was no electricity), she felt among the tins and packets of rice and curry for the bowl of vegetables, worked it free, and used it to replace the pan. The contents of the pan went out of the window through the iron bars that protected the house from burglars. There were no window panes or shutters, just wasp screens. On nights like this, Archana would lie under the weeping roof, her imagination vivid: an elephant in heaven was squirting water from its trunk, making the rain fall on the earth and the houses.

But then how munificent a sun greeted the morning after such a stormy night! Even the town dogs, scruffy, lazy, and cowardly, were emboldened and crept out of all the nooks and crannies of the bazaar, blinking in the bright light. They grinned contentedly and basked shamelessly at the side of the road, stretching their spindly, flea-bitten paws, and airing the sodden skin that covered their mouldering bones. Small boys raced past along the street, which was running with water. They screeched like a flock of parrots, vying with one another as they begged their friend and leader of the pack for an object much coveted in small boys' games: a wheel with a worn tyre bowled along with a wooden stick.

On days like these, the Guhas' mother would summon all her children and, squatting in a circle, they would all indulge in the well-known game of airing and drying their father's books, a dozen hands (and that's more than the Goddess Durga) flattening the damp and swollen pages. The little ones sniffled with colds, giggling and listening to their elders. The latter discussed which of Durga's daughters would be their statue for that autumn's Puja festival. According to legend, Durga had two daughters — Lakshmi and Saraswati. Lakshmi served to attract wealth, was depicted as a heavenly ideal and regarded as the goddess of all things — beauty, abundance, happiness. Saraswati, goddess of learning and wisdom, by contrast, was extremely modest, pale, her skin clear, her only jewellery a small string of pearls. Year after year and by consensus, it was only ever an earthenware figure of Saraswati that was solemnly borne into their home.

How many of Archana's memories were bound up with Puja! Every year, when autumn arrived, her father set off to the bazaar to buy clothes for the children. There was not much money and sometimes none at all if the flow of students had temporarily dried up. For reasons of economy, Father would chose the clothes at the bazaar himself. Sometimes he took their mother along but she merely observed him make the purchase without getting involved or giving advice. When they got home, Father would open the bag and without looking would say: "So, this one's for Emmy." The next would be for Archana and the third for Anjali. And it turned out — always — that Archana did not like her sari. Either the colour was wrong or the cut. She would call for help from her older brother, Sibendra. He had been her chief adviser, even on matters of fashion, since childhood.

"Sibendra, tell me, which of these three saris do you like the most?

"Well, this one!" Sibendra offered.

"Me too. But that one isn't mine. This is! What should I do?"

Only now cottoning on to what was happening and thinking on his feet, Sibendra quickly revised his opinion, even before Archana could begin to cry.

"I was only joking, silly. I just wanted to see what you'd say. To be honest, this sari's the best. Yours! Look how it goes with your hair! And your eyes! It really sets off your eyes!"

Slightly taken aback, Archana immediately went over to the mirror and tried to see with her brother's eyes. Gradually, she changed her opinion, melting and smiling. Yes, of course, Sibendra was right. How had she failed to see it herself?

When there was rather more money, the clothes were ordered from a tailor. He would come to the house with samples of material. Their father never got involved in colours, textures, or cut, just immediately bought twenty metres of the same fabric for all his daughters. It worked out cheaper. Archana was bubbling with rage but didn't dare challenge her father. Once, she couldn't bear it and rushed off to seek sympathy from Sibendra. Her brother, who was already doing odd jobs to earn money and had saved a few coins, came to her rescue for the umpteenth time. Sibendra bought some fabric Archana had chosen. Too embarrassed to speak to the tailor directly, Archana fled into the women's room and from behind the door, called out, grateful and enraptured, her feelings overflowing in exclamations:

"Sibendra! Listen carefully! I need a dress! Tell the tailor it needs to be slim-fitting and cut to fit. With buttons, here, here, and here... Tell the tailor, it's got to have a round neckline! Definitely not an oval one! And we'll make the skirt from two different fabrics! Yes! And no gathers at the waist! Sibendra! Can you hear me? Gathers make you look fat!"

"Right! No gathers at the waist! I can hear you! Gathers make you look fat!" Sibendra repeated everything word for word and everyone, even the imperious little sister behind the door, burst out laughing.

Once, during the Puja festival, Sibendra was due to take his sisters to the town square. People were gathering to watch the procession of the gods. Ramendra and Saumen had been gone some time but Sibendra was standing waiting for his sisters — not all of them, just Archana — finally to finish getting ready.

Archana was fifteen that year. She had just moved from dresses to saris and had not yet got to grips with the intricacies of the new garment which was simply a seven-metre bolt of cotton. Her mother and older sister Emmy took two minutes to get dressed but Archana needed forever. She was so embarrassed by her awkwardness that she made her sisters leave the room. She took up the whole room, stretching the material out to one side, and began wrapping it around her waist the way grown-up women do. It was important to make sure it hung gracefully, with the folds facing left, for the hem not to leave the floor. Once the wrap rounds were finished, the free end of the sari went over the shoulder and was fastened with a decorative pin to prevent it falling down. And that's where the problem arose. If the layers around the waist were too tight, it was hard to breathe. If they were too loose, the sari flapped around the hips like an empty sail without enough wind.

Finally, Archana came out of the room. Sibendra, Emmy, and Anjali sighed with relief, showered their sister with compliments, and hurried off to the square. They had hardly left the neighbourhood when they heard an ominous whisper:

"Sibendra, something's wrong with my sari! It's going to fall off!"

"Keep calm, don't panic," Sibendra said quietly and, keeping his sisters in view, he dashed between the houses and stalls, looking for a suitable space. There, fenced around by her relatives' backs, Archana hastily unwound her sari and just as hastily wound it up again, constantly checking what was happening outside:

"Sibendra? Girls! No-one's coming, are they?"

"No! The whole town's been in the square for ages. Hurry up or the gods will have gone… and you won't see hide nor hair of them till next autumn!"

Sibendra was a small man with a big personality and thick tufted eyebrows that jutted out like a rain shelter. His whole world consisted of sounds. When he began a conversation, people often felt he had been completely transformed into a listener and his gaze was so long, lingering, and penetrating that he seemed to be listening even with his eyes.

From early childhood, Sibendra had been wedded to the violin. Since then, not a morning had passed without the family waking, at five o'clock as was their wont, to the usual assortment of scales and etudes. As the oldest brother, Sibendra had responsibilities. It was his job to take his mother and sisters into town. Sometimes they would go to the cinema. Sometimes it was the girls themselves who asked:

"Sibendra, Sibendra, shall we go and see this film?"

"I'll have to ask Father. But first, do your lessons for three days in advance," said Sibendra, setting his terms.

In the morning, hardly had Sibendra got out of bed and picked up his violin case, quietly whistling a Tagore song, when three sets of murmurings first crept then burst out of the girls' room. The sisters had risen earlier than usual, each taken out their books and were theatrically reciting their lessons aloud. This went on for three mornings in succession, whereupon Sibendra went to his mother.

"Ma, the girls are studying hard. May I ask Father's permission to take them to the cinema?"

Then he went to his father.

"Babu, there's a new film on in town. Mama and the girls want to go."

"Have you seen it yourself?" his father asked, momentarily tearing himself away from his books.

"No, but I've heard good reports."

"Take them, then. You have my permission."

After the trip to the cinema, the morning muttering stopped.

* * *

And so time went slowly by. Then, all of a sudden, Sibendra began to disappear. Sometimes in the evening and sometimes overnight. It wasn't as though he had plunged into a personal life either, although he was the right age. In those old-fashioned years in India, in Bengal, personal lives began only after marriage. He had found … a hobby? Something else? Whatever word you choose, it won't be the right one.

When he was still a teenager, Sibendra started visiting their neighbours, collecting rice and rags, and taking them to the slums to give to the poor. At that time, the door to hell stood ajar and he glimpsed inside with fear and pity. He saw putrid wounds, looked at teeming lice, gazed on hunger, death throes, and death itself and realized that life, like the Hindu god, has not one but many heads. One day he went home and, almost in tears, said:

"It's a good thing people only have one mouth. If there were as many mouths as Vishnu has arms, the whole world would turn into a slum."

When he was a little older, Sibendra found himself a far from simple task. At that time, people used to die on the streets of Calcutta and Howrah. Sometimes, you could leave for the bazaar in the morning and there, amid all the trading, in a damp and stinking corner, would be a fresh corpse, crawling with maggots and flies. A man had fallen asleep and died, and there was no-one to bury him. Homeless in life, he remained so in death. There was no specialized service in the town — everyone relied on good will. But who could bring themselves to do this with plague and cholera all around? Sibendra could. He and his friends rustled up stretchers on bicycle wheels and began to patrol the town. They might come across several corpses in one night. They took them to the cemetery and laid them to rest. Incidentally, this was kept from Father because he was very much afraid that contact with infections might kill his children. Sibendra would leave the house when their father was sleeping soundly but their mother knew, of course. He acted under her protection. Later on, his brothers found out as well. Sibendra couldn't conceal his reasons for coming home late at night for long.

Was it not then, in those harsh times, when people were dying like flies and Sibendra's goodness was fraught with mortal risk, that his younger brother, Saumen, was so inspired by Sibendra's fearlessness that it would mark the whole of his future life, giving it direction and focus? Sibendra was looked upon as an ideal. Saumen did not lag behind. The youngest in the family, he was everybody's favourite — the most fastidious, the most intelligent, and the most learned, not just of those at home but in the street, the neighbourhood, and the town. He was advanced for his age. He was known as the little genius. He was an asset to the family, their pride, and their treasure. His delighted mother, father, brothers, and sisters, loved him more than all the others put together.

And how could they not love him and be proud of him when, at only three years of age, he learnt the entire alphabet in just three days? And this in a country where not every adult could read. From the moment he began effortlessly building letters into words and then easily seeing between the lines of what he read, his only interest was in books. Knowledge was a treasure that was always with you, a priceless trophy, the key to conquering the world. By the age of twelve, Saumen had collected a library and would share his books with everyone in turn. The earthenware Saraswati could be proud of him. His gifted childhood was noted at the state level. Even the newspapers wrote about it.

What happened was this. Somehow, as he was going through some ancient manuscripts, Saumen's attention was suddenly drawn to an unknown letter. There was no doubt that he was utterly familiar with the Bengali alphabet and could even toy with it like a true linguist but he had never come across this letter before. Nor had anyone else. As it turned out — and Saumen studied and researched it thoroughly — it wasn't in any of the dictionaries or other literary sources. What was it? How was it pronounced? Why wasn't it used? Could it be revived? Saumen did the research and wrote an essay that was published in a newspaper. A civil servant came to the house and presented Saumen with a certificate and a financial prize as a thank you for his great discovery. Saumen gave the money (one hundred rupees, which was a huge amount!) to his parents and they bought the vastly expensive tabla he had been dreaming of for ages. For a long time, his mother would show the newspaper to the neighbours and for a long time the neighbours would whisper, delightedly:

"Look who's coming! It's Sudharani's son. He found a lost letter of the Bengali alphabet!"

However, all this happened after Saumen's sisters had given him his most important gift: a tilak mark on his forehead. The dab of sandalwood paste the colour of dry blood could mean only one thing — that the boy had a sister who would offer prayers for him to live a long life and even, should the need arise, sacrifice herself for him. The mark is a sign of love and a sister's loyalty. A special connection. A charm.

Saumen was five when the drop of ochre first adorned his forehead on Bhai Phota — Brothers' Day. Before the ceremony, the whole house was cloaked in the utmost secrecy. A commotion of rustling could be heard in the male half of the house. Sibendra and Ramendra were wrapping up surprise presents — pencils, rulers, and other small items. Saumen was too little to have anything to do but, like an adult, was thinking about the gifts he would be giving his sisters.

Well before the festival, Saumen's mother had come up with a game for him to play. He was the owner of a little shop where he sold and stored sweets and vegetables. When she needed something for supper, she would ask him as, if it were a matter of national importance:

"I wonder whether I might purchase a kilo of aubergines from you?"

Saumen would weigh them all properly and receive a coin for his pains. Since his mother was the bank, she gave him the money. In the end, she had provided her son with funds — he had amassed a couple of rupees– and they took them to the bazaar and spent them on the cheapest things the girls liked — powder and kohl. They set the gifts out in a mandala on a small, earthenware plate, which Saumen painted with ashoka flowers and gave to his mother to look after.

On Brothers' Day, when the tilak had blossomed on Saumen's forehead, he suddenly shouted:

"My darling sisters, wait a minute! I've got something for you too. Ma, come in!"

And their mother, the leading actor in her son's theatre,

solemnly bore in the plate. They were all so touched they cried, pretending not to have expected a surprise, and saying over and over as one:

"Wherever did you find it? It's exactly right. Oh!!"

"Really? Do you really like it?"

Beside himself with joy, Saumen galloped round his sisters and the third eye on his forehead positively beamed with happiness.

The kohl and powder soon ran out but the plate, the earthenware plate with its painted ashoka flowers, would decorate the girls' bedroom for a long time — a memento of childhood, a sign of the bond between brothers and sisters and the mystery of the tilak. Later, when they moved to Calcutta, when everything in the house was out of place and upside down, the plate was smashed. Not on purpose, but by the absurdity of chance, presaging misfortune. This could happen to anyone. It really does. That's life for everyone.

Chapter 3

The Teacher

If we want to unwind the tangled skeins of the past even further, and catch hold of those distant years when mangoes were redder, the Ganges water like a mirror, and the war-cry of the mongoose in the high grass — rikki-tikki-tikki-tikki-tchk! — trumped the noise of the bazaar in even the most garrulous town... If we want to dip even deeper into that time when it seemed the suns were molten gold and the moons silver, when clothes were simpler and smiles broader, and when *that* had not yet happened, then we need to remember that Archana never went to school. Not for so much as a month or even a week. For her father would not countenance the beating of children. And since, in Bengali schools, this vile expedient was and is considered normal practice, he would not even entertain the thought of his mischievous little girl's back feeling the teacher's cane — just because, for example, she laughed at the wrong moment, or suddenly started singing, or her bird-like legs set off with a skip. And this often happened, for she was a singer, a dancer, as jolly a girl as you could hope to meet.

No, her father could not even think of that back and the teacher's cane. So he himself taught his daughters, while his sons, yes, they were sent to school.

Her father was a strict teacher, but his discipline was no harder than pine resin. His classes — be they mathematics, physics, literature, history — seemed to be just one long sequence of pleasures, filling the time as it flew. After the lessons there always lingered a curious impression of things left half-said, producing an explosion of impatience in her immature heart, a need to know more, to find out more. Or to understand more. To penetrate something her father had not yet said, or had not finished saying, planting a seed that would germinate tomorrow. Or in the future, when he, her father, would no longer be on this earth.

After these lessons, in the evenings Archana would find Emmy in bed with a book, under the soft light of the paraffin lamp. She would curl up next to her and, while Mother and the youngest, Anjali, were getting washed and putting on their night-clothes, she would ask Emmy to read aloud. She read with expression, but very quietly, in an intimate whisper, trying to give voice to the meaning of the words — not just the words, but even the letters:

"The deeper man's reason penetrates into the mystery of time as it flies, the easier it will be for him to withstand the blows fate deals him... Our fear of the dark is unbearable, because the dark is the unknown..."

"Oh no, no, no!" Archana was insistent. "Not darkness, anything but darkness. That's dreary! Isn't there anything a bit livelier?!"

And Emmy would skip that page and read on:

"... beauty roams, invisible, along the paths of life, never fading under the burdensome attention of the crowd. The whole of creation lives by this wisdom..."

"Ahhh...," Archana gave a deep sigh and blew into the pillow in an attempt to stifle a yawn. "Maybe that one's all right, but it's not quite... Er... what's on the next page?"

"Well what else are you looking for?" Emmy frowned, seeing that it was time to put the tales of Kabi Guru (as Bengalis call Rabindranath Tagore) away under the pillow. "Fine, here's the last thing I'm going to read! After that — sleep!"

And again, half-whispering, in warm, mellifluous tones:

"And this is the way of human life, with truth and story intertwining: something from the creator, something from man himself, and something from the people around him. Life is the coming together of a variety of opposites: the natural and the unnatural, the invented and the real..."

"Oh Emmy... that bit, read that again, 'something from the creator, something from man himself and something from the people around him'," said Archana, slowly, as if nursing a liquorice sweet inside her cheek, which must be sucked slowly and sparingly, so as to extract every bit of its taste. Then she fell asleep under the spell of a truth, a truth of the kind that flashes before you for an instant, when you do not yet recognize it as a truth — you have not yet taken it in, just sensed it.

* * *

When, at the age of sixteen, Archana was called to the education department commission for her school leaving exams, she had no trouble gaining her certificate. After that she chose to go to a college where, after four years, she could take her bachelor's degree. Just like Emmy, who was two years older than Archana, she had decided to continue their father's work.

But things did not immediately go smoothly at college. Having hardly begun her studies, Archana broke off for a while. She returned to college and later came another break and another return. For times were hard in Bengal and the family had money problems. Poverty had struck the household, raining down on them like the monsoon in June. The children were already teenagers and they all needed an academic qualification. They economized on food and clothing. Father could no longer support the family, and even once the older brothers had started work there was still not enough. Sibendra had graduated, become a music teacher, and opened a small school teaching the violin. Ramendra was still studying, but had a part-time job on the railway.

In 1961, when Archana was still at college, Emmy graduated and opened a school in the village of Kolorah, on the outskirts of

Howrah. There were four classes in the school, from years five to eight, and two hundred pupils. It had not yet been granted state registration, so the teachers could not be paid salaries. The school fund set up by the local villagers could pay only their bus fares.

When the education department sent Emmy on a course to gain a higher qualification, someone had to take her place and Emmy offered the job to her younger sister. So now Archana would get up before five in the morning, pack her rice for lunch, go to college, and from there to the village school. At last she became acquainted with a school blackboard — she herself, of course, had studied at home.

Her first pupils were about two years younger than Archana. Year eight, and they already wore a little kohl on their eyes; already the fabric of their saris lifted over their breasts. They would soon be of marriageable age and the match-maker had already made arrangements for some of them. They seemed to Archana to be too shy, timid, limp, alienated from everything — as if they were all deaf mutes. She couldn't find a way to make contact, to get them talking, rouse them, ignite a spark of curiosity in their eyes, or break down the glass wall that cut them off from her as soon as she came into the room. Archana longed for them to rush up to her after the class, form a circle round her desk, and besiege her with their noisy gabbling, irrepressible as a flock of chattering magpies. But there was none of that. All Archana could read in those silent teenage eyes was resignation and obedience to her status as teacher. And no interest in her as a mentor.

After a couple of weeks of this fruitless existence in the role of substitute village teacher, Archana started to wonder what she was doing wrong. Why did those village girls not see her as a teacher? She looked at herself in the mirror. Trapped in that glass box was an awkward, narrow-shouldered girl, a bit dumpy, no longer a teenager but not yet a woman, with a shock of dark brown hair, coarse as a horse's mane, pulled into the nape of her neck with a rubber band, with exuberant curls around her brow and temples, like the actress Nargis in the film *The Vagabond*.

Her face bore no sign as yet of those soft, calm, smooth forms that appear as a privilege of age and immediately inspire confidence. Village aunties, *mashimas*, have them and are able, with nothing more than a prayer shawl thrown on their heads, to command respect in society. But neither was there movie gloss in the form of plump, quivering lips, artificially moistened with peach-pulp, dragonfly eyelashes separated into black arrows, or the sparkling crystalline lenses of rhinestones in the nose, or bracelets around the ankles.

All she had was a simple, absurd sari, a chaotic rainbow, a crimson blur, a splodge on the palette of an avant-garde artist. A garish zigzag flashed erratically, its gaudy spots dazzled. After seeing the sari you were blind to the owner's eyes, face, and movements.

Recoiling from herself, from that overpowering, flowery apparition, Archana could picture clearly the class and the teacher's desk and, at the desk, that splodge with the tar-coloured blackboard behind it. Not a silhouette but a splodge.

"No, that will never do," she decided. "I have to become a real teacher. Not from the outside but from within."

From that day, Archana went to school only in white — a white sari and white shawl — and now did not wait for her pupils to gather round and throw questions at her. Instead she did the gathering round herself. She dipped them into a river of stories. She gave them riddles, then answered them herself. Unexpectedly, the wall fell away. Teacher and pupils became close. So that when, on Emmy's return, Archana had to say goodbye to the school, she took away in her heart a soaring, triumphant joy, tinged, though, with a wistful melancholy, nostalgia for the life that had called her and captured her, and which she would like to try out once more. Or even plunge all the way into, rush into headlong the way, for example, people rush into their first love.

Less than two months had passed when one day, returning from college, Archana found guests at home. A little group of people from the "school authorities" were talking to her father, trying to persuade him.

"The children want Archana as their teacher. They say they'll stop studying unless she comes. We don't know what to do. Would you allow her to come and work for us? Especially as Emmy is going off to another school."

"Mmm... But Archana hasn't finished college yet, she needs to study..." her father started to object. But Archana threw herself at his feet:

"Baba! I can do both. I can work and study, if you'll only say yes. You'll see, I can manage everything."

And so Archana became wedded to the school.

* * *

It took three stuffy hours to get from home to the village of Kolorah. The 61A bus hauled itself lazily along Andul Road, always having to tack with the current of people loaded down with bast-fibre bags, and carts stuffed full of hay bales, and between oncoming buses and those travelling alongside, from the dusty sides of which the sign for the sacred sound "Om" — or dozens, hundreds of "Oms", liberally emblazoned in Devanagari script — looked out, like so many pairs of sharp eyes. Hindus believe that Om is the quintessence of the Word, and that everything comes from its vibration. And if you chant it repeatedly, forgetting everything on earth, it is possible to chant until the distant expanses of the other world open up, open up, and call you. But who's in any hurry?

On the right-hand side of Andul Road a classic Indian sight amused her: palm trees stood on their single leg, lanky as models on the podium, and baring breasts of coconut bunches. Along the left-hand side stretched the long, tedious frontage of the largest botanic garden in Asia. It was separated from the road by concrete and barbed wire. In fact, the barbed wire was merely for show. If you touched it, it would crumble away with age.

On Bombay Road Archana would change to the 62 and then, near the village, she would get off and, her light, hardy feet paddling in liquid mud during the summer or through coppery dust in winter, would walk another three miles along a twisty road. A bamboo forest rose up like walls to left and right, interspersed with mangoes, pines, and bananas. But in one place the crowns were thinner and the heavens were revealed. The forest gave way to the grounds of a brick works. In Kolorah, bricks were shaped by hand and spread out to dry in the open: a draughts board spreading mile after mile, entirely covered with ingots of terracotta.

Nearer the school, the picture changed and an island of habitation came into view: huts of different sizes among chaotically planted pines, lopsided stalls set on bicycle wheels, an overgrown temple on a lifeless pond, as well as wandering packs of feral dogs. To tell the truth, they did not go for humans, but it was worth throwing them some fish gut or an onion paste wrapper — then they could kill each other for it.

One day, on the way to school, Archana unexpectedly found herself face to face with the local drunk. Scruffy, his hair in a tangle, totally inebriated, he was sitting on the ground, dejected, at the entrance to the village shop, and arguing with someone unseen, sometimes friendly, sometimes yelling, waving his arms around wildly like swords. A major fight was brewing in his invisible world. Catching sight of Archana, he stood up abruptly and started towards her, ready to share with her his maudlin joy or melancholy. But at that moment the shopkeeper hurried out and shouted at the drunkard:

"Shh! Shut up! Shut that shameless great mouth of yours! Can't you see who's coming?! It's the tea-cher!"

And from the genuine respect with which he pronounced the word "tea-cher", slowly, each syllable emphasized, Archana understood that she had nothing to fear.

"Don't be frightened didi, go on sister, go on," said the shopkeeper, raising his hands to his chin, and bowing almost to the ground, remaining in that position until she had gone past.

The drunk clutched his head in horror and fell to the ground like a stone, pitching his face, already a dirty red colour, into the hot dust. And, for a good while still, Archana could hear behind her:

"Has the teacher gone? Has she? Has the teacher gone…? I'm ashamed! So ashamed!"

And this is how Archana saw in practice what she already knew from her father: being a teacher means respect, even from drunks.

This road, by the way, this unfinished country track, would one day lead Archana to the top job.

Time passed and the number of students at the village school increased. There were now five hundred, and the state authorities decided to grant the school public sector status. Teachers in state schools received a wage that was regular, if pathetically small. But for that every teacher had to take a state examination.

On the appointed day the corridor was thronged with teachers. The test was rumoured to be tricky. But what really caused a sinking feeling in the stomach was the inevitable encounter with Sisirkana, chief inspector of schools for the region. Her inspections were legendary: after them, heads would often roll and school leaders lose their jobs.

"Ooh! Terrible questions the old woman asks," moaned the teachers after the test.

Some sat crying, sure that this year too no wages would await them. Archana was nervously biting her lip. She could certainly not have imagined that the interview would end as it did.

"So you're from the school in Kolorah village?" asked Sisirkana, the moment Archana stepped into the office.

"Yes, that's right, madam."

"I inspected that school three times this year."

"Yes, madam, I remember."

"And it wasn't long ago, was it, that you got your bachelor's degree? Two or three years?"

"That's right, madam."

"And all the time you were studying you were also working at this same school?"

"Yes madam, that's correct."

"I have no more questions, child. I don't need any exam to tell me you're a teacher. If you didn't have the heart of a teacher you couldn't even have endured the travelling to get to school. I know that route — two or three buses and three miles on foot. Three hours just to get there. Six hours in a day. I don't have anything else to ask you, child. I'm sure you're a real teacher!"

While Archana was trying to come to terms with this unexpected stroke of luck, three of her fellow-teachers were ushered into the office.

"I shan't test you either, dear colleagues," said Sisirkana, her enthusiasm plain to see. "You'll now be working under Archana's leadership. She's been appointed headmistress and you are her assistants. And we can be confident that from now on I shan't have anything to worry about regarding the school at Kolorah."

That year Archana turned twenty-five. On the very first day of her new role, she forbade her teachers to beat the pupils.

* * *

But I must also tell you about Archana's personal life. Even if it had been today, her life would still have followed her parents' example, in accordance with the preconceptions of the clan. And those have not changed since the Laws of Manu were written. Every girl's calling is, primarily, to become a good wife. Not even a good mother so much as a good wife. And the earlier she acquires that august status, the earlier she dons the marriage bracelets-cum-handcuffs, the better it is for her. In her role as wife she is in the presence of her guru, her spiritual mentor, her only god. She is under his protection. In vain did Tagore argue that it was only in the nineteenth century that girls were given into marriage like puppets, and that when he wrote, at the beginning of the twentieth, girls were quite different and did not want to become playthings in the hands of a mashima. He said it in the time of British India. In the past. That was long gone.

Even today, in many Bengali families daughters are given away, sold, passed from hand to hand after the parents or the extended family have lined up the partner. And if the girl has an academic qualification and long hair, is small and a virgin, with pale skin (in memory of her Aryan roots) and is not too slender (which by Bengali standards would be a sign of sickliness), there will be plenty of willing matchmakers. In that case you don't even have to organize a dowry — you can demand cash from the bridegroom.

Obviously, the Guha family was considered to be in an enviable position in the marriage market as long, of course, as one was not too concerned about their lack of money... but who was not poor in those days? This awkward circumstance meant they had to count their rupees, but when in the early sixties Sibendra and Ramendra decided to get married (which they did, by the way, according to their personal choice), the parents did not feel the need to ask for dowries from their daughters-in-law. They firmly refused the money offered with the brides, which made for greater equality in the marriages. This was for those times a generous gesture and very avant-garde behaviour.

After her brothers, Emmy also married, and this time it was the relatives who arranged it. Soon, overtaking Archana (for it was really her turn), the youngest, Anjali — who now taught dancing and singing — donned the red wedding sari. Her parents had allowed her to choose for herself. Her husband was a former student of her father.

So what about Archana? From time to time marriage brokers would appear at the house, and tender-hearted sisters and sisters-in-law were for ever urging her to "Make up your mind! It's your turn, Archana!"

But Archana was letting no one into her personal life. She did not want any changes. And indeed her parents, seeing their daughter's frame of mind, did not hurry to insist. Which of us has not encountered workaholics so caught up in their profession that they have given themselves over to it entirely, both head and heart, postponing life until later? There was Lavanya, for instance, in Tagore's *The Last Poem*. Her learned father, reflecting on his daughter's future, was convinced that "if his daughter's heart might incline to thoughts of marriage at some time, it was now securely protected by the armour of history and mathematics, and no amount of tender feelings could sink their roots into it." He even accepted that Lavanya might never marry. "What of it?" he said. "For she is now betrothed to knowledge and learning for the whole of her life!"

And I too say, "What of it?" How easy it is to recognize characters from literature in real life!

Archana considered herself betrothed to the school. And when she turned thirty, a second major reason descended on to the scales and was even weightier than the first. And that reason, that reason only, swollen as if with child and inspiring a sense of duty, that reason occupied every inch of her personal universe, leaving not the smallest chink open for a retreat into her private world.

But forgive me — I'm getting ahead of myself again.

The story of that second reason — a reason of flesh and blood, bearing the same family name and a tilak mark on the forehead — that will come later. Now is a different part of the story. May this halcyon period, my heroine's youth, while her clothes are simpler, her smile broader, and she still walks through the bamboo forest in a white sari and white shawl — may this time continue, if only for a day, a month, or a year.

* * *

The day before the May holidays began, Archana returned from school with a garland of wild flowers like the disc of the over-ripe sun. Her pupils had made it for her, but when she got home she presented it to her father, as if bestowing a medal or passing on an heirloom. Her father admired the interlacing of the flowers and stems and then gave it a firm yank to test its strength. The garland did not give.

"Do you know why this can't be broken?"

"Yes, Baba! The stems are so tightly entwined that they support each other."

"Exactly. But look what happens to each flower if they are separated..."

Father carefully pulled out a champa or a jasmine and, with a light motion, split the stem with his nail. A thick bubble of milky blood emerged.

"So it is in a family where brothers and sisters support each other. As long as they are together, they will be as strong as this garland."

That morning, when her father took to his bed — he was not ill but he suddenly needed to lie down — Archana was getting ready for work.

"Don't go — stay at home today," he said.

"But what about school, Baba?" said Archana, undecided, for her father's appearance gave no particular grounds for staying home. "I must go!"

She had almost reached the village when suddenly everything went dark before her eyes and she felt a pain in her chest. Once in the staffroom, she immediately turned back and rushed as fast as humanly possible — through the village, the brick works, the bamboo forest. Three hours later, sweating and sickened by her premonition, she ran into the house. Her father was lying unconscious. And for those two hours, while his exhausted heart still fluttered, and then when it came to rest, this time for good, Archana sat at her father's feet and silently prayed. Old women from outside the family were already beginning to rustle around the house. One, a sallow-faced widow who lived nearby, had taken the marriage bracelets off the arms of Archana's mother — who was now in a daze — and started to rub the red bindi off her forehead, which was now that of a widow.

Some years later her mother, Sudharani, would be ready to believe that half-crazed old woman's story that widowhood is a curse. She would say to herself and her children, now grown up:

"It's a good thing your father's gone. If he hadn't died in 1970 he'd have been shot in '74."

And yes, he would have been shot because that scum would not have left an old man alive who had thrown himself across their path. And father would most certainly have thrown himself across their path. To protect his family. That night. That same night after which there was no dawn.

Chapter 4

At the Back of a Crowd Scene

I think I should drop into the story myself at this point, but not for long — to quote a fellow-writer and fellow country-woman. She is also my namesake, and a lady of unshakeable Jewish principles, with an inexhaustible sense of humour.

So, here goes: "I think I should drop into the story myself at this point. Not for long. I shan't obstruct your view, despite being its author — I am, rather, one of the minor characters at the back of a crowd scene."

The back of a crowd scene — that's the edge of the world. Or, as they used to say where I came from, "in a dormitory suburb worlds away". Or, as they say where I live now, "in the endless jungles of Faroffistan". Well, if the endless jungles actually have a furthest corner, then it is there, in that region, blurred by haze, buried deep in the backwoods, that I am taking up residence. That place — at the very, very back of a crowd scene — suits me even better. There I swim like a fish in the fog, roaming the waters like the Flying Dutchman. I've been getting acclimatized to such places since I was a child. Right back to when I was inscribed in the birth register of our incomer nation. Or when I stood, last in the line-up (I was not conspicuous for my height) in gym lessons at school.

You probably remember those classes, do you? They went on everywhere, all identical.

"Into height order — go! Two teams — count off, one-two, one-two. Go!"

Your head swings violently to the left and your mouth barks the next number, a signal spat out to the class-mate next to you.

"One!"
"Two!"
"One!"
"Two!"

In a flash the echo is carried, reverberating into a roar, from first to last and back again, until finally... The last to call is a One — and whoever is a One now becomes a Two...

Do you think I'm rambling now? And what I've just said has nothing to do with the tale I'm telling? Don't forget that chickens always come home to roost — and please, keep reading. Just take this as an interval until they've finished the scene change on the other side, on the main stage. And while this is happening, the author can indulge herself. A caprice in three sentences. An extravagance of one paragraph. The briefest of eccentricities. An innocent word-game in which, lying hidden between the letters — and they have to be hidden — are vestiges of my real import. What to do? I cannot deny myself this pleasure. I cannot but port arms, aim my rifle, my pen, and fire — as old Aesop taught us. He was accused of blasphemy, though, and thrown off a cliff. Yet Aesop's fables were far more innocent than mine.

And so, as a minor character at the back of a crowd scene, I will gradually tell you — drop by drop, a teaspoon at a time, and only in the margin and between the lines of the main story — how this story came to reach your door. It is yet another tale of challenges surmounted, another swerve on the twisting road of human life. But do be patient, dear reader!

I was born in the early 70s, shortly after the death of Archana's father. (As you see, even here, in my first effort to raise myself above the ranked extras in the crowd scene, to get a distant glimpse of my heroine, I have managed to find my first parallel with her.) You could say I was born on a bridge between East and West. In one of the Asian colonies of a giant empire. At the junction between different worlds, languages, and cultures.

The year of my birth was not marked by revelations and

catastrophes on a worldwide scale. Except that on one side of our bridge the third Indo-Pakistani war was raging while the other saw the death of Coco Chanel, Arne Jacobsen, and Louis Armstrong, and the birth of Disneyworld and of Denmark's Freetown Christiania. My parents, though, knew nothing of this, and they could not know because they lived behind the iron curtain.

But even so, no matter how impenetrable that curtain, foreign phantoms did get through. They reached us despite the firmly shut borders and the strict conformity of local industry — thanks to which all the girls in our class went round in identical boots made by an industrial combine that used the same material to make caterpillar tracks for tanks. Those foreign spectres had forenames and surnames. Sumptuous forenames and surnames, to our way of thinking. Names you could pronounce with a bourgeoisified in-breath and an exclamatory out-breath. Mademoiselle French Perfumes, Frau Finnish Plumber, Japanese Tape-Recorder-San, Pani Bohemian Glass, Herr Meissen Dinner-Service, Sir Persian Carpet, Mrs Chinese Silk, Mr Indian Tea...

Stop! Indian tea! There it is — another parallel with my heroine.

Where I was born, tea is something special. They drink it anywhere and any time — at breakfast, lunch, and dinner, at home, at work, visiting friends. No coffee, juice, water, fizzy drinks, or alcohol can rival tea. Old people savour it a dozen times a day, nibbling sugar-cubes and oriental sweetmeats. Children mix cherry plum seeds and sea-buckthorn honey into an amber sludge. But best of all is to drink tea on its own. And the best of the best can only be Indian tea.

The whole of my childhood was imbued with its slightly bitter aroma. The roasted, spiky leaves were spooned out of a silvery cube with three elephants on the yellow and red label, which then became a bookmark in our school-books. How often in physics lessons (for Pascal's and Ohm's laws never set my heart aflutter) did my eye bore into that little picture where — beyond the silhouettes of those noble elephants, their voluptuous, rounded forms caparisoned and craggy brows crowned with tiaras — mountains and forests were seen, painted in with a squirrel-hair brush. Old, good India was shown as both old and good. And we discovered a new India at the cinema — the whole class would race off there after the final, sixth lesson of the day.

In our colonial province the Indian cinema was popular: the demand was higher than for Fellini films. On days when an Indian film was showing, it was a job to elbow your way into that eight-hundred-seat cinema. On those days we, scions of an incomer nation, the offspring of white colonizers, political exiles in a southern land, felt like the British in India on the eve of August 15, 1947 —minor characters at the back of a crowd scene. But this did not stop us getting as involved as the rest of the audience in the excitement of the story and falling in love with the Bollywood actors, their fine costumes, their singing and dancing. As the film reached its climax the entire auditorium would shed a companionable tear. And with good reason.

The Indian cinema is the weepiest of all. There are three basic, two-dimensional plots and nothing more. There is the parable about a prince who gives up everything to save his loved one; the action film about a terrible revenge; and the family drama in which the brother is the golden boy of the family, dreaming of great things, and the sister melts into the background for the time being. Suddenly something terrible happens to the brother — an illness or an arrest. The parents die. Friends betray him. And only the sister steps out of the shadows to help the brother as he passes through the circles of hell. This third plot is about sacrifice in the name of the family, about a summons from deep in the blood.

Among the other Indian pages of my colonial childhood I recall the name Indira. In every school and in every year there was a dark-eyed girl who had been given that name in honour of the premier of that distant land. The rulers of our empire idolized that prime minister and were seen on the news embracing her.

I also remember Ganges, the enormous Indian store, spread over two floors in the centre of our southern capital, a magnet for our women of fashion. For many years, as long as the shop flourished (and it flourished until the empire breathed its last), the town was bright with fancy garments of muslin and delicate gauze. I remember a dress my mother bought from that shop — a frivolous affair with a bell skirt, a carousel of frills and flaps, with splashes of sparkling lurex. I remember how, like a circus conjuror, she would feed the dress through a ring she had taken from her ring finger. And I would give an admiring sigh: goodness knows what ethereal beings Indian women must be if they only needed fabrics of mist and air to cover themselves.

Why, half-forgotten pages from my childhood, do I leaf through you now? Surely not because I am trying to find where, when, at what time, in what era, on which side of which page I first brushed up against my heroine? Or maybe I am returning to you to try and understand which line it was, which moment, when you deceived me? And you did deceive me! You deceived me when you created, in my naïve, child's heart, that sublime image of a country that was not sublime. No, it was not.

So what was it? What was there instead? In place of that? What was hidden behind the monolithic backs of the Indian elephants on the tea label? What was it that the films for export kept quiet about? What could the insubstantial fabrics woven from air not tell me? And that little girl, that young lady, that woman I am now hunting down with my net, as if she were a rare butterfly — what is she to me? And what is my interest in the twists and turns of her fortunes, which I am now following so closely, collecting up the fragments, flashes, murmurs of elusive memories? Why am I endeavouring to grasp by the tail the evasive ghosts of a vanishing past? Why bring them back to life? Why restore their lost voice? Why try to find out what she wore, how comfortably she lived, what books she read, what she talked and dreamed of? And what kind of line it is, by which she, all unknowing, has drawn me to her, through space and time?

Chapter 5

The Hand

The night of July 17 to 18, 1974, was no different from any other Calcutta night in the rainy season. Sticky, lustreless as an old woman, it was suffocating, with a steamy closeness in the air that could not be relieved even by the fine drizzle. The town settled into long-awaited silence, and there was only the squelching of a rickshaw-boy's feet running through puddles to disturb the sleepy quiet of the dwellings that lined the road, their windows like empty eye-sockets, knowing neither shutters nor glass.

Looking back, across the impregnable barrier of time, it is no longer possible to say what Inspector Runu Niyogi was doing that night. It is, however, known for sure that he was not at the police station. They were expecting him there in the morning. And so… what else could he have been doing? On a Wednesday night? Between two working days? Probably catching up on sleep, getting his strength up.

Here I should stop for a moment and try to describe him — although a portrait is always a fantasy. Police Officer Runu has barely appeared in our story — he has not really begun his part at all — yet he has already formed a protective coating to ward off questions. It is as if he had donned a black bag. All I can tell you about him with absolute certainty is no more than a series of external details. A massive, square-ish oval body, the carcass of an oak, a scattering of gaudy rings on his massive fingers, a cigarette, a gobbet of spittle, and the rictus of a shark. And that, I suppose, is all. Though it's not inconsiderable. After all, in Boris Vallejo's picture *The Hand*, all we see is a great claw of a hand —

we don't see the monster himself, but nor do we feel a need to. Our mind escapes the frame of what is shown. Sliding out into the realm of the unseen, we build the reality for ourselves.

Runu usually returned home after dark, often just before dawn, after a slap-up midnight supper in a restaurant for "people in the know" somewhere in the Beniapukur district. He arrived home reeking of cheap Indian whiskey, which he treated himself to more frequently than the meagre salary of a Bengali policeman could possibly allow. But discussion of Runu's finances is hardly relevant here. In Bengal, as in India, they say "police" and think "perks", say "perks" and think "police".

Runu's work was neither easy nor pleasant. It was a nasty, dirty little job, but he loved it. He even fantasized about it, just as some indulge in lustful fantasies about a young but bold and experienced courtesan, who knows how to debauch a lusty male ego and maintain it at the peak of satisfaction.

In this job there was no knowing what the next day would bring. In the course of twenty-four hours Runu would go off on several assignments — he never knew where he would be going, who he would be meeting, what he would hear. He would appraise the situation, propose a solution and implement it, taking a few notes, appending the odd signature, reprimanding some people, being reprimanded by others; he would give orders, carry out instructions — and all the while on the go, on the hop, in a rush. No iota of weakness, not a jot of fatigue, not in his legs, his body, his voice. Always and everywhere hard and resolute. Always and everywhere in the autocrat's mask that had become so much a part of him over the years in this job that it had eaten away the skin, as though there never had been a face there, just a pitted, rutted crust made of clay and papier mâché.

Returning home, Runu would ease off his black-as-kohl work boots, releasing into the air the putrid stench of his feet, drop heavily onto the rickety divan, and quickly consign his curved police-issue dagger to the folds of his pillow, before his eyelids could grow heavy. Even the ritual couplings with his wife did not awaken in him that long-forgotten languor, transporting him to the dream kingdom of nirvana that he had known as a thickset, sporty youth, before he went to police college.

Aeons had passed since then — almost twenty years. People, feelings, attachments had all sunk into the Ganges mud. What did you love, what did you laugh at — do you remember? Can you really see anything now, beneath the murky deposits of slime that cover the windows onto your youth, your past? And why would you want to look through those windows anyway, to recall those sentiments, when the present is so much clearer than your yesterdays? Today you have strength, accolades, and power. Your blood is cooler now.

But no, there *is* something more to pull out of the slime and scrape free of accretions. It is — and feast your eyes on this! — Runu's native Cooch Bihar, in the north of Bengal, at the foot of the Himalayas. There he was born and grew up in the family of a town court functionary — and not the lowest grade at that. When he finished college, he got his first job, on the tea plantations of a member of parliament, Mr. S. P. Roy. But he only took work there during the off-season. His main passion was football. Runu played for the district team — I have to admit he was a brilliant player. One day his playing attracted the attention of someone high up in the Calcutta police, Ranjit Gupta, who then suggested that Runu should join the police.

The training was not easy, being far from home, with discipline as tough as in an army at war, work as hard as in a penal battalion and, worst of all, the ever-present, suffocating animal fear instilled into him from the first minute. Fear of the top brass, whose trust must not be betrayed. Fear of an order that must not be disobeyed. Fear of a task that must not be refused. Fear of yourself, if you showed yourself a weakling.

But then, at the end of the day, when the new intake from police college — bad-tempered, sweaty, and hungry — formed a line for roll-call, the commander would reward them a hundredfold for their agonies. His bass voice even now assaults Runu's ears, booming like a gun salute:

"Don't forget! Get this into your noddles! *You* are the cornerstone of the regime! *You* are the guardians of the nation! For *you* — everything's legal! *You* are the elite! Repeat after me! Ay! Leet! All the rest — peasants!"

This, the last comment, impressed Runu the most. Yes, of course he was not scum, not a bad smell, not a servant, like the rest of humankind. He was, as the commander had said, the cornerstone of the regime. The elite.

Runu's service record after leaving college is not of great interest to the reader. When he finally ended up with the Calcutta Metropolitan Police he wore the sub-inspector's insignia with two proud five-pointed grey stars and red and blue transversal stripes above the legend "CP". His curriculum vitae sparkled with brilliant arrests of killers and burglars. But what really impressed his bosses was the network of informers that Runu had cobbled together out of rejects from the criminal world.

Only football no longer featured. Playing in a police team, Runu had damaged his knee during a match. The doctors said no more football.

On his arrival in the capital, he first served for a time in Central Division, with constant moves from one station to another, with all that tedious patrolling — come heat-wave or monsoon — of streets and squares smelling of samosas, frankincense, and urine, before finally becoming his own man in the CID and at last settling down, with an office, his own desk, and toilet. He settled not in some little niche fighting robbery and prostitution but in a special unit. Its name was spoken in a stage whisper, index finger jabbing up to the heavens. Just listen. "Special". "Cell". The cell with a *special* function.

Here he exchanged his uniform for civvies, trousers with a European-style shirt, and became the most devoted, most obedient, almost a spiritual son to the legendary Chief of Police,

Debi Roy. But Runu soon became more renowned than the Chief, earning himself the indelible reputation of an inspector whose interrogations would make even corpses talk.

We need only remember that guru of the partisan war, that elusive avenger, that damned revolutionary, as Runu would sneeringly refer to him, that home-grown, Indian Lenin, Charu Mazumdar. What eyes that old man had, how sunken, how hollow, how full of doom they became when he understood who it was that he saw standing before him.

Exactly two years had passed since then, but Runu could still not get enough of it, kept replaying it in his mind, kept trying to fix the details of that unforgettable operation in his memory. Runu was just bursting with pride at the thought that he, a simple policeman, Runu Niyogi, had been a part of it. Or not quite. He — *he himself* — was its creator.

* * *

Well, since we are going back to that event... You do, of course, remember that resounding word, that glorious word? That banner, summons, clarion-call. That word for freedom: "Naxalites". I would even say it was the word for explosions, the word for gunshots. For they certainly liked to blow people up, when there was someone to blow up. And when all the bullets in the magazine were used up.

It was only later, years later, that the Indian government officially called them — those of militant Maoist, left-wing extremist, anarcho-communist persuasion — terrorists. At the time, however, as the '60s became the '70s, at the dawning of that time of romantic youth, when passions had reached boiling point, the Naxalites considered themselves and were perceived by ordinary people to be solely patriots and revolutionaries. Whole villages of peasants threw down their hoes, whole cohorts of students left universities and colleges, all to join the Naxalites, to join together in a revolutionary guerrilla war.

What did they want, those despairing, suicidal young people, who were not martyrs for any faith yet still scorned death? In fact, they did not want anything special. They wanted what the whole world wants. To live, just to live. With enough to eat, not starving.

But they — or rather their leaders — added in another demand, on top of these basic needs. They also wanted what, for example, the Bolsheviks wanted in Russia and the Maoists in China: power and a change of government. Revolution. These, as we know, are accomplished by popular mass movements. For them to be successful, the masses need to be given weapons. Lots of them. The sources of these were government troops and the police — so it was these that the Naxalites attacked: fledgling constables in the traffic police, well-fed senior ranks in the CID, and dapper officers and men in armed units.

Over and again the newspapers reported exchanges of fire in the suburbs, police vans blown up, police officers kidnapped and held for ransom, weapons snatched. Over and again rumours went the rounds. Here peasant committees were being cobbled together, there poor people's debts to money-lenders being cancelled, somewhere else death sentences being pronounced in people's courts. Somewhere else money-lenders had already been beheaded — along with informants and agents — and their bodies festooned round lamp-posts.

Maoist ideas even made it into criminal circles, so swindlers, thieves, and killers also made for the Naxalites — and were not turned away. Everyone was accepted. They were re-educated and given a grounding in ideology along with weapons.

Do I need to explain the hysteria that seized pro-government sectors of the population? Or how many rich land-owners fled the state, especially Calcutta, in fear? The police were scared too, and tried not to show themselves on the streets. And not only the police.

Runu recalled how four years earlier, in 1970, the wives, children, and parents of all police officers had been moved en masse into barracks in the middle of towns. And there they lived — in fear and trembling, and without even the most meagre of home comforts — under military protection. They were very strictly banned from telling anyone that their husbands, fathers, and sons were in the police.

The police themselves were issued with secret orders to keep their arms at the ready. Always and everywhere. Even at home, even in bed, where they had to keep daggers and truncheons with them.

As for leisure activities — restaurants, weddings, cricket — they were told to forget about those. The only place they were allowed to go was to the bazaar, and then only when accompanied by a fellow-policeman. While one bought provisions, the other had to keep a lookout.

There were reasons for this paranoia. Not a week would go by without the Calcutta police gazette reporting new losses in police ranks. Twenty-five killed… Four hundred wounded… And as for kidnappings… And all this in a single year of unrest.

At the end of 1970 Indira Gandhi's government woke from its stupor and agreed that an act designed to stamp out terrorism should be applied to the Naxalites. Also, to be sure of success, they wheeled out heavy artillery in the form of all-embracing bills to "avert acts of violence". The advantage immediately shifted to the police. They went from defence onto the attack. One single clause — the freedom to arrest all and sundry without a warrant — was the deciding blow. A vendetta now roared through Calcutta, waged on behalf of dead colleagues and of the families in barracks — and the nights with knives under pillows. Compared with this, the Wars of the Roses were a game of pick-up-sticks in the top year of kindergarten.

Runu would never forget the night of September 9, 1971, when he and his brigade combed block after block, dragging boys out of bed, boys suspected — barely suspected — of being Naxalite sympathisers. He didn't even arrest them. Oh no. He just ordered them to stand in line and loaded his gun. That night he was rewarded for his bravery with a medal and an emotional speech by the Chief to the massed ranks of the Calcutta police about him, Runu Niyogi, "a model of courage and devotion to duty at risk to his own life". And with a promotion, of course: the sub-inspector's insignia was exchanged for that of an inspector.

And what do you know — nights like that would occur over and over again.

But something surprising happened: no matter how great the slaughter, what kind of informers and killers they hired, what ingenious pogrom-organizers (for a hundred and fifty rupees a month!) they sent into suspect areas of Calcutta, the number of Naxalites — of whom no fewer than two thousand had already been killed — did not decrease. On the contrary. As with the Lernean Hydra, when one head was cut off, two new ones grew in its place. And the malice and vengefulness even tripled.

And it was all down to the man who gave the Naxalites their ideology and promised the simple people a life without hunger — after the victory.

His forehead was high, broad, and proud, his nose large and beaky like a Tibetan crow, his lips delicate, mobile. His hawk-eyed gaze was youthful, within the funereal frame of his glasses. His chin was pointed, sharp as an elbow, reaching forward, as did the whole persona of this standard-bearer, brooking no criticism. He was the height of a child — a gaunt, scrawny, little shrimp. A walking corpse with tenacious fingers, long as a spider's thread. Age somewhere just past fifty.

He never stopped preaching that power understands only one argument — a bayonet in the throat. He called for vengeance, vengeance, and more vengeance, for every comrade shot or tortured — for one should never fear to take revenge. And the whole of India listened. People prayed to him, as to Mao and Stalin. He had a melodious name — Mazumdar. The people called him simply Charubabu.

He was the most wanted man in all India. But it looked as

if shoeing the proverbial flea might be easier than finding that genius of conspiracy.

* * *

In the spring of 1972 Runu and his team did nevertheless pick up the trail. When, later, after some high-society dinner, he was asked how he'd done it, he gave his interlocutor a cunning smirk, rubbing his rotund stomach. "Sleight of hand and no cheating!"

The bit about sleight of hand was, of course, true. Later, in his memoir, he would describe how the police discovered, among twenty-eight Naxalites they had arrested, one who was personally acquainted with Mazumdar. Of course they *elicited* from him, in the way that only the police can, the fact that Mazumdar had a courier network and what time and at which station a courier was to arrive.

They set up an ambush at the station.

The courier did not arrive on the expected day. Nor three, nor five, nor ten days later. But they kept the ambush in place, feeding it up like a bride before her first inspection by the groom's family. Not a single bench, not an inch of floor-space, not one corner, not one crowded, jostling platform was neglected.

At last the courier appeared. Fast-moving, nimble, light on his feet, and sharp-eyed. Slippery as an eel. One of the boys who collect up scraps from under the samosa stalls. The pack of letters extracted from the boy's trousers on July 15 produced a long-awaited surprise. No address, no signature, but...

"... try and come to Calcutta..." wrote Mazumdar to his wife.

"To Calcutta... To Calcutta? So he's in Calcutta!" guessed Runu. Until now his network had told him Charu was hiding out beyond the state boundaries.

There was not a minute to be lost. If Mazumdar was really here, it was important to complete the operation within twenty-four hours. After that the courier's disappearance would be discovered and Mazumdar would leave town.

By evening they'd extracted from the boy the address where he'd collected the letters. At midnight they picked up nine sleeping men at that address — Mazumdar was not among them. But those who were turned out to be no small fry: they were members of the regional party committee and commanders of partisan units.

Within the hour Runu heard the young constables beating information out of them in the cell next to his office. And the lighter the night sky, the louder the screams from next door and the clearer it became that only one out of this whole group knew where Mazumdar was. The poor devil finally talked at three in the morning. Just a few words — but so much pain. 170A Middle Road.

"That's Entally area," Runu quickly worked out. "The other side of Sealdah station."

Still not believing his luck, and fearful of losing a star on his insignia, Runu ordered that the Naxalite be dressed in women's clothes. Two constables rushed into the street and spotted a rickshaw-boy at a junction, sleeping in his two-wheeled bullock cart. And before the boy even realized what was happening he was knocked out and pushed into a police van.

Runu harnessed himself between the shafts, quite prepared to pull that bone-shaker, and waited while a policeman climbed in with the Naxalite, now under a burqa, so they looked like an ordinary married couple.

When they came to the end of Middle Road and stopped outside the three-storey slum that was number 170A, Runu, soaked through with the excitement and the unwonted exertion, threw down the shafts, grabbed the Naxalite by the elbow, and they both made their way soundlessly into the entrance-hall. The prisoner nodded silently towards a door on the ground floor. Runu took him back to the van.

Fourteen armed men had the whole building surrounded in half a minute, beneath a strontium-yellow moon that hung in the sky observing the goings-on below. One policeman stood outside the window. At half past three Runu returned to the entrance-hall and started thumping on the door impatiently with his fists.

In five minutes they heard sleepy footsteps coming from inside the flat. The brief noise of the lock and bolt being opened suggested strong, youthful hands. Without a sound they pulled the door slightly open. The narrow crack revealed to those in the entrance hall a sliver of unshaven cheek and the pupil of a dark eye. Someone asked, calmly: "What do you want?"

Runu did not answer. He pushed the door open and crossed the threshold towards the room where he expected to find Mazumdar. The person who had opened the door trotted after him, mumbling:

"What do you want? What do you want?"

The door of the room he was making for was ajar. There was a bed against the wall and on it, back turned on the world, a tiny body was breathing regularly.

"Who's that?" said Runu, jabbing with his finger, already feeling his heart swell with a paean of joy.

"It's my grandfather," the other answered.

Only now cooling down, Runu sat on the corner of the bed and touched the old man's shoulder politely.

"Sir! Sir!" he addressed him, respectfully.

The body gave a little wriggle and a shudder as if only now waking up, and turned round. Thus each looked the other in the eye, both knowing what lay in store.

Finally, the old man was shaken by an asthmatic cough.

Waiting patiently for the paroxysm to subside, Runu said thoughtfully (how long he had spent polishing the intonation!):

"There is truth in bloody victory, but it is not the ultimate truth. Why did the poet say these words?"

Neither the old man nor the one who'd said he was the grandson made a sound.

Runu took a cheroot from his pocket, the kind they smoked in the days of the British Empire.

"Smoke?" said Runu politely, holding one out to him.

"Can I?" said the old man, suspiciously, betraying for the first time the existence of a voice.

Runu struck a match deferentially and helped the old man get the cheroot lit, and from the way he started waving away the smoke, the policeman on watch outside understood that the denouement was close.

Even before the old man finished smoking his cheroot, four men burst into the flat and lined up all the inhabitants — they had found another man and a girl in the next room — against the wall, before starting to turn the place upside down.

Meanwhile, Runu went out into the hall and upstairs to the landlord, who had a telephone. He called the police station and asked them to send reinforcements, as if detaining a sick enemy might incur risk to life and limb. Only then did he clear his throat and, expanding the bellows of his chest like an accordion, dialled his chief.

"Good news, sir. We've arrested Mazumdar."

"Sure it's not just someone who looks like him?" asked Debi Roy.

"No possible mistake, sir. I recognized him immediately, though he doesn't look like the photograph any more. He's shaved his beard. But I'd have known him anywhere. I gave him a cheroot and he smoked it. You know how he likes cheroots, sir."

"Yes, yes, my son. I'm on my way!"

Satisfied that he'd done his duty, Runu went down to the ground floor. The walls within which, only ten minutes earlier, he had lit a cheroot under the nose of the Bengal police's greatest trophy, had now changed. The smell of death was in them. There was only one way to leave them — or, rather, there was no way out.

Runu was no longer in the mood for poetry, so he went up to the old man and, noticing with distaste that class enemy number one did not even come up to his chest, spoke without haste:

"Charubabu, I'm Runu Niyogi. You're under arrest."

And Runu guessed, from the way Charu Mazumdar swallowed, tensed up, that he recognized the name. At that time Runu was not generally known by name. At least, not *until* that time.

Somewhere in the depths of his demonic being, that was what Runu was striving for. Loud acclaim would not stop him moving noiselessly. That bulky frame knew how to stay invisible. Very few Bengalis knew Runu's face, but I doubt there would be anyone who would not, later, run for cover when his name was mentioned. Which was quite understandable. Calcutta is just one big crowd, a great jumble of people. If you shout something in Barabazar in the morning, they'll be shouting a response in Kushtia that evening. Within the bounds of adjacent districts, rumours spread more rapidly than the anopheles mosquito, landing on a rickshaw-boy, can sink its proboscis into him.

In other words, many people knew about Police Officer Runu but could not recognize him. And in that there was something of the Grim Reaper, who everyone had heard of, but no living soul had seen.

* * *

Twelve days after the arrest, Mazumdar breathed his last. At four in the morning, in an interrogation cell in the central jail.

They did not give the body to his family and did not even allow them sight of it. Having surrounded the area and cleared everyone out, even the stray dogs, they took it under police escort to the crematorium and cremated it. And for a long time yet there were whisperings in Calcutta and its underground groups to the effect that even Lenin and José Mariátegui died a natural death but Mazumdar, our poor Mazumdar, died a martyr.

As the authorities had thought, after the liquidation of Mazumdar the Naxalites lost their anchor, their charisma. It was as if the heart had been ripped from a strong body once the brain had lost its inspiration. The movement splintered and dispersed.

Shooting was heard less and less in the streets. More and more often in news bulletins it was "situation normal". The police went back to their cricket and their families left the barracks.

But there could be no question of total pacification.

With the arrest of Charu Mazumdar, a heap of papers had come into the hands of the police, and with them lists, lists, metres-long lists with names of Naxal members. Where had all these people gone? Where were they hiding? What were they planning? Had they gone underground to lick their wounds? Were they planning a new strike? The government could not allow them to return.

This is why the night of July 17 to 18 in Calcutta was no different from any other Bengal night. Deep into that night police informers were, as usual, earning their living, denunciations were being written, raids organized, arrests carried out.

And the next day, at ten o'clock, Runu will once more go to his office and someone will already be sitting there. One unfortunate wretch? Two? Three? But that is tomorrow — everything will happen tomorrow. It is still to come. But for the moment the clock tells us it is today. Outside, it is a July night. It is suffocating from the steamy closeness of the air, a closeness that cannot be relieved even by the fine drizzle. The town has settled into silence, and there is only the squelching of a rickshaw-boy's running feet to disturb the quiet of the dwellings that lined the road, their windows like empty eye-sockets, knowing neither shutters nor glass.

Night, night, stifling night. And with it come all the phantoms.

Chapter 6
The Iron Age

Did I promise you a night? A stifling night, with rain and phantoms? After which there will be no dawn? From which, once you are in it, there is no return? Which can begin but never end...? No matter how much I have drawn out the lines, trying to put off the inevitable moment for paragraph after paragraph, trying to loiter a moment on the sunny side of destiny, the inevitable is just that, inevitable. Well now, I'm afraid, we've arrived. Hanna, silent Hanna in the film *The Secret Life of Words* — how right you were when you said, "Your whole life is about to change and you're worrying about an old Fiat Turbo."

Yes, and I too might say that to my heroine: "Your whole life is about to change and you're worrying about such nonsense."

That day (that day would, of course be followed by that night) Archana arrived at work earlier than usual and looked at the clock more frequently than usual, willing the hands to speed up. At the head teachers' department they were paying out the salaries. After her classes she had to rush there, to the centre of Calcutta, by foot and by bus, to get there before the cashier's office closed. Getting paid today would be opportune: the department paid salaries haphazardly, once in a while, whenever they got round to it. And at home the butter had run out, the shelves were empty of food, and, come to think of it, they had guests for the night, the daughters of her brother Ramendra.

"Now I'm getting paid I can do a week's shopping and Ma can work her magic in the kitchen and give the girls a real treat," mused Archana happily.

When the hour hand reached one o'clock, Archana left school. Not even noticing that she had come out of the bamboo forest that had thrown itself on the mercy of the July rain, she was bumped around as usual in the bus, got out in Calcutta, walked two blocks through town, and ran up the steps of the head teachers' department. At a wooden hatch with an iron grille, a lady in an expensive muslin sari counted out a hundred rupees, Archana's salary for the month.

Another quarter of an hour at the little local bazaar and Archana was happily packing mustard-seed oil, beans, quinoa, spinach, vegetables, curry, and rice into bags. And she also bought some sweet desserts for her nieces. Weighed down with this festive fare, she ran again for the stuffy bus with the enormous "Om" signs on its sides — this time heading for home.

* * *

Archana had been living in the working-class district of Dum Dum in the north of Calcutta for three years now. She had moved there with her mother and Saumen after her father's death. Two shabby little rooms and a minute kitchen in a two-storey, concrete nesting box at 7 Jawpur Road could not, of course, rival the brick walls of her childhood. The decision to move from their home in Howrah, where everyone knew everything about everyone, to the cramped, self-centred metropolis of Calcutta had been for Saumen's sake. To help him lose himself in the capital's human anthill: lose himself and live unnoticed, work unnoticed for the cause to which he had now dedicated himself.

Before the death of his father, Saumen, an exceptionally brilliant student, was training to be an engineer. His years at university had coincided with the Naxalbari uprising, from which the Naxalites emerged. Caught up in this romantic whirlwind, with its admixture of patriotism, Saumen began to take an interest in politics — an interest that had its origins even earlier, in his childhood, in the hunger and harshness of life around him, in his paternal home with the door always open — for his mother and father had taught the children never to refuse people their help.

Soon that simple interest escalated into an immersion in Marx, Lenin, and Mao, into all that communist nonsense, cleverly shaped into various "isms" with the same old revolutionary slogans. But that was no surprise — for it is only today that communists are unloved, along with racists, Nazis, nationalists, and extremists. But then, half a century ago, half the world went by that doctrine. And why not, when you were promised in exchange equality and communal ownership, when it was "one for all and all for one," "from each according to his abilities, to each according to his needs," "he who was nothing will become everything?" The chains smashed, a happy future, a just life without hunger. Who could not fall in love when the bride brought the promise of such a dowry?

In his last year of university, which he, therefore, never completed, Saumen became an apprentice engineer at a well-known organization, the Calcutta Metropolitan Development Authority. He was soon promoted to the prestigious position of Overseer (Mechanical and Electrical), where he came to know real life, toiling by the sweat of his brow, without political slogans, but with a reassuring sense of economic wellbeing.

But after his father's death he suddenly turned his back on the largesse that life was starting to offer. He turned his back in the name of that other, new world, which he had already believed in as a student and to which he now decided to dedicate himself one hundred percent — and in the name of which he had even left home, offloading his mother's care on to Archana's unmarried shoulders.

Three years had passed since Archana and her mother had settled in Calcutta, three years since Saumen had gone into hiding underground.

But even so, they did see him sometimes. Once a week or once a month he would come home — emaciated, dirty, dead tired, dusty, permeated with the smell of the earth, as if the underground were literally underground. His appearances were always unexpected — sometimes at night, sometimes during the day. None of the family knew exactly when he would come or for how long, a couple of days or a couple of hours.

Both Archana and her mother knew that Saumen was a Naxalite. Not only did they know, but they were proud of him, even supported his activities. Though exactly what he did in the underground remained unclear. Saumen did not want to talk about it, other than saying airily that "we help the peasants to get the movement going…" and "we help the poor to organize their lives." His family did not ask for any more detail, understanding that it was better not to know. They did not even try to find out where this underground was, just guessing blindly: somewhere in the back of beyond, somewhere in Bankura district…

Despite the deep secrecy that shrouded their relationships and meant they had to stay on their guard, even with neighbours who were close friends, neither Archana, nor her mother, nor the other family members ever thought about the possible consequences. About the fact that they were walking through a mine-field, like all the families of Naxalites. For they knew that every night the police were carting young men off from the neighbouring houses and districts. But did they perhaps not *want* to think about it? Not dare even to entertain thoughts of that kind? As if Krishna himself had endowed them with a blessed simplicity and ordered them not to be afraid.

"What could be wrong with that, with helping the poor?" Archana would say within the family group. "They're tackling the peasants' problems. They're fighting for freedom."

"Helping the poor is noble!" her mother would fervently concur.

Yes, mother was especially unstinting in her support of her son. When Saumen came and leaned his head on her shoulder, she would put her arms, like vine tendrils, around him and say with a catch in her voice that would not discredit any film star:

"I know, son, I believe in you — it's a good thing you're doing. All my thoughts are with you, and all my strength as a mother."

Sometimes Saumen arrived in a bad mood, limp, doubting himself, arguing with himself.

"I can't go on like this! I can't stand it!"

But his mother would again comfort him:

"You can... you can, son. I'm with you. I've given you my blessing."

But what exactly she had given her blessing to she did not and could not know. She had heard about the raids, the kidnappings, the killings, the explosions — she'd heard all that. But she believed, she fervently believed that her son was not like that, that he took no part in killings, that he was only helping the peasants. And helping is noble. And he would not sign up to evil deeds — he wasn't brought up like that.

And his mother's feeling about it was correct. Saumen was among those Naxalites who did not accept violence and tried to keep out of the way when it arose. They called people like him "theoretical leaders." His particular task was to "organize the poor against the feudal system and ensure they have sufficient knowledge to stand up for themselves." But what lay hidden in the ironed-out folds of those red calico formulas? Could it be that, while he himself took no part in the shootings, kidnappings, and explosions, he was nevertheless teaching others how and why they should?

The underground is the underground, but even within this obsessive milieu love burgeoned. During one of his sorties to visit his mother, Saumen told her that he was going to get married.

No one could say for sure when and where he had first seen Latika. Some said they had met by chance, at the home of friends; others were sure they were brought together by shared interests.

That year Latika, a lecturer at a women's college, was writing a first draft for her dissertation on the role of women in Indian politics from the 1920s to the 1970s, and in that connection she was meeting activists from various parties, including the Naxalites. She never hid her sympathy with the latter.

Archana and her mother greeted the news about Latika with joy. They also saw no problem with the difference in ages, the bride being ten years older than Saumen. Latika was on the verge of becoming a professor and a Ph.D. in political science: she bore the indelible mark of one worthy of respect. And the fact that she, a serious lady from a prosperous, well-known family (her father was a high-ranking police official, though now retired), suddenly wanted to marry a poor man who was not indifferent to the work of the underground… The Guha family saw in that a sign that fortune had smiled on them.

Latika's parents did not accept the marriage and broke off relations with their daughter.

After a quiet, slightly awkward wedding in the family circle, the newly-weds rented very modest accommodation in Calcutta. Their honeymoon over, Saumen returned to the underground and Latika, as tradition demanded, moved in with her mother-in-law in Dum Dum.

And there the three of them lived, mother, Archana, and Latika.

* * *

The wan eye of the late sun was still glinting playfully through slits in the palm fronds when Archana, weighed down with bags, stepped off the bus. Turning off the made-up road, she had to walk past blocks of flats, on the balconies of which skirts and saris waved like flags. Here and there, behind the waving hemlines, housewives' hands would flit about, grabbing the coloured rags and pulling them into the cave-like flats.

An unseen hand was working assiduously to spur on the evening and slowly, mile by mile, up-end the sky. From its extreme edge immature clouds came creeping, ready to ripen by nightfall and burst into leaden bullets.

The building where the Guha family rented two rooms and a kitchen had the air of a wretched little two-storey hovel. Its foundations had subsided, soaked through in the monsoon, and its walls faded to the colour of boiled cod. The one window, with vertical bars, and the blue, scratched door of their ground-floor flat gave on to a narrow balcony with an iron grille. And only from there, once you had opened the rusty bolt of another barred gate, could you get out on to the street.

Archana was met with a hubbub and a fug, and the extreme vitality that soon pervades the air when children arrive. The little girls — Sanchayiya and Samhita, six and ten years old respectively — were sitting on the double bed and slapping their knees, beating out a tap-dance to accompany the merry recitation of a children's tongue-twister "agdum-bagdum". In the kitchen, heated butter (her mother had obviously borrowed some from a neighbour) was sputtering in a pan, diffusing a smell of mustard and turmeric, and announcing that supper was imminent. Archana planted a kiss on the top of the girls' heads and went into the kitchen to unload her bags.

"So what story do you want to hear today? The one about how Iron Age outwitted Bronze Age, or the one about the Vaitarani River?"

"How Iron Age outwi-i-tted!" cried the girls, clapping their hands. "Let's leave the Vaitarani till tomorrow!"

Soon Latika got back from work and then Gouri, Archana's friend and almost one of the family, arrived. She'll be no stranger to this story, so let's take a look at her as well.

Gouri Chatterjee was single — as single as the spire on a church tower. She lost her father when only a child, and became an orphan despite her mother being in good health. For, laid low by widow's grief, by poverty, and by a petulant character, her mother could no longer — no longer wanted to — take care of her daughter. So from a backwoods Bengal village they sent the little girl to Howrah, to be looked after by her uncle.

Despite the fact that Gouri belonged to the highest caste, the Brahmin, the most sought-after in the marriage market, the matchmakers were taking their time — and that was the source of an impenetrable melancholy and sometimes a wet pillow by morning. The reason for her solitude was not a dark skin or anorexia: it was her height, which was unusual for a girl — the height of European fashion models. This was regarded as nature's blunder, fate's practical joke. Few Indian men would not feel diminished, even degraded, alongside a tall wife. Potential mothers-in-law turned up their noses if Gouri cropped up in conversation.

Now Gouri was nearly twenty-three and had found work in Calcutta, in a small, private workshop in Beadon Street, where they embroidered bedspreads, cushions, and saris. She started as an apprentice but quickly rose to become foreman and started teaching embroidery to the newcomers. She liked the work a lot and didn't want to lose it, not at any price. So she would arrive at the crack of dawn and leave after the others. She would work overtime, demonstrating her usefulness to the workshop, and knowing that she had only herself to rely on. When she didn't have the energy to get back to Howrah, she would go to Archana's. In the Guha home she was welcome at any time.

And now, the minute Gouri appeared in the doorway, they all rushed up to her.

"Gouri, my child, how lovely that you've come," said Sudharani and gave her a hug. "By the way, I've got something. Look. I saved it for you."

The few letters that Saumen sent were no longer than a page. They were not even letters, but the kind of chitter-chatter you get on postcards, always with an innocuous text, the kind you can send from the underground. His respects to his mother, his gratitude to his wife and sister, his wishes for their endurance and their good health, and always with the same postscript: "Please look after Gouri — she's like a sister to us. Parimal also sends her his best wishes."

It was Emmy who brought the letters — the postman would throw them to her, or else a little boy would hand them over, running the message for a stranger in the street… Mother read them first, then Archana, Latika, and Gouri. Whoever read the letter last was supposed to destroy it.

Now, again, Gouri's eyes bored into the words "Parimal also sends best wishes to her" and she pressed the letter to her cheek, wiped a tear from an eyelash, and was about to tear the letter up when they were called to supper. She hesitated, then began to hurry, and thrust the sheet of paper into the book-case, thinking to herself that she would be able to read it again when she went to bed, or in the morning before work.

* * *

At ten o'clock, they drew the curtains and all went to bed in the same room. Mother, Archana, and the nieces were on mattresses on the floor. Latika and Gouri had the bed.

"Archana, you pro-mised…" came the well-rehearsed whine.

"Of course, of course! I promised, so I'll tell the story."

Sanchayiya and Samhita snuggled up either side of Archana.

"Once upon a time, long, long ago, when the sky was higher, the sun brighter, and the moon lighter," began Archana slowly, bringing her voice into tune with the night — and the night is lyrical…

She no longer remembered where this story came from, from which of the sacred books in the Brahmins' care, and had even forgotten where she herself knew it from. Perhaps she had heard it somewhere, or read it, or maybe seen it in street theatre. With the years some bits had been erased from her memory and others added.

"Once upon a time, long, long ago, when the sky was higher, the sun brighter, and the moon lighter, the waters of the Ganges began above the sky and poured down below the earth. They were clearer than the purest tear of a babe in arms — because they were not loaded with the ashes of dead souls, for there were not yet any dead souls. At that time a father had four sons, called Golden Age, Silver Age, Bronze Age, and Iron Age. And they were the four legs of the sacred cow of the whole of creation.

"One day the father called his sons and ordered them to go down to the earth and rule its people. He commanded them to rule in turn, alternating like morning, midday, evening, and night; spring, summer, autumn, and winter; childhood, youth, maturity, and old age; conception, birth, maturing, and death.

"Golden Age was the first to come to the throne. The fair-skinned infant lay in a cradle of golden lotus petals. All who held the baby in their arms and clasped him to their breast were filled with boundless love. For the child was Love. And the more people reached out for him, the more his laughter rang out, the louder the bells of creation rang out — and the less sorrow remained in the world. One day it disappeared completely. All the people became happy and all became equal. The aim of their life from then on was to preserve the sound of the bells. Its vibrations filled their hearts with the breath of eternity.

"But in the clear, mirror-like sky, a small cloud appeared. This was when the next son, Silver Age, ascended the throne. A silvery wreath adorned the head of the delicate youth, a mark of selection, of rank. The era of equality, truth, and purity had come to an end. The time of separation had come. People were divided into castes. They no longer simply loved others, taking no account of who or what they were: they loved only those like themselves. And only because they did not yet know sinful passions could they still hear the bells of creation.

"Time passed and clouds crept out, a yellow bronze, like the leaves of a withered banyan tree. This was the third son, Bronze Age, coming to the throne. The giant's beard had a reddish tinge and behind his back hung a bow and arrows. There were bracelets round his arms and legs, his body was covered in golden brocade, and on his head sparkled a crown, symbolizing wealth and power, but also the rule of law. The people had to be reminded of what was bad and what good — for alone they were liable to forget. Bronze Age walked down the stairway leading from the sky. People threw themselves to pay obeisance. The strongest and nimblest could get higher than the others. From up there the world seemed spread out before them as if it lay at their feet. This gave a feeling of superiority, and they enjoyed being above the others. The cow lost its second leg. And only because people still helped one another, and particularly those who remained below them, could they still sometimes hear the bells of creation.

"When it was the turn of the fourth son, he did not send any leaden clouds but instead found his way in unnoticed and hid in the mango grove. He was a youthful-looking old man with a golden head, silver chest, bronze hips, and calves cast in iron. His metal-heeled boots concealed the fact that his feet were made from old, dried-out clay. Iron Age waited till his brother was coming past and then stepped out to meet him.

"'You?' cried Bronze Age. 'How dare you appear and walk in my grove?'

"'It's me, your brother! Don't you recognize me? It's my turn to rule over the people!'

"Bronze Age flew into a rage:

"'That's as may be, but I know what you're up to. Your kingdom is the incarnation of evil. My kingdom is the law. It will be better for the people if I remain their ruler!'

"'But, brother, you cannot change the laws of the Universe. Admit it, my time has come.'

"'It's not up to you to decide what I can do!' said Bronze Age aggressively and pulled out his bow and arrows.

"Iron Age fell to his knees.

"'Stop! Stop, great Emperor! Have it your way. You stay here and rule. But don't send me away! Give me sanctuary. You respect the law, and the law says that we must be virtuous. Please, give me sanctuary!'

"'Good,' said Bronze Age, softening. He liked it when people knelt before him. 'You shall have it, but on one condition. You are allowed to be in only four places. Your domain is gambling, alcohol, depravity, and violence.'

"'But people don't go to places like that! I'll be all alone!' And Iron Age bent even lower, banging his forehead on the ground and sobbing. 'O my great Emperor! Have pity on me! Give me one more place. Just one more!'

"'Fine, you can also live in gold, glory, and splendour. These are three dark reflections of pride alone.'

"'Oh, thank you! How great you are and how merciful!' laughed Iron Age, and immediately disappeared.

"Bronze Age did the rounds of his domain, returning home towards evening. His lips were dry with thirst and blood dripped from his blistered feet. He called people to help him, but for some reason they did not hear. No one gave him water. No one washed his wounds.

"'This is all very strange. Very strange, indeed, frowned Bronze Age." This morning everything was fine but now these people are deaf.'

And then Bronze Age heard a metallic whisper above his ear:

"'But it is in your power to teach them a lesson! Punish those cold-hearted little nobodies! Kill them! Kill!'

"Obeying the summons, Bronze Age grabbed his bow and arrows and drew his bow. But his hand shook. All at once he understood whose voice it was. Iron Age had outwitted him and had settled inside the gold crown on his head. Bronze Age was the last Emperor who obeyed the law. He knew what was bad and what good. He could not kill a human. He could hear the bells of creation.

"Bronze Age threw his crown to the ground in despair and from it was heard metallic laughter. He started climbing swiftly up the stairway to the sky. And the cow lost its third leg.

"'Away from this place!' he told himself. 'Lawlessness has

arrived! Dark times have come! Evil incarnate has come to the earth!'

"When he hid in the feather bed of the heavens, the clouds formed into a curved sabre and — from beyond this wide earth and beyond the heavens — cut the sky away from the earth…"

The younger girl, Sanchayiya, had fallen asleep before the end of the story. But Samhita lay back, thinking.

"Archana, what happened then, when Iron Age became the ruler?"

"We can see that now. The Brahmins say the Iron Age hasn't come to an end yet."

"What a sad story, with each new time turning out worse than the one before. It should be the other way round!"

"Yes, that'd be good. But it is only a fairy-tale, my dear. Let's go to sleep now! Look, the others are already asleep."

"And that's right," thought Archana's mother, as she rolled over. "Sleep now. The morning brings wisdom."

* * *

In the middle of a very run-of-the-mill dream a thousand suns seemed suddenly to explode. All at once it was light in the room — you could sense it on your skin — and not just light but bright, blinding, sharp, caustic spikes into eyes still closed and vacant. The light was discharged in a powerful flow, like water from a fire hose, from the side of the room with the window, dissolving the curtain on the way and penetrating under sheets, creeping under saris, ferreting around bodies, burning through legs and chests.

"What? Is it morning already?" thought Archana in surprise, pulling the sheet up to her face, trying to hide from the brazen rays.

Only now did her auditory system open the sluice gate, closed in the depth of the night, and a hollow, drumming sound assault her ear; nearby, thousands of a woodpeckers were hammering frenziedly away, apparently just outside their wall and door. Her brain had not yet woken up — it was rolling around, staggering drunkenly, assembling itself from atoms into ribbons of molecules. But her heart had already lurched with fear, as at a cobra-bite, and fallen over a precipice, settling into an uneven rhythm as it fell.

Archana forced her eyes open, fighting blindness in a space drowned in light — a space that knew no electric lamps but had now burst into flame — and discerned, above her, Latika and Gouri, frozen in a dumb attempt to work out what was happening.

But mother had understood it all immediately and rushed to open the door.

She had been struggling with the tricky lock for about a minute, shouting all the time "Just a moment, just a moment!" to the as yet unseen force that had already started kicking the door in from the other side. At last she got it open. She herself, cold and pale, shrank back to the side, making way for disaster to enter.

Eight spotlights piercing the darkness, each the size of a moon, now ringed the room. Searchlight spears crept across the walls, impaling the folds of concrete like pins in flannelette. They thrust into bedding that still exuded feminine warmth, cut into the mattress and pillows, and finally came to rest, stopping dead on the faces of the occupants. Sanchayiya was snivelling: Samhita, very grown-up, hushed her sister and squeezed her doll-like hand.

When Archana's eyes got used to the light, she could make out legs standing by the spotlights. A pair of boots came forward. A low-browed face came into view and asked disdainfully:

"Which one's Latika? Latika Mukherjee?"

"I am," said Latika, without mentioning that a year ago she had become a Guha.

"And what relationship are these women to you?"

"This is my mother-in-law. This is my sister-in-law. This is a friend. And who are you?"

"Calcutta police!"

"What do you want?"

"What do we want, boys?" brayed the most senior, with a stentorian guffaw. "First, madam, just get this straight. *We ask the questions here!* And secondly… we've got to search this place."

For an hour and a half the evil dervishes of light whirled about the room, blocking out the air, walls, and floor with their surges. Skirts, saris, and linen, potatoes, rice, carrots, peas, and flour — round they all went on the same carousel. Household utensils crashed to the floor; cushions released a fog of down. When they got to the shelves where Latika kept her books, the air filled with an archival dust that made your nose itch.

Archana sat, neither alive nor dead, propped up against the naked wall, and mentally mending the hem of her grass-coloured night sari. Sometimes sounds would penetrate the fog in her brain. Someone was yelling at Latika. Yes, they knew everything! On such and such a day of such and such a month she went to such and such an address! On such and such a day at such and such a bazaar she bought such and such and such and such! Then another voice reached her: "Manash, look at this! This'll do you nicely!"

And again, silence. Like in a silent film. There is an image, a picture: a moving picture, the mouths open, but there are no voices.

Then another sound penetrated. Somewhere above her and to the right someone said:

"We've finished the search. You, you, and you are coming with us. Get them into the van, quickly."

About three in the morning, a paroxysm of knocking resounded in the first-floor flat at 7 Jawpur Road, where the Choudhury family, who owned the house, lived. The family was not asleep. For the last hour and a half, since being awoken by the noise in the flat below, they had listened to the sounds in the entrance hall, looking out of the window from behind a thick curtain. The courtyard was full of police, the house surrounded. The landlord's wife was trying to count the uniforms from the window. She lost count at thirty.

When they heard the knocking, the father and son, Badal and Panchu Choudhury, hurried to the door. They couldn't refuse to open: a policeman was already just outside. Not waiting to be told the reason for the visit, the head of the family spoke first:

"Why are you taking those women? What have they done?"

"Shut up and sign this!" And the policeman handed him an official-looking form. "Get a move on! Sign here!"

"But can I just…" said the old man, now trembling. "Why do I have to sign it? It's a blank form!"

"Because we're telling you to. Sign it! Because… you've got a son."

The old man said nothing more. He signed. He bowed. He stood back. Then the son added his own squiggle.

Both accepted sin into their heart — and stopped disaster coming *their* way.

* * *

In the dark, blue-black van with grating over the windows, there was room for more than three people. Archana, Latika, and Gouri sat in different corners, and all the time the van bumped along the city streets they said not a word.

Somewhere along the byways of their consciousness they realized they had to do something, keep their eyes busy, if only by looking out of the window with no idea where they were being taken. But the windows seemed to have been smeared with wax on the outside. The silhouettes of streets, houses, and trees flashed by in a cavalcade of shadows. Archana tried to pull herself together but she had difficulty putting her thoughts into words.

"So it was Latika… they came because of Latika?" And she

struggled to recollect the night's events. "Well, yes. The first thing they said was 'Which one's Latika?' Why, why? Why do they want Latika? But why is that so odd actually? She's not got much common sense, she always blurts out whatever she's thinking… someone must have informed on her…"

Archana now looked at Latika. She was sitting stock still, riveted to the spot like a temple Buddha, reflecting on her own concerns, maybe about the same thing, interlacing her fine, intellectual fingers under her delicate breasts. Her cornflower-blue night sari shimmered purplish black. Archana was thirty-three and Latika a little older. For a year now they had been such close friends that no one ever referred to them as sisters-in-law.

"Yes, but why did they immediately use her maiden name? Didn't they know she's taken her husband's name? Perhaps they didn't even know she was married?"

The deep, melancholy wail of a giant cowrie shell was wafted their way by a gust of wind. Somewhere nearby was a workshop making wedding decorations, which hummed with activity even at night.

"But if they don't know Latika's married, does it mean this has nothing to do with Saumen? How come they didn't ask about Saumen? Looks as if it's not…"

The van swerved sharply into the kerb, gave a snort, and stopped. In the driver's cabin, the passenger door slammed, bringing the window grilles to life. The constable ran to the building where they had stopped — a building with a sign-board, white as a wall eye, saying "Cossipore Police Station."

"But if it was only about Latika, then shouldn't they let us go? She's not a politician or activist, she's just an academic and lecturer. There's nothing wrong in that. The main thing's to keep quiet about Saumen. Lucky he wasn't at home. What do they do to women? Nothing. They'll ask us a few questions, for the sake of form, but then they'll let us go. But Saumen — they might have killed *him*."

The constable, drenched, rushed into Cossipore police station and asked to use the phone.

"Who've you got today?" asked the duty officer, pulling the phone over from the desk to the counter.

"We don't know that ourselves yet," answered the constable, as he started dialling the number. "One of them's got the same surname as someone on Charu Mazumdar's list. We brought the others with her for company… We'll have to check."

"Ah, terrorists! They don't come here, they go to Runu!"

"I know. That's where we're taking them."

The constable emerged from the building into the rain, jumped into the van next to the driver and told him, with a yawn:

"To Lalbazar."

Chapter 7

A Test of Character

The detectives at Calcutta Criminal Investigation Department had such a surfeit of women at their disposal that not even the young and lustful constables who had only just joined the service could be bothered to rape them to force a confession. As a warning to particularly unaccommodating women, most of them Untouchables, they kept half-drunk thugs at the entrance to the station, primed to have some fun with a woman when ordered to do so to work off their own petty crimes. These hirelings were not often needed, however, except perhaps during major festivals, like the month of Ashvin, when the sky, a bright, saccharine, eye-watering turquoise barely shed a tear of its own; when the weather was wonderful and the crowded city teemed with the painted effigies of a myriad Indian gods, the air tantalizing with its milky aroma of rasgulla balls, signifying the end of the fast and luring even the dynasties of beggars out onto the path that led to a full stomach. On days like this, people didn't want to work but to run down to the banks of the Ganges where on the tenth day of the waxing moon the peasants, arrayed in their festive best, lowered rafts onto the water, bearing ten-armed Mother Durga who protects the world order from demons.

But at this time of year, in July, with the autumn festivities still a long way off, the policemen did most of the work themselves. On days like this, the hired thugs were used just as intimidation. The belief that the more experienced the officer of the law, the greater his skill in handling women and using rape in order to extract a confession was, if you like, a thing of the past — old-fashioned, out of date. Interrogating a woman like a man, as if she was a man, now that was an art. But it meant effectively making the woman as much like a man as possible. And that was an even greater art and all the junior staff assembled to observe it.

However, I'm getting ahead of myself again. But then, how are you supposed to tell the story of life? It has to be as you see it from the very first word, the very first line. With all the stops between stations and all the smoking breaks. With all that is only partially said or partially seen. And a mysterious purpose between the lines.

* * *

As the night drew to a close, Police Officer Manas — Manas Roy Chawdhury–loose-limbed and lanky, his dark eyes like iron buttons in his beetroot face — gave a long yawn. The night had been unusually calm — no alarms, no raids, no chases — just one planned arrest that brought a long period of surveillance to an end. He had made the arrest and joined in the search, led by his friend, Amit Mazumder. A snatch squad had played a part but had not been of much use. In a show of strength, the lads had cordoned off the house. They had sowed terror in the residents. No one had tried to resist arrest, which meant there had been no shooting either.

The arrested women had already been brought in. At 04:30 A.M., they were sitting in CID on the first floor at Lalbazar in the Special Cell Corridor, in their nightclothes, expressionless. They were calm, deathly still. As though they were dead already, thought Manas, with a smirk. There was no wailing or keening. They didn't ask for anything and they didn't talk among themselves. They didn't even gesture at one another.

Political, though not prohibited, materials had been found in the flat where they were seized. The fact that books like that had been found there at all pointed to the owners' interest in certain issues. It was enough to make the detectives ask questions.

As it turned out, the flat with the dangerous books was entirely empty of men and that thought irritated Manas like a grain of cayenne pepper. There was no getting away from the fact that all the arrested women were of marriageable age. Particularly the one they had been following, who was essentially the reason they had arrested the others.

"If some woman's itching to get involved in politics, and this one certainly is," Manas thought as he fixed the confiscated volumes of Marx and Engels with a glare, "it has to be under the influence of a brother or husband. So where the hell are the men?"

His shift came to an end as the day began. He couldn't stop the yawns. They were wearing him out.

"I'll send them for questioning and then sleep. Runu can handle it in the morning," Manas decided, flexing his fingers as he kneaded his long, stiff neck.

The door was jerked open. The duty officer called Latika. Her frozen face seemed sealed shut. Everything about her said she was there by mistake.

"Now she's going to play at Little Miss Know-Nothing," thought Manas. "Fair enough. Let her. It'll do for a first time."

Drily and politely he gestured to the wonky chair opposite him.

"Take a seat. There's no need to be frightened. I have to put this on record. Please give precise answers to all the questions. This conversation is just a formality. We know everything. There's no point telling lies or making a fuss. You will only make your position worse. So, here goes. What's your name?"

"Latika."

"Surname?"

"Guha."

"Now, listen, I warned you. We know everything. You're not a Guha. Your name's Mukherjee."

"That's my father's name. My married name is Guha. I haven't been married long."

"Aha! I see. You're married... Congratulations!" Manas was so pleased he even raised his narrow eyebrows, curved as a scimitar. "In that case, yes... of, course, let's write about your husband. Who did you say was the lucky chap?"

"My husband's name is Saumen," Latika said through gritted teeth, aware that the conversation had taken an undesirable turn.

Manas brightened. The yawns vanished. His suspicions that a man was involved had suddenly proved grounded.

"Does your husband live at your address, 7, Jawpur Road?"

"He does."

"Hm... so you say, but he wasn't at home last night. Can you explain where he was?"

"I don't know why he didn't come home."

"Okay. Let's put it differently. Where is he now, this what's his name?" Manas looked at the statement and read out carefully, "Sa-u-men?"

"I don't know."

"Think about it. Where does he usually go? Relatives, friends?"

"I don't know. I'm telling you, I don't know."

"Oh, come now. A wife doesn't know where her husband is?" Manas half stood up in his impatience. "Who's going to believe that?! Cut the comedy! You're a grown woman! Give me a proper answer. Where...is...your...husband...Saumen?"

"I don't know. Honestly, I can't tell you anything. I don't know."

"Fine. Let's say I believe you." Manas sank back onto his chair. "Who else lives at that address?"

"My mother-in-law and my sister-in-law."

"And their names?"

"Sudharani Guha. Archana Guha."

"Good. Where do you work?"

"At the girls' college. Gokhale Memorial Girls' College.

"As?"

"A professor. A doctor of political science."

"Really? Political science…" Manas smacked his lips in satisfaction. "So, politics. Active in politics, are you?"

"No, I'm just a teacher."

"We'll see. Do you have connections to the Naxalites? Do you?"

"No."

"I warned you. There's no point telling lies. You do have connections to the Naxalites." Manas put the stress on the wrong syllable.

"I really don't!"

"Fine. Let's say I believe you. So, Mrs. Guha, here's what we'll do. You want to get out of here, don't you? Alive and well? We can help you to do that. But first you help us. Look at this list!" Manas produced a long list of names. "Which names do you know?"

"None of them. I don't know anyone."

"You haven't even bothered to look!"

"That's because I don't know anyone. At all."

"Everyone says that to start with. Everyone thinks they're a hero."

Latika was taken out and Archana brought in. Archana was taken out and Gouri brought in. We won't go into the details of the questioning. It was all quick and unemotional — just for the record. It was merely a prelude, a test of character. A testing of their mettle. A game of cat and mouse when the cat really needed a nap.

* * *

Towards six, when the bazaars woke up and the puddles on the pavement evaporated, giving back what the heavens had rained down overnight, Archana, Latika, and Gouri were removed from the Special Cell. A bull-headed guard in squeaky-new boots ordered them to put their hands behind their backs and strode along the lengthy corridors. Heavy doors opened and closed. Rusty bundles of keys scraped. Eventually, they all reached a grey-brown inner courtyard, the walls a lighter shade of brown. They eagerly took a gulp of air that carried a sour taste of sweat then plunged immediately into the central block.

Now that we're in, let's have a look around. Provincials like myself will immediately think of a travelling zoo — a prison on wheels, its sedate line of trailers, standing wall to wall, their cages with strong iron bars, containing one or more animals. American films, the century before last admittedly, had something like it, but for people, with prisoners in cages rather than cells, all under one roof and the gaze of the guards and of one another. There's something like it in our own day in the footage from Guantanamo. But this was the prototype, here in one of the loveliest buildings in the state, once home to John Palmer, prince of merchants, whose residence later became Calcutta's main police station. Several hundred men, women, and even children have whiled away their worst days here. The central block was a holding block not the real prison. Moving on to the prison was more a dream than a punishment.

A small, unsteady woman with crab-like claws carried out a body search, a cursory stroke of their breasts and a thorough grope of their bottoms. Suddenly standing on tiptoe, she stretched up to speak into the ear of a mortified Gouri and mawkishly breathed, "and you still a virgin," before she dropped back, swearing.

The lock screeched like a seagull. Once their eyes were accustomed to the dark, Archana, Latika, and Gouri found themselves standing next to some fifty or so twisted bodies, half-lying or sitting on the wet ground. Some still slept under prison-issue rags, others used theirs to lie on.

Archana swayed backwards as if struck on the forehead and turned back the way they had come in confusion. In the gloom, on the other side of the iron bars, another cage could be made out — that was where the men were. Thieves, con-men, prostitutes, fare dodgers, murderers, and political prisoners. Here you go, move up — here's another three.

There was movement in the furthest corner. A figure detached itself from the mass. Broke away and began writhing, tearing at her hair.

"What have I done? What have I done?!"

Another immediately rose, walked over, and hugged her, swearing under her breath.

"Why did you tell them? Why?"

"Because they took you … right in front of me… What else could I do to stop them?"

"Mama!" the other said more loudly. "What have you done? Now they'll get my brother. They'll find him and kill him."

Latika dropped like mown grass and whispered to Archana and Gouri:

"Listen, girls, just don't be scared. This won't go on forever. In 24 hours, it'll all be over. They have to take us to court… The court will let us go."

And then, silently, just moving her lips, she said:

"But we can't betray Saumen."

* * *

Before having the papers put in the safe and handing over, Manas took another look at the confiscated books and read through a letter found during the search:

"Dear Sezdi!

"Allow me to express my respect. Thank you for taking on the job of looking after Ma and letting me devote myself completely to my work. My heart is at peace because Ma is in good hands. Thank you for your support, my dear!

"I know how hard it is for you but you are the strong one among us. You are an example to me and the others. I draw my strength and my inspiration from you. Look after yourself and stay well. I hope we will see one another soon.

"Your loving brother.

"P.S. Please look after Gouri. She's like a sister to us. Parimal also sends her his best wishes."

There was no doubt that this was a brother writing to his sister and that sister, this Sezdi (Sezdi means sister number three in Bengali), was the arrested woman, Archana Guha.

"But what's this work he's talking about?" Manas wondered as he checked the safe was locked. "I have a hunch he means the underground. But why does he talk to her with so much respect? What normal guy would talk to a woman like that? Only a subordinate! Does that mean he's her subordinate? Well, why not? He even says: '*You are an example to me and the others. I draw my strength and my inspiration from you.*' Ha! But of course! She's the leader. She's *their* leader! It's obvious! Wow, are the lads going to have some work to do today... so much work."

Chapter 8
Timoka

I shall be frank. For a long time I was unable to approach this chapter, this topic, this page of our story. I kept putting off the month and the hour because I didn't, or rather don't, know *how* to write about it — what letters there are in the words for cruelty, how many sounds a voice needs to express weeping, or where to put the commas and full stops in the pauses in the pain. I naively dreamt, like my heroines, that I could seek refuge in unconsciousness and there, in oblivion, in that quiet and unfeeling death, write the lines of my lament. And come round only when it was over and didn't hurt any more.

Alas, that's not what happens in real life. There's no skipping a rung on the ladder, no snapping a link from the chain. No crossing an hour out of the day, a day out of the month, a month out of the year. Man cannot throw off a single one of the burdens placed on the toiling shoulders of fate. They must all be borne to the very last one. Even if he has no strength left. Why life is made like this, with no right to choose, I cannot say. I just don't know, although I would very much like to find out. I'd like to find out, together with you, why we are given this cruel knowledge. Does humanity really need to learn what kind of world must be avoided in order to understand what kind of world to seek? Is human progress really just a way to avoid its own antithesis?

Before I open the door to that world — and, you know, it is not a world, it's hell — I want to ask a favour. All you have to do as of this minute and this line is to imagine yourself in Archana's place. Or Latika's, or Gouri's. Just that. Go on, take that step. Try and put on their skin, their hearing, their eyes. Be their shadow. Breathe with their lungs. Burn with their fear. Scream with their very being. Don't be afraid. Imagining yourself in their position is far from the same as being in their position. And I'll be there to guide you. There, where they were alone.

And if you suddenly change your mind, if you suddenly don't want to step into someone else's shoes because you are used to drawing wisdom and light, not gloom and doom, from a book, just read. Don't walk away from the spy-hole, keep reading. Without picking up on at least a shadow of distress, an echo of pain, a smattering of sorrow, can you really penetrate the essence of things — that the heart does not die when we think it should. But why not? Why not?

* * *

When he, Police Inspector Runu Niyogi, entered the Special Cell it was ten in the morning and Archana, Latika, and Gouri had already been brought to his office. Hardly had his foot touched the threshold (and he moved quickly, ridding himself of a cigarette butt as he went, taking great strides), he immediately filled half the available space, the other half crushed by the weight of his shadow. In the mornings after breakfast, his fleshy cheeks shone like a glazed bun, his trousers had been repeatedly ironed by an accommodating female hand, and his shirt crackled like freshly milled sugar. He appeared to be in an exuberant frame of mind. And how could it be otherwise? He had long been his own man in the Special Cell. Or rather everything in it was his.

But what was the *Special Cell*? It wasn't just a prison. It came into being along with the Naxalites. It was created especially for them: "for the freedom-fighters," whispered the people; "for the terrorists," hissed the police. Only in size did the Special Cell fail to match its predecessors — in the KGB and the Gestapo, and its successors Guantanamo and Abu Ghraib. D Unit consisted of only three rooms. The first and biggest was a general office: it was here that Archana, Latika, and Gouri had been questioned the previous day. It was here that the junior staff did their paper work and waited for assignments. The second room with its oak desk, its safe the shape of a small coffin, and a worn bench served as Runu's office. The third and final room was the toilet but there was no toilet in it. The first room gave on to the second and the second on to the third. The third was at the edge of all things. Not a sound could escape.

The third room was Timoka.

If anyone remembers, the original title of Ingmar Bergman's film *The Silence* was *Timoka*. In his memoirs he recalled seeing a heading in an Estonian book and, without knowing the translation, deciding that it was a suitable title for the city where his three main characters end up. Only later did he discover that the word "timoka" means "appertaining to the executioner". A place where God falls silent forever.

Lalbazar, the Special Cell, and especially the third room are all then timoka. Ti-mo-ka. Appertaining to the executioner.

The first to be taken in was Gouri. Latika and Archana stayed behind in Runu's office. After 20 minutes, fairly quickly, when Runu had scarcely set out his papers to prepare for their interrogation, the door to the third room opened a crack. A choice expletive slipped out. Archana was ordered to go in.

Archana stood up. She set off. Her heart pounded with terror. She had no more control over her legs than a cotton plant over leaves sprayed with defoliant. But she braced herself and set off. Walking independently. The door, the threshold. She was inside.

She was assailed by the strong smell of a den of iniquity. Damp, sweat, tobacco, and wine, rotting skin, blood, traces of vomit, burning, even milky tea: it was a heady mixture. To the left of the door was a tattered mattress on the concrete floor. Opposite was a bundle of Indian lathis of various sizes: truncheons, rods, canes with metal grips. There was a black hole in the wall. To the right were two high-backed armchairs. Between them a pole sagged under its burden. The ends were propped on the arms of the chairs. There was something on the pole like a roast on a spit. A person? An animal? A huge embryo? All four limbs were twisted into an impossible knot, bound up with nettle rope.

Suddenly ... Archana felt as if she had been scalded. The sari! The familiar colour... Gouri! It was Gouri!

Police Officer Kamal towered over Gouri's body. Next to him stood Constable Santosh. Kamal was flaying the soles of her feet with lathis. The flayed skin hung in a fringe of lace. But Kamal kept up the bastinado, saying, this time for Archana's benefit:

"Look! Take a good look! If you don't confess, it'll be you next.

Bizarrely, Gouri wasn't crying or moaning. She wasn't even begging for mercy. It was as if she wasn't there. Her consciousness had been unable to withstand the horror, the horror of the pain, and had fled a body that no longer belonged to her.

Archana was taken back into Runu's office. A quarter of an hour later there was a glimpse of a doctor's coat as it disappeared into the room that still contained Gouri. Kamal came out.

"Now deal with this one!" Runu ordered Kamal, nodding towards Latika. He was still sitting at his desk, rooting around in his paperwork.

Kamal yanked Latika out of her chair and shoved her against the wall. His right hand, fingers stiff, flew up like a butcher's knife, and came down on Latika's left cheek. Again and again. To Archana on the sidelines, it seemed as though Latika's eyes jumped out of their sockets with each blow. Her forehead, ears, nose, chin — everything began to protrude. Her cheek showed the marks of Kamal's fingers. Her eyes showed her intense fear.

Fifteen minutes. A backhander every time. Then, a chair was shoved under Latika.

Out of the third room, clutching the wall, crawled Gouri. They had brought her round (it was why they had needed the doctor) but she couldn't walk. Santosh looked out after her.

"Now this one!" Runu directed.

Archana was lifted from her chair and dragged through the door. A pack of police constables, who had been waiting in the general office, piled after her, their gestures obscene. A little while later, they were followed by Runu.

* * *

"We've got to make a man of her!" Santosh ordered.

Four of them, Santosh, Kamal, Aditya, and Arun, vying with one another, their faces a dull red, forced Archana to the floor. They pushed her sari up above her knees, knotting the front and back folds between her legs. The end of the fabric that covered her chest like a scarf and fell from her shoulder was also yanked down, torn, and folded around her stomach. The sari wasn't a sari any more but a pair of men's shorts — *kachka*. A Bengali woman would choose death rather than be seen like that.

And yet they went further.

There was the thick rope. There were her thin wrists. They were bound tightly as if welded to her doomed ankles. Her chest and stomach were soldered to her legs. Her body could no longer move or unbend. It was hard to breathe.

And yet they went further.

A teak pole was forcibly twisted behind her knees and through the bend in her arms. There was no room and the skin resisted but blow by blow, push by push, the ends soon poked out on either side of her legs.

And yet they went further

At an order from Runu, two of them grabbed the ends of the pole, wrested it off the floor, carried it to between the chairs, and lowered it onto the arm rests. The arm rests were strong. The supports didn't give. Her body hung from the pole like a roast on a spit. Soles of the feet up, head down.

And yet they went further

"You first," Runu nodded to Santosh. He moved across to the wall — from where he had the best view — took out a cigarette and struck a match.

Santosh bent over the lathis. He made his choice, examined it closely. Tried it for size. Tested to see if it slashed through the air. It whistled! Then every blow, every blow of the lathi on the soles of Archana's feet, was an explosion in her head. And her head was no longer a head that could see, smell and hear, but lava... Seething lava.

Was that it?

No way. They went further.

Now it was Runu's turn. He came over to Archana and rained kicks on her thighs. His boots were drumsticks for the tom-tom. The tom-tom is an instrument played to proclaim a death.

Tchaikovsky. Symphony No. Six. But there the drums come in only at the end whereas here they were only the beginning.

Did they go further?

They went further.

A favourite trick.

The burning cigarette Runu had until then been holding between his teeth now ate into the soles of Archana's feet. It stung, took off, and came down on the pads of her toes, counting them off one by one. Then it landed on her nails and counted those off one by one as well. Having had its fun with her feet, it moved to her hands. Ten finger pads, ten nails and then on to her elbow. After that, for symmetry's sake, it sank into the other.

"Commie bitch! Red slut!" Runu kept on yelling all the time. "I'll make you confess. You'll confess to everything!"

A lot of what he spewed out, Archana didn't hear. Her consciousness had abandoned her body. But Latika saw

Archana's torment. She was told to watch it. To watch and once again to hear the words:

"If you don't confess, it'll be you next…"

* * *

Forty minutes. The cigarettes had burnt out, the lathis were still. Arms had grown weary, too tired for beating. Two constables lifted the pole off the chairs and lowered it to the floor. The ropes slackened. The pole rolled away from her knees, catching, ripping away, tearing off a layer of pulverized skin. Archana was dragged off to the mattress, her cheeks slapped, doused with water. It took a long time for her to come round. Her jaw quivered.

When Archana finally managed to force her eyes open, there was something wrong with the lighting in the room. One minute it was like a flame from an open stove, the next like plunging into a freezing night. Someone raised her to her feet and told her to go and wait in Runu's office where Latika and Gouri still sat. It was three in the afternoon, a mere twelve hours since their arrest. Archana stumbled towards the exit, grasping at the air for support but the floor dissolved, the walls spun, and the rank fumes from her burnt feet hung in the air.

A little later the women were sent to their cell. Gouri and Archana limped half the way, clutching at the wall, the other half they crawled. When they finally made it back and the bolt slid home, they could only say to one another:

"How on earth will they take us to court?"

"It's not to their advantage any more."

In general, however, they sighed with relief. They were still alive and they hadn't betrayed Saumen.

After four, they were summoned back to the Special Cell. The constables and police officers had already eaten and the same gang greeted the women with obscene gestures. Archana was taken into Timoka first. Everything began again, without a break until late in the evening. Latika was forced to watch. But I lack the strength to say more. I lack the strength to write more. My hand is numb, paralyzed. My gaze is blurred and seeks to leave the page. Will even I really have to turn back, shy away like a coward, and depart, leaving them there alone? Why? For whose sake? For yours, reader? So that you don't say: it's too much, this is too much? Perhaps, but there may be other reasons.

It isn't always possible or necessary to recount every last detail of the abuse that goes on in police basements, nor is it the aim of this book to describe torture. Like my heroines, having undertaken to recount what happened, I am paralyzed by shame— by shock, pain, and shame. And the more delicate the parts of the body subjected to torture, the less the victims have to say and the more taciturn I, the author, become. It is a human characteristic and a human problem to cast the silence of the grave over what does most damage. Even so, I do have a slight hope. The one that ate away at Solzhenitsyn when he wrote "The Gulag Archipelago". He wrote it but worried that he got *everything* down. But "to taste the ocean takes only a single drop."

Chapter 9

The Ogre Does What Ogres Can

I think I should drop into the story myself at this point, but not for long: after all, I did promise to tell you how this story came to reach your door.

In the early 2000s, I was invited to Copenhagen City Hall: majestic ceilings, burnished balustrades, a clock tower, and a golden statue of Archbishop Absalon. The woman to whom this book is dedicated was bestowing an award from her foundation on a Turkish doctor. When the official speeches finished and a monologue entitled "Impunity", and written for the occasion by Isabel Allende, had been read out, the guests broke up into smaller groups or, without waiting for the break, headed off to the food table. The hostess and organizer of the event then led me over to one of the guests, former Prime Minister Poul Nyrup Rasmussen, and introduced me briefly as a "journalist and writer." Then, more quietly and in the lowered, confidential tone people adopt when they tell you a secret, said, "a torture victim. Uzbekistan."

It was so unexpected that, despite my self-control, I shuddered at the thunder clap of the truth I knew so well. Three years separated me from the hateful day that I stepped into the same boat Archana had been in thirty years before. Did those around me attach any stigma to this, a stigma for all time? Or was it a visiting card I was now meant to carry ?

The ex-prime minister gave me a fatherly nod, touched my sleeve in a friendly fashion, and said that he was delighted to meet me, of course. I said the same. We chatted a little about the Danish weather then went our separate ways. He headed for the drinks and snacks, and I went out into the fresh air and away. Before I left, I said goodbye to the organizer. My affection for her was undiminished so I simply said:

"If it's really impossible not to go into that kind of detail, call me a *survivor*. But not a victim. Never that. Please!"

The small, serious woman in glasses that covered half her face looked at me in a new way as if was seeing me for the first time.

"I like that. Don't call me a victim. And yes, I know, pain and suffering make people stronger."

She would probably have said more but the circumstances were awkward and, anyway, that was enough for me. How many people — in the last hundred, the last thousand years — have uttered these words, sometimes as a consolation, to explain or to demonstrate — to themselves or others — that life is a laboratory of human qualities, that suffering is always positive, and that only someone who has suffered knows the real value of life. And I would have agreed with this last assertion had I not known from my own experience that people are as fragile as they are strong. Had I not known people whose suffering had in fact killed them.

But I held my tongue. It wasn't that I couldn't take her comments. Moreover, my observations of people had long since convinced me that even after Auschwitz — yes, even after Auschwitz — it is possible to return to playing the violin, to painting, or to writing poems. Let's not delude ourselves, however. It takes people more than one night and more than one effort of will to recover from a terrible experience. For a long time, if not for the rest of their lives, they will be torn between periods of time, one foot in the present, the other in a distant past that remains too close and strives to take the place of the present. Why is this so? Because the goal of any torture is not to hurt or even to kill.

Death is too little. Death is only a moment, as the hero of a film once said. Suffering should last forever.

So now, let me tell you how you would feel if you had been in the same place as Archana, Latika, and Gouri. In the same boat, the same trap.

It is many years since the world learned about the five techniques, the Belfast methods the British government used in interrogations in Northern Ireland in the early 1970s. The human mind devised (or, more likely, simply adopted from the times of the Inquisition or perhaps even from Ancient Greece or Rome) a set of ways of torturing people in phases, moving from one gradation to the next or simply emptying the whole arsenal at one and the same time. Years and generations succeeded one another. Humanity moved from caves to skyscrapers, swapped axes for computers, and yet even today it is not enough for the torturers just to have their prisoner up against the wall, crucified, and immobile for days on end, utterly detached from a body grown weary of begging for mercy. The prisoner must now wear a black hood, be bombarded with unbearable noise, forbidden to go to the toilet, deprived of food and drink, and not allowed to sleep.

In combination, these methods rapidly induce psychosis: eyes that stare like headlamps, excessive trembling and paralysis, inability to stand, sit, or lie down, to think, or answer simple questions, to count to ten, to give your own name. There are bouts of insanity. Some people hear funeral marches and believe they are attending their own burials. Others suddenly see God ordering them to cooperate. When they come round, if such it can be called, one thing and one thing only blocks out the whole world.

"I can't take it any more… I can't. I can't stand it… I'll sign whatever they want… say I'm whoever they want… Hard labour, prison… as if that could scare me now! The only thing I'm scared of is what they're doing to me here and now…"

That's exactly what happens. People cannot stand it. Healthy people never can. It's not a question of spiritual strength. Anyone can be broken. And pretty quickly too. Particularly in our own day when torturers do not have only criminals at their service but also psychiatrists, psychologists, physiologists, experts in anthropology and culture.

The deeper our knowledge of the human soul, the easier it is to destroy the protective armour nature provides.

My notebook contains extracts from various people's recollections of what they feared most when they entered the torture chamber. The range is extensive: charting the household gods of human pain. I can study the state of the world and of ourselves as individuals. I judge humanity not in terms of technological advances but of how many trouble spots continue to smoulder.

One of my notes belongs to Menachem Begin, seventh prime minister of Israel and winner of the Nobel Peace Prize. Before taking office, he headed an armed organization, Irgun Ha-Tzvai Ha-Leumi, which waged a terrorist war against the British in Palestine, up to and including bombing cafés, hotels, buses. At the beginning of World War II, Begin, a Polish Jew, fled from the Nazis to Vilnius, where he was arrested by the NKVD. In his memoir, *White Nights*, he says that sleep deprivation was the hardest thing to bear. Prisoners whose will had not been broken by other cruel forms of torture gave in immediately when denied sleep for just a few days.

"Anyone who has experienced this desire [to sleep] knows that not even hunger or thirst are comparable with it. I came across prisoners who signed what they were ordered to sign, only to get what the interrogator promised them. He did not promise them food to sate themselves. He promised them — if they signed — uninterrupted sleep! They signed… And, having signed, there was nothing in the world that could move them to risk again such nights and such days. The main thing was to sleep," Begin recalls.

"… to sleep, to sleep just a little, not to get up, to lie, to rest, to forget…"

Believe me. Anyone who has experienced this knows that non-physical torture has a similar effect to a cane on the soles of the feet. The same explosion in the brain. The same rush of madness. The same paroxysm of despair. The same pit of helplessness. The same desire for it simply to stop. Even at the cost of departing this life altogether — as long as it's over soon. And there's no need ever to go back there again! The torturer knows what he has to do and does precisely what you fear the most.

What are you scared of? The dark? They'll shut you up in a crate the size of a zinc coffin for a month. Insects or rats? They'll put you in a box where these creatures can crawl over you. Death? They'll put you in front of a firing squad. Dirt? They'll feed you excrement. Are you devout? They'll make you fornicate. Are you pregnant and about to give birth? They'll arrange an abortion. Do you fear for those you love? They'll bring them in — your children, spouse, relatives — and torture them right in front of you — or worse, they'll make you do it. Are you a man? They'll mutilate your genitals. A woman? You'll be lucky to become a mother by the time they've finished with you. A musician? They'll dislocate your hands. A footballer? They'll damage your feet. A politician? They'll rip out your tongue. An artist? They'll put out your eyes.

Human cruelty is highly inventive. "The ogre does what ogres can."

And what if the torturer is tired? Is there a break then? There is, but for him not for you. There's no break for the prisoner. The pauses in the torture are the most terrifying part. That's when a fire starts to burn under your skin. "What's going to happen next? What will they do next time? They can't let me go… So are they going to kill me?"

A break is always an expectation of death.

I'm afraid to say it but I am more and more inclined to the view that there may be less torture in our century but its quantity is more than offset by its quality. The equipment for breaking the human spirit stands on its old foundation and is striding confidently towards the peak of perfection. Violence is a handy, multi-faceted option, the torturer's many-chorded instrument, brought into play when the state extracts a confession, when it has to find something out, to punish, intimidate, alter someone's core beliefs.

But violence is not the goal. Punishment of the body is necessary for punishment of the soul. All torture aims not to "obtain information" or to "force a confession." The main thing is to kill the personality and to do so in such a way that when you leave, whether for home or jail, you will still see, hear, listen, look, and breathe but not live, experience joy, or dream. You will be a living corpse, dead in life. To paraphrase Brodsky: life might well be possible but it will have no meaning.

Chapter 10

Cricket

It was the second day since their arrest, only the second, but their hearts had aged an entire lifetime; their bodies were no longer bodies but tenderized meat, although protestation had become firmly lodged somewhere inside them, preventing their spirits falling right through the abyss.

Night — that first night in prison, bent over the damp earthen bed, like a black-skinned siren, casting a loop around their necks like a poacher and drawing them into a jungle of uneasy sleep, but their bodies put up a fight and snapped back, throwing off the rope of oblivion. Wandering between dream and reality, Latika blew on Archana's burns, Archana bewailed Gouri's feet, and Gouri grieved for Latika's face. The women cared for one another as best they could so that they did not vanish in a vortex of pain.

Then, in the morning, hardly had the arrestees received an earthenware cup containing a few splashes of sour tea, when they came for them. They didn't take them to the Special Cell. They took them outside. They put them in a police van that sped along Calcutta's avenues before pulling up short in a burst of exhaust fumes.

The women recognized the place. It was Sealdah Court. Bullets of hope and relief exploded in their hearts.

In the court, they were taken into a bare cell the size of a cupboard and locked in. Outside, on the other side of the door, those not behind bars went on with their busy, noisy lives. Someone was calling names in officious, stentorian tones.

Someone's steps came closer, then moved away. They always went past though, past the door they sat behind. Time crept by at a snail's pace.

"There's probably a queue... a lot of people... they're studying the case," said Latika soothingly.

"They should have called us by now!" Gouri fidgeted nervously.

"Poor Ma! How is she managing?" said Archana, wiping her eyes.

"Come on girls, don't be down-hearted," Latika kept saying. "They haven't pressed charges. There's no reason to detain us. The judge has to let us go. It's just for today!"

Each of them imagined that after their arrest, mother would no doubt have raced round their relatives, and the relatives would have gone to a lawyer. If that was the case, there was hope that he was somewhere close by.

It was two hours or so before the door opened. A guard brought the prisoners out of the cell and led them along a winding corridor, past doors, one of which concealed the judge. Suddenly, they found themselves outside. They were swallowed up by the police van, which reversed, hit the kerb, snorted and set off.

"Lalbazar," the guard told the driver.

The women's hearts began to thump. What was going on? How could it be that they had been to court but not appeared before a judge?

Hardly had the women been delivered to the Special Cell when Runu, Aditya, Kamal, and Santosh all half-rose, delighted to see them, and broke into heated applause, as if they were greeting Hollywood stars.

"Ha! Familiar faces! Ladies, we missed you," they guffawed, trying to outdo one another's clowning. They began to pour out confessions of how cleverly they had outwitted everyone by giving the arrestees false names.

It turned out that the police documents submitted to the court registered Archana as Nanda, Latika as Urmila, and Gouri as Tuku. Realization dawned on the women — the court, the judge, and the police were all in it together.

The excited, self-satisfied police officers stood round in a circle. Tutting and wiggling their hips they began to hand the women from one to another.

In the end Runu said, "You've had your fun. Now back to work!"

Police Officer Amit Mazumder came out of Runu's office. Archana recognized him as the young man who had searched the house. Mazumder told her to sit at the desk. He spread out a fan of blank forms.

"Sign them all. Right here! If anyone refuses, I'll send a patrol straight round to get your mums and nieces. We'll rape them right in front of you. So, it's up to you. It's them or your signatures!"

"Oh, great, you've all signed!" Mazumder said after a little while, scraping up the forms like a deck of cards and putting them into a black file.

"All we need's a confession. You don't want us to arrest your mum or for her to have to beg in her old age if we arrest your other relatives as well."

Three blank forms landed on the desk.

"Sign. I'll tell you what to write."

* * *

Signatures there may be, but they testify only to the fact that during those dreadful days in July 1974 the women were being stitched up. At speed and in clear white stitches. A case was being fabricated.

It was customary to kill many birds with one stone in the Special Cell in order to demonstrate the staff's aptitude for the job and their commitment to their employer, i.e. the government.

As a result, the ritual question of Saumen's whereabouts was no less frequently posed once the signatures had been obtained. Runu was convinced Saumen had sent the letter that was found in the house from the underground and that Archana, as his *leader* (and they continued to maintain this — there was no other way they could explain such a respectful tone from a brother to his sister), had to know where he lived. He and his fellow conspirators.

At around four in the afternoon, Archana was taken to Runu. He was sitting with a Howrah police friend, Arun Banerjee. They had agreed on a game of cricket. Runu was the bowler, the player who issued the instructions. Arun was the batsman, the defending player. Archana was the ball.

They reached agreement and began. Runu would ask: "Where's Saumen?" Archana, as before, would reply, "I don't know." Whereupon Arun flicked the ball that was Archana's head, as if he was hammering in nails. This went on for a quarter of an hour.

"Where's Saumen?"

"I don't know."

Flick.

"Where's Saumen?"

"I don't know."

Flick...

Acute, sickening pain skittered from the back of her head into her neck. From there it ran down her spine, its rivulets snaking into her arms and legs. Over and over again. Until it immobilized her altogether, taking away her capacity to see and hear.

But that was only the warm up.

In the evening, Archana was taken back to the Special Cell. Runu was sitting there with Kamal.

"This is Saneka Hath. The Golden Hand!" said Runu, introducing his subordinate and clapping him on the back. "End up with him and you won't be going anywhere again!"

Gentle and homely to look at, the pock-marked Kamal, pimples reddening his cheeks and forehead, nodded in time with each word.

"We're giving you a chance today," Runu continued. "You won't get another. If you don't tell us where Saumen is, you won't see tomorrow. We'll kill you tonight and throw you in the Ganges. And no-one in your family will ever be able to prove you were in Lalbazar."

Archana said nothing.

"Get on with it!" Runu ordered Kamal.

Kamal grabbed Archana by the hair, wound it like reins around his hand, and heaved her body up off the chair. Then he took a wide swing intended to smash her against the wall but just when her head should have made contact with the panelling, Kamal pulled his arm back. Archana couldn't keep her footing and crashed to the floor. She was lifted up by her hair and sent flying again. Her head flew back and forth between the wall and Kamal like a leather ball on a string. Twenty minutes later Kamal was fading and, staggering back, he took himself off for a rest. Aditya took his place.

"This Naxalite slag has got very long hair," Runu remarked.

Aditya bent over Archana and tore out a clump of her hair.

"It's not just long, it's strong too. We know what to do with that!"

Aditya left and came back with an assistant. They pushed Archana to the ground. One grabbed her hair from the left, the other from the right. On a count of "one, two, three" they pulled in different directions as if in a tug of war, then decided that didn't hurt enough and began to lift her off the floor by the hair.

"Where's Saumen?! Where are your accomplices?!" Runu roared constantly, kicking Archana's backside.

"Confess, you red whore! You know people on that list!"

"I don't know where Saumen is," Archana groaned. "I don't know the people on the list."

She drifted in and out of consciousness.

When her swollen eyelids finally began to open the smallest bit, it was already close to midnight. With her peripheral vision, Archana could see she wasn't in Runu's office but in the torture chamber, in Timoka. Snatches of sentences reached her:

"… Has she come round? …"

"… Yes…"

"… Confessed? …"

"… No…"

Archana opened her eyes with difficulty — there wasn't enough light or air — and closed them again in terror. Around her stood not two or three but a dozen people. Each was holding a flashlight. It was this searing light that was setting everything at the edge of the room ablaze, from floor to ceiling.

"I'd be better off dead," Archana thought.

She was forced to her feet and pushed against the wall. The remains of her clothes were ripped off. When the last flimsy protection that had covered her body and held her soul together was gone, Archana began hurling herself around, calling out:

"Ma! Save me, Ma."

"Look at that. The idiot's calling for help!" rasped Runu. "No-one's going to help you. You're on your own now."

Runu moved closer to Archana and began to drive a cigarette into her like a needle. The others skewered her with the burning beams of their flashlights, blinding her and firing orders at point blank range:

"Confess! Where's Saumen?"

"Confess! Name his associates!"

In a world of diminishing strength and illusions, this barrage of voices and shadows was more than a single wave. It rolled on in a giant force — a typhoon of raging criminal passions overwhelming heaven and earth, and sweeping Archana off into the maelstrom — away from the shore, from any shore, and down, down to the lowest depths. To Archana it seemed that the cup had been drained, she had crossed the wilderness, and only now, not the day before when her feet had been flayed, or even at midday when she was forced to denounce herself, or in the afternoon when her head was used as a cricket ball, but only now when she was left wearing nothing but her own skin had she hit the bottom. She had touched the depths and looked into the abyss. She had looked and was struck dumb. She was struck dumb and nearly died. She died but she did not turn away. God, if he still existed and forced the living into such desperate straits, must be the most cruel torturer and so must all the vast multitude of India's gods. Otherwise, he would have left the way open for a withdrawal. He would have provided awareness with an off switch. Or turned us into a particle of dust, a grain of sand, a speck of dirt so that we could merge with the air or slip between the cracks. He would have torn our souls from our bodies to deliver us from evil.

But no, even at the height of the very worst pain, Archana remained alive. She was still in her heavy sack of skin, muscle, and bone. She remained there so that she could feel. So that she could feel it all. The whole, heady, hellish brew that eventually poisons the brain. And leads to a sudden loss of the will to live. And the loneliness in which a person dies in long-suffering captivity, one on one with the elements, without finding so much as a molecule that might become a hand to pull them out of the abyss. Who do you call on at these times? Who can you rely on? Who can you trust?

Archana tried to look through the ceiling, out through the raging swarm of her enemies and her executioners' flagellating lights, and her numb, dry eyes wept. It wasn't the bestial Runu that she faced all alone but life itself. And if there was nothing outside herself to grasp hold of and to trust, then surely there had to be something inside.

Archana came round. Froth trickled from her mouth. She shuddered deep inside and so much unexpected fury, so much sharp and desperate fury suddenly blazed within her that, unable to deal with the fire, she stepped into its flames. Wrath. She was in the grip of wrath. It gripped her and bore her away. Bore her up and did not let her fall through the abyss.

"I'm not a criminal!" was what she wanted to shout but her voice was a faint murmur.

"I'm not a criminal! I haven't done anything wrong! I can't give in to this scum."

As she turned, not to the heavens or the walls but to somewhere inside herself, her real self, and at the same time to memory, to life, to all that had ever been good in the past, she suddenly remembered her late father, remembered him and begged:

"Baba, give me strength! Give me the strength to bear all this! I don't know how to stand it! Baba, give me strength!"

Later she never forgot this moment, when she had had nothing left, and everything was given to her. She spoke to herself and gave the order not to die, not to die before her time.

* * *

Long after midnight, Aditya and his partner dragged an unconscious Archana back into her cell. As he passed the office that registered arrestees being taken out of the Special Cell, he gave the duty officer a form. The officer looked at the subject of the transfer — a motionless, bleeding mass — and nodded permission to pass, signed the paper, and read out:

"No complaints. No injuries."

Back in the cell, Latika and Gouri hurled themselves at Archana. They had been taken into the Special Cell twice, tortured a while, and again forced to sign and denounce themselves. They had been made to listen to Archana's cries. Then they were taken away.

Gouri sank down at the foot of the mattress in tears.

"What have they done? What have they done?"

Latika squatted at its head and placed her hands on

Archana's forehead. She howled with the pain. Latika leapt back in fright. Clumps of Archana's hair had come out.

Watching the scene, Aditya guffawed:

"We gave her such a beating! Such a beating! I've never beaten anyone so badly let alone a woman!"

When he had gone, Latika and Gouri leant over Archana in tears, soaking her body, and covering her in the prison-issue rags.

"We're together… we're still together," they wailed as one

"You can drop the sloppy stuff!" the warden suddenly yelled. "Your friend's about to go into solitary!"

Chapter 11
The River Vaitarani

Most frightening of all is being face to face with your torturer and then face to face with yourself. It's like crossing the River Vaitarani — the crossing to Hell. Perhaps though the scriptures are lying and no such river exists? Perhaps it flows only in our imagination and then only at the height of delirium, full of pus, blood, and filth as it separates the world of the dead from the world of the living.

Just one prison cell separated the world of the dead from the world of the living. Archana came round in howling darkness. She came round because of the noises that were rending the air. Someone's cry drilled and sawed away at her temples. "Archana, Archana! Say something!" It came from somewhere beyond the jungle of walls but the walls let through only a confused whisper.

An eternity passed before she realized that the shouts came from Latika and Gouri. Another eternity before she remembered who she was, where she was, and why. A third before she recalled that she had been there for more than twenty-four hours, and yet another before she could push off the great weight of sleep. Perhaps it wasn't sleep but a vision, delirium? Aditya was binding her arms with a rope. Runu was stubbing cigarettes out on her skin and beating her about the head with a leather whip that ended in a great knot. Each blow sounded like a coconut splitting open. Then everything came crashing down, collapsed, plummeted down to the very depths of hell. She was blindfolded by darkness. As she had been at the cinema when she was little and the reel broke, leaving the audience alone in the dark. She had not been scared then, though. Her brothers and sisters had been right there with her. Now she was utterly alone. Alone with herself and her own body, a constant reminder of what happened yesterday.

And yes, it was yesterday. Only yesterday. Although now it seemed as if it had been going on forever.

She was desperately thirsty. Her tongue was as dry and swollen as if stung by a bee. It no longer fitted in her mouth. Swellings blistered and bloated her body. Archana cautiously rolled off her back and onto her stomach and stretched out a hand, trying to feel with her fingers where other people might be. Overcoming the pain, she began to crawl.

This was not Nabokov's *Invitation to a Beheading* with its furnished jails. Archana's prison had no door with a peephole for the jailer, no cot, or table, or chair, no books, or dressing-gown, or clean sheets of paper and "beautifully sharpened pencil" with "an ebony gleam". No golden electric light, no ugly little window just below the ceiling, no spider on a thread, no zinc tray of food. Just two walls, two sets of bars, four corners, an earth floor, a concrete roof, and a vast amount of space — you could dance to your heart's content. As if you had been put in an aircraft hangar and locked in.

Moreover, if you sat with your chest and face pressed up against the grille, you could see a bit of the corridor and even the corner of the cell holding Latika and Gouri. And, if you pushed your face through the bars and gave a really good yell, Latika and Gouri might hear. Just as Archana heard them. Heard them and started crawling.

It turned out to be already morning. The detainees were let out for their morning tea. That was the only reason Latika and Gouri could come over. Frightened, they peered into the depths of the solitary cell, saw Archana crawling and, as one, they burst into tears.

"She's alive! She's alive!"

At the risk of attracting the wrath of the guards, Latika squatted down by the grille and thrust a hand through the bars.

"Sezdi… yesterday… when you were brought out of the Special Cell… we yelled and called you so much… all night… but you didn't hear us. What did they do?"

Archana was still unable to speak. But she was happy that she was able to see Latika and Gouri at least for the moment, while they drank their tea.

Her solitary cell was so much bigger than the one that held fifty women. An echo took at least a couple of minutes to travel from corner to corner. The ceiling bore down like a tombstone. The smell of decay brought desolation with it. Silent spectres spawned in the absence of light (day or night, it was always dark here).

But it was not the darkness that did the most to break her. When she was with Latika and Gouri, she knew they were all alive. That helped to overcome the pain. In solitary, though…

Solitary achieved its goal through the unknown. Every time Latika and Gouri were taken to be interrogated and not brought back for a long time, she would sit facing the grille and flay herself with doubts. "What on earth was happening? Something had happened!" The body, our own body, that crude sack of bones, can stand a great deal, more than just stand it, but anxiety and fear are both Trojan horses. They enter at will and when you lower your defences during the night, they place even those defences at the mercy of the enemy.

Each time anxiety and fear had almost reached their peak and the only way out was to come crashing down, Archana would open her eyes and with a loud whisper, a quiet cry, would drag herself out of the slough of inner darkness.

"I haven't done anything wrong! I can't give in to this scum! Baba, give me strength!"

Who could say what this was? A prayer, a curse, or an order. Or perhaps, it was character. Just her own character. And character is destiny.

* * *

It was precisely this that irritated Runu most of all. Infuriated him. Made him boil. Explode. Fly off the handle. Scoff. Rampage and play the tyrant. This inappropriate insolence. This excessive resistance. This inability to kneel. This reluctance to plead for mercy. This stubbornness. This heroism. Naïve, stupid, senseless heroism. Just like in the cinema. And where? On his, Runu's, patch where he reigned supreme, where he had already resolved not to release her but to wear her down, to break her.

In the first 24 hours, all three arrested woman signed blank forms, whatever they were forced to sign. There was enough to fabricate not one but several cases. Signing was all very well but the women had not asked for mercy. They had denied any connection with the Naxalites and had not given away Saumen's whereabouts and this cast a shadow over the torturer's skill. If a victim stays silent, has the will to resist, it means the main aim has not been achieved. And it has to be achieved! Over and over again, the women were summoned to the Special Cell. They were returned to their cells in the evening only to be taken back again in the morning.

This went on for twenty-seven days. For twenty-seven days, they were held hostage. A hair's breadth from death. On a knife-edge of pain.

Mutual support was what got them through. Latika, Gouri, or their cellmates, would scarcely have regained consciousness after the Special Cell when they would be surrounded. Someone would examine their wounds. Someone would put a bundle of rags under their head. Someone would massage their hands and feet. They would be asked cautiously: "What did they do to you? Beat the soles of your feet? Hang you up by your hair? Lay you on ice? Burn you with cigarettes?" Some would resist putting what they had been through into words. By contrast, it simply poured out of others. There was no need to conceal what had happened to them. Suffering openly was accepted and the poison came to the surface: a brief respite for the spirit.

But they did not only help one another to verbalize their pain.

Once Archana was waiting for Latika and Gouri to be taken away for interrogation. An escort guard appeared in the corridor. He had a new detainee with him. When he saw Archana, the latter muttered:

"You slut! Sitting there in full view of everyone! I'll…"

"Latika! Gouri! Did you hear that?" Archana yelled.

At this, a shout from Latika rang out of the communal cell:

"What did you say to my sister-in-law? Apologize, go on!"

And from the men's side came a growing roar:

"Just try not apologizing, do you hear, you bastard. It's us you'll have to deal with …'"

Anticipating some fun, the guard initially encouraged the detainee to answer back but then had second thoughts.

"Can't you hear, you idiot? Go on, say you're sorry!"

And the detainee — what else could he do? — took it all back.

They even decided to revolt.

It so happened that once Archana was not brought back from an interrogation or was kept longer than usual. Latika and Gouri despaired of keeping watch on the corridor. The warders had arrived and had already handed out the evening rations and Archana was still not back.

"We won't eat until we see Archana!" Latika and Gouri declared.

Suddenly, someone in the men's cell said:

"I won't either… Let us see Archana!"

Which of the detainees it was — a political prisoner, a thief, or a murderer — Latika and Gouri did not know. After him, however, others began to call out:

"We're not going to eat either!"

"We've got to see Archana!"

They began to stagger around, rattling the bars.

"Ar-cha-na! Ar-cha-na!" The cry arose on all sides.

Closer to midnight, when she was brought back and tossed into the solitary cell, a shout swept through the cells from one wall to another, even passing through the walls: "Archana's here!"

Here, more than anywhere else, people knew the value of action. If you didn't help someone today, who would help you tomorrow?

Please don't think, however, that the detainees were not kept in line. Public punishments were frequently carried out to intimidate the rebels. Once, a teenage boy was brought in and the first interrogation carried out in the corridor. In answer to everything, the boy said: "I don't know." He was put in the communal cell.

A day later, two old men were allowed into the cells. They were very smartly dressed. They turned out to be his father and his uncle. When the boy had not gone home, his family had set out to find him. And they did. In Lalbazar.

"Is this your son?" a police officer politely asked the father.

"Yes, yes. That's my son!"

"And what's his name, pray?"

His father gave his name. The boy in the cell shuddered. He had given his interrogators a different name.

"You see, he's only young…" The father and uncle continued to apologize. "But please don't think… we'll pay you… as soon as the boy comes home."

"Now, now, what's money got to do with it?" said the guard, playing along as he escorted them to the exit. "Don't worry. Your lad will be back. He'll be released in the courtroom tomorrow."

When he came back, the officer dragged the boy out by the hair.

"You lied. You told us a pack of lies. But you'll talk now!"

For the first hour, they beat the boy in front of his cellmates. Then they took him to the Special Cell. When they brought him back to the shared cell, he was no longer himself. Within twenty-four hours, he had incriminated all his friends and acquaintances. And personally escorted the agents from one door to the next, revealing the addresses of meetings and assemblies. That night, his evidence led to the arrests of a hundred people. But was it really his fault that his spirit was still immature when his body betrayed him? Indeed, does the spirit exist at all when the body is destroyed? Is that not just a tale told by poets, theologians, and fools?

* * *

And so it was that during their endless time under arrest they were dragged through all the circles of hell. They also gained a new understanding of people, however. And a new understanding of feelings. And they learnt something too. To sleep on the ground, to use the toilet bucket in front of everyone, to comb their hair with their fingers, to tie knots to mend the holes in their clothes. They even learnt to breathe to one side as Untouchables are commanded to do: they were forbidden to wash or clean their teeth.

Fear of being separated taught Archana, Latika, and Gouri not to let one another out of their sight — to push their faces through the bars of the grille and watch the corridor for hours. Just so that they did not miss a friend being taken off for interrogation or dragged back again. And then, from their crazed eyes, their dishevelled hair, from their bent spines and shackled hands, they could at least tell what had happened in the Special Cell.

As the third week came to an end, three new people were brought into the communal cell — two fifteen-year-old prostitutes and their elderly madame. Everyone knew by then that their kind didn't stay in Lalbazar. They would pay a bribe and be released after twenty-four hours.

Latika immediately asked:

"Please can you help us? Since we were arrested, we've had no contact with our families. They don't even know where we are…"

"What are you in for?" the madame asked.

"They say it's for politics."

"Aha. I see, well, okay. They'll let us out today. What's the message and who's it to?"

Latika found a tiny scrap of paper. She broke the edge off a tea bowl, wet the clay with spit, and wrote down her name and address. The madame hid the letter under her clothes.

They never saw one another again but the madame kept her promise.

* * *

On the evening of August 13, Archana, Latika, and Gouri were once again taken to court. Once again, they were locked in a cell and held for a couple of hours.

No charges were brought. Perhaps they would be allowed to go home after all?

But they never appeared before the judge. They were taken back to Lalbazar where they were told that the Presidency Jail of Alipore, was now expecting them and they would be sent there straight away. They were no longer detainees. Now they were prisoners.

Chapter 12

Aurobindo's Cell

The Alipore Presidency Jail — known in earlier times as Alipore Jail and now, in the vernacular, as the Government Hotel, Alipore — was no lost isle in the jungle of Calcutta's prison system. Along one side ran a clamorous, rattling, narrow road frequented by rickshaws, cows, buses with "Om" signs, and cars with horns — whoever had the loudest horn was the champion. On the other side, a wide pedestrian path snaked its dusty way up to prison gates the colour and size of elephants. Along the verge sprawled tumbledown huts and in the yards old women pottered about carrying basins, and anaemic dogs and children formed packs to greet the sunset with yelping and the dawn with whining.

Despite the barbed wire atop the rough, forbidding wall, with the years this place has become a centre of pilgrimage. For it is here that the thirty-six-year-old underground leader and terrorist suspect, Aurobindo Ghosh, achieved enlightenment. And that was… when was that actually? Good grief, it was back in ancient times… in 1908. A year later the court found him innocent anyway, and he left both prison and politics. He no longer saw it as his life's work to fight for the freedom of a single people, even his own. He was thinking about spiritual freedom, and not just for himself. Later he became well-known as the father of integral yoga and a new kind of philosopher and thinker — Sri Aurobindo. Reflecting on his life experiences, including Alipore Jail, he wrote:

"All is not settled when a cause is humanly lost and hopeless; all is settled only when the soul renounces its effort."

That's worth a second look — especially this bit: "… all is settled only when the soul renounces its effort."

So perhaps that's it — the solution? Or one of them?

The reason Archana's soul had not already given up the struggle was that in Alipore she was blessed with an easing of the regime, and it was that respite — if only for a day, a week or a month — that loosened the strings and offered some slight relief to nerves so tightly wound they were ready to snap. There was no torture of the Lalbazar kind there and they did not separate the women into different cells but put all three together. Visits were allowed twice a month. And at last they could look human again, wash, and clean off the dirt of twenty-seven days, from their bodies, that is, not from their hearts.

Their new cell was very similar to Aurobindo's, so it would not be inappropriate to look at their environment through his eyes. There were no windows, just three cement-coloured walls and bars instead of a fourth. Beyond the bars was a tiny, dark area of corridor with a massive brick wall and a low, old-fashioned plank door, smeared with filth, which gave onto the cramped prison yard. Towards the top of the door, at forehead-level, was an imposing curved gash. When the door closed, a spying eye would hover in the gash, as in the slits in a mask. It would blink, and blink, and blink. Aurobindo's door to the yard was often left open, and beyond it at least some kind of life would flit past. There were six cells of this kind, all together in a row. They were known as "decrees" and were for those placed in solitary confinement. But even in these cells a hierarchy prevailed, and those deemed to merit severe punishment did not have their yard door opened at all.

To say that Archana, Latika, and Gouri were deemed to merit severe punishment would not tell you the half of it. They were held in the political prisoners' wing, where the door to the yard was nailed up. Their wandering and inflamed eyes saw only mouldy bricks. When the British were in charge, walks in the open air had been allowed but now that was an idle dream. The women were never let into the yard, only from their cell into the corridor while the morning rations were handed out, and again after dinner when the prisoners cleaned their cells and brought out their buckets.

As in Lalbazar, a concrete floor was their mattress, the ceiling their counterpane. They would stick a bundle of rags behind their head or form them into a bolster to lean back against. During the rainy season, after a particularly furious downpour, their habitable island shrank to the size of a water-lily leaf. Water would flow through the bars and race towards their feet, rubbing their bare heels with rough lumps of pumice, slowly nibbling away at them, and forcing the prisoners towards the back wall.

And yet even here, in this unsmiling place, the kind of place that would drive anyone of flagging heart or enfeebled body to thoughts of suicide, heaven did smile on these women or offer, at any rate, a hint of a smile.

It was this smile that sustained them.

There were twenty of them in the cell, women become old while still young. Most had ended up there thanks to a Naxalite connection. If they had anything in common with the others, it was only that they kicked against their situation, not wanting to give in to the torturers. They were being persecuted for their fighting spirit, for their independence.

But they did not divide up into groups — they all supported each other as best they could. When one fell into the meshes of melancholy, the others rushed to help her out. If she was troubled by insomnia, they sang or recited poems. They distracted the fevered memory and soothed the poisoned brain. It was like communicating vessels, where liquid is poured into one, flows into the next, then settles at the same level in both. Melancholy, as we know, hates company. It picks off isolated individuals.

But there was also some friction. Once Archana had started to recover from the cigarette burns, which had continued to suppurate for a long while, and was gingerly attempting to stand on her battered feet, she suddenly became aware that tension between Latika and Gouri was casting a shadow. From the very first days of their captivity, Latika had been their nurse and it has to be said that no sister of mercy was ever more generous-hearted or more considerate. But when she tried to get close to Gouri, the latter was seized by an access of irritation.

"No, stop! Don't touch me!" Gouri would growl, and turn a hostile back on Latika.

Archana thought about this a lot. And after a while she understood. When the police burst into their home, they gave Latika's name. It was clear: they were after Latika and it was she who had brought them to the house. They only found out about Saumen later. And Gouri had not forgotten that. She blamed no one openly and endured the Special Cell with fortitude (she too had suffered a great deal and nearly died on two occasions). But that thought was eating away at her, the thought that they had been arrested because of Latika, and that she herself was suffering only because she was a friend of the family and had, on that hellish evening, been at their home only by chance.

Gouri could not reconcile herself to this situation, and could certainly not forgive.

* * *

Not long before her arrest, Gouri had already received a slap in the face from fate. Strangely enough, the roots of this story also lead back to Saumen, though Gouri knew him only slightly through his letters and the tales his family told and had seen him only a couple of times in her life.

Saumen had a friend from student times, Parimal. Poor as a church mouse (and he had his mother, three brothers, and a sister living with him), Parimal was often faced with the choice of eating or paying for his studies. Saumen did not know this but he guessed when Parimal fainted during a lecture. He invited Parimal for a chat and then went round his friends with a begging bowl to scrape together the fees. And when Saumen himself went into the underground, he brought Parimal's family home, saying:

"Ma, they don't have anywhere to live now... We have to help."

And so Parimal's family moved in with the Guhas for a while. And because Gouri also turned up, they could not help but meet. Once Saumen asked Parimal whether he wanted to get married and Parimal answered that yes, he himself would like to, especially since he had taken a fancy to Gouri — but there was a problem.

Parimal's mother did not believe her son's wife should be taller than him, even if she was from the highest, Brahmin caste. Parimal did not dare go against his mother. When Gouri found out, she drooped like the boughs of the banyan tree and from then on she was wedded to melancholy.

When she arrived in prison, she was absolutely sure her chance of marriage had gone up in smoke. If, before, the problem had been her height, now she would be "unclean", for people were not stupid and would, of course, guess what they do to unmarried girls in Lalbazar. And even if someone was lucky and nothing did happen to her, who would believe it? Prison was an indelible stigma.

Gouri's heart was full of gloom. She was the victim of coincidence and a monstrous injustice. It was like an ordinary citizen who pops into the bank for five minutes and arrives during a bank robbery — and only when taken hostage does he recognize that life has washed its hands of him.

* * *

When they had stopped flinching in the mornings at the rasp of the prison bell, blaring at them to wake up, but were still counting the weeks, days, and hours, hoping despite everything to come to court, some news arrived via the many-mouthed postal system that crept from cell to cell, and even from one prison to another. It was the news they had feared most of all: Saumen had also been arrested and had already been through the Special Cell.

If we remount the river of time and look again at its waves, it turns out that Archana, Latika, and Gouri were moved to Alipore a week after Saumen's arrest. By this time it is almost impossible to know whether this was pure coincidence or if there was some link between the two events. But one thing is certain — Saumen's arrest was not as a result of information extracted from the women. And they paid a terrible price for not divulging where he was — information that they did not even have.

Saumen had been captured near the underground base, in the provinces. At a fork in the road near the bazaar as he went to buy provisions. He was sick with a fever and had not eaten or slept for some days. Some say the arrest came about by chance, that the police had set up a raid on the bazaar, surrounded it and all approaches to it, and had rounded up into a coach all the men who happened to be within the cordon. According to another version, someone had betrayed him and pointed him out as he went to the bazaar.

But anyway, even a chance arrest, part of a general sweep encompassing a whole crowd, cannot be called pure coincidence. "There is a proverb," wrote Solzhenitsyn in *The Gulag Archipelago*. "'Shoot the crow and shoot the raven — in the end you'll hit the swan!' Just keep shooting, one after the other — and in the end you'll hit the one you want. The primary idea of mass terror is exactly this: even the strong and well hidden, who could never be rooted out singly, will be caught and will perish."

Anyway, they caught him. They cast their poachers' net and, along with a few useless minnows, they caught a white swan…

Ten days into August Sibendra received a postcard. The name

on it was female and unknown to him; the writing was lopsided and shaky, dense with errors. It said that Saumen was at the police station. According to the postmark, the card came from Bankura district.

Sibendra, by this time already the father of two small children, rushed in a lather from Howrah to the Calcutta district of Dum Dum.

"Ma! Saumen's been arrested! I've got to go to the police!"

His mother demurred.

"Just think about it before you rush off. We've already got three in prison. And we don't even know who sent the letter. What if it's a provocation? What if you turn up and they arrest you?"

"I don't care!" fumed Sibendra. "I've got to go! He's my brother! I need to find out what's happening."

At the Bankura district police station no one was being held under the name of Guha. Sibendra thought Saumen might be using a different name. Not betraying that conjecture, he quietly left the station and found a lawyer, who later confirmed that Saumen was under arrest and would soon come to court.

The sight of Saumen in court upset Sibendra tremendously. He saw them bring him in in a police van, push him out, and drag him along the ground. His body was sagging like a rotting rope bridge, black from all the bruises. Sibendra guessed he'd been tortured, and brutally. He started begging the lawyer to do something, if only to get Saumen moved into prison, for if he went back to the police station they would surely kill him.

Sibendra was right. For six days solidly Saumen had been tortured in Bankura police station and then, for two weeks, at Lalbazar in the Special Cell, where he fallen into the hands of Runu, among others.

Once, when Saumen had been beaten till his blood was congealed like sealing wax, he came round on the floor with a policeman standing on his chest, prodding him below the belt with a red-hot skewer, and the phone rang. The policeman picked up the receiver and, still standing on Saumen's chest, started cooing endearments into the phone.

"…yes, dear…good, dear…everything's fine here, how about you? What are the children doing? Ah, asleep already…Yes, yes, I'll be back soon…Miss you…Love you…"

Saumen gritted his teeth, broken and crushed to dust, mashing scraps of his tarry mouth into his viscous, slimy blood, and trying not to howl. His defenceless body, unable to move, his derided, beaten ego — everything in him was swearing vengeance.

* * *

As September drew to a close, and the women were in their second month of incarceration in the Presidency Jail, there was an unexpected development. In the morning, after the distribution of rations, a policeman came into the cell and shouted loudly at the girl lying motionless, face to the wall:

"Prisoner Gouri Chatterjee!"

And while Gouri was anxiously turning round, staggering to her feet, legs still weak and with a bad limp, the policeman was clearing his throat, hand over his mouth, as judges do when about to pronounce sentence. In stentorian tones, punctuated by pauses, he announced:

"Gouri Chatterjee! All charges have been withdrawn. You are free to go home immediately!"

She broke out in a sweat. Her arms hung down like liana ropes. Her legs felt a great weight lifted off them, as if the cobblestones in them had just melted away. She felt as if her throat was full of old rope. It tickled. She did not know where to look. Spots floated before her eyes.

It struck like a wind.

It rose like the sun.

It burst like a bomb.

The policeman was breathing heavily while he waited.

"Follow me! Pick up your document at the office and that's it."

Gouri, pale, threw up her hands as if struck dumb. Her friends, her cellmates surrounded her in a sweaty circle, nineteen mouths expressing their joy. Hugs. Tears. Parting words whispered: "Be careful… take care of yourself…" Gouri looked down guiltily from her great height: here she was, leaving now, while her friends were staying there. The ceiling had split into two halves, to show a sliver of open sky. But it was still there, that ceiling, hanging over her like a monolithic tombstone.

In the office they gave her an official document franked with a blue stamp. A policeman led her out of the gates, above which the legend "Presidency Jail, Alipore" stretched in a wide arc.

"That's the way to the bus stop. They go every hour. Where are you going, anyway?"

"Mm… first to Dum Dum," said Gouri timidly. "I'll go home from there…"

"How are you going to get there? You haven't got any money, have you?"

The policeman, like a conjuror, deftly produced a rupee from his breast pocket.

"Here, take this. It'll be enough for the bus!" he said, and disappeared through the prison gates.

Gouri looked around in all directions. To the right of the gate nestled the cabin where they checked documents and passes, its walls covered with announcements. Nearby a little group, waiting for visits, broke up and scurried away. To the left stretched the yellow brick wall — unassailable as the Great Wall of China — that encircled the prison. The dry undergrowth lining the road clung tight to the base of the wall. Gouri moved fearfully, quietly, like a fish over the sea-bed, feeling how unaccustomed to movement her feet had become, and suffering constant pain, now in her heels now in her toes, as if she was walking on pebbles. She was already imagining how she would get on the bus and, in a couple of hours, knock on Archana's mother's door, and how while travelling she would avidly gaze out of the window, and how roughly-painted effigies of Indian gods would bare their teeth and grin at her in every square and in every district. It was the month of Ashvin and the air would soon be filled with the milky aroma of rasgulla balls and the peasants, decked out in their best, brightly-coloured glad-rags, were already finishing off their rafts. On these, on the tenth night of the waxing moon, they would launch onto the water the ten-armed Maa Durga, who defends the world order from the demons.

"Gouri Chatterjee!" She heard the call behind her, when she had gone barely a hundred steps.

She turned. A policeman, his face unfamiliar, was looking at her. He had emerged from the same gates through which they had just released her.

"Gouri Chatterjee! You're under arrest! I'm arresting you under MISA!"

People's legs would go numb instantly at the sound of this word — even legs sprinkled a minute earlier with the water of life. Even the blinding gloom of solitary confinement cannot kill the human capacity to oppose demonic forces — for there is always the hope of deliverance, enshrined in the verdict handed down by the court. However many years of misery it may be, three, five, or ten, when the period of incarceration is known there is both a starting point and a final destination. The final destination is where the battle stops — where, after a long, sleepless night, dawn must finally come.

But for anyone imprisoned under MISA (the Maintenance of Internal Security Act) there was only a departure track — no end station. This cunning law was adopted in 1973, and it granted unlimited, unreasonable powers to a government that was sitting on a time bomb. The authorities were empowered to arrest all malcontents and imprison them — without the necessity of a trial — for an *unspecified* period, a period that could expand to a whole life.

That evening Gouri returned to Latika and Archana.

When, three days later, a policeman came into the cell and announced, "Prisoner Archana Guha! All charges have been withdrawn. You are free to go home immediately!" everyone already knew it was a trick. Archana left the prison gates and was immediately re-arrested. Three days later the heroine of the story with the now-familiar ending was Latika.

The sentences they were given were like carbon copies — only the names were changed:

"You, (name), being an active member of the Communist (Marxist-Leninist) Party of India, took part on 27th May 1974 in a secret meeting of the above party held at 10 Bipin Mitra Lane, Calcutta. At this meeting, you together with others decided to kill police personnel and seize their weapons, so as later to effect an armed revolution with the aim of violently overthrowing the government."

Later Saumen and all Archana's, Latika's, and Gouri's cellmates received the same sentence, along with more than a hundred people the women had never heard of.

Latika tried to protest. For the whole week after the infamous word MISA was first suspended like an axe above their heads, cleanly cutting off their way home, she thought about what to do. Finally she managed to get herself taken to the office, where an elderly female functionary listened to her arguments before, with an irritated sigh, throwing her paper and a pen. Latika decided to send a petition to the state government's department of family affairs. Having made up her mind, she started writing:

"I hereby affirm that, in the course of being arrested and imprisoned, I and two other women in my family suffered serious physical injury ..."

Here she paused — she needed to put into words everything that had happened in the Special Cell. But at that moment she was halted by a sudden shout from the hawk-eyed employee.

She ordered Latika to take out "physical injury" and she herself dictated the ending of the letter:

"...financial and mental hardships."

And so the waters closed over their heads.

* * *

And how about Mother? We haven't talked about her yet. What happened to her? That night, when the police left her home, taking with them her nearest and dearest, she was already a different person. It was as if they had cut out her heart and given her a new one.

Until the children's arrest, Sudharani was, you will remember, a stay-at-home. She would never go out alone, or get a bus, or ride in a rickshaw. But now she was unrecognizable. She had moved into a looking-glass version of her world.

The whole day, from dawn to dusk, Mother haunted the thresholds of police stations, trying to glean any shred of information about the fate of her children. Guessing where they might be held, she would walk around under the walls of Lalbazar, trying with a mother's intuition to work out in which of its wings they were tormenting her girls. Or she waited in the quadrangle of one or another courthouse, hoping they would be brought there.

When visits became possible, her so far haphazard itinerary acquired an organized trajectory. By that time her son too had been taken from her — Saumen was being held at the Central Prison. At the crack of dawn his mother would make her way there — just to find out when she could visit. She would sit there, under a tree, for half the day. Then she would get up and walk to Alipore. She did not worry about hunger or thirst, or her sore feet, or the pitiless assault of the sun, or the fact that her clothes were soaked through. She was driven by a single obsession. It was what kept her going.

With the arrest of Latika and Archana, who had taken care

of the household expenses, Mother was left penniless and could not pay the rent. Her sons begged her to leave Dum Dum and move in with them, in Howrah. But Mother refused outright and went to ask Emmy for help.

"It's so far away... so far from the prison... I must wait for them here. This is their home."

Emmy sighed and went cap in hand to the landlords, the Choudhury father and son. Fortunately they had no objection.

"Fine, fine!" said the old man — who had earlier been made to put his signature to an accusation against Archana, Latika, and Gouri — hurrying to reassure her. "I too am happy for your family to carry on living here. If ever Sudharani wants to move out, then she should do it with a smile. She must not leave with tears in her eyes."

As a result, Emmy paid rent on only one room, not two. The old man locked the other room, promising that the Guhas would live in it again, as soon as their children came back home.

"They'll come back, Emmy, you'll see! I'll bring them home myself!" cried Mother joyfully.

Whenever she was laid low with exhaustion and, at night, her heart ailed her, Mother would shed tears into her pillow, but only a few. Then she would turn to — to whom? To the darkness.

"I mustn't die now! No one can take my life now! Even if the Grim Reaper himself turns up, I'll say 'You'll have to wait, dear, till my children are home! I won't let you take me away! I have to see them first!'"

And, strangely enough, the pain would go. Even colds and flu gave her a wide berth.

* * *

After six months, Saumen was moved to Alipore. Mother had spent a long time writing petitions, hanging around entrances, imploring and explaining that it would be easier for an old woman to walk to a single prison than to two. But Mother had not been thinking of herself. In Alipore, when she visited him, Saumen could also see his wife and sister.

Once a fortnight Saumen, Archana, Latika, and Gouri were brought to the visitors' wing and ordered to stand by the wall with the others, in random order. Talking was not allowed. All the families were crowded together at the other end, on the other side of the bars. When they announced the start of visiting time, they all started yelling. Half an hour later they took the prisoners back to their cells.

Arriving home after dark, Mother would open the diary she had been keeping since the arrest. She loved all the children equally, but she began each entry in her exercise books with the words "My dear Sunu, my little daughter Archana, I came to see you today. I came to Alipore…"

Latika's parents did not go to the prison. Having once decided not to accept their daughter's marriage, they shunned her now as well. Gouri's mother, on the other hand, did appear, and a couple of times when she had been to Alipore she would come to Dum Dum, where she tried to hold Sudharani responsible for what had happened.

"My poor Gouri is suffering because of you! Because of you!" she shouted, wringing her hands and holding her head in her hands.

Once Emmy saw this and she told Parimal.

"Emmy," said Parimal unexpectedly. "When Gouri gets out, I'll marry her for sure. Get your mother to tell Gouri when she next visits."

Emmy was dumbfounded. Then, in a fit of temper, she really let rip:

"When Gouri gets out? And when's that going to be? Do people ever get out? Have you forgotten? Have you forgotten that damned MISA?"

Chapter 13
A Critical Case

In those balmy days of late autumn, in that most mellow month of Ashvin, when the peasants, decked out in their best, brightly-coloured glad-rags, at last lowered the rafts bearing ten-armed Mother Durga onto the water and celebrated the triumph of good over evil, Archana lost the ability to walk. If fate decides to strike you down, then it will be straight from the shoulder — so you can't get up again. Literally can't get up.

The paralysis of her once fast-moving, frisky, spindly little legs did not develop immediately but, like gangrene, a predatory serpent gradually devouring its environment, picked away at them centimetre by centimetre. On the first day in the Special Cell, Archana had not been able to keep her balance: the constables had dragged her across the floor and in the cell she had got around on hands and knees. Later, in the Presidency Jail, Archana had gradually recovered. First she learned to stand without falling over and, later, to crawl slowly out into the corridor. When they allowed visits from her mother, she overcame terrible pain and, clinging to the wall or her friends, limped her way inch by inch to the visiting area. But even when the blackened skin fell away from her body and scars appeared in place of the burns and ulcers, the pain in her legs never disappeared. Instead it went into hiding, lay in wait. And when the prison clerk delivered the MISA sentence, it shrank down like a coiled spring only to expand again to its fullest extent.

It happened to the left leg first. It grew numb and more and more frequently just dangled, dragging helplessly as she walked.

Archana tried to put all her weight on her right foot, holding on to Latika and Gouri, and biting her lip. And so she managed to walk — she walked, frantically, desperately — for she could not miss her mother's visit. When the weakness appeared in the right leg as well, she had to relinquish her right to visits, although she still tried to get around a bit in the cell. Then she could no longer manage that, though she still attempted to stand up. And, finally, she could no longer stand. Her legs wasted away into two little stalks, two wisps of straw, hollow bulrushes, their milky blood sucked out.

And so, after a few months, life deserted her legs entirely. What does it mean to live without legs? It means your back is to the concrete, your face to the ceiling, imprisoned by your own body, which is itself locked into a jail of bricks and mortar.

Of course, they sounded the alarm. They both did, Latika and Gouri, who were now both looking after Archana like a small child and understood everything about her condition. They shouted. They rattled the bars. They demanded that a doctor be called. They argued with the guards till they were hoarse. They cursed them till they were blue in the face. But there was no response to their entreaties. The best they ever got, if the guard was in a good mood, was a couple of tablets thrown in, to dull the excruciating pain. But what pain could they really dull? That of a sleepless body? The sleepless heart, the insomniac mind did not yield to these half-measures. Not to mention the state of her soul. She was now consumed not, as previously, by raw hope but by anger, hurt, confusion, and decay.

Archana was asking herself some difficult questions.

For example, they say that God is in everything, in every blade of grass, in every individual. Does that mean he's also in Runu?

No, her intellect could not allow that.

And they say that the torments of torture are also the touch of God, the breath of his boundless love. So the touch of the lathi and of cigarettes on her heels — was that the breath of God?

No, her intellect could not allow that either.

Or how about this: God is the greatest of torturers because he loves us. But how are we to understand that? And to accept it? Can a loving mother knowingly cripple her child? And — the main thing — why? What for? What kind of blessing would she thereby confer?

If God can be a torturer, then can a torturer also become a god?

Or again: why should an innocent person suffer? Why? What, then, is justice?

Questions — questions, morning, evening, night and day, were numbing her brain. She had never till then had such a fertile inner life. She felt so many feelings, thought so many thoughts. Being deprived of freedom and of legs, her life was now measured not in steps but in ideas. Or rather in an idea. One idea. If God is, among others, Runu, and bastinado, and the execution of innocent people, then she had better renounce God. Or, even better, scorn him and rebel against him. But how? Where could she find the strength?

And as she had before, in the Special Cell, she again turned into herself and forced out, sobbed out into the infinite depths of darkness:

"Baba, give me strength! Give me the strength to bear all this! Baba, give me strength!"

* * *

During these overwrought days two tiny miracles occurred. It was already six months since Archana had seen her mother. Latika, Gouri, and Saumen had all been begging for the same thing — that Archana be allowed a visit in the cell. But they were always refused. The idea of allowing family into a cell was absolutely unheard of here. But suddenly, like manna from heaven, with a grating of bolts Emmy appeared in the cell, followed by Mother. It was so very unexpected, and just so unnatural to see them there, behind bars, in that brick and cement nowhere, among prisoners as if they themselves *were* prisoners.

In the half hour they were allowed, they uttered not a single word. Emmy gazed mutely around, her tear-filled, frightened gaze feeling its way round the malodorous dungeon. Mother sat next to Archana, holding her hands, stroking her head, and kissing that tired brow — and looked, looked, looked… until a pock-marked prison guard insolently clanked the lock.

Then two weeks later, after Saumen had bombarded the prison office for months requesting a meeting with his sister, they carried her on a stretcher into an interior prison yard and allowed her to see her brother. They were not given much time. Saumen spoke immediately:

"Sezdi, do you remember our neighbour, the teacher? What she said to you, when you were about ten?"

No, Archana didn't remember. Saumen told her the story rapidly, as he himself had heard it once, from his father. And as his hurried story took on more detail a picture was reawakening in Archana's memory.

Yes, she'd been about ten when she'd learned to knit. Knitting needles, stitches, yarns, skeins… One day she'd been left with an elderly neighbour. Archana was sitting at a window on the first floor, knitting away avidly. Suddenly the ball of wool slipped and flew out of the window. Archana stretched out to catch it, hanging over the windowsill, but the ball lay on the ground, still linked by a woollen umbilical cord to the sharp needles she held in her hands. Archana pulled at the wool, trying to raise the ball, but it stayed put, merely executing a succession of *fouettés*. Archana was standing with a mass of tangled yarn in her hands when the neighbour, the teacher, came in.

"No, listen — that won't work," she said calmly. "Break the yarn and then go out into the street and get the ball."

Archana did as she said, came back, and looked at the ringlets of spoiled wool.

"What can I do now?" she sobbed.

"Come here, child," said the neighbour gently. "Sit next to me and copy what I do. But don't rush. If you rush, nothing will come right."

And she set about showing Archana how to disentangle yarn and wind it into a ball.

"You're still small, but try to remember this from now on. You'll have other problems in your life, bigger problems than this one, and you'll have to deal with them. So always work it out carefully, patiently. Not like you did just now, when you were trying to pull the ball of wool up. In everything, my dear, you need patience. Without patience you won't solve a single problem. Do you understand?"

Archana did not really understand. And at home she told her father all about it.

"You must remember this advice all your life," was her father's response. "In everything, you need patience. Without patience you won't solve a single problem."

That night, Archana lay awake, thinking. How wonderful that Saumen had remembered that, and had reminded her. Patience. She needed patience. How could she ever have forgotten?

* * *

More than a year had passed by the time Archana was finally allowed to see the prison doctor. Bhaba Ranjan Sengupta's entry in his medical log read "Patient is suffering from weakness." But he did not specify what kind of weakness. A prison doctor answers to his paymaster — but at least he passed Archana on to a woman doctor. A woman can be of more help to a woman.

Gynaecologist Geeta Chaudhury had seen it all in the Presidency Jail — but even her tough heart flinched when she felt Archana's legs — or, rather, what remained of them. She understood everything immediately: with that problem, no one could survive in Alipore. What should she do? How could she help? If she sent the patient to a hospital in town on some innocuous pretext, doctors there would examine her, and not the way the prison doctor had. Maybe they would come up with something? Maybe there would be a chance? It wouldn't be hard to find some pretext. After all, people who'd been through the Special Cell had more reasons to need help than they had haematomas on their arms and legs.

Geeta Chaudhury sent Archana to the women's clinic. She could not know what a dramatic reversal that would put in train.

The armed prison escort assigned to Archana was constantly in the ward, so the chance the good doctor had been banking on never materialized — the doctors were frightened to speak to Archana over and above the imposed limits. But, on the other hand, Archana could see her mother, who came on whichever days she was allowed to. She would sit in the ward quietly, until Archana's guards decide to throw her out. However, this spell of pure heaven did not last long. One day, arriving at four o'clock as agreed, Mother found the bed empty. An orderly told her that they had taken her daughter off on a stretcher just a minute before and that she was now on her way back to prison. And Mother bellowed, trumpeted like an injured elephant.

In the prison van, they had already battened the door when Archana heard it — when she heard *that*... and something snapped inside her.

"Why are you taking my daughter away?! Why are you taking my daughter away?! Why are you taking my daughter away?!" roared Mother like a madwoman, and hurled her frail little body against the side of the van, trying to bar its way. "Don't take her away! She'll die there! She'll die there!"

The van pulled away, indifferent to her pleas, and moved out onto the highway. Archana lay, as if entombed, unable to see the outside world. But she could hear her mother running somewhere nearby, a couple of metres away. Running and roaring. Running and wheezing. Stumbling, falling behind. Sobbing, choking, moaning, begging, imploring, cursing.

"Why are you taking my daughter away?! Why are you taking my daughter?! Why are you ta—"

The cry broke off suddenly. It did not grow more distant, it did not disappear round a corner. It broke off. Archana did not know what to think, how to explain it. Had her mother fallen behind? Stopped? Had the police seized her? Seized her and hauled her off? Or had she fallen? Fallen and died?

Her head throbbed as if pounded with a sledge-hammer. The air was steamy as a sauna, piercing her with red-hot needles. The roof of the van tilted like the lowering sky before a thunderstorm. Her heart beat like a butterfly fallen between shutter slats.

You were wise to this in advance, Seneca, when you said, "Pain, you are mild if I can bear you and short-lived if I cannot".

* * *

In the cell, among the familiar nineteen woman she had not seen for a month, Archana thought only of her mother. She did not eat or drink but lay delirious for a week, floating between this and other worlds.

On the morning of February 9, she once more half regained consciousness, her eyes once more half groped for Latika and Gouri, she half winced in a half smile and half wept. Then she greedily closed her eyes, as if she had never slept her whole life long. And she sank into unconsciousness.

It was the twenty-first month of their incarceration.

It had been hours now, and Archana had still not regained consciousness. Her cellmates slapped her cheeks and pounded at her arms and legs, while Latika and Gouri were hammering at the bars in desperation and shouting:

"Come here! Help! Hey, someone come and help!"

"Help! Come quick!"

There was no reaction. Not the slightest.

When, at five in the afternoon, it was time for cell-cleaning, the guards finally showed themselves. They opened the bars and ordered everyone out into the corridor. The prisoners came out but refused to go back.

"Get Archana to the hospital! Right now!"

From the cells to left and right a buzz of voices could be heard:

"She's dying, Archana's dying…"

"She's got to get to the hospital!"

Other wings joined the storm of protest.

"Get the governor here!"

But more time passed before the prison governor appeared, promising to do something.

"No promises! Take her to the hospital right now!" The walk-out had now spread to the men's side. "You can kill us, but we're not going back to our cells! Get Archana to the hospital!"

That lasted until late in the evening. The mutiny surged on from one wing of the prison to the next. Neither orders nor threats from the guards could quell it.

At midnight, two of the warders brought a stretcher in and carried off the half-dead body that was now white as a sheet. They pushed it into the van. And when, in the reception area of the Medical College Hospital, the duty doctor and nurse came to look at Archana, when they felt her carotid artery for a thread, or even the tiniest filament, of a pulse and tested the reaction of her pupils to light, they positively screamed:

"She's critical. It's an emergency!"

"Into Resus. Right now! Critical case!"

Chapter 14

The Milgram Experiment

"You know, that's a really good idea for a book, Dina, the story of a woman who fell into police hands and became a hostage. What they did to her, how they made fun of her, the state they reduced her to, trying to torture her brother's whereabouts out of her. It really struck a chord when I heard about it at the PEN Club and I decided to ring. You've really hit the nail on the head. You're not just writing her story. You're writing the story of lots of people. I wonder if even you can imagine how many there are in the world. Millions! Millions, really... A few days ago I read that in Africa alone ... well, not even all of Africa actually, it was just about Zimbabwe. In Zimbabwe, a woman, a doctor... her name was... something nice, you know... Love...No, hang on, not Love...something longer... Lovemore! ... Anyway, this Lovemore person has recorded people like Archana. And you know what? Every month there are another thousand. Can you imagine? Another thousand every month. In five or ten years, that's a whole city! And then there's Asia, the Middle East, Latin America, not forgetting Russia and all those 'stans', those 'Faroffistans'...

"But the reason I rang, actually, is that I'm not new to this subject. I have a connection to it, so to speak. Not like Archana, no. My grandfather, a run-of-the-mill book-keeper, was a member of a punishment battalion during the war. The family didn't know about it, or kept it quiet. Just imagine what it was like finding that out as a teenager, a genetic burden like that. I wanted to drown myself in shame. At the time, you see,

I thought being a torturer was an illness, a pathology, in the genes… hereditary. I spent a long time looking for the 'traces' in myself. That's why I studied psychology. I sifted through so much information, went through so much research. I wanted to understand where these inhuman monsters come from. And do you know what I discovered? They're not inhuman at all. They're people, ordinary people. And they're not born like that. It's something they become. It turns out that anyone can become a torturer. Did you not know that? Anyone! Or, okay, that's going too far. Not anyone but two-thirds of us. Eight out of ten… The majority! It's been proved by science. And it's got nothing to do with genetics. So what is it, you say? You must have heard of Stanley Milgram's experiment? That's right, the psychologist. From America. Yes, the one who came up with the six degrees of separation theory. You haven't? I'll tell you then, just quickly. So much has been written about it, in magazines, on the Internet. It's a really famous experiment. One of the most significant in twentieth century psychology. And most of all, it was a really shocking discovery. The findings are just frightening.

"You've heard of Adolf Eichmann? That's the one, from the Gestapo, one of their chief torturers. He was one of the architects of the Holocaust. After the war, he managed to escape to Argentina. He spent many years there under a false name but they tracked him down in the end and took him off to Israel and, of course, they put him on trial. The sentence was what you'd expect… he was hanged. Eichmann defended himself in court. He said he wasn't to blame, that he was just a soldier who'd carried out his commander's orders. And as for conscience, that was no business of the law. So your conscience is like underpants — wear them if you like, don't bother if you don't. And you know, the court ruled that he was utterly sane … that he was normal in other words. Not psychologically disturbed.

"Hannah Arendt, the philosopher and political theorist … she covered the trial for *The New Yorker*… said that basically Eichmann and his ilk embodied the *banality of evil*. Many people at the time agreed. I do too. The greatest harm to humanity was done not by fanatical terrorists or the mentally ill but by simple, normal, ordinary people carrying out the orders of their superiors.

"Well, anyway… Milgram was working on that notion at the time too. *The banality of evil*. He was interested in how German citizens during the war had been able to torture and annihilate several million people. Obviously, the decisions were taken at the very top by a gang of politicians. But they were carried out… all these mass executions and murders … by ordinary people. They were the ones who herded people into trains, transported them to concentration camps, delivered the canisters of Zyklon B, boarded up the gates, turned on the tap. It doesn't happen that an entire nation is sadistically inclined. Something else was evidently going on. Milgram decided to find out what. He had some guesses. He planned to go to Germany to carry out his experiment but to start with he decided to try it out in the state of Connecticut. What he discovered meant he didn't need to make the trip. Whether in Germany or the state of Connecticut, people are the same everywhere. Or, rather, they show the same inclination to cruelty everywhere when they are carrying out their superiors' orders.

"So, you ask, how did he do it? It was quite simple. He recruited volunteers through a newspaper ad. He chose people of all ages, by the way, from twenty to fifty, and all races and social classes. Labourers and postal workers, businessmen and engineers, housewives, teachers, and academics. They were told they'd be researching the effect of pain on memory. They were lied to, in other words. They didn't know they were the ones being studied, to see how far they'd go in causing pain if an authority figure required it.

"Essentially, the experiment was this: one of the recruited volunteers was designated the 'teacher.' Another — an actor, a plant that the 'teacher,' of course, didn't know about — played a 'pupil.' The 'pupil' had to learn sentences and repeat them off by heart. If the 'pupil' got it wrong — and you'll understand that he did nothing but get it wrong — the 'teacher' had to punish him. And do you know how? By giving him an electric shock. What's more, the voltage had to go up with each wrong answer. Up to 450 volts. Everything was designed so that the 'teacher' believed he was really, genuinely, delivering electric shocks — though in actual fact there was no current.

"So, what happened? How did all these people behave? You might think that at least someone... at least one of this mob... refused to deliver the shock! Nothing of the sort! It was stressful for them as well. Many were very nervous. Their hands shook, their armpits sweated, they gasped, laughed guiltily, shed a tear... hiccupped and stammered... There was one sturdy looking chap, a flourishing business type, he sold encyclopaedias... within twenty minutes he was on the verge of a nervous breakdown, clutching his head, and pleading, 'God, no! Let's stop already!' But the 'instructor' said, 'Stay focused, please. We have to keep going.' And he did. He didn't want to but he did. He increased the voltage again and again to the very highest level.

"By the way, the instructor was played by Stanley Milgram himself. He sat in the room, wearing a white lab coat, the very picture of an authority figure. If the 'pupil' hesitated, expressed doubt, or objected, Milgram urged him on: 'This is a very important experiment' or 'It's extremely important that you see it through.' And as a rule that one second, that tiny nudge, that slight encouragement on his part was sufficient for people... no matter what conflict might be tormenting them ... to set aside any moral qualms and keep on increasing the current.

"Then there was the actor. He didn't just sit there either. He gave a realistic performance of how much it hurt: he yelled, writhed in agony, groaned, went into convulsions. He even complained of a heart problem. 'Call a doctor! Let me go! Let me out!' In the end, when the voltage was up to 250 or 300 volts, he simply stopped responding as if he'd lost consciousness. The 'instructor' again told the 'pupil,' 'Carry on, please.' And these dear, delightful people did just that.

"Only one or perhaps two out of ten refused to take part once the actor clutched at his heart. They said, 'We shouldn't give him so much… It's dangerous… I don't think it's humane… No way, I can't do it… No, no, it's not right…What a hellish experiment…. The kid's really hurting… I don't want any part of it… Let's stop. This isn't normal.'

"Just think… Only one or two out of ten… All the rest, no matter how their hands trembled… kept on and on. And yet the conditions of the experiment were like nothing we encounter in real life. The 'instructor' didn't threaten to sack them or offer them any reward. People were free to leave with impunity at any point.

"That, basically, is the way it is. People, adults, altered the way they behaved. The point here is that they were not so much naturally drawn towards cruelty as inclined to obey. It's easier to become a torturer than to say no to a superior.

"And do you know what? This has been done all over the place. From Italy to Jordan and not long ago in America again. And the results are the same. Two-thirds…again, the majority.

"What did you say? That the world is a horrible place and people are frightful? Well, yes, basically. Unfortunately, that's true. But isn't the whole of our history proof of that? Just compare how much violence is carried out on the order of superiors and how much under the flag of revolt! Have you made the comparison? There you are then. If you take only the most recent… Hitler, Stalin… How many people engaged in active resistance? How many were they? Exactly. Hardly any. Passively, sure, — passively! — lots of people hated the torturers although it's hard to say exactly how many today. Then there was rampant propaganda. When the Germans were asked afterwards how it could be that they'd sent whole peoples to the gas chambers, they answered: 'Personally, I didn't agree with it.' Or: 'But we didn't know.' What can you say to that?

"In nature, in theory, there are not very many people who can say no. And even fewer who can go against the current.

And, although they're the very ones the torturers will have it in for they can't be called victims. Victims are those who *don't* resist evil. Those whose silence gives assent. Who are prepared to adapt, lie down and roll over. I presume it was for them, these two-legged plankton, that the commandments were devised, all these 'shalt not kill's' and 'shalt not do harm's.' And quite right too. After all, if there were no laws at all and life was lived solely according to conscience, the world would soon go to hell. It would be, what did you just say? The world is a horrible place and people are frightful? Well, yes, exactly, unfortunately, that's just what would happen."

Chapter 15

Maya

Her vision was not yet free of the veil of blindness that had descended on her, and the world was only showing through in unsteady, blurred patches, as the bed of the sacred Ganges shows through a miry residue of sludge and dust. Her hearing, however, had already smashed through foul blockages in search of the quiet just before dawn; her mind was coming home, timidly, on tiptoe; and her sense of touch was just making an entrance. So she knew her cocoon was no longer damp, low, and uncomfortable but, on the contrary, dry, elevated, and warm. Her head could feel the gentle fluffiness of a pillow, her back a soft, comfortable firmness, and the air... the air no longer tore the delicate membranes of her eyes and nostrils into spiky tatters but clung to her and soothed her with the herbal aroma of a pharmacy. Archana moved her hand and, as she returned to her paralyzed body, her weak, enfeebled fingers encountered something long-forgotten, the edge of a sheet. Where am I? Where am I?

"Are you back with us?" a soft voice above her asked.

An unfamiliar face, with high, kohl-accented eyebrows, came into view. A small hand touched her brow and started straightening the sheet so as to cover Archana up to the neck. It also, carefully, prised open Archana's fingers under the sheet and put something into her hand — a small ball, the size of a pea. It was inserted, and the hand firmly closed it away like a pearl in an oyster shell.

Archana's ear caught a barely audible whisper: "Hide it!"

The unknown woman sat with her a little longer, then looked round, opened the drawer of the bedside table and straightened the case-notes. With a "Sleep well!" she moved soundlessly to the exit, and disappeared through the doorway, which was, Archana noticed only now, framed by two great hulks in uniform.

Until morning, never opening her fist, she kept thinking, guessing, wondering what it could be. She had already realized that she'd come back, come back to life again, to life under the sword of Damocles, and that she was in a hospital ward guarded by a prison escort, and that the night-duty nurse was called Sandhwa. In the morning a nursing assistant arrived and helped Archana to wash and go to the toilet. The guards had to go out into the corridor for a few minutes then. As the door closed, Archana opened up her now damp fingers. The pearl in the shell proved to be a note: "Archana, all of us here, all the nurses, have decided to help you. Please tell us what you need."

That night Sandhwa appeared again. Having sent the guards outside ("I have to examine the patient!"), she whispered:

"Archana, if you like we can tell your family…"

In the morning, after her shift, she knocked on the clinic director's door.

"Doctor… we, the nurses here… well we all think… we've got to help Archana. She mustn't go back to prison — she'll die there. You must (and Sandhwa stressed the word 'must')… keep her here."

The elderly Professor Mondal pulled the horn-rimmed, roughly repaired spectacles from his pitted nose.

"Yes, I realize that… The new patient in the single room… her condition's critical… it's very difficult… a difficult case."

And she could not tell what he meant. Difficult in the medical sense? Or what?

* * *

It was the head of the medical team, Kumar Bishnu, who took Archana to a ward in the neurology clinic on the third floor. And it was he who made the first entry in her case notes. Unlike prison doctors, who played according to the unwritten rules of the prison chiefs, Doctor Kumar did not hesitate to call a spade a spade.

"After being arrested, Archana Guha was in the Presidency Jail from August, 1974. In July, she had been subjected to physical torture. On 9th February, 1976, she was admitted to hospital due to the gradual paralysis of her lower limbs and other medical conditions…"

A disapproving whisper went round the guards.

And, yes, there were a large number of them, those guards. Not two, not three but seven of them — for the one, immobile Archana. Two, from the Presidency Jail, were in the ward round the clock. Two, from Lalbazar, stood outside the door. The fifth, also from Lalbazar, sat at the desk by the door and scrupulously, jealously noted everything he saw and heard around him: which hospital staff called into the ward, how long they talked to her, what they talked about. The sixth was on duty in the corridor by the lift and the seventh by the lift in the lobby below.

At first they kept Archana in a single room. The hospital allocated these rooms to wealthy patients on payment of a special rate, but sometimes, on instruction from above, they would give one to the police.

There was so much space here that all seven guards would sprawl in a smelly, red-faced heap, lounging impudently in front of Archana and smoking and chatting, telling tall stories peppered with oaths and innuendoes.

"Make the most of the rest cure while it lasts, my lovely — it'll be finished soon! You'll be back to your 'permanent place of domicile', hey?"

Their lowing, grunting, and cackling over, they allowed themselves a snooze, taking their nap in lordly fashion, anchored to their chairs by legs spread at right angles, heads dangling to one side, their dribbling, gap-toothed mouths agape and reeking of exhaust fumes. Each clawed vigorously at an unresponsive fly, the fast, simian stroke of his sweaty paw causing it to rise like a soap bubble. One after the other — especially at night.

A month later, Professor Mondal moved Archana into a twelve-person ward, despite the protests of the escort guards, who were thus deprived of the chance to plague her with their nocturnal intrusions. In the communal ward there was no room. It was congested, smelly, and stuffy. All they could do now was to station two guards by the door while the rest had to hang around outside. When the Professor came to examine his patients, the guards left the ward.

Archana asked the Professor, sotto voce, not to take her back to the single room as the police wanted.

"Don't worry, my dear," he said, hastening to put her mind at rest and straightening his spectacles. "No one can move you without my permission. And I'm not going to give that permission. D'you hear? No one, not even the chief of police, is going to take you away. You can get a good sleep now."

For some reason she trusted him — or she was desperately anxious to trust him, just as she trusted all these new people around her, these easy-going people who were good to her and had decided for themselves whose side they were on.

And how this angered the police! How hard they tried to hurt her!

"But she's a terrorist," the first would confide hoarsely, puffing out his sagging jowls so they looked like dough rising in a baking tray, as he guided one or another of the doctors by the elbow into their little nook.

"D'you know how many of our people she's killed?" the second would whisper to every nurse coming on duty, smoochily screwing up his little currant-like eyes.

"They found pistols in her house!" the third would tell the nursing assistants excitedly, when they went to the kitchen for their meals.

"She had a whole arsenal at home! She was blowing people up, the bitch!" the fourth would say, gossiping with Archana's neighbours in the ward.

Yet this was not their territory, not their world. They were incomers here, outsiders, forcibly billeted on everyone. The masters here were the people — not these escort guards. Some people believed the police goons, but the naïve types who were taken in could be counted on the fingers of one hand. The rest — and that was the whole department, the whole floor — openly laughed as the policemen walked away, dismissing their importunate, overdone nonsense, and giving the index-finger-to-the-temple gesture. And even those humbled by their caste, unable to read and write, the wrinkled old women cleaning the toilets (and such people were the easiest to frighten), they too were rooting for Archana, as for one of their own. Auntie Gita for example. As soon as she had cleaned the commode, she immediately hurried to Archana so that she could be the first to use it. Then she sat on the corner of the bed, took her by the hand, and stroked her head:

"Daughter... you're my little daughter..."

The nursing assistant, Maya, was forever nagging her about it.

"Gita! How many times do I have to tell you! Don't touch her! You've come straight from the toilet! Have you forgotten what the doctor said? She has a weak immune system! Any infection could kill her!"

Ah, Maya, Maya... those words, about immunity and infection, would turn out to be prophetic. But we'll get to that a bit later. Now I'd rather talk about you. Everyone must know about you. Our world has not yet seen the end of the simple, mutinous individual who not only can shout "no", but loves to do so, and whose character, thoughts, and actions are a shining example of the refusal to submit to evil — and more than that, of active opposition to it.

* * *

All the patients unable to walk had nursing assistants, and this included Archana. There were two of them, the day nurse and the night nurse — who were as different as day and night. The day nurse was noisy and hyperactive, like a new Soviet transistor radio, but also tender as an angel. The night nurse was silent as a deep gully, somewhat heavyset and something of a coward. The day nurse was Auntie Maya, from Bangladesh, and she was just under fifty. The name and age of the night nurse are lost in the mists of time.

When the nursing assistants were looking after detainees, it was the police who paid for their work although they were hired by the hospital. In other words, the assistants reported to the doctors but were materially dependent only on those who paid them. And in every case the police would try to recruit them to their cause.

"Be strict with her!" they would urge the assistants, as if drilling troops. "You're being paid by the police! You've got to represent us! Archana's a criminal, a terrorist! She's got to be scared of you! You're representing the authorities — so show her who's the boss!"

The night nurse became puffed up with her own importance, strutting like a turkey-cock — but Auntie Maya would brush such talk aside with a gesture — fastidious, squeamish. It seemed to say: "Just get away from me, gentlemen, you big cheeses, with your advice — get far, far away…"

And she had a hard time, did Maya, thanks to her intractability. Whenever the time came to take Archana for treatment, two policemen would stand in their way and not allow them into the lift. No terrorists allowed! And Maya would demonstrate her irritation by spitting at their feet, and call a friend to help. Both would grumble, moan, and curse, they would be running with sweat, but they would selflessly haul the wheelchair, clattering, up and down the stairs. From the third floor to the ground and back.

And what an operation Maya had going in the kitchen! A secret service, a conspiracy, a band of partisans. It was a real people's militia!

Archana had stopped eating while in the Presidency Jail and showed no sign of improvement even in hospital. A month, another, and another — and still no appetite. She was thinner than a wraith. A diet of better fare was prescribed — but what sort of diet could she get in the hospital? Only watery gruel and a few pitiful scraps of fish with rice. Detainees were not allowed to have food brought in. So Maya decided on a ruse.

Before she left for work, she would cook at home. And when the food was being served out in the hospital kitchen she would fill her patient's plate with the home-made food and eat the hospital rations herself.

Archana was puzzled for a good while as to why her rice was whiter and looked more appetizing than the other patients' and her piece of fish was bigger than theirs. And the curry sauce was not the slightest bit fetid or watery like hospital food but real, fresh, hot, aromatic curry. And there were even vegetables, mung beans, and peas, things that had never been seen in hospitals.

The policemen were seething with rage.

"We've never seen this kind of food in a hospital," they complained, looking at Archana's plate.

When the truth was revealed, Maya was forbidden to go into the kitchen, but she found a way round that too. Other assistants came to the rescue and set their female cunning — all sorts of manoeuvres and signals — to work. If one of them cleared her throat three times it meant a guard was approaching the kitchen. If they clanked a bucket in the corridor it meant the coast was clear.

"Carry on with your silly games and you'll be out of here like a shot!" the policemen would yell at Maya, sensing some new ruse.

"So what?" she'd laugh. "Go on then! I won't be out of work!"

"Don't kid yourself! You're just a ragamuffin, a serving girl!"

"Yes, I'm a serving girl, yes! I'm serving an innocent, crippled woman — while you're grovelling to Runu!"

They could do nothing with her — they couldn't scare her, they couldn't win her over. The only thing would be to get rid of her somehow — to fire her, send her packing. But their threats were like water off a duck's back. If you gave Maya a ruled exercise book she would write in it crosswise.

* * *

But one day even Maya ran out of steam. She could not bear to watch the goings-on. She didn't fear for herself — she could stand it — but she feared for others…

Once a week Archana's mother was allowed to visit her daughter. But as soon as she set foot in the hospital the guards set up a marathon for her. They would not let her use the lift. Sudharani had to get to the third floor on foot (and the ceilings here were so high that each floor was the equivalent of two). She would climb up, scramble up, out of breath. Since she had tried to keep up with the police van taking Archana away, her health had deteriorated — her legs and heart had both weakened. And now they were punishing her feet — pursuing her, spurring her on, always with the same stupid comments:

"Run, old woman. Better get a move on before your hour's up!"

"What's it like to have a terrorist for a daughter? Not much fun, eh?"

And then something happened — something seemingly insignificant: Archana's sari got torn. Her mother promised to bring another one — in a week, the next time she came. But a guard told her she could come the following day.

"But that's not allowed!" Archana broke in. "Visiting's only allowed once a week."

"Just calm down. Your mother won't be able to see you — she can leave the sari with us."

The next day, as the clock struck four, Archana did not take her eyes off the doorway, through which she could see the whole length of the lobby. Her mother did not like to be late — in fact she always arrived early so she could get up to the third floor in time. But four had struck and her mother did not appear.

Instead a guard came, the one on duty at the lift, and whispered something to the policeman at the entrance to the ward.

"... rid of her," Archana managed to lip-read.

At half past six Auntie Maya appeared. She seemed to have lost her purposeful gait: she walked up unwillingly, at a snail's pace.

"What's happened, Maya? Tell me the truth!" said Archana, almost in tears, in fear and trembling.

Maya frowned and said nothing.

"Did she come? Tell me!"

"Let's not talk about that," snapped Maya.

"Yes, we will talk about it. Tell me. Tell me!" screeched Archana, beating the bed with her fist. "I must know!"

Maya sobbed, then blew her nose.

"Yes, she was here."

"Carry on!"

"What can I tell you...?" and Maya, not finding the words to explain, coughed nervously until she was hoarse. "They followed her all the way up the stairs again. She was gasping for breath... When she got up to the department they sent her packing. And didn't take the sari of course."

Archana squeezed her fists so tight that her nails drew blood. Her mother was her Achilles heel. If they wanted to give her a thorough hammering they just had to hurt her mother.

Archana turned towards the door where the guard was standing and croaked, falteringly:

"I knew... everything would be like this... you tortured me... and now you're torturing my mother... yesterday you promised, in front of everyone... everyone here witnessed it... you told her to come... and you sent her away... I won't let you torture my mother any more... I... I'm going to do something about it... I'll do... I'll do..."

The whole upper part of her thin body crumpled as if on hinges. She could not hear what she was saying or how far out of the window her broken cries carried. The weary heart does not think, it only screams. The weary heart screams and breaks loose. It no longer wants freedom, or peace, or life. It wants nothing — just to end all the humiliation, all this wretched weariness. Just to end it quickly. To put an end to everything.

The guard rounded on Auntie Maya:

"Who gave you permission to blab? Right, you're out! Tomorrow's your last day in this hospital — and good riddance!"

Maya flushed, as if she'd been slapped in the face. Her eyes narrowed to needles of black pine, her fists resting on her hips like the handles of a china soup bowl. She sprang towards the door:

"Well you know what you can do with your tomorrow and your constant ordering people around! I won't be here tomorrow! I don't want to watch this any longer! I'll find another job — and it won't be hard!"

And red in the face, as if from stinging nettles, she turned to Archana:

"Forgive me, Archana… I won't be here tomorrow. The night-duty assistant will have to stay tomorrow morning until they find someone else."

"Are you leaving me, Maya?"

"I'm sorry. I can't watch them tormenting your mother any longer."

For the first time since the day of her arrest, life had smiled on Archana. It had smiled in that hospital ward, making her believe that suffering also had its limits, that there would be an end to her nightmares. But how short-lived that smile was… Perhaps it was a grimace, rather, fate sneering at her? What was she to think now? Who could she trust? People are this world's greatest riches — and they are also its great affliction. They can decide for themselves — making choices and decisions — where they stand, with whom, on whose side. They can vote with their hands, "a collective promise of good", or with their feet. When they vote with their hands they nourish hope: they restore the suffering soul to consciousness with a drop of life-giving moisture. When they vote with their feet, they trample on that hope. The forces of someone deprived of mercy will then march off at the double. Not to fight for themselves but to beat the pain. That pain is like the pulsating universe — the only thing that knows no end. And how can we avoid its clutches? How can we not lose our way? Not get bogged down? Not sink without trace? How to live with that pain? How to live at all?

Archana told the night nurse she could go, that she didn't need anything. She wrapped herself up in the sheet as in a shroud, slamming herself shut, closing herself off from the world. And so she lay in her cottony tomb, until she heard:

"What's this, nine o'clock already and you haven't eaten anything? Come on then!"

Archana opened her eyes and closed them again. Auntie Maya was leaning over her.

"Oh, it's you… did you come to say goodbye? You don't need to, you can go."

Her calmness was fused with exhaustion and teetered on the brink of desperation.

"Whatever gave you that idea, saying goodbye? I'm staying!"

"But… why?"

"Well, because…" And Maya started gabbling away, "…when I went home yesterday… d'you know what my husband said? He said… 'You're working for Archana, aren't you? Not for the police, are you? Archana needs your help, doesn't she? Not the police. And what have you done? If you leave you're helping the police. They'll hire another nursing assistant… and she'll do what they say… You don't want that, do you? Of course you don't! I know you love Archana, and Archana loves you. So just you go back and stay by her side!"

In short, Maya was back. And back, too, was maya:

illusion and the chains of suffering and change.

* * *

That morning termites seemed to be running over her skin, then it felt unusually warm, and in the space of a minute she was assailed by heat — a clammy, stifling heat. As if someone had opened up the damper valve on the stove and stuffed her head into the heat of a thousand hungry suns. Or had surrounded her with firewood, like a body on the Ganges steps — and set fire to her.

Archana was already used to being able to move only the top part of her body, while the bottom stayed motionless, attached like useless ballast. But now, unexpectedly, the top also lost all feeling. Just before this, Maya had been called into another ward. Archana was suddenly frightened by a darkness that reeled her in and attacked her eyes. She just managed to cry out "Nurse! I'm losing conscious…" And that was it. She burned up. She went out. She left. She went out so very quickly.

A nurse came running when she heard the cry and within fifteen minutes was hurriedly applying ice to the convulsing body, and a doctor was talking to the police commissioner:

"It's malaria… She won't last till morning. Inform the relatives."

At midnight there was loud knocking on the door at 7 Jawpur Road. Sudharani leaped up. Nocturnal guests bring bad news. At the door was a policeman, who handed her a form.

Hearing the noise at the entrance, Choudhury, the landlord, came downstairs. The paper in Sudharani's hand was shaking like a leaf. "What… what does it say? I don't understand…"

The landlord looked and gave a sigh.

"Your daughter… is dying… Archana."

"Is she alive? Right now… is she alive?" she asked over and over, looking right through the policeman.

"This evening she was unconscious, but more or less alive… but now… They said she wouldn't last till morning."

The door closed. Sudharani wanted to be alone.

But she did not fall face down on her pillow, did not collapse on the floor. She did not run into the street looking for a rickshaw and beg the man to take her to her daughter. The whole night Mother stayed in the corner. On her knees, in the corner, before the portrait of her late husband. In her thoughts, she was carried far, far away, to where he might now abide. She tried to call him, tried to ask him one thing. Or not, in fact, to ask but to implore. Or not to implore but to demand. This was the only time in her whole life that she allowed herself to raise her voice when talking to her husband, with tears in her eyes and a spikiness in her tone. As if the world had been turned upside down.

"Can you hear? Can you hear me? I know you can hear me! You've simply got to hear me now! You've got to! Your daughter is dying. Can you hear me? Go and ask! Ask on her behalf. Do everything you can. Save her life! She must live. Go and ask! I want to see her! Alive!"

An hour passed in this way... and another... and a third, and a fourth... Mother did not get up off her knees until daybreak.

All this time Archana was wandering somewhere — wandering, clearly, in a place of no return. It was only here, in this hospital ward on the third floor, that twenty-four hours passed in this way: there, where she was — either on a short visit or perhaps she had already got to know her new sanctuary — time did not exist. But suddenly she was called back, or rather not so much called as ordered back. She was being ordered back in a fairly peremptory fashion... as if someone had taken a deep breath in and then immediately breathed out again. And she understood. She now saw that her time was not over; *there* it was not over... and *here* it had not yet begun.

Archana regained consciousness — awoken by the voice of Emmy. Emmy was shouting outside the door, cursing and screaming.

"We've got to see her! I don't believe you! Let us in!"

"You're not allowed in!"

"It was you who sent for us! So we are allowed!"

Silence. And the same voice again.

"All right, you can look… from the corridor… Look… she's stopped moving."

"She's ali-i-ve…" Mother yelled happily. It was not her eyes, which were blinded by tears, but her clear-sighted heart that had picked up, from that distance, a quivering in Archana's pulse and the twitching and shuddering of her almost-frozen eyelids.

* * *

Yes, she survived. But Professor Mondal warned them that, "if she doesn't get any little pleasures, she won't progress now. Whether they like it or not, we have to seek them out, those pleasures!" He called the police commissioner and insisted that other members of the family should also be allowed to visit Archana.

It was now more than two years since Archana had last seen her relatives; and suddenly her nephew appeared at the door of the ward. Goodness, the boy had become a man while she'd been away!

The next time, Mother brought her son Ramendra's daughter with her. And another surprise! What a beauty! Such long hair! Archana laughed and cried — in all the wrong places.

The third time, Mother brought Ramendra's wife. They had had a baby six months before. The nurses and assistants all played auntie to the baby girl while Archana's mother and sister-in-law sat with Archana. At six o'clock, in accordance with the rules, the guests left. Just before seven, Maya rushed in to Archana, looking alarmed, and said in tragic tones:

"Archana, something's happened."

"What?"

"That one… over there, at the desk… he's scribbling away at something the whole time."

At midnight the guards changed. The night-time assistant, dozing in her armchair, was awoken by an unaccustomed noise and looked out into the corridor.

"Archana, something's happened."

"What?"

"I don't know. But their boss is there… he's talking about you the whole time."

In the morning, when the assistant went for water, she came back saying:

"There really is something going on over there. Now the boss's boss has arrived. And they're all talking about you again!"

Soon the boss's boss himself appeared in the ward.

"And how are you getting on?" he addressed Archana politely.

"No change," she replied.

"Your mother is still coming to visit?"

"She came yesterday."

"Did she come alone or with someone else?"

"With my brother's wife."

"And how was that? Everything went well?"

"It always goes well when Mother comes."

"Are you sure your mother brought only your sister-in-law?

"Yes."

"That's a barefaced lie!" yelled the policeman. "We've been informed that there was someone else. An extra one! Who was it? Answer me!"

"An extra visitor?"

Then Archana understood.

"What kind of extra visitor did I have? She wasn't an extra one — she wasn't even an extra half, not even a quarter. She's a babe in arms, just six months old. She can't talk yet. Do you hear? She… can't… talk… yet. And that means… (and now Archana lowered her voice to a dramatic whisper, like a spy in an Indian film, revealing a military secret) …she couldn't talk to me about politics. And that's what you're driving at, aren't you?"

He did not hang about. The door of the ward slammed but some choice language could still be heard outside.

"You idiot! What's this nonsense you've written! Three visitors!"

"Yes sir, there were three of them and only two are allowed. Strictly speaking, I was right."

"Strictly speaking you were right, but in fact you're a complete idiot! You should have written that the third visitor was a baby! A baby! A babe in arms! We came all the way from Lalbazar! D'you think we've got nothing better to do?"

In the ward they were roaring with laughter.

* * *

Life went on, meagre, poor, sometimes full of conflict, sometimes with none, sometimes frightening, sometimes kind, and so winter, spring, summer, and autumn went by, ten months under hospital arrest. The whole of this time they were trying to get Archana back to Alipore: the police were pressuring the nurses, even threatening the doctors, but Professor Mondal stuck to his guns.

And suddenly, there was a great change in fortune. The Professor was to be transferred to a new job. As soon as he heard about it, he called in Archana's mother and brothers, trying to explain to them — disconnectedly thanks to his agitated state — that they must get to Lalbazar immediately and ask, ask as soon as possible, for a transfer to house arrest, while he, Professor Mondal was still in this job.

"You know, don't you," he said, anxiously, "that there's been no improvement in her condition. As soon as I leave here they'll take her straight back to prison. There's only one way to save her — house arrest. Go and ask them, promise them, give them a written undertaking!"

Mother needed no persuasion. She understood everything immediately. She rushed to Archana, but Archana didn't want to listen. House arrest, being on parole was a trap, a risk, a snare for the whole family. For with that written undertaking they would be offering their own freedom as collateral. Must her brothers and sisters take that risk? But she remembered that she was not her mother's only concern, that there were still, in the Presidency Jail, three family members and Mother was dividing herself among them — how much longer would she be able to manage? In short, she thought about it and agreed.

Sibendra was spinning like a top, whirling up and down the stairs of Lalbazar with the request from the head of the clinic to certify to the prison authorities that his patient was no danger to anyone: "Think about it, where could she run off to, a woman who can't even walk?"

They gave permission, but only for a month.

It was the end of the working day when the Lalbazar clerk brought the order for house arrest to the ward. It still needed to be stamped by the head of the clinic, but he had already gone home, so everything was put off till the following day. The five Lalbazar guards left their posts immediately. The two from the Presidency Jail stayed till morning. That evening Maya vented her anger:

"Well, what about it, you jackals? You're not in charge of Archana now! *Not in charge!* You're not to come in any more! So you can just leave this ward right now! Quick march! Off you go!"

"Just you wait, you viper! You can laugh now!" growled the guards. "But your legless wonder'll be back in jail in a month. And they'll be waiting for her…"

* * *

In the morning they got Archana ready for home. The whole department came to watch. The family gave the nurse and the assistants each a sari and the others Bengali sweetmeats. Her brothers supported Archana and lifted her quickly to a taxi, rushing as though frightened that the guards would suddenly change their mind and send someone after them. On the way, Sibendra was shouting "Let Archana come to us! She'll be more comfortable with us!" But Mother stood firm, as firm as only such a woman can be, a grey-haired woman whose dream — the one she has been dreaming for the previous eight hundred and sixty-two sleepless nights — has just this very minute come true.

"Home! Nowhere else! Archana is coming home!"

At last they drove up. There was still the same sunken foundation, soaked through in the monsoon. Still the same window with vertical bars, the same blue, scratched door. Still the same narrow walkway with its iron grille. And only from there, once you had opened the bolt on yet another barred door, could you get out into the street. But there was no getting out for Archana. They carried her in from the taxi. As for how she would fare later, surely this was no time to think about that? Let her at least be happy now.

Archana's home greeted her with the same furniture and fittings as she had known before her arrest. Plus a special kind of untouched, unlived-in cleanness. The clothes, the household implements — all were as before. The books lay tranquil in their place. It was no home but a museum. All that was missing was the hubbub. Saumen, Latika, and Gouri were still in prison. They still had no fixed term… was it a life sentence? But Mother still repeated her mantra:

"They will come home!"

* * *

At the end of the first month, and in January, and in February, Sibendra went to Lalbazar to beg for and to sign a new parole pledge. Each time he sought an extension of two or three weeks, prolonging the house arrest for a short while, and to his surprise they did not refuse him. Either they really were convinced that the paralyzed woman was no threat, or they were ridding their budget of an extra mouth to feed, while still not giving Archana her freedom.

The reason for these new extensions might have been the country's political situation. That winter, when India was waiting expectantly for the results of the parliamentary elections, things were hotting up, and not only on the streets. People were finally running out of patience. The prisons were bursting at the seams, like over-ripe chestnuts. The government had its tail between its legs, but they put on a brave face. The opposition were sharpening the political knives. Both sides were currying up to the public, promising that if they won the elections they would set political prisoners free.

And at the end of March everything — the radio, newspapers, bazaars — everything exploded: Indira Gandhi lost and fell from power, and the opposition came in. The Guhas silently thanked heaven and, still disbelieving, still fearing to jinx their luck, said nothing — just waited. The wicked witch had disappeared, but would her sorcery also melt away?

They had to wait forty days. In May a policeman knocked at the door. Not for an inspection but to announce that Archana's MISA sentence had been lifted. As of now she could get up and go (that's what he said—"get up and go") to the four corners of the earth.

Two weeks later Mother heard the cry:

"Mother! Gouri!"

Mother ran out of the steamy kitchen where she was cooking dal, thinking Archana was delirious (as had happened before, when she had malaria). She froze: there, on the threshold stood a figure lanky as a stork — her Gouri. Her eyebrows were like the new moon, her lips an upturned rainbow, her eyes… her eyes had turned grey, the colour of rain.

"Gouri! My little girl! You've come home!"

There were exclamations, there was sobbing, there was tearful laughter… After three years apart, all their emotions were mixed up.

That same evening Latika came back.

And in a month Saumen arrived.

And there we could leave them, in a tight family circle, to rejoice and chat as much as they wanted. To dote on each other and, finally, to get to know each other all over again. And then — to try to understand how they were to live now... with all that... after all they had suffered.

For most families the story would end there. And no one would ever know what they felt, what weights were rolling round inside their heads, what cats were scratching at their hearts, what hedgehogs were scurrying around in their bodies; with what toxic thoughts, with what agonizing, bloodthirsty wakefulness they had come back into this world, into their previous, now extinguished life — a life that now could not, not for a day, not for a minute, be what it used to be. This is what happens — with the majority of families. After this, they no longer live — they survive, they wait out their final years.

So is our story nearing its conclusion? No — what an idea! However could it be? Of course not. Our story has not even reached its twilight — much lies ahead... Our story is only just beginning.

PART TWO

Crime Without Punishment

"You who weep, who suffer and tremble, who dare not expect an end to your ills, an issue to your pangs, behold: there is no night without dawn and the day is about to break when darkness is thickest; there is no mist that the sun does not dispel, no cloud that it does not gild, no tear that it will not dry one day, no storm that is not followed by its shining triumphant bow; there is no snow that it does not melt, nor winter that it does not change into radiant spring. And for you too, there is no affliction which does not bring its measure of glory, no distress which cannot be transformed into joy, nor defeat into victory, nor downfall into higher ascension, nor solitude into radiating centre of life, nor discord into harmony — sometimes it is a misunderstanding between two minds that compels two hearts to open to mutual communication; lastly, there is no infinite weakness that cannot be changed into strength."

The Mother

Chapter 16
The Historic Metamorphosis

But they never did manage to get to know each other all over again. Nor to have their fill of one another's company, conversation, or affection. Their time was cut short, to a bare minimum. One day, two, no more than a week, and Saumen began working on the family. He set about persuading them to talk, not about emotional issues but more pragmatic ones. How to live from then on. How to live with it all, after everything that had happened, immediately, right from the start, out of the frying pan into the fire. As if they had not been apart for three years. As if during all those years in prison, he had thought and seethed about just one thing. About one thing only.

And it was true. He had seethed. About the historic metamorphosis: the victim rising up against the torturer. The victim in pursuit of the torturer. The victim finding the torturer. The victim seizing the torturer. The victim accusing the torturer. The victim putting the torturer on trial. In other words: the prosecutor becomes the accused and the former accused is now the prosecutor. Victim… torturer… they can still change places. Heaven… earth… everything can change places. And for everyone to see.

That's what he wanted. More than anything in the world. What he, Saumen, wanted. Punishment. Justice *and* punishment.

The justice of punishment.

So, let's jump ahead so that we can say:

Torturers and would-be torturers: be afraid of your victims. Alive or dead, it doesn't matter. Be afraid of their relatives, even.

How can you know whether they might include people willing to give up their whole lives — and not theirs alone — simply to bring the moment of vengeance closer. The minute you do wrong, do violence to a human being, be afraid, right there and then. For there is no torturer who cannot become a victim and no victim who cannot become a torturer. For there is no pain that does not inspire even as it kills. So be prepared. It could be today or tomorrow but be prepared. Always. Even when you despair of being prepared — don't stop, not even then. There is a shadow over you, as implacable as a wall. And it will be with you to the grave. *Your* grave.

* * *

Reader, if you only knew how many unhappy people lie unsleeping on this earth — tossing and turning, worrying, going over things in their minds, making choices, calculating: as if they had tracked down their torturer, lain in wait in a dark corner, attacked them, had them at their mercy, overwhelmed them, beaten them up, and battered them over the head with a heavy implement. How many such people, as their torturer writhed in his dying agony, drooling rusty, vile spittle, would peer into his hateful little eyes and wonder: "Does he recognize me? Does he know who I am?" If he was too slow to recognize them, it would be easy enough to help him along. "Remember, scum… it was in such and such a year…" And then, what will be, will be. "Let them clap me in irons. I've done what I had to do." Simply, and without any claims to sanctity. What does it matter? We have nothing to lose but our chains — but that's one less evildoer in the world.

Reader, if you only knew how many unhappy people there are on this earth for whom it is easier to be dubbed a criminal or even a terrorist than to end their lives as victim.

But no, that was not how Saumen thought. Or rather he did, but not quite like that. He had already tried to seek justice through violence. And failed. Now he wanted to find it through the law.

Saumen used to think about it in the Presidential Jail. About how, as soon as he was released, he would do the rounds of others like him, ex-prisoners. He would do the rounds, persuade them, talk them round, get them together. Put together a group of witnesses. There would be nothing amateur about it. Together, they would bring a collective court action against Runu and the other police officers, against the whole pack that he had once fought on ideological grounds and now hated more than anything and on personal grounds as well.

Were these plans dictated by his earlier views, a continuation of his far-left struggles before he went to prison? Or was he overwhelmed by personal pain on behalf of his family that would never wholly heal? Both, it would seem, but there might be something else as well, something we will never know, at least not for certain…

Only one thing is known for certain: Saumen did not go back to the Naxalites after he left prison. He had lost faith in the movement and left the party. He did not believe in the new government either. He believed in something else. What? What could he still believe in?

In some abstract universal law or human rights, perhaps? Or in personal protest, the counterpoint to individual destiny? Or in the path of the lone warrior, the defender of the afflicted? Which, it seems, is what he had wanted to be since childhood. Be that as it may, his main target was still the police. To forgive and forget meant allowing them to do it all again. Was he capable of generosity? Now when his mother could be taken ill any day? When his wife and his sister's friend could scarcely walk? When his sister herself was disabled? And when his own body and soul called out for vengeance?

No. He believed in justice. It was all he needed. Not through violence but through the law. *That* was now his number one plan in life. No others were envisaged. There is no need to ask where he acquired this asceticism. Is it for us, who sympathize, to put our fingers into still bleeding wounds? Is it for us mortals to delve into the highly-charged darkness of someone's soul, particularly a crippled soul that has been through things that heaven forbid others should experience?

* * *

The ex-prisoners turned him down. Everyone he went to turned him down. Despite his expectations, although it was understandable. They had been through enough. They were intimidated, their health was none too good. Most importantly, however, people did not believe. They did not believe that truth would win the day. Was it a joke this taking the police to court? Waging war on Runu? Who are we? Who is Runu? What forces does he have? What forces do we have? It would be like sand against the wind, a mouse against an elephant. No, get used to it, wipe it from your mind, get some treatment, find a job — basically, support your family and lead a quiet life…that's the way to do it. Justice, well, yes, it is important… but let God think about that…

And so the dream of collective court action died.

In those same days, Saumen approached Archana and his mother. He had prepared Latika beforehand.

"We've got to do something… We have to punish Runu," Saumen said forcefully, forestalling any refusal, and immediately gaining their attention. There was no a hint of a question in his voice. He wasn't asking but telling. "Use the law to do something. Do you see?"

Without giving them any time to think or to gather their wits, he immediately tackled Archana:

"What do you think?"

"I don't mind," she said, confused and not yet understanding what she really meant, namely, "Do what you like" or… "Are you in your right mind, little brother? Where can I go on these legs?"

"Let's make up our minds today," Saumen went on. "Sezdi, you're disabled. We can't forgive that. We just need to get started. I'll gather evidence, go to the doctors. Latika will be a witness."

"And," he said in conclusion, "I want to see Runu in jail!"

Time passed and it should have been time to start forgetting but the horror endured in those days had not vanished at all. On the contrary, it had grown a second skin, like putty or ready-mix concrete. It oppressed them, ruled their lives. In hospital, the doctors had introduced Archana to sleeping pills but even when she took one and closed her eyes, allowing the darkness to envelop her consciousness, she would suddenly tremble, helpless, as a seething mass expanded inside her. Back at home, she learnt to deal with it (her mother was tossing and turning on the bed beside her). She would rein in her tremors, stamp them down in her chest, preventing a howl escaping, and only as morning approached and she was exhausted by the unequal fight would she find fifteen minutes' sleep as weak as under-brewed tea.

Nor were her days any better. They were quite simply empty. Her life was on hold while the lives of the others gained meaning with each passing day. At least Gouri's life did. Immediately she came out of prison, Parimal proposed and, at last, to the delight of all the Guhas, they were married. Things had also worked out for Latika: she had gone back to her job at the college.

Only for Archana did nothing change. She had her bed and the window. Scarcely a month ago, her assistant from her old job appeared at the window. Her place as headmistress had been held open while she was in prison. It was what the villagers had wanted.

"And the job is still yours," her guest informed her. "Everyone is waiting for you. Just come along…"

But she looked at Archana's legs and added in embarrassment:

"When you're better, of course…"

And what about Archana? The school was her whole life, everything she thought about. Had there been a chance to go back, would she really have wanted anything else? But she never thought she would be able to walk again which meant she had nothing to deaden the pain.

Mother was the first to agree. She did not keep Saumen waiting long. Once Mother had given her backing, Archana also said yes.

"Let's get started right now!" said Saumen. He jumped up, hugged them and went off to get the ball rolling.

* * *

By the way, what do you think he is like, Saumen? Vladimir Nabokov had people like him in mind when he wrote: "He felt over keenly the social side of things."

It should also be said that his family doted on him. Saumen was the youngest in the family but they tended to respect his opinion as if he were the eldest.

Even as a teenager, inspired by Sibendra's example, Saumen had dreamed of a mission of his own: either opening a school for adults who could not read or write, or teaching the arts to children of the poor. Tirelessly and unsparingly he plunged into science books and there was no subject or amount of it that he could not devour. When he was studying to be an engineer under the auspices of the exact sciences, he could also take a stroll through the humanities and engage in highly academic research that could bring glory to the Bengali language. His appetite knew no bounds. No matter what he turned his hand to, it was a huge success. He was a man of many callings. Over time, he began to resemble a reinforced safe packed with exclusive knowledge. His enthusiasm was like a volcanic eruption and would have borne him higher than the seventh heaven had it not been for the disaster of going to jail.

What's more, he knew his own worth and was not averse to raising the bar to a level few could reach. If they had called him their little genius when he was a child, then later they would come to idolize him. When anyone happened to talk about a complex matter, whether in maths, biology, physics, astronomy, theology, or God knows what else, Saumen would spontaneously, without any preparation, dredge up at least a dozen rare and eloquent facts and a storm of references to a store of unique sources known only to him. No matter what the subject, even psychology and the history of music, he had the understanding of an expert if not more. He had only to be asked, "Do you know anything about this?" and he would simply catch fire: "But of course, listen and I'll tell you!" When he expounded, a thrilled and approving crowd would gather around him. "Wow! Brilliant! A real genius!"

Recognition and praise dogged his steps, becoming as much a feature of his daily life as brushing his teeth, and it was already hard to tell which was cause and which effect: whether recognition was the spur to genius or whether genius could not survive without recognition.

And yet, all the respect and admiration accorded his family hid one thing. When it came to ordinary life, Saumen spent more on himself than his brothers and sisters did. On one occasion, his bedside table even held expensive hair wax that he raffishly applied to his wiry locks like the fashion icons of Indian cinema. He might have managed without it when they were destitute. But even before that Saumen had never given any thought to daily life, knowing there was always someone to look after these matters for him — first his father and Archana, then Sibendra and Emmy. Whereas now…

He could still spend hours firing up his intellect in conversation about, say, the teachings of Freud, lipid exchanges and synergetics, dead languages, or the monoammonium salts of glycyrrhizic acid, but when he was asked what potatoes cost at the bazaar or about the health of a mutual friend, he was obviously bored rigid. It was a kind of emotional apathy, a splinter in his soul. He was not used to talking about the humdrum or about feelings.

* * *

A family council decided not to get Gouri involved so as not to mar her joy at being married. How could they do otherwise? They had wronged her so much already.

Saumen acquired a machine (no one knew what it was called) and began to record their voices — everything that Latika and Archana could recount about their arrest and Lalbazar. Later, they pulled something together from these ragged fragments, broken by pauses, embittered by shame, pricked by rage, and soaked by salt tears. Saumen showed it to a lawyer. Arun Prakash Chatterjee was eager to offer his help free of charge. He dictated a statement. Saumen attached no importance to why the lawyer did not insist on a full account with all the details and was content with just a rough draft.

"Nothing else is required. This evidence is sufficient."

Saumen went to the Medical College Hospital where Archana had once been a patient. He tried to secure the support of witnesses. No-one was willing to appear in court, however, bar two doctors. The paperwork took nearly a month and a half, during which everything was kept secret. Once the papers were ready, Saumen ordered an ambulance to take Archana to court. And this is what happened:

At 10:30 A.M. on August 20, 1977, the Guha family crossed the Rubicon.

The brothers and sisters, their mother and friends, even Latika's relatives, had gathered to watch the event and, of course, to offer their support. All the seats were taken. People crowded in the doorways. Only Gouri had not come. Archana decided she was either ill or pregnant.

In came the magistrate. Everyone rose respectfully leaving only Archana to lie in the middle of the dusty courtroom on a stretcher lowered to the ground, fenced around by male and female legs of all ages. Their nerves were wound so tight it was hard to breathe properly. How could they speak in public about things it was frightening to acknowledge even in their own minds?

Saumen addressed the magistrate, explaining Archana's condition. The magistrate gave her permission to speak from her stretcher. Amid the quiet, her testimony flowed from floor to ceiling: how she had been working as a teacher, how they had forced their way into her home, how she, Latika, and Gouri were taken to Lalbazar. One by one the police officers' names rang out — those she could remember for certain: Runu Niyogi... Kamal Swapan Das... Santosh Dey...Arun Banerjee... Aditya Karmakar...The hour hand on the clock jumped forward several times before Archana uttered the words:

"My life has been destroyed. Their special methods made me an invalid."

At this, the magistrate closed the session and sent people home.

The evening edition of the *Hindustan Standard* wrote about a thirty-six-year-old paralyzed woman who, that day, August 20, had declared war on five Special Cell police officers, headed by their well-known leader, Runu Niyogi. It was broadcast on the radio later that evening. In the morning, Saumen went to buy a paper and found Archana's and Runu's names opposite each other in every language — Hindi, Bengali, English, and Urdu. In the bazaars, on market stalls, in the hospitals, on buses, in doorways, ashrams, banks, pharmacies, tea shops, in smoke-ridden family kitchens, and at rickshaw stands there was only one topic of conversation:

"You must have heard? That woman? Archana Guha?

Runu should go to jail!"

So, quite unexpectedly, Archana woke up famous: her case was the talk of the town.

* * *

Autumn was packed with events without pause or respite, as if someone up above was threading beads closely onto a new prayer string.

Throughout September, Saumen, Latika, and Mother travelled to court: Latika began to give evidence. After her, the doctors from the Medical College Hospital and the Presidential Jail began to be called.

By October, it was announced that a criminal case would be brought. The five police officers were summoned to court. Saumen asked and was permitted to deliver the summons personally to Runu. At the end of the session, signatures were taken from Runu and his sidekicks and they were released on bail. They were glib and cocky, saying, "It's a smear campaign, simple revenge." But they came into court by the rear entrance, trying to avoid the press corps.

Strangely enough, local human rights societies were in no hurry to offer the Guhas their support. Rather, they distanced themselves as much as possible. On the other hand, ordinary residents of Calcutta, some openly, some in secret, rushed to help them. Secretaries at the hospital looked up their medical cards and gladly handed them over to the court. Doctors offered insights into matters of jurisprudence. One of them spent many nights helping Saumen draft the medical arguments. Typists undertook to bring their documents to the top of the pile. Against the rules, a banker and a notary went to Archana's home to certify her signature. Once a messenger delivered a letter from Runu's auntie. She wished the Guhas "a speedy victory over her scoundrel of a nephew".

Meanwhile, that autumn, Mother began to grow frail, so much so in fact that running the house and caring for Archana all devolved upon Latika. She alone was bringing money into the family since her salary as a college teacher was equal to the pay of two clerks. Saumen was in no hurry to become a breadwinner. Just as he had once abandoned his job as an engineer to fight the Naxalite war, so now he was utterly absorbed in the court case — and everything outside that struggle was of no interest to him. He bought up piles of old law books and became a real book worm.

The newspaper frenzy drew attention and doctors arrived at the Guhas' house. One was a neurologist, the other an orthopaedist. Both said Archana could be treated. Exercises of some kind, hydrotherapy. They were sorry, however, that these options existed only in the private hospital and that was exorbitantly expensive.

As they instructed, Saumen wrote to the state government but a reply came immediately to say that they could not help with treatment. They offered an allowance or rather a hand-out — one hundred rupees a month, when a single massage cost the family 50. Archana shrugged her shoulders: "I need my legs not money." The government wrote a second time to say it could do nothing to help.

Then, in December, some foreign guests arrived. Three men and a woman. One was Canadian, the others from London. Archana couldn't recall the men's names but she did remember the woman. A face as white as snow and so fine-boned she seemed about to snap at the waist. Probably about 30. Wheat-blond hair pulled back in a bun, held up by a rubber band. Her nose was straight and high as the crest of Kanchenjunga. You could sign letters and even dot i's with a nose like that. She was the leader of the group. Yvonne, Yvonne Terlingen.

* * *

People from Amnesty had been trying to get there for ages but the Gandhi government had dug in their heels more than ever before, as if they were being asked to mount the scaffold. Now that the authorities had changed, Amnesty had applied again and met no further resistance. Delhi, Calcutta, the detention centre, the jail — the whole caboodle.

"God, she's so pretty... and so unhappy," Yvonne thought as she looked at Archana, for whom Saumen was speaking. "I can't just leave." She leant over Archana, clasped her shoulder as she would a friend, and said firmly:

"We promise to do something. You will get treatment."

Even before this reached her brain and her awareness began to process it, Archana's heart leapt in sheer joy but then came to its senses and shrank back, full of doubt as it whether it was really possible and how. "After all, they're strangers. They'll leave soon...," she thought. When the door closed behind the visitors, Archana began to pinch her unresponsive legs — she slapped them, poked them, beat them like laundry in the river, trying to see whether she could squeeze out even a drop of good health. But no. Her legs lay like dead logs.

Mother, though, was looking younger. Mother had put her faith in Yvonne.

The Guhas learned later on that when she got home Yvonne contacted the state government. A correspondence began, with one side seeking to persuade the state that it should pay for the treatment of a woman it was responsible for maiming. One side sought to establish a precedent, the other to avoid it: "Just you try. Make concessions, just once and there'll be a whole crowd in a flash. This Archana Guha isn't the only one."

The game of ping pong went on for over a year until one of the sides gave in — that's how it seemed from the sidelines at least. To the naïve delight of Bengali officialdom.

* * *

Meanwhile, life was a rollercoaster. Mother was laid low by hemiplegia — her right side paralyzed. Latika was now torn not just between work and home but between Archana and Mother: each needed to be washed, given a bed pan, fed, dressed and the weekly massage paid for, although it didn't do any good. Saumen was also on call but as a man could not be allowed to provide intimate care — all that became Latika's responsibility. She was still not 40 and yet her head was threaded with grey. Her face, in its owl-like glasses, had set in teacherly strictness and taken on a somewhat sorrowful look. Just as in prison, however, there was no more generous nurse than Latika. If there was anyone to whom a person without the use of her legs might entrust herself, she was the one.

That same year the Guhas left their home in Dum-Dum and moved to Kushtia where Latika had found a cheaper flat of the same size on the first floor. Nevertheless, there was still not enough money. What they were able to save on rent was immediately swallowed up by the trial. Poverty was killing them, beginning with their stomachs.

On one of those anxious, half-hungry days when there was not even a handful of rice left in the kitchen, Latika set off for work feeling guilty but still hopeful that she might at least be paid that day and return home with food. Archana was waiting by the window as usual, her gaze wandering over the buttercup yellow wall of a neighbouring house. Suddenly, there was a knock at the door and someone came in. A girl she didn't know put a bucket down on the floor.

Latika came back in the evening and froze on the doorstep. She was dazzled by the array of carrots, potatoes, and tomatoes inside. Latika squealed in surprise and hurriedly sat down as though she had seen a miracle.

"No, but isn't Emmy clever! She must have been able to sense it!"

"It wasn't Emmy," said Archana, smiling.

"Sibendra? Has Sibendra been round?"

"Or Sibendra."

"Oh, I see, the neighbours," said Latika, embarrassed at not being able to guess. "Never mind, we'll pay them back."

"No, no. What neighbours?! It was Maya! Maya! You remember the nursing assistant, Maya? I didn't even know they had an allotment just outside Calcutta. There... Maya sent it with her daughter."

Latika buried her face in her hands. Her sharp shoulders shook.

"Ma... Sezdi... you won't believe it... they didn't pay us

today... I walked the whole way, in tears because I didn't know what I could give you to eat."

"Oh, now, my darling..." To their left Mother reached out from the bed left. "There, there, don't cry... you see, there is a God ... there is."

* * *

There wasn't or, if there was, He either had more important things to do or was leading humanity a merry dance. Otherwise He would not have allowed the Guhas to sink into the mire. Initiating a criminal case had absolutely no impact on Runu's career. He was not removed from office as the rules required and could therefore exploit his position. Of course, he did not simply await an outcome but lodged an appeal and the case was immediately halted pending a decision from the higher court.

Runu was protected at the highest level. Not just in the police force but among Congressmen as well. And the fact that power had changed hands meant nothing. He had pandered to both sides at different times. Under the Gandhi administration, he had catered to the democrats. Now, he gave equally devoted service to the Communists. If an arrested person belonged to the Communist Party, Runu would let him go. A non-Communist was just tossed into the system.

He was useful to the Congressmen in another way. Those he fawned over on friendly terms kept him as a fighting dog to be unleashed when needed, to intimidate an opponent, for example. Runu helped his protectors consolidate their power and in return they hand fed him. Runu's position at Lalbazar was not a lofty one but his real power knew no bounds. As before, he continued to be Calcutta's most influential police officer.

Reliably protected, he not only showed uninhibited zeal in the Special Cell, he also engaged in organized crime. When Archana Guha's case reached the newspaper, the weekly *Darpan* carried a story about the Zenith Hotel, where Runu once burst in with a couple of cronies and beat the staff to a pulp — why? To get into the safe and clear it out.

Nor was he a novice when it came to legal battles. He had already been accused of rape at the police station and of the murder of two village boys. In one instance, the case was closed, apparently for lack of witnesses. In the second, there were as many as 15 witnesses but the verdict was overturned by a higher court. When Archana's story began to appear, another woman went to court. She accused Runu of killing her sons but soon retracted her statement: Runu had threatened to kidnap her daughters.

How many people tried to put up a fight but gave up halfway? There were far more, however, who did not even think of fighting back, because they were no longer capable even of thinking. Srimati Roy, for example, who was taken in after giving birth. The cigarette burns and ice left her paralysed down one side and psychologically damaged. Only then did they release her although no-one heard any more about her. Just as they heard nothing about a boy named Ashok Dutta, who also lost his mind, when Runu's assistants inserted a skewer, spread with chilli, into his anus, then threw him into the Ganges.

Runu had taken lives. Many complaints had been made against him and were lodged in various courts. Yet no-one was able to break open this vessel, full to the brim with evil. Evil simply scoffed behind the door: there were no witnesses and since that was the case, how could anything be proven? The stone age would end and a new age would be born, but even then blood to a torturer would be like water off a duck's back. It was always the victim, the victim alone, who was left to pay the price. Only the victim.

Saumen was not naive. He understood all this. His brain had been reprogrammed, however. Just one thought drove him on: "I want to see Runu in prison! I want to see Runu in prison!"

He pored over his textbooks. Studied other cases in detail. Got to grips with the wording of the law. Listened to lawyers.

Took notes of courtroom speeches. Gained insight into lawyers' tricks. Gradually got the hang of their subtleties. Came to understand a great deal. He hoped to win the case within five years at the most. It was all he thought of during his days of constant activity and nights of deepest sleep.

The historic metamorphosis: the victim in pursuit of the torturer. The victim finding the torturer. The victim seizing the torturer. The victim accusing their torturer. The victim putting the torturer on trial. The prosecutor is the accused. The former accused is now the prosecutor. Victim… torturer… They could still change places. Heaven… earth… everything can change places.

He was right, the seer who said: "Our future will arise and walk but it will our damaged feet that take it forward."

Chapter 17

God Does Exist! He Does!

On the first day of autumn 1979, the letter box that looked like an unpainted bird box once again spat an envelope out onto a step in the entry. It had a British stamp and a London postmark. More than a year had gone by, during which Yvonne had kept them informed about her correspondence with the state government. She had enclosed the Bengali officials's replies — refusal after refusal after refusal. The Guhas had grown used to these letters and no longer expected anything of them. Then, all of a sudden...

Saumen read it out five times. Latika repeated it three times word for word. Then it was Archana's turn. She was so astonished and excited that she read it out syllable by syllable. Then Mother cast her eye over what was a just a lined page torn out of an exercise book. She couldn't understand a single letter — what was it written in? English?

She gave it back to Saumen. "Read it again, son!"

"So... Yvonne ... You remember Yvonne Terlingen, Ma, don't you? She came to see us two years ago..."

"Hurry up! I remember everything!"

"She writes that Archana is being invited to go to London. There..."

"Where's this ... this Lon...don?" Mother broke in excitedly, savouring the unfamiliar sounds on her tongue. To her, even the Andaman Islands were like the ends of the earth.

"Oh, Ma, it's such a long way away! I'll explain later. She says... Amnesty is inviting Archana to London. They have a group of doctors. First, they'll look at what's going on with her legs, then think about how to treat them. Shall I read it again?"

"Yes, son, do! Read it again. Keep reading it! I told you! God does exist! He does!"

"It's not God, Ma. It's Amnesty. People from Amnesty, Ma."

"And what's the difference? They're one and the same!"

They had hardly come to terms with this first piece of news when a second arrived hot on its heels. This time Yvonne wrote: "We were a bit hasty about London. Doctor Inge Genefke, the head of our medical section, wants to examine Archana: she lives in Copenhagen."

"And where's that? Cop…pp…" For Mother, in her agitation, this too was beyond her.

"For goodness' sake, Ma. I'll explain later," Saumen said. "Doctor Inge Genefke? Is it a woman or a man? You just can't tell with these foreign names…"

"Lon–don… Cop…ppp… a woman or a man… what does it matter to us?" Mother simply could not be calmed. "The main thing is they're going to treat my daughter!"

They had hardly had time to digest the second piece of news when a third arrived. A letter from Doctor Inge Genefke herself. They still could not tell whether it was a woman or a man but they did establish something else. Archana was being asked to go in winter, right after New Year. They did not say how she was to get there, however.

Saumen spent all night trying to decide what to do and in the morning raced round their friends to try and collect the money for a ticket. No-one turned him down. Everyone gave what they could. The money he collected, however, was scarcely enough for a taxi to the airport. Saumen swallowed his pride and wrote to Yvonne; "I'm sorry but we cannot afford the fare." The reply from London was quick to arrive: "You don't need to bother about that. The state government has to pay. We're in negotiations with them."

Presently, an assistant to the finance minister came to see the Guhas. The woman gazed around as if she was afraid of someone, and spoke in a rapid, nervous whisper.

"Really, Archana, this is not good. If you go for treatment abroad, it will be a disgrace for our country. Agree to be treated here. We'll give you the money. Really, we will!"

"Not now, no!" Archana replied, gesticulating. She was afraid of giving in to the pressure. "I wanted to have the treatment in Calcutta but you didn't provide it. And now… well, now it's too late!"

"But this is a disgrace for our country!"

"I don't care."

"You don't care?"

"Well, what do you think? I want to be the way I used to be! I want to learn to walk! I want to be a teacher! I don't want to depend on other people all my life!"

The minister's assistant took her leave. Soon afterwards, they learnt that the state government had backed down.

The orthopaedist who examined Archana warned them she couldn't travel so far on her own. "The government will have to pay for someone else to go and look after her." They began to think who should go. Mother had her hemiplegia. Latika was earning a living. It left only Saumen. The orthopaedist wrote to the state government and secured their agreement.

"They should have agreed to a private hospital in Calcutta at the time, two years ago. It would have been cheaper," the orthopaedist said contentedly as he read the letter. "But I'm pleased for the poor girl. God, am I pleased! Let her get her treatment over there!"

* * *

All through the autumn and the beginning of winter, until Saumen arrived with passports, tickets, and visas, Archana was either consumed by a foolish joy, or frightened, and keeping that joy at bay, afraid that she might inadvertently jinx a benevolent fate. What if fate deemed her joy immodest and simply laughed and went away? Or the doctors changed their minds? Or suddenly told her she would never walk? Could her mother survive such a verdict after expecting a miracle? And so she lived with a feeling that she was pulling petals off a daisy: believed them, believed them not, believed them not, believed them when they said that soon, really very soon, she would arise and walk.

The day before their departure, a little book, its paper beginning to decay, appeared in the house. Saumen had found it at the flea market. It was set out simply, like a child's ABC. A — Andersen, B — Bohr, C — Copenhagen, D — Dannebrog… They learnt that Denmark was a toy country the size of a cowpat, with 400 islands, a royal family, and a hole in its coins; that it had fewer people than you find at a Calcutta Puja, and that some of the numbers were read from right to left. This idyll was marred by weather like a freezer. The book said that in the winter the roads were covered in ice but once the ice had had enough, it turned into water. When she heard that, Emmy felt so pierced by the cold herself that she set off to the flea market where, among other items quite unnecessary for life in Bengal, she discovered, haggled over, purchased, cleaned, brought back, and triumphantly presented a nice-looking pair of Siberian mittens, a camel fur hat, and a scarf. One of their old friends lent Archana a coat. As their departure drew near, Mother slit open the mattress and took out her wedding bracelet, a gift from her husband, which she had held onto even when prison had consumed everything else she still had from her marriage. She clasped the keepsake to her bosom, asked her husband's forgiveness, and let it go with instructions to sell it. They didn't know how things would turn out over there in an alien land and they had to have money on them. The money raised by selling the bracelet was sewn into the hem of Saumen's clothes. Last of all, the brothers and sisters each gave Archana a sari.

"But why so many? It's more than enough for a lifetime!" said Archana, blushing.

"But they're not for a lifetime. They're for the hospital. Wear a new sari every day."

The next 24 hours were a simple sequence of events. A taxi. The airport. A wheelchair. The flight from Calcutta to Bombay and from Bombay to Frankfurt. Saumen didn't leave his seat throughout the flight. He had his hand on Archana's forehead. She lay with her legs sticking out into the aisle. And the magnificent white aircraft, the third flight of the day, eventually left the sinful earth behind, soaring up in a cloud of hope reborn.

Chapter 18

The Siddhartha Effect

While they're in the air, why don't we take a break as well? It's time for me to explain why I've been chasing this person since she was a little girl, on through her teens to a grown woman as if she were a rare butterfly. To explain what interest I have in the many miles of her fate as I creep along in its wake, gathering the snippets, sparks, and susurrations of elusive recollections. And why I am endeavouring to grasp by the tail the evasive ghosts of a vanishing past. Why I am trying to bring them back to life. To restore a lost voice. And what kind of line it is by which she drew me to her through space and time. It's time … time for explanations.

Three things made me sit down at my desk to write, essentially on bread and water, in the silence of solitary confinement. I had formerly worked as a journalist, earning decent money, no worse than others, but these three things turned my world completely upside down — divided it between two shorelines, split it into "before" and "after".

It first capsized during my own final interrogation (readers familiar with my *Sandholm Diary* will grasp the reference). Blinded by a burning cigarette, I spent I don't know how long in the dark convinced I had lost my sight for good. Blinded on the outside, albeit temporarily, however, I suddenly gained inner sight. Then came my overlong experience of refugee camps (and six months of a metaphysical death that were more like six years), cut off from my family and children, and struck dumb by grief and sorrow. During that time, as I held night-time conversations with myself on a bottom bunk, my inner voice awoke. And again later, when a conventional court dealt me the blow, or bestowed the gift, of exile.

Now, years later, this collage of extreme experiences may be seen as the turning point. The turning point in my destiny. At the time, however, the judges did not know that, by the day of the verdict, I had exiled myself in any case and stepped off the merry-go-round of the social whirl. Or that the silence of solitude had become more precious than the media fame that later caught up with me.

I did not rest in that silence. No, I pushed myself to the very utmost every day. I had to find myself again, gather myself into a single whole, knit my ego back together. Out of what, I didn't know. I grabbed whatever came to hand. Sometimes, fragments of the broken past, sometimes a presentiment... of the future, sometimes people going by. It all went into rekindling my soul.

And so not just one year and not just two went by, and mentally it was an entire lifetime before I understood. Everything that had happened in the past had been necessary for an encounter with destiny. For a meeting with myself. It's odd, isn't it? I had to go blind and regain my sight, become dumb and then hear *my own* voice, lose everything and move so far from my roots, perhaps even hack them off, in order to come nearer to the main root, the root of my soul.

Years later I am able to say that it worked. I was able to glue myself back together. To do so, I had to acknowledge that even in tragedy life is good, that there is joy in overcoming tears, and that a human being is not a crystal vase but a chipped and sturdy pot, and tragedy its firing. If the pot cracks when it's fired — the clay was worthless. If it withstands the heat — it's fit for further use.

As it turned out, my own existential pot, while not in fact broken, was certainly covered in cracks. And yet it was still fit for further use. But what had given it the strength to withstand the heat of the fire? Perhaps the fact that not for a second did I believe in an "evil" fate? That I have never inclined towards talk of karma? On the contrary, I have always and everywhere sought to control my own lot and have learnt to see dangers not as a punishment but as a challenge presented by fate — as trials that are sent us before we are given something of importance. Like the pot. If it fails to withstand the heat — throw it away. If it survives, perhaps (and it is important to say "perhaps" here), it will be given a protective skin and put to further use. Was Cardinal Newman right when he said that if we are intended for great ends, greater than simply living and idling our time away, we are called to great hazards?

All this is personal, however, what happened to me. But what gives other people the strength to withstand the heat of the fire? Why does one person survive and another, in similar circumstances, does not? Is it something within us? Around us? External to us? As long as I live, I am constantly seeking, constantly trying to solve this mystery, including between the lines of this story.

* * *

The year my first book was translated into Danish, the translator, Sten Jakobsen, came to see me to discuss some issues with the text. As he left, he said:

"The course of your life is like a variation on the Monte Cristo story."

"Monte Cristo? That's Dumas, isn't it? I remember something from when I was small…what's it about?"

"Well, the hero … everything in his life's fine just as it was for you. But then he's arrested and sent to prison for political reasons. After several years, he manages to escape and goes back to normal life. Then he sets about repaying everyone in kind."

"Who?"

"The people responsible for his misfortunes."

"So, he repaid his enemies in kind when they had stopped even thinking about him?"

"You could say that."

"And did he do good to those who helped him?"

"That too, sometimes."

"I'm sorry I haven't read it."

"You don't really need to. You know everything about him anyway. He *is* you."

"Maybe. If life insists, there's a touch of Monte Cristo in all of us."

And yet, life is not made up of alternating stripes, where to start with everything is fine and then it's bad and then it's good again, and you can start "repaying everyone in kind". Rather, it's a cocktail of good and bad, half and half. If you try and get even with evil, it will mock you behind your back.

My *Sandholm Diary*, which I called "therapy for the soul," my opponents "emotional pornography," journalists an "important testimony," and critics "a beautiful piece of work," suddenly became the subject of debate at a national level. Hundreds of people I didn't know wrote to me in friendship and solidarity. But there were others who were losing sleep. The day after I was interviewed on the TV show "Deadline", I received an email from one Freddy H. Christensen, a qualified carpenter and engineer, born in 1938 and now retired, which said: "You will never be a fellow citizen, but always persona non grata."

Before three months had gone by, my postbox spat out an anonymous letter: a photocopied picture of Death from Ingmar Bergman's *The Seventh Seal*. Threats appeared on the Internet. The police began to look into it. Someone was trying to control my feelings.

But the extraordinary thing is that, having been through this particular mill in another country, I had come out of it with a different attitude. Now, when it was all happening again,

I didn't just sit there terrified and I no longer wanted to run away. I kept on working. I had a new lease of life. I suddenly realised that I could go to meet the threat. I could do so, not because I had decided to be brave (like everyone else, I am becoming more cautious with the passing of the years) but because like Timudjin in the film "Mongol: The Rise to Power of Genghis Khan," to whom it was said, "All Mongols fear the thunder … but not you," I could now cheerfully respond, "I had no place to hide from the thunder… so I wasn't afraid any more." I must have realized that life is not about fear. And simply trusted to the old principle: do what's right, come what may. Should a hand appear to drag me back into the abyss, two more will appear also to help me not to fall.

* * *

At my first meeting with readers in Copenhagen in 2006, the organizer of the event, Elisabeth Møller Jensen, came over and asked whether I needed a certain Danish author to mentor me. She gave me the name: Suzanne. And a surname that I, not the most gifted student when it comes to languages, could not make out. Rocco? Brocco? Barocco? It sounded a bit like the Russian word for fate and indeed fell, full and fateful on the ear.

"Of course, I need a mentor," I replied, without finding out who she was talking about.

A week later I had a letter confirming the offer. The letter clarified the name but even when it was properly spelt it failed to jog my memory. My Eurasian baggage, weighed down by the Soviet curriculum, easily recalled the Danish triumvirate of Hans Christian Anderson, Johannes V. Jensen, and Søren Kierkegaard. I knew about Karen Blixen from the American film.

The following day, a Saturday, the phone rang. A voice with the tone of a cello, slightly hoarse. The thought occurred that she was deliberately articulating slowly and drawing out the words so that it would be easier for me, a foreigner, to follow them.

I said I would be pleased to meet her. She said she was happy to make my acquaintance. I issued an invitation. She accepted. She would come to me. When I ended the conversation, I still didn't know who I had been talking to.

When my husband found out who had rung, he said, joking:

"Brodsky had Auden, you've got Brøgger."

"Dear God," I said, "you don't make jokes like that about the Danes. Remember Jante's law."

On Monday, at a Danish lesson in the Studieskolen language school, I told my teacher what had happened.

"Suzanne? Brøgger?" said Hanna, disbelievingly, her eyes big as circles. "Are you sure? Is it definitely her?"

Then she gabbled excitedly, "But she's a very famous writer! One of our greatest! Just imagine… She wears such interesting clothes! Always with such elaborate hats. Journalists go crazy about her."

"And," she went on nostalgically, "one of the abiding memories of my childhood is of her walking through Strøget, in a broad-brimmed red hat and carrying a basket of cherries, and us children, following her in a line half the length of the street, running and shouting: "Suzanne Brøgger! It's Suzanne Brøgger!"

"So she puts on a bit of a show?"

"I don't know about that but there's some kind of mystery about her. She's our most exotic writer. Another Blixen."

During the break, Hanna went out and came back with a pile of papers.

"Here, I found this on the Internet. You can read it on the way home."

I started looking through it on the train — biographies, bibliographies. Among the stream of dry reports about her childhood and her youth, my eye lighted upon what seemed closest to me. As a student, Suzanne had studied Russian and her first experience as a writer had been as a journalist sending back dispatches from the USSR. Her writing was autobiographical, something between novel and essay. The subject matter was distilled from her own life. Fact and fiction vied with one another, and the age itself was revealed through one small woman's private history. A feminist. Not afraid to shock the public. In recent years, however, she had withdrawn to the countryside in an attempt to escape the media that was always on her heels.

"It's not just the media, either," I thought, looking at a photograph of a woman with a long, aristocratic face and a vague, closed smile. My inner eye shone a light on the concealed sadness in eyes as liquid as adagio scales. Sadness of the kind that eternally puts the exile or prisoner on a pedestal of solitude.

* * *

She arrived in a shower of rain, two days before the start of the Danish summer. She alighted on the railway platform and I recognized her straight away. She wore no hat or complicated arrangement on her head. Just a black and red headscarf with tiny green flowers and filaments of lurex thread. No one wears or ever has worn these in Europe, but for older ladies like us they are a family standby. Her Isabella raincoat was open like a book. Fawn cord trousers. A long cardigan over her hips. High-top trainers, high cheekbones, musician's fingers with brown, slightly scratched nail varnish, as if she had come straight from pruning roses in the garden. And heavy, hazel coloured beads of old stone. My great-grandmother wore beads just like them all the time and my mother has kept them as a charm. "The scarf and beads are just a coincidence," I thought. "She couldn't know about that." Generally, my emotions were alight even before we touched cheeks there on the platform.

I took her a round-about route home from the station. She seemed to have forgotten some of her Russian and I had not yet learnt Danish. We switched to English, which was foreign to both of us, and there were a lot of awkward pauses.

"You must know… yes? …I've been to your country… to Tashkent and Samarkand… but you know that already, yes?" Suzanne asked cautiously.

"No, I didn't know. When were you there?"

"Before you were born. 1969. When I was working as a journalist."

"And what did you think? Did you like it? The Uzbeks are a hospitable people."

She did not reply, however.

"Did you do the forty plaits? I've seen it. It's pretty"

"Well, sort of. Just for fun. When I played with my sister when we were little. It's something Uzbek girls do. I'm not Uzbek."

At home, we sat in the living room, facing one another. The tea in its china teapot went cold more quickly than usual. I went off to the kitchen to make some more and to make up a plate of filling Danish pastries, some plain, others with honey, cinnamon or poppy seeds. I had long since got out of the habit of baking myself but the bakery nearest the house saved my innate instinct for Asian hospitality.

"Is there anything I can do to help? Perhaps I can help you find out about grants? You're planning to carry on writing, aren't you?"

I shrugged. I never ask well-known people for anything unless it's a matter of life or health. Now, though, with her here, when I had taken to her just because of her scarf and my great-grandmother's beads, I was even less keen to ask for anything.

"I'll keep writing with or without a grant."

"You can't feed yourself on literature. Why are you doing it?"

"I don't know really… I need to for some reason… maybe it's a kind of resistance… or a way of remaining myself…of gluing a broken heart back together…"

"Gluing a broken heart back together?" she said in surprise. "There's nothing so whole as a broken heart."

She said this so quietly, in a half-whisper almost, that it was like hearing a petal drop.

On the way back to the station we talked about our childhoods. It turned out that the word exile was not unknown in Suzanne's house. Her great-grandfather had been born in Poland, but her mother grew up in Riga, then fled to Sweden during the war.

The last thing she did was to give me her latest book of essays. When the train had swallowed her up and pulled out of the station, I opened it and read on the first page: "To Dina from your 'mentor' and friend." I smiled at the word "friend" then pondered the rest: Why was mentor in inverted commas? Wasn't that what she came for? And if not, what was it for?

* * *

The day that I was invited to take a look at her world, to look inside those walls where all her books were written and which they say will one day be a museum, was the hottest that summer. We agreed to meet at Slagelse station, a hundred kilometres from Copenhagen, and "in terms of time a thousand," as she herself explained. Because of the heat, which was so unusual in that country, the train was thirty minutes late. I went into the station square but couldn't find anyone. I hazarded a guess and went down to the underground and, indeed, there she was, wearing a full-length grape-coloured jelaba. It suited her surprisingly well although it lifted her out of her current context. We joined hands and went to the car park. Suzanne took the driver's seat and for another fifteen minutes we travelled through fields of rape and manure, leaving straw-hatted peasant huts behind us, going further and further away from the world and closer and closer to the edge of the earth which, as I was beginning to realize, could be seen from the windows of her house.

"I live in an old school house... there are 28 windows," she said as we approached ash-grey gypsum walls, covered by branching shrubbery.

"Look, there, under the awning… it's my husband," she said, her eyes twinkling either at me or into the corner of the yard as she parked the car in a garage that had once been a woodshed or stable.

There was someone standing beneath the awning. I said hello but he didn't seem to hear, although he was staring in our direction the whole time. I moved towards him and burst out laughing. It was a mannequin in a man's suit.

We went into the house. The all-exposing light stayed outside. We were enfolded in quietness and shade right from the threshold. A tired sofa greeted us in the hall. To the right of the entrance was a bathroom, nothing glamorous, the same as anyone else's. The living room was to the left, with a piano, a mezzo-soprano with a cold, and so many paintings of various people scattered across the paprika-coloured walls that they dazzled the unaccustomed eye. A narrow passageway from the far side of the living room led to a kitchen that was only big enough for three. A Turkmen camel rug, three times my age, and a creaking bench in the corner, covered in sheaves of linen cushions.

I was given permission to explore the house and set off to wander between walls that had absorbed an aura of books when it was a school, and now gave off a meditative air. I came across another two reception rooms. The first, looking onto the garden, was a monastic cell, full of books. They did not lie in disarray nor stand neatly on the shelves. Rather they were quite haphazard — in pairs, piles, or on their own — on the table, the chairs, the windowsill, the arms of armchairs, on the floor, on the little table with a lamp, or on the sofa cushions. The second was a classroom, where models and sketches still littered the desks as though it was an artist's studio. There was no hurry within these walls. The pulse of time beat at an easy pace as if its heart had slowed or possibly stopped altogether.

I was called out into the garden. I saw no perfect, crew-cut lawns here, no stiff and formal flowerbeds, plucked like a model's eyebrows, no symmetrical trees, their roots baked into clay pots.

Nature made do without a gardener. Here, it was good to cast off the armour of public attire and bare the soul.

"I like things to grow wild," Suzanne said. "If you go for a look, mind you don't trip."

I did go for a look. I did trip.

Immediately beyond the garden, which had no fences, the world spilled over its banks. The garden seemed to be a threshold on the edge of the world. It was like visiting my parents' home where, beneath the window of the bedroom my sister and I shared, just such an endless field billowed out. We would see how tall we were by standing under the ears of grain.

I seemed to walk for a long time, everything forgotten. When I came back, the table had been laid for three. Spring water in fluted indigo glasses sparkled with ice confetti. Suzanne served a fruit salad with pieces of unsalted feta and marinated melon. A mannequin sat at the table... the one from the yard, and smiled, its eyes lifelike.

"So, what did the publishers say?" Suzanne asked, referring to my story about Archana.

I told her how things stood. This book had already taken up residence within me that summer, in embryonic form. I had tried to outline the concept in a synopsis, which I had sent to an editor who was thinking about it. "You see," the editor had said, "it needs to be translated and the reader isn't familiar with the country you're from — it's not in the news. What if the book doesn't sell?" I smiled. Publishers are so funny. A book is a commodity to them. For the person who wrote it, it is a major feat. What's more, there are some books that should be handed out free of charge, the way food parcels and water are thrown out of aircraft when there has been a natural disaster. Publishers know that but still say "but what if the book doesn't sell?" They had promised to think about it and I was waiting patiently.

"May I see the synopsis?" Suzanne asked.

"*Don't Call Me a Victim*"? she read out in surprise when she saw the working title, and went into the house to read the rest.

When she came back, she asked whether I had read *A Century of Victims*.

"No. What is it?"

"*A Century of Victims* is by Danish historian Henrik Jensen. He believes that as a species humans have a tendency to see themselves as victims and to present that image as attractive. And here you are, suggesting investigating how people who have survived the very worst still manage to gather their strength and attempt to move on. This deserves support. With your permission, I'd like to write to the editor and explain how I see your idea. It's a book of ideas rather than plot. We have to realize that it can be read on two levels"

Suzanne returned the synopsis. At the end of my title was a green exclamation mark like a traffic light. I don't like exclamations. My favourite punctuation mark is dot-dot-dot but I decided to keep it. After all, we agreed, it did add a certain something.

Don't Call Me a Victim! And, incidentally, don't. This is not a request, or a complaint, or a plea. It is my position. It is the stamp of someone who is building their destiny not thanks to but in spite of circumstance. It is, ultimately, respect for life. Respect not just because of its delights but because of its hardships as well.

"But, if it's okay, I'll do it tomorrow and now, could you read me a little in your own language?" Suzanne asked.

She brought over a tiny old volume of Akhmatova, and while I read aloud in Russian she listened to the music of the words, without understanding their meaning, and was gripped by thoughts and recollections of some kind.

* * *

Touched by her friendliness, which I did not yet understand, I decided to get to know what she had written herself. How else to get under her skin and find out about her non-public self? No matter how you look at it, artists, whatever their chosen topics or heroes, clothe them in thoughts and feelings taken from their own heads — and if they are not describing themselves, they are (Oh, Hesse, Hesse!) writing the biography of their own soul.

At the library, I was given a faded 1970s paperback. "That's her first book," the librarian said. Before I left, I had begun to leaf through it, to look at the headings, when suddenly something familiar flashed past on one of the pages: Uzbekistan and Tashkent. I went back. A chapter entitled "Rape". I stumbled in the third paragraph and shuddered. "My own rape story, which deserves a title such as 'The Prickly Path to Humiliation'…" she wrote. It pierced me like a rapier. I couldn't believe it. The story was, briefly, as follows:

… A young journalist from Denmark (age twenty-five, the looks of a model), studying Russian, goes to Soviet Uzbekistan to produce a series of sketches for her magazine. In Tashkent, she finds an assistant in a local lad who helps her with the interviews. The young man and woman come to like each other. They go off to a park to be alone. Suddenly they are surrounded by policemen. The boy urges her not to say she's a foreigner. Contact with foreigners is not encouraged in a country with a KGB.

"Tell them you're from Riga!" he whispers to her. "Otherwise, it'll be prison and Siberia."

And the girl believes him. No, she trusts him. What's more, she wants to help.

She has no documents in her bag, only dollars, and her broken Russian is like a Baltic accent. The policemen decide she is a prostitute. A prostitute from Riga working for hard currency, obviously. They let the boy go. He walks away without a word. The girl is arrested. She's interrogated, dragged along by the hair, hit in the face… She is released only towards the morning.

Back at her hotel, she cancels her trips around the USSR. A telegram is dispatched to the magazine: "The other republics are of no interest to us." She cannot tell the whole truth because she is afraid her editor will decide that a person who gets raped cannot be a good journalist. Years later she would write eight versions of what happened. She wrote solely to wipe out the pain. And to understand whether she might have escaped.

I don't know whether she could have escaped but she did escape the worst. It was naïve on her part not to have said who she was, where she was from, and why she was there right from the start. But it did make sense not to say anything when it was over. She would not have been allowed to leave the country. In the Cold War years, it would have provoked a scandal. Exile to Siberia wouldn't have been enough to cover it up. In the place where that happened, people were not hidden away behind walls under these circumstances, they were simply buried in concrete.

Back at the hotel, she grabbed a notebook and the first thing she wrote, her hand shaking, was "I am so scared, I am so scared, I am so scared…" She wrote these words and set out her pain in the notebook until it was full.

* * *

We began to meet up again after that. Each time I wanted to ask whether it was true, but could not bring myself to do so. I just couldn't. On the one hand, I understood that yes, it was true. On the other, we shouldn't tread on the snakes that dwell in the recesses of our memories. They can still bite.

Six months later she herself helped provide me with an answer. It came on a page of the notebook into which she had poured out a stream of consciousness on the train after our first meeting, two days before the start of the Danish summer.

"North Zeeland — it's such a long way by train from the western part of the island where I live but it's important to me to meet her exactly where she lives, especially as it's a home for refugees. I think about her. Her fortress is here now…

"She's on the platform. At first sight, I realize I have always known her. 'Love at first sight'.

"We drink tea but the attraction is in the conversation. The Art of Conversation. Listening to one another. When you understand that there are no differences — ethnic, or religious. We are always changing. Every morning when we wake, we are not who we were the day before.

"I once studied the art of conversation at a seminar run by physicist David Bohm. It isn't the banks of the river that speak in a dialogue, first one then the other, but the current of the river, its flow. It is a new place.

"I didn't tell Dina about my Uzbek tragedy (being raped by the policemen) because we were talking about something completely different. Even so, I felt that Dina had helped me, had helped me heal the young girl inside me, who was once so unlucky and who once, a very long time ago, was unable to defend herself."

When I read this, I could not hold back the tears. My question as to whether or not it was true burst like a soap bubble. The inverted commas fell away. We were joined by an umbilical cord. We had found each other. We had become each other's déjà vu. Just as she had sat in a southern country and cried and written with tears for ink for as long as she had paper, "I am so scared, I am so scared, I am so scared," so I now am sitting and writing somewhere in the north as long as I have paper and do not run out of letters — every letter is a bullet — yes, that's right — so that literature is a firing range where the greatest shooting practices take place. For the heart does not die when one thinks it should. But why, why does it not die? Why does it break, but not die?

* * *

From my correspondence with Suzanne Brøgger, January 2009:

"Dear Dina,

"There is nothing so whole as a broken heart. I chose this old Jewish saying as the epigraph to my autobiographical novel and over time it has become my very own hallmark. I see this broken heart as a symbol of victory, like the one in the Christmas hymn: "broken hearts are the best to feel

what this great and blissful festival has to bring of joy."

"It's hard to believe but people can be happy in unhappiness. The Hungarian writer and Nobel Prize winner, Imre Kertész, experienced many moments of happiness in a place where no-one would want to end up. Where he spent his childhood. In the Nazi concentration camp, Auschwitz.

"What allows someone to survive mass murders, violence, treachery, loss of family, tragedies, disasters, exile? And why is it that, sometimes, having survived all this, a person lives with a feeling of deeper joy and thankfulness, breathing fully and deeply? Because they have been tested. And through that has come an understanding of how great life is! Someone who has not been through such trials cannot be relied upon fully. What they say cannot be trusted because, as the Jewish saying puts it, 'Du bist nicht geprieft, men Sohn!' You have not yet been tested!

"Author Karen Blixen is usually considered an expert in this field. She knows what she is talking about when she writes about pride. A person's real value is not increased or diminished by what other people think about them or by what has happened to them.

"One of my family sagas ends with an episode in which it becomes clear to the heroes that the right to be an artist sometimes comes at a high price. You may risk being crushed by an elephant. This doesn't necessarily mean you also have to carry an elephant all your life. But you can of course be proud that you survived the confrontation.

"But what is a tried and tested response to the vicissitudes of fate? How can one look Dame Fortune in the face with dignity?

"Throughout their lives, people derive strength from art, religion, and philosophy. I have always been inspired by the Buddhist practice that is based on everything being determined by thought. The point is to be the master of your own consciousness rather than the servant of the unconscious instinct to repeat what has already been learnt and experienced.

"Agitated thought leads to suffering. Calm thought leads to happiness. In the Dhamapada, the Buddha says: '"He abused me, he beat me, he defeated me, he robbed me," — in those who harbour such thoughts hatred will never cease." "He abused me, he beat me, he defeated me, he robbed me," — in those who do not harbour such thoughts hatred will cease.'

"In *The Muslim Jesus* Christ says: 'If people appoint you as their heads, be like tails.' In other words: Be the opposite. People should be the opposite. And I was too.

"At the time I made my debut with *Deliver Us from Love*, it was widely thought that a woman should feel like a victim in a male-dominated society. I refused to be a victim. Instead, I opted for the opposite strategy of sarcasm and irony. I made a fool of the authorities. Held the oppressors up to mockery. I laughed at the rapists.

"Laughter is a good strategy against the totalitarian mind-set and fundamentalism. Life, seen from a frog's height, seems very tragic. If you turn the binoculars round and look at life from the height of a bird's flight, it becomes a comedy."

And it is really only now that I can go back to the beginning of this chapter and explain why I am chasing after Archana, what interest I have in the many miles of her fate, why I am trying to grasp by the tail the evasive ghosts of a vanishing past, why I am trying to bring them back to life, and with what line she drew me to her through space and time.

As I write her life story, I am walking in the path of Siddhartha who contemplates the fate of another person but understands in the end that that other person is himself. In writing her life story, I am also setting out my own biography and my own crucified soul. And however heavy the stone, I roll it and roll it like Sisyphus, and am determined to roll it to the very top. As if, when I have done so, when I have taken the story to the highest peak, I will know how it ends. As if, knowing that, I will understand how my own story will one day end as well.

And not mine alone.

But that of many others too.

Chapter 19

Groundbreakers

The plane touched down at around four in the afternoon. It lowered its iron paws onto the frozen asphalt and glided rapidly along the runway, wheel-speed slowing as it went. Snatches of an alien, foreign landscape flashed past as alien, foreign people in strontium yellow high visibility jackets swarmed and slithered on the ground. The day had not yet burnt itself out completely but the air was visibly leaching colour. Just as the ramp was wheeled over and the doors thrown open, the sky went out like a light and dusk stole slowly in.

Damp, windy, minty cold Copenhagen. January.

Exhausted by the flight and excited to be on the threshold of something new, as if they had landed on an island where wishes come true, Archana and Saumen awaited the steward's instructions. When the final passenger had left the cabin, a welcoming voice called from the other side of the door:

"Archana! Saumen! I'm here!"

When the wheelchair was brought over and they went down the steps — whereupon they were struck by a searing wind and a touch of frost — when a border guard came over and a dog suddenly jumped up, its wet mouth probing, and when they were squeezed into a cheery yellow ambulance that left the airport and sailed along the street, all that time Archana could see a fair-haired woman of average height beside her, wearing huge glasses that covered half her face. So, that's what she's like! Inge Genefke! Doctor Genefke was a she, not a he.

* * *

Inge Genefke was seriously upset by the incident with the dog that had suddenly loomed over Archana. She had seen plenty of dogs in her forty years and had always liked animals, but she wouldn't have expected one to jump up at a paralyzed woman. She blushed when she saw it, afraid for Archana, and in the end she lost her temper. She was on the point of shouting out and leaping into action to drag the wretched creature away, but she gritted her teeth and managed not to give vent to her displeasure. In order to access the landing field to collect her patient, to support her from her very first minute in a new country, Inge had been obliged to spend a long time seeking permission in the most august quarters.

It was more than five years now since Doctor Genefke had plunged into her demanding work. It was not for the fainthearted.

In late 1973, Amnesty International's London Office had appealed for doctors to become involved in a campaign against the use of torture. The impetus was the recent military coup in Chile, which brought Pinochet to power and with him brought torture, torture, and more torture.

Bad news was coming in from all over. From India, Greece, Ireland, the USSR. Half the population of our planet lived in countries where the government relied on torture to shore up its power. Survivors did sometimes go to court but the accused would deny everything and claim with one voice that the plaintiffs had only themselves to blame: that they had fallen of their own accord, hit themselves, cut themselves, hoisted themselves off the ground, and scalded or burnt themselves. There were no other witnesses to the crimes.

Only the victim ever paid for it all, no-one else. The torturers revelled in their impunity.

But the time had come. Amnesty decided to put together a group of doctors to visit prisons. And to harness the services of science so that they could specifically state and indeed prove that a victim of torture really was a victim of torture and not of an accident. If there were shown to be medical techniques for proving crimes of this sort even without witnesses, the situation in the courts would be very different. If proof was possible, so was punishment.

That, at least, was Amnesty's thinking.

Doctor Genefke responded to the appeal. Only to discover that she was, for the moment, the only one. You can't fight a battle on your own. You need reinforcements, so in April 1974 she advertised in a magazine for Danish doctors. Three men responded: Ole Vedel Rasmussen, Helmuth Stadler, and Peter Moltke. And so Amnesty International's first medical group came into being, composed of Danish doctors. A few months later they were joined by another six people.

When she embarked on this new work, Inge naively imagined it would be easy to prove that someone had been tortured. They would just need to study the recommendations that had come out in recent years. Suddenly, however, she discovered that the scientific world had in fact written nothing about the issue. Or at least not in any accessible resources. People had always been tortured, of course, but what happened to the person being tortured apart from physical pain? What happened to them later? How could that be studied, exposed, proved, healed? Libraries and medical centres unconscionably turned up nothing at all. It was like throwing yourself in the sea to save someone from drowning only to find out once you were in the water that you couldn't actually swim.

"So, we're going to have to learn it all ourselves," Inge told her colleagues.

And so off they went on a journey without a guide and it would be the soles of their feet that paced out all the roads, all the labyrinths and dead-ends, all the pot holes and danger zones, that felt all the splinters and sharp stones. It was they who would put together a detailed map, researching, paving the way for those who would come after.

These ten doctors were groundbreakers.

The first patients (or more precisely, volunteers, who let themselves be studied) were Chilean and Argentine refugees, who had recently arrived in Denmark. Inge knew one of them. He was called Miguel. He introduced her to friends who had also been imprisoned under Pinochet.

Inge arranged to pick them up after she finished work. When she arrived, however, half of those who had previously agreed failed to turn up. Only years later did Inge discover that they had set out but then taken fright at the last minute and hidden around the nearest corner. They didn't have the strength to put themselves in a situation where they would have be willing to lay bare their memories once again.

The doctors worked in the evenings with those who did manage to overcome their fears and put themselves in the doctors' hands. A session lasted four hours. They had compiled a general questionnaire. They offered a medical examination. The doctors studied everything they could: muscles, reflexes, amputations, scars, haematomas, burns, sight, hearing. And suddenly discovered something that had never even entered their heads.

They were studying the body when it became apparent that the most insidious wounds were in the psyche. And these wounds were no less incapacitating even than losing an arm or a leg.

These people's anguish was far more severe than the pain of someone who had survived the experience of war or any other man-made or natural disaster. The torturer was no longer present but the pain, once ignited, never went away. It would rise up in the night. Nightmares generated terror. Terror produced agitation. Agitation led to debility. Debility spread into blame. Blame kindled shame. Shame nurtured obsession. Obsession honed hatred. Hatred was eager for justice. Justice sought revenge. Revenge appeared to be a cure. And, unfortunately, the only one.

There were signs of neurosis everywhere. They pulled their captive in different directions until they had shredded his soul.

It was impossible to live with this pain. Or to love or bring up children. All you could do was suffer torments and torment others.

But it seemed even more peculiar that all these wounds to the mind developed significantly later. Once people were in their own worlds. There, even an innocent thing could trigger a flashback.

What's special about about a water tap? You turn it on the mornings and get washed. Nothing, of course, unless you've been repeatedly dunked in a vat of water.

What's special about a silk tie? The kind worn in respectable company. Nothing, unless you've been choked with one.

Or about a cigarette? Everyone smokes everywhere these days. Nothing, unless they've been stumped out on your skin.

Or a box of salt? You can't cook without it. Nothing, unless you've been thrown down onto salt when your back's been lacerated by a flogging.

Or a dog, for instance? A dog that just won't shut up in next door's yard. Nothing, unless you've been raped by a trained dog.

And it was not only memory that ate away at these unfortunates. It was what they had learnt that was killing them. Their knowledge of what people were like. They no longer had any trust in the world of human beings.

Having peered into the hidden recesses of human misfortune, the ten doctors were at first glued to the spot, thunderstruck, asking themselves and each other: "What's going on? What on earth is this?" They recognized that they were seeing the consequences of the most powerful means of destroying human souls. They also realized that the time had not yet come to put the torturers on trial. Trials were not what they needed to think about first of all. They needed to learn how to help these people.

Archana was the very first person they decided to treat. And no matter what came of the attempt, of the experiment, essentially, involving this small woman, it was the start of a great adventure.

* * *

The University Hospital, the *Rigshospitalet*, is not just huge, it's a monster. Its grey pagoda rises like a mountain amid the magnificent but squat Danish capital, where nothing is over five-storeys tall or higher than the trees — chestnuts, beeches, and pines. The roof of the main building towers into the sky, outdoing the churches' twisted spires. Walkways stretch in all directions. Outside is the rapid breath of the city, inside the cool and measured pulse of labyrinths, passageways, corridors, and lobbies. Immediately outside the lift, dotted lines in various colours run along the floors of the departments, like lanes in a swimming pool or safety ropes along the walls of homes for the blind. On checking in, you are inevitably told to follow the white (red, blue, or yellow) line. Otherwise, you'll get lost. It is difficult even to imagine how many people arrive at one and the same time. And yet the merest glance is met with instant respect.

So, what if there are walls? Walls in themselves don't matter, however high. What matters is that people smile and here there are too many smiles to count! Archana was taken up to the eighth floor. The neurology staff came out to meet her, all in the same uniform of white trousers, indoor shoes, and tunic. Without the badges on their chests, stating their name and role, it was impossible to tell at first sight who was a doctor, a nurse, a healthcare assistant, or a porter...

Incidentally, that was a new word. Porter. You won't find anything of the sort in India. The profession — neither paramedic, nor assistant, but rather a combination of the two — does not exist there. Danish porters are responsible for moving patients around. But they also carry out resuscitation in cases of clinical death. When someone's heart stops in hospital, an alarm brings a crash team running. A cardiologist commands the field, is in charge in other words, taking decisions and managing the resuscitation process. An anaesthesiologist performs the tracheotomy. A nurse puts the catheter in a vein. But it is the porter who massages the heart.

This is a sweaty, muscular, Herculean task. A hundred compressions a minute is no joke. For ten to twenty minutes without a break. With each push, the breastbone has to go down six centimetres. On occasion, ribs break. The dual with death cannot countenance limp, gentle, compassionate hands. The typical porter is always a sturdy chap, built like a soldier. But with a nurse's caring heart.

In the ward, Saumen opened the suitcase. Archana took out a clean sari. The nurses and assistants admired the garment's many layers, like the leaves of a cabbage, the wrap and its train, and handed her hospital clothes.

"Miss Guha, this will be easier for you and the doctors," they explained delicately, unfolding the pyjama bottoms and top.

Archana was embarrassed but took them nonetheless. How could she have known that these foreign hospitals handed out clothes? The dozen saris her relatives had so kindly packed vanished under the bed.

Everything was different here — devoid of colour and light, purified, without any smell of grime or piles of dust in the corners, as it if had been shampooed. Archana immediately decided that she would not let the wonders of this world, what was called a life of luxury in Calcutta, trouble her. She had come for something else. She was expecting to get better. She already had everything else — at home, at her mother's feet.

It turned out just as she had thought. She came to the hospital straight from the plane and left the same way. She had no time to see anything apart from the almond-paste walls of the hospital, the pale, blue-eyed staff in their white uniforms, and the water-colour cityscape behind the glass. When she was taken over to the window, she would become absorbed in the intricate tracery of slow, smooth, branching roads the colour of wet foil, and the sloping, tiled roofs of the marzipan and liquorice houses. From her bed, however, all she could see was a sky the colour of ashes, as grainy, frothy, and cloudy as the ferocious June monsoon. Sometimes, a forlorn and restless bird would wander across the sky, having forgotten the way home. One minute the wind would hurl the poor creature sideways, the next backwards, but somehow it would manage to right itself and, a couple of seconds later, it would resume its flight.

If only I were like that, Archana thought, and could recover from a setback in two ticks. But it's not like that for people. People are too heavy to take flight like that. They are weighed down by their past.

Archana's neighbour in the ward was called Agnes but Archana used her surname. An energetic woman with a goose neck and comical little curls on a fluffy golden head that looked like a dandelion, Fru Christie was jauntily living out her days, racked with cancer (unbeknown to Archana). Her husband visited twice a day and the two of them entertained Archana so much with their chatter that they sometimes missed the soup and sandwiches for lunch. Archana nodded and smiled and Saumen spoke for her.

Saumen spent the first night in a cheap hotel, provided either by Amnesty or by the local refugee council. After that, Inge Genefke put him up at her home in the picturesque setting of Værløse, enclosed by two forests with herds of fallow deer and a third with swans and lakes, two of them crowded with kayaks, canoes, and sailing boats, the third a nature reserve, smelling of sweet, fresh water. Saumen, however, didn't even look at this Danish idyll. That wasn't why he was there. From early morning until late in the evening, apart from two days when he was taken to Amnesty's local office, Saumen never left Archana's side. He was her interpreter and a member of the family and when the doctors examined her he could go into all the details even more thoroughly than Archana.

By contrast to the shy and almost silent Archana, Saumen appeared over-eager. Garrulous, pushy, hyper-active. "But then, he's been through a nightmare of his own!" Inge would think, watching him. She felt guilty not to be able to offer him a medical assessment. The funds simply wouldn't stretch to it. Her science and her mission were still only looking for ways to get off the ground. They had no centre of their own.

And Saumen himself didn't ask for anything. He was happy for his sister and proud of her and of the opportunity for her to be treated in Denmark. His joy was doubled when he met Amnesty, however. Saumen secretly hoped that their role in treating Archana might have an effect on the court case, their international name bringing it greater recognition.

Saumen was eager and ready for action. His response to living under the sword of Damocles was uncompromising and unnuanced and had made him power-hungry. He wore any advance in his sister's case like a medal on his chest. He didn't even seem to realize that he had been the cause of his sister's misfortunes. In the pyramid of their relationship, he saw himself as her saviour. He took care of her and loved her dearly. He held nothing back. At the same time, he controlled her. He controlled everything for her. Even Inge raised her eyebrows. "He's her little brother yet he bosses her about so much! He's always taking decisions... on Archana's behalf ..."

Archana had long grown used to this state of affairs, however, regarding it as only natural. The smile never left her face. For a couple of weeks now she had been taken to various floors, to have her heart checked, or her lungs, her spine, or her kidneys, or to have her nerves, skin, and blood examined. The minutiae of these sacred rites stoked Archana's faith. She expected good things from this city and these people.

Two weeks later, when there was a clearer picture of Archana's paralysis, Saumen left for Calcutta and she was on her own. She no longer mixed up people's faces, could say all their names, and knew the Danish for "hello", "how are things?" and "thank you". She had even got used to being called "Arkana", with a "k" that broke the flow of the word rather than the correct, melodious "ch". The only thing she couldn't get used to was the rice, tasteless despite being as white as snowflakes, and she was still too shy to say that she wasn't a big fan of meat. Fru Christie noticed and had a word in Inge's ear. Inge went down to the kitchen and asked the cook to provide her patient with a Bengali diet despite hospital regulations.

She already knew there was a chance of getting Archana back on her feet. It was such an atypical case, however, that Inge was full of doubt as to how and indeed whether to tell Archana.

* * *

The picture that had emerged was as follows. The vital organs were fine, generally speaking. Her frame of mind was that of anyone in her position. Absolutely all the doctors had shuddered on taking a close look at her skin, however. Faint in places, less so in others, there were crescent-shaped scars with a faded, brown film. Their size corresponded to cigarette burns. It was the neurologists who explained their effect. They said:

"The patient has been bedridden for five years, during which time she has not walked independently but only with support on both sides. There has been a perceptible loss of muscle strength in the arms and shoulders, although she is still able to move her arms. The leg muscles have atrophied and the flexor and extensor muscles are also wasted. However, the reflexes — reflexes! — remain. This means there has been no damage to the peripheral nervous system or not sufficient to impede walking. All the signs are that Archana's body has not lost that ability, and if she is not walking it is because her brain will not let her. This is probably because a chronic focus of excitation has developed in the recesses of the brain and is suppressing the area of the cortex governing movement. In other words, there is a blockage. Or the paralysis is *psychogenic*. This may be the result of shock caused by the very great pain of being tortured.

"Overcoming such a blockage is an individual process. Some patients respond to authoritarian methods. The patient is simply given an order: "That's it. You can walk. We're starting tomorrow." If there is belief, *trust*, on the part of the patient, it can sweep the blockage away like a cyclone.

"This approach is harmful to others, however. Can someone who has been bedridden for five years understand and immediately accept that their inability to move is nothing but a decision of their brain? There is a risk that the patient will rebel and reject medical support, whereupon the cause is lost. There should be no bald statements under these circumstances. The patient is won over by tiny, roundabout steps."

In Archana's case, no-one could tell which would be the right approach.

Safest of all, Inge realized, thinking it through with her colleague, Gudrun, would be to put Archana in an environment where she would slowly begin to exercise, start to feel her muscles respond, gradually remember and sense that the ground beneath her feet was firm, and begin to get used to the thought that she didn't just *want* to walk but was able to — already *able to* — and should try to do so.

"Intensive massage, training in the gym, hydrotherapy — first, let's see how the muscles respond and then we'll be able to see what to do," the doctors agreed.

* * *

Per Jensen had been a porter at the university hospital for twenty years, since he had been twenty years old. A native of the city, he was one of those townspeople who like to spend their days off in the countryside, far from the crowds, thinking, reading, meditating, and thinking and reading again beneath the canopy of a centenary pine. On work days, life seemed prosaically simple, and sometimes dull and boring, since from dawn to dusk it lay along the bus route from Tårnby station on the island of Amager, where he lived in a one-bedroom bachelor flat, to the hospital on Blegdamsvej. Was Per a workaholic? It's hard to say. He looked forward to and enjoyed his breaks. Once a year he was happy to go off on holiday, but there too he avoided the crowds. The bus for Lake Garda (a resort popular with Danes at that time) went without him. Per would go by himself to geysers in Iceland, icebergs in Greenland, or Sampo in Lapland. When he came back, he was caught up in his work all over again. Apart from his job, however, Per had no other constant concerns. He had never had a wife or children.

His childhood had been spent in a yellow, two-storey block in the working class district of Hvidovre on the outskirts of Copenhagen, with the traditional appearance of a perfectly ordinary, post-war family home: ruched lace at the windows, floors polished till they shone, royal blue, fluted porcelain from the flea market in a mahogany corner cabinet, a wooden trunk with a curved lid and carved designs, containing all sorts of odds and ends, and on birthdays the Danish flag on a bleached linen table cloth, and a rosy duck stuffed with prunes at Christmas.

Per wasn't even 14 when his father, a hotel waiter, died. His mother was a cleaner at the library but when she was widowed she had to take on even more work, and only saw her son at suppertime. Fortunately, Per gave her no cause for concern. Long before their father died, Per's only brother, nine years his senior, had taken a job as a junior waiter at the D'Angleterre Hotel and not long afterwards went to work on a cargo ship and was away at sea for months on end. He had friends, of course, but mostly for playing football. Per dealt with all his questions, thoughts, and feelings on his own. No-one interfered but no-one gave him any help either.

When he finished secondary school with the relevant certificate, Per discovered that he still had no idea what he wanted to do. He applied on the off chance to train as a lab assistant but within three months he knew it wasn't for him. Rather than waste the rest of the year, he attended the college classes. On graduating, he went into the army, where he only lasted two months — he refused to handle weapons. He had to come up with something.

He couldn't be a burden on his mother. Someone mentioned that the University Hospital was hiring porters — he would never be out of a job. He went, essentially, without being particularly drawn to it, again, on the off chance. He moved out of his mother's after his first pay cheque and rented an ancient room with no conveniences whatsoever in an old villa on Amager.

Per had already worked for several years when he enrolled on an evening psychology degree at Copenhagen University. Three years on and that went wrong as well. The course was split into thirty-three units, none of which took him where he wanted to go. He wanted something about meaning, about why we are here, but that subject didn't exist. Next, he decided not to tempt fate but to settle for the bird in the hand. It was a steady income, after all ... what more did he need?

So, as he approached middle age, Per had acquired no lofty ambitions and no ideals, with the exception of those he still sought to find in Dostoyevsky, Kierkegaard, and Sartre. Even there, though, there weren't so many ideals — just poor folk, Christian discourses and nausea.

* * *

It was already half way through the winter of 1980 when, one chilly afternoon as snowflakes slid down the window panes and the walls in the hospital gleamed cobalt, Per was told to collect a patient from physiotherapy.

Sara from physio asked him to take Miss Guha to her ward on the eighth floor after hydrotherapy. The foreign prefix, the gentle harmony of that "Miss", told Per who the patient was.

For a week now, the physiotherapy department had been talking about the patient from India. Such a lovely, attractive woman but, damn it, she couldn't walk. Anyone who asked how or why would shake their head in bewilderment: "How could something like that be inflicted on a living person, what kind of monsters were they?!" But they got over their discomfort and went off about their business once again. So did Per. It was like reading it in a book — he shuddered, found it rather distressing, sympathized with the heroine for a moment, but then turned the page and that was it. Gone, forgotten.

The door to the pool was open. Archana was in her wheelchair. Grey hospital trousers, a baggy dark-blue top: a Danish "small" was too big for her. A rubber band held back a long stream of mermaid's hair.

"She's as thin as a toothbrush, her belly's touching her backbone," Per noted immediately. His heart contracted with pity. How could someone possibly be so thin?

He went over to the wheelchair, put on his official smile, took the handle, released the brakes, and, without a word, calmly and confidently, pushed it out into the corridor and along the passageway towards the lift and onto the eighth floor. Archana knew a little English, which Per spoke well, but she didn't say a word, just stared ahead. Per was also silent and pensive. From his great height, he could see the glint of her milk-white parting against her coal-black hair, her forehead the colour of tea with its mark of distinction, the still damp eyebrows, the flourishes of her inky eyelashes, the hump of her birdlike nose, and her knotty fingers on the too-large knees of the hospital trousers. It was a standard-issue wheelchair but it drowned Archana.

"Like the heart of a flower… the pearl in an oyster…" Per reflected as he pushed the chair along.

When they reached the ward, he lifted her onto the bed, noticing with sympathy once again how unhealthily bony her back was. He wished her a speedy recovery and dashed off to another job. Once in the lift, he became lost in thought and for the first time ever he missed his floor:

"But it's so strange though… it's one thing to read about it… but when you see the person for real and you know what they've been through … well, that's different… it affects you differently… You can't just turn away… you mustn't… you can't shut a person like you can a book."

* * *

It was the last day of February. Snow swirled outside, unremitting. The sky was thick as wax, coming between night and day like a curtain, when Dr. Gudrun Boysen, a severe, rather brusque woman with a pageboy haircut and eyes like a baby owl's (her husband fondly called her Guddi) came to do her rounds. She said:

"Archana. Good news. You can walk."

Archana was sitting on the bed and a minute before had been writing home about her daily existence, the people who surrounded her, what she could see out of the window, the treatment she was getting. At the end, she had underlined with a thick squiggle: "Mama, I can feel — and I feel it every day — that everything will be alright." She had just put it in an envelope when Gudrun came into the ward. She sat on the corner of the bed and asked how she had spent the night then said, calmly but firmly:

"Archana. Good news. You can walk."

Archana shuddered, numb, her face frozen. A shiver ran over her shoulders. Her mouth fell open — she couldn't get her breath. Should she believe it or not? Was it true or not? While her brain cursed and turned somersaults of doubt, her body was swept with the balm of happiness and she suddenly had a vision of herself running through a grove of trees... independently ... running into the village school...

"I can?" gulped Archana, her throat constricted. Her hands covered her face. Her voice remained firm.

"Yes, Archana, you can," Gudrun said calmly. She leant forward and hugged her. "We'll start today!"

Just before midday, Archana was taken to the gym, a blissful expression on her face. Sara, the massage therapist, called for a porter. It turned out to be Per. He lifted Archana out of her wheel chair and put her on the treadmill — a track between two bars that provided support. Archana had been on it before but to no avail. When she was sure Archana was supporting herself and that Per was standing guard behind her, Sara walked forward. There was about half a metre between her and Archana. Sara said:

"Now, Miss Guha… take a step towards me!"

The look of bliss vanished. Archana's face crumpled like dried ashoka flowers. She shook with tension. Every vein, every nerve, every muscle, and every bone was as taut as the bit in a donkey's mouth when it turns a millstone. Her breathing was heavy and uneven. A wave of fury swept over her. Drops began to trickle from her face and back like melting ice. Her legs felt like lead, as if nailed fast to the floor.

"Miss Guha, step towards me!" Sara said loudly.

"Go on… just a step!" urged Per behind her.

A shudder leapt to her forehead and temples, like a rat that goes for the throat when no chink is left as an escape route. It leapt and fell back. Fell back and exploded. The lead in her legs cracked. The crack began to ripple like a snake. The snake pounded like a hydraulic hammer, smashing her flesh to pieces. Everything came tumbling down like an icefall. And kept on pouring, pouring, pouring… pouring, pouring, pouring… until darkness pricked her eyes. Just a second before the darkness, however, her body, with a howl, responded to the summons and threw one leg forward, just one.

Per gave a sigh of relief and carried Archana back to the wheelchair. Stunned, as if she had just seen an entire universe unfurl, Sara went out of the gym, unsteadily and clasping the doorframe, and shouted out to the whole corridor:

"Miss Guha… our Miss Guha… one minute ago… took her first step!"

Applause broke out. Someone dashed to the flower shop. Someone else into the gym. There was a hubbub of congratulations. Archana heard none of it. It was all just a pattern of spots. Everything was swaying.

When, supported by the rails, she had thrown one leg forward and placed the sole of her foot on the track, she had been overwhelmed by a single feeling, as if, in an instant, she had been showered with gold. Someone's cry of "yes" rang out.

A deluge of happiness.

The touch of a dream.

* * *

Inge Genefke was working in another department that day. When she heard the news from her colleague, Gudrun, she was delighted — and scared. It was the first case of its kind in her career. "Now what? What happens next? Will Archana be able to cope?"

Barely waiting for the end of the working day, Inge raced to the shop to buy chocolate and flowers and went up to the eighth floor.

Achana sat alone in the ward. She broke into a happy smile when she saw Inge, pale and anxious, holding a lavish bunch of gerberas.

"I can walk!"

Tears slashed her throat like a knife but Inge got a hold of herself. No, no, she mustn't cry! It was important to keep calm right now. Calm and optimistic.

"Inge, you will be the first person I walk with unaided. Come on, help me!" Archana said determinedly but her voice was not her own. It was low, staccato, authoritative.

Inge came right up close to Archana. Giving her no time to think, the latter hastily stretched out both arms, dug sharply into Inge's shoulders, cautiously put her feet on the floor and stood up — by herself. And suddenly transferred her weight forwards. Inge could barely support her forty-five kilos. As if this physical earthquake — the typhoon of trembling that had suddenly been set in motion, first spinning, harmless as a top, then whirling into a demonic centrifuge, beginning to howl and roar within the tiny body, shattering it, splitting it into pieces — had added to her weight.

Five minutes went by. The trembling didn't lessen, it dispersed. She puffed out her cheeks. Her chin and jaw shook. No, Inge thought, it wasn't time yet, she needed to go back to bed. At that moment, Archana tensed again, like a sprinter on the starting blocks, detached herself from Inge, straightened, and thrust one leg forward. Then again and again. More than that, she couldn't manage.

"I've got to lie down!" Archana said her voice mechanical, not her own.

Inge helped her back onto the bed. "This girl doesn't realize herself just how strong she is! Such quiet courage!"

When her trembling had finally diminished, her face brightened and the tears came.

"Did you see? I did it myself! I did it!"

For the second time that day, Archana almost fainted, dizzy with happiness. For the second time that day she was touched by her dream.

Inge hugged her and burst into tears.

"It will all be fine. The most important thing now is to rebuild your muscles. It will take a lot of work, an awful lot."

Before succumbing to blissful exhaustion and sleeping right through the night for the first time in years, Archana opened the bedside table and took out her exercise book. This letter home, hot on the heels of the one sent that morning, was the shortest and yet the greatest. Seven words and a tsunami of exclamation marks in every square of the page:

"Ma! Latika! Saumen! Your Archana can walk!"

* * *

When, a month later, she was allowed to go home, the results were evident but not enough. Archana had learnt to walk but in an unsteady waddle and barely two metres. True, the doctors gave assurances that it was now down to physio to rebuild the muscles. Intensive exercise at home, every day, every single day, and in two or three months everything would be fine.

How her heart sang! Everything would be fine!

Saumen flew in a week before she was discharged. Once again, he stayed with Inge. On the last day, he brought along a camera he had borrowed, but photography wasn't allowed in the hospital and he went outside. A cameraman from Amnesty was already there, making the film, *Archana Can Walk*.

The kindly physiotherapy team gave Archana presents. In the past few days, they had been teaching her how to stand up and sit down, how to get onto a bed properly, how to open the door, how to go down stairs, how to put on her sandals, how to use the toilet and have a shower.

Amnesty International staff member Gunhild Nielsen was assigned to take the Indian guests to the airport. She arrived by car then waited curiously for an hour outside the hospital. The staff of two departments were huddled by the entrance — nurses, porters, doctors. Per was there too. When Archana was brought out, he moved away from his colleagues, lifted her out of the chair and carried her over to the car. This pleased Saumen and he called out:

"Per, Per! Let's take a picture!"

Per slowed for just a second, embarrassed at having to pose, then proceeded at a brisk pace. Once he had put Archana in the car, he awkwardly placed a tangerine muslin scarf on the seat. Archana smiled in reply. Was she remembering the person with whom she had struggled through that first step? Per didn't stick in her mind for any other reason. Their whole conversation amounted to good day, goodbye, and get well soon.

When Gunhild Nielsen and her guests reached Kastrup, she had parked the car and taken the key out of the ignition when the door opened and someone offered to help. To her astonishment it was Per. He had got there before them. Saumen and Archana smiled broadly, assuming Per had been sent by the hospital, and nodded in reply.

And only Gunhild, watching how Per lifted Archana and carried her carefully into the terminal, was puzzled, unable to make sense of it. There wasn't a trace of romance in it — just trust and good will. Gunhild trotted after them and simply couldn't understand:

"How odd that this porter's come to the airport. It's really not his job at all."

Chapter 20

The Impatient Heart

On the morning of April 1, when Archana and Saumen were due to return to Calcutta, Latika bought roses at the bazaar and gave one to each member of an excited reception committee, electrified by what was about to occur. The brothers and sisters, their wives, husbands, and children, the neighbours, and the neighbours' children went to the airport as festively attired as a band of gypsies. Even Mother, feeble with age, her right side paralyzed, and long since housebound, asked to be taken along. She simply could not believe that Archana, her Archana, could walk. "I want to see it. I really, really do!" she insisted, always the mother hen.

An hour went by and then another, and there was still no plane. It had not landed.

Worried and visibly flagging, like a hot air balloon, its joy deflating as the gas is turned off, the same festive horde went home again and there they found a telegram. Saumen reported that the flight from Bombay had been delayed, and would not be in Calcutta before that evening. Latika decided that Mother would stay at home — there was no need to put her health at risk — and so would the neighbours and the children. The second time around the reception committee was smaller—Latika, the brothers and sisters, their wives and husbands.

Finally, they landed.

Saumen brought Archana into the arrivals hall, helped her out of the wheelchair, and, scooting a few steps ahead, aimed the camera. He called out to the family — who were transfixed —

instantly focusing their moist eyes, now unblinking lest they miss the performance of a miracle:

"Look at this! Sezdi can walk!"

Archana gave a blissful, cheery wave, and eagerly took an unsteady, jerky step forward. Then another and another. She began to walk slowly, heavily, haltingly, criss-crossing her feet at odd angles, until she reached her two-yard limit. Then Saumen settled her back in the wheelchair.

A fragile silence hung in the air, viscous as a drop of spittle preparing to fall from an elephant's tusk: everyone was in shock. First to give a sob was Anjali. After that, all the other relatives began to weep and wail, giving thanks to heaven.

On the way home, Saumen had instructions for Archana.

"Sezdi, you know that Ma has a bad heart. Try to go gently, or it might be too much for her..."

When Archana was carried up the steps, Saumen asked her to wait in the entrance while he went into their mother's room.

"Ma, try and stay calm. Sezdi's about to *walk* through that door."

"I don't believe it," Mother said, her voice trembling. She was on the verge of tears, as if afraid of the long-awaited happiness she had prayed for during many years of sleepless nights.

"Just make sure you don't upset yourself!"

The door opened wide. Archana appeared in the room, albeit supported by relatives. The latter stood to one side, and Archana moved towards her mother with her uneven, child-like gait.

"Look! I'm walking!"

Mother, only now believing, reached for her daughter with her good, left hand and sobbed. Could she ever have thought that this hour would come, back when she stood amid the wreckage of her home, or dashed around Lalbazar's various floors, demanding to know what had happened to her children; when she emerged from police interrogations on her brittle legs, liable to fracture at any time, or waited for visits at Alipore or the Central Prison; when she learned of the paralysis and began the secret diary in which she talked to her children at night, keeping her heartache at bay; when she prayed for a daughter consumed by a deadly infection, when she received her home again, although without the use of her legs, or when she herself was immobilized but still strove to convince Archana: "You are going to walk…I want to see it… you are going to walk…?" Could she ever have thought she would see this hour? That the heavens would be so merciful as to let her live to see it?

That night, only the children at the Guhas house got any sleep. The others gathered in Mother's room. Archana recounted in detail what had happened over there in Copenhagen, and the family wiped their eyes, and came to believe forever that it was a miracle.

"She's walking slowly now," Saumen kept repeating, "but it will improve in time… really soon… definitely."

* * *

After seeing their Indian guests off at Copenhagen Airport, Gunhild Nielsen offered to drop Per off at home — it was on her way. They had a cup of coffee at a filling station. En route, Per recounted how Archana had been taught to walk, and admitted that he was worried, very worried actually, as to whether she could cope on her own. Gunhild was as puzzled as before, and wondered about this once again: Why was he bothering so much? Weren't there plenty of patients like this? Per, meanwhile, was effectively talking to himself, tossing new wood on the fire of her vague surmises:

"But you saw how skinny she is! Is it really possible for someone to be so skinny?"

At the beginning of May, the hospital received a letter from Calcutta. Archana told them about their journey home (Latika had helped with the English grammar), said that generally everything was fine, and she would never forget all the people who had given her her legs back. The whole department composed the reply. As Per added a couple of lines of his own to say that Archana must do her exercises, he glanced at the envelope and wrote down the address.

On October 1, the first day of his leave, having saved ten thousand kroner for the ticket and without telling a soul, not even his mother, Per flew to Calcutta.

It was a crazy thing to do, as well as an expensive one, if you bear in mind that Per had never, ever been drawn to Asia. Even now he was indifferent to these places and preferred the north. He could happily travel for a fifth time to Iceland's geysers, but the south and the east... No, nothing attracted him about that stifling, dusty, sweaty world: all those ashrams and taj mahals, the gilt and the clothes as lurid as spices, all those fakirs and snake-charmers, Mowglis and tame elephants, the kitsch films, its actresses decked out in beads, the saccharine mummery of a million gods, the mantras, the comatose yogi, samsara, and the concept of karma.

He went, surprised at himself. He was surprised at what was driving him: a heart-felt disquiet. A disquiet about someone he didn't even know. Apart from the spine-chilling tale he had heard in the hospital. This disquiet was spurring him on and he was letting it. And he was even pleased to do so. Pleased that he could go and put his mind at rest. Check that everything was okay. Put an end to the worries of recent nights.

"I'll just take a look and come right back," he said to himself on the plane, trying to convince himself as he read *Nagel's Encyclopedia Guide: India and Nepal*, the latest, 1979, edition of the little pink and white book.

He had his visa and his ticket, and a return date. Two weeks, then home.

At Dum-Dum Airport, Per exchanged his kroner for rupees and went out to the taxi stand in a damp and fragrant noontime. The sight of a white man in a Western suit drew a swarm of drivers in an instant. They fastened on him like gadflies on an elephant, promising the very heavens. Per didn't try to find the cheapest, but did what he would have done in Denmark, and took the first taxi in the line.

"Could you take me to a cheap hotel, please."

The hotel owner, a prim English lady with a hint of blue-grey above her top lip, could not get over the green Danish passport. In his photo, Per was clean-shaven whereas in real life he had a thick, luxuriant moustache, the colour of cinnamon nougat. Eventually, she gave him the key to an attic that looked out over a tiny formal garden. As Per climbed the stairs, the jaundiced faces of the servants feigned a welcome. Those of the other guests did not. The corridor brought to mind a homeless shelter or a den of thieves. Per was not particularly perturbed by any of this. He just wanted to lock his door and sleep. He had hastily freshened up from his journey, endeavouring not to examine the vagaries of the plumbing too carefully, or the walls that bore the traces of splattered mosquitoes and woodlice. He had wearily straightened the bed when there was a knock at the door. The floor attendant inquired whether sir might like to buy ganja or hashish, or to sell his camera. Per pulled a face: Er, no, he didn't. An hour later, the knock came again, with the same question. And so it went on — until midnight.

In the morning after downing a glass of unknown juice with a slightly sour, rancid taste, and breakfasting on toast with banana jam, Per put his presents in his bag, asked for a taxi, and gave the driver Archana's address. He had already checked on the map that he should head south-east. As he drove through the residential areas, he was astonished and even embarrassed: not so much at the weeping windows as at his inability to make sense of why so many house fronts bore the Nazi swastika. Later he realized that the swastika shape of the air vents was only obscene in Europe. For Indian peoples it was an ancient sun symbol of the movement of life and abundance.

There was no abundance here, however, anywhere, ever. From

the taxi windows, mere holes without glass (it would be entirely appropriate to put up a sign saying, "Ride with the wind in your hair"), to the tired, dead eye-sockets of the decrepit houses, their prison-like bars stuffed with tattered rags. The city stood bravely on its rotting legs and continued to decay. Posts and trees bore badly spelled signs: "Physiotherapy & Yoga: we treats arthritis, spondylosis, paralises, etc. Dr. P. Mandal". These services were evidently in great demand.

"Here you are!" said the driver at last.

Per paid and got out. Now what should he do? Ten or so houses huddled around, all of them alike: four-storeys of muddy yellow concrete panels. Either their windows or side wall looked onto a mossy pond, where a pack of children frolicked. Old ladies sat at its edge, washing clothes and dishes. The pond was protected by a thin-stemmed palm tree like a wooden pasha with only one leg, and by a mighty tree, festooned in aerial roots, the name of which Per did not know. Spotting the foreign-looking stranger, the children clambered out of the murky water and galloped over to him yelling, leaving puddles on the copper earth. They crowded round and began to inspect him, giggling with curiosity.

"Do you know where Archana lives?" Per asked in English.

All the children could understand of what he said was the name Archana and they raced one another as they hurtled into the middle entrance, from which Saumen shortly emerged.

"Per? Is it you?" Surprise shone in Saumen's face but he immediately suppressed it: it wasn't nice to let a guest know he was unexpected even if he was.

"Well, why on earth are we standing out here? Come on in. Come in!"

Even as he showed him into the first-floor flat, he laughed in sheer delight:

"Oh my goodness! What a surprise! You've come to see India!"

"I've come to see Archana," said Per, immediately revealing his hand.

A cluster of guests, Sibendra and his wife and children, were already sitting in the twelve or so square metres of the room Per was shown into, which served as a bedroom at night, judging by the bed that took up as much as half the space. It seemed the family had come together to eat: a dish of rice and stewed vegetables stood untouched in the middle of the table. On seeing Per, everyone stood, bowed, and cleared a place in the middle. Per was astonished at how small they all were: they didn't even come up to his chest. Saumen alone was like a Gulliver among them. Forgetting their manners, the children stared wide-eyed as if at the cinema or the circus. They had never seen a white person before. Saumen said something in Bengali, and Latika left the room. When she came back, she put a knife and fork in front of Per. No-one else had any cutlery that he could see.

Firstly, of course, they asked if he was in India for long. When he heard the address of the hotel, Saumen pulled a critical face. "A terrible place. The pits." He suggested moving to a safer area, both nearer their house and offering cheaper board. Per was happy to agree. He kept looking towards the door, expecting Archana to come in, but there was no sign of her.

"Would you like to see Archana?" Saumen asked eventually, when the guests had had something to eat. Latika went into the next room, said something to somebody, and invited Per inside.

Archana was sitting in the position he remembered her in in hospital — on the bed, her legs dangling down. This room, no bigger than the first, was occupied by a big bed, a makeshift armchair like a fold-up bed, and book shelves up to the ceiling. Next to Archana on the bed, frail as a mummy, sat Mother, swathed in a white sari. She had greying hair that was smoothly combed, heavy black glasses, a sharp, pinched face without an ounce of subcutaneous fat, a delicate neck, and slender arms, and was even more petite than Archana. Despite all the severity in her dry face and her fine-boned, bird-like body, Mother was the epitome of caring and of home. And of strength, real strength.

Per gradually came to realize that everyone in this family was particularly stubborn. Despite the precariousness of their lives they had none of the submission to karma that keeps people backed into a corner — the corner of their own lives. Nor was there any burning cynicism, nor the cunning and rapacious superiority that alternates with hardened outrage. On the contrary, their wide, clear-eyed gaze was innocent, even naïve, entirely out of step with the times, although as intense as sorrow.

When called, as if under a spell, Per first leant over Mother and cautiously squeezed her hand. Mother was not used to being touched by men she didn't know, but Per was not aware of that, which Mother guessed. Only then did Per greet Archana.

"Hello, there. How are you?"

"I'm fine, thank you."

He could see that Archana was pleased but embarrassed, that she could answer questions but not hold a conversation. Not sure what to do next, Per fussed over his presents. He placed a sumptuous, satin-papered volume of views of Denmark published by Gyldendal besides Mother, gave a pair of earrings to Archana, and bracelets to Latika. There was even something for Saumen. Finally, he took out some of Denmark's famous pastries, twisted into spirals like a Sikh turban, frosted and flaky sesame and vanilla *wienebrød*. Even he was surprised that they had arrived safely.

A little later Saumen suggested sorting out a hotel. As he left the room, Per noticed the smoke-darkened kitchen. There was no sign of a stove — food was cooked over an open fire and the walls were covered in the dangerous residue of cooking oil. This was not what shocked Per most, however. During the fifteen minutes Per had talked to Archana, he had realized what was most important: it was exactly six months since she had been discharged from hospital but her situation had not improved one whit. The two-yard limit had not been crossed. Just as before, she couldn't cross the threshold of her own bedroom.

To say this came as a blow to Per is putting it mildly. He had never found anything so painful before nor been so close to making a huge commitment.

* * *

A new hotel with the airy name of Bliss (the windows opened onto a shared balcony overlooking a city that was choking in its own fumes) really was only a kilometre from the Guhas'. The next day, it took Per only ten minutes to reach them, without getting lost once. Shaking hands with the family, he said without any preliminaries:

"I want to show Archana how to go up and down stairs."

He helped Archana into the entry way and asked her to perform a couple of movements on the steps. He was saddened to see how helpless she was.

"Walking two metres really isn't enough," he remarked in some agitation. "Six months have gone by and there's been no change."

"I have massages," Archana said, apologetically

"That's not enough. I think you should continue your treatment in Denmark."

Archana looked at Per in amazement and immediately lowered her eyes.

"But is that really possible?"

"You can go with me."

"I don't understand what that means, going with you."

"I can marry you, Archana. I've never been married. It would make me happy if you were to accept my proposal."

As is customary on such exceptional occasions, Per wanted to explain his family and lineage, his education and income, where he lived and what he could offer her, but he recognized from Archana's stunned expression that he had already said a lot. Archana had paled with a tremulous pallor that left her face the colour of egg white, chalk, ice and pearls, and brought tears to her eyes. She asked him to take her to her mother.

"Ma," she said, sheepishly, as she reached the doorway:

"Ma, Per would like to marry me."

Mother trembled too. Without delay or hesitation, as if she had known in advance and prepared her maternal response, she voiced the first thing to arise from the haze of her awareness:

"That man has been sent by God."

Per himself was overjoyed when he realized what he had done. It had been like a solar flare, like being hit by lightning: she had said, "Yes". He had no clearly formed ideas. And no clearly defined emotions. He could simply see from the outside that he was flooded with happiness. And it was perhaps only then, at that minute, there on the stairs, that he finally realized that he was in love.

His was the late, mature love that needs only to give, not to take. For the rest: what would be, would be.

* * *

The rest of the day and all that night the Guhas held a council at the house. There was a real mixture of concern and delight. Despite liking Per very much, Saumen plagued the family with his suspicions as to why a physically healthy and apparently prosperous man had decided to marry a woman who was no longer young ("Sezdi's already thirty-nine!"), who could only look after herself with great difficulty, and could not take care of a husband and a home. Ramendra felt the same. He had not yet met Per and was at a loss, unable to grasp why a foreigner was asking to marry his disabled sister. What if his intentions were not honourable and he took her away and did something? Emmy was also confused. How could they give their sister away to someone from far away? There had to be some skeletons in his cupboard! If anything happened, they wouldn't even know. They couldn't just go and help, or bring her back!

"I've got to talk to Per!" Saumen decided in the end. "Sezdi's in no fit state for married life. We have to be sure she'll be safe."

The events of the next three days were like a test. Saumen asked Per to take a trip. At first sight, it was a hospitable gesture — to show a visitor places off the tourist track. On a second and closer viewing, it was a chance to get to know the man better by being with him round the clock, and observing him in unfamiliar settings where he might reveal different aspects of himself.

It cannot be said that Per was ready for the kind of travel that involved changing buses several times a day, squatting down to eat straight off palm leaves, and absolutely no toilets. His sense of balance was playing up — hours of rally racing the Bengal hills was like bouncing on a trampoline. Every bump slammed the top of his head into the tin roof, and only a cargo of wood could have been unaffected when they braked.

Saumen, meanwhile, appeared to be running like clockwork. He couldn't stop talking, asking Per about his family, his job, his wages, and his accommodation. Per, struggling to keep his balance and to register the scenes outside the pane-free window, held nothing back as he talked about himself — he had never married, he lived in a small, one-bedroom flat, and he wanted to help Archana.

When, as the third day drew to a close, Saumen, his voice solemn, made an awkward speech about the purpose of marriage, and the family duties of a man and woman, Per realized that their trip was coming to an end. He endeavoured to listen attentively, nodding now and then in agreement, and respectfully interjecting a "yes, yes, yes", but had he been asked a minute later what the conversation had been about, he would not have remembered. Indeed, his head was swollen, as if he had been stung by a bee, his stomach was dancing a jig, and his eyes rolled in all directions...

When they got home, Saumen declared:

"Ma, I think Per will make you a good son-in-law. You and Sezdi should say yes."

When he found out that the family did not oppose the match and even agreed to solemnize the marriage before his visa ran out, skipping the traditional sentimental parade of pre-wedding festivities, Per felt all the exhilaration of a hero of yore.

"Luck is on my side!" he mumbled into his moustache as he arrived back at the hotel from the Guhas'. And the palm trees he had only seen before in ports, and the tree with its garland of aerial roots, whose fabled name of banyan he had heard the day before, screened off the bright, falling stars, and rustled overhead: "On my side, my side, my side."

* * *

There was still a week left on Per's visa when Latika set off to see how to register the marriage and Saumen undertook to introduce him to the family. He began with his sister, Monobina, then went to visit Sibendra, then on in order of age. Per could still not get used to the fact that the moment he arrived he would be taken to sit at a festive table and all the women of the house from the hostess to her daughters-in-law and daughters would circle in silence, ensuring he did not feel crowded. The guest was meant to begin eating while the others sat opposite and watched as if he was in a silent film. They found literally everything endearing — how Per used a knife and fork, how he chased his rice around the plate, how he lifted a napkin to his lips. Fortunately, Per already knew that local custom dictated that he should only take food with his right hand — the left was used on the toilet. If you're India, never ever use your left hand to put something in your mouth or people will think you're incredibly uncouth.

Strangely enough, Per experienced no culture shock. He experienced something like astonishment, tinged with an indelible sadness during his three-day trip when he came upon the nadir of poverty, and staggered back, frowning, unable to process it. It is not the same as seeing it on television where a diminutive, prettified version of the world is revealed behind protective glass, and can be switched off with a flick of the finger. Nothing here can be switched off or beautified. Here everything grabs you by the hand, pulls at your leg, thrusts into your vision, pours into your ears, sticks in your nose, and grabs you by the throat. Everything acts differently on your foreigner's soul, turning it completely upside down and inside out. Right down to the last tiny grain of thought — the thought that certain life forms are not well-adapted to life but in people the instinct to keep breathing is so fierce that it carries on even when they are suffocating.

At the Guhas' house, however, Per experienced no culture shock. They were people just like himself with two arms and two legs. They read no fewer books and knew rather more about life, not to mention so paltry a thing as its meaning. That was something Per should probably learn from them — the art of life as survival, while remaining human. But what could they take from him apart from reasonably good English with a Danish accent, mastery of a knife and fork, and the polite application of a napkin to the lips?

But they did take things from him and came to like him in the process. Things that seemed mundane to Per, not even worth mentioning, such as brushing his teeth, had all the impact of a bomb going off. Per promised the anxious Mother that Archana would come to see her whenever she wanted and certainly once a year. He didn't know that an Indian family is ruled by the man, or that a married woman would not dare to visit her father's home, even if her parents were just around the corner, other than very rarely, and with her husband's consent. Whereas he was planning to let her travel from over the hills and far away. Whenever *she* wanted. Per's promise occasioned such a tearful response from the family that he blushed in embarrassment. At which point the family elevated him to the status of a higher being.

Latika was told at the register office that representatives of different religions could not get married whenever they liked: the procedure took many months. There was no way it could be done in just a week. Hearing this, Per did not take even a minute to think but said with an ease that captivated the family all over again:

"All religions are one. If it speeds things up, I'm willing to become a Hindu."

That same evening, Latika took Per to a temple. An old man in crazy rags lit a fire on the ground then spent a long time tediously sprinkling him with ashes and chanting something like a shaman. Finally, he lifted filmy eyes to Per and asked him to repeat a few words. In the end, he issued a caution: you must be tolerant of other points of view and not eat beef. Per replied that he would try. The ceremony ended by conferring a name. Per was now called Pinaki.

There were no other impediments to the marriage.

It's hard late to say whether Per had read Stefan Zweig's *Beware of Pity*, in which the hero falls in love with a woman who cannot walk but, in the grip of the eponymous emotion, loses his courage, retreats, and runs away. Stefan Zweig's generous spirit was the first to emerge from the mists of consciousness, in which the mind could not articulate nor the brain yet process, but emotion had become his constant companion and infallible guide, and swept him along a winding river, its eternal meaning dawning only in the final loop.

"There are two kinds of pity. One, the weak and sentimental kind, which is really no more than the heart's impatience to be rid as quickly as possible of the painful emotion aroused by the sight of another's unhappiness, that pity which is not compassion, but only an instinctive desire to fortify one's own soul against the sufferings of another; and the other, the only one that counts, the unsentimental but creative kind, which knows what it is about and is determined to hold out, in patience and forbearance, to the very limit of its strength and even beyond."

* * *

The wedding was simple, quick, and crowded, without priests or rituals — their good will was sealed in mundane ink. Latika managed to send out invitations only at the very last moment with the modest P.S. "Mama will be grateful for any support." They were expecting hardly anyone bar the family and their neighbours. They were very wrong. People kept on coming until late at night. Everyone wanted to see for themselves, to hear with their own ears, a story that seemed more wondrous than even the most incredible Indian fairy tale or the vanishing statue of Ganesha

In her deep red, bridal sari, a medallion glittering on her forehead, Archana was flushed with happiness. Her hair was decorated with milk-white jasmine and her fairly long parting, from the top of her head to the middle of her brow, had been painted with red sindoor: the longer the sindoor, the longer the husband's life. Archana's wrists were encircled by shell bracelets in the colours of a married woman — and they tinkled and tinkled and tinkled. Per, with this dark moustache, wore a white shirt that so set off and deepened his tan that he looked as if he had southern blood himself. Garlands of flowers were placed on the bride and groom, which moved Per to tears. Not good at talking about emotions, he was unable to express the feelings that overwhelmed him. He simply knew that this was happiness and his smile never left his face.

Late into the night, Per and Archana were surrounded by children holding flowers. The guests whispered that even though she couldn't walk, she had flown over the hills and far away and come back able to walk … and then her angel had flown after her.

When the wedding was over, Per took Archana by the hand and carried her carefully to the taxi to go to the hotel. Before allowing him to put her down, Archana looked her husband in the eye and sensed everything, understood everything.

She understood that even if she was never able to walk properly, she could rely on his wings.

For the rest of the night and the day after the wedding, they learnt about one another through words. There seemed no lack of things to say despite the differences in their English.

Overcoming their lack of similarity, two lives began slowly to merge into one, forging a shared path against the current on the map of human destinies.

The following day, Per's visa expired and he left. He went to draft an invitation. Back home, he sold the collection of royal porcelain he had been amassing all his life, and sent the money for the ticket. The Guhas' didn't have a phone. When she wrote her reply, Archana asked Latika to correct her grammar, but this time Latika said: "In private letters? No way. You'll have to do that yourself!"

At Christmas, Archana flew north on an SAS direct flight. When a member of the customer care service carried her out in her chair, Per was already waiting. He hadn't brought flowers but he had brought a warm coat.

Hastening home by taxi, he carried Archana into the entry and up in the lift to the fifth and final floor. At the top of the stairs, he gently set her on her feet to take the keys out of his pocket. Looking around at the landing, the lift, and the door to the flat, Archana asked cautiously:

"Is this where you live?"

"Not me, no!" said Per with an enigmatic expression.

Joyfully he turned the lock and flung the door open, as wide as his heart.

"We do. You and I. We live here."

Chapter 21

Free At Last

But it was a long time still, before Archana could manage without a wheelchair. For about two years, every morning soon after Per left for work, the social services minibus would drive up and the driver would knock on the door ("I'll give you a hand, Fru Jensen!"), and take her to the physiotherapy centre of the University Hospital, where she had taken her first step. Later they would take her to the rehabilitation centre for patients like her, which had recently opened thanks to the efforts of Inge Genefke.

It was another three months or so of training in the gym, hydrotherapy, and therapeutic massage, before Archana first walked out of the room and round the whole apartment without support. After six months she could leave the apartment independently, and slowly, slowly — arduously dragging her right leg, bringing it towards the left with a sudden jerk, and clinging hard to the handrail — go down three… no, four… no, even five stairs. For sheer joy she did not sleep for over a week. Her brain could not relinquish the euphoria of her triumph.

Her outdoor walks were punctuated by frequent pauses. When the lingering pain seized her ankles and calves, pierced them with its suckers, as convolvulus overwhelms thyme, and worked its way into her back and further — into her neck, the back of her head, her temples — Archana would turn to the nearest bench. There she would take Per's hands and use them, as people apply plantain leaves to bleeding wounds, to warm up the painful places. In time Per learned to have this conversation silently, with his hands: "I-feel-your-pain-and-I'll-take-it-away".

But for walks further than the back yard they needed the wheelchair a lot longer. To the sales staff in the supermarket on the corner just by Tårnby station they were instantly recognizable — the moustachioed man in the white shirt under a sleeveless woollen pullover, wheeling a woman in a brightly-coloured sari along the aisles, taking products off the shelves, and explaining things to her in English. When, one or two years later, Archana called into the supermarket alone, without Per, walking at a snail's pace and dragging her right leg, they did not recognize her immediately. But when they did, they were amazed — and happy for her.

To mark this event — her liberation from the wheelchair — Per and Archana had a visit from Amnesty. On the day of her discharge from the University Hospital, they had filmed the event and called it *Archana Can Walk*. Now they had decided to make a film entitled *Free at Last*.

There was a bird-cage in the room. The cameraman, happy to have found a metaphor for the film, asked Archana to open the cage door a little. The parrots — all four of them — got into such a frenzy at this hint of freedom that they did not hop out one after the other, but rushed through the little gap en masse, lashing Archana's forehead on the way. The shot was not very cinematic, and the cameraman decided to re-take it. But the parrots had settled high up on the curtains and could not be lured down. The guests tried repeatedly to recapture the runaways by throwing towels at the ceiling. They caught them in the end and returned them to the cage. Archana opened it. The cameraman stood ready, but the birds, now terrified, crowded into a corner of the cage. With difficulty, just one was coaxed out. Disbelieving, and still ready to retreat, the bird scrambled on to a windowsill and flapped the fear from its wings. The camera whirred in a contented bass. This became the final shot of *Free at Last*.

And was she? Free at last?

If I could orchestrate lives, if I could plan people's destinies, this story would finish here — it already contains as much of everything as a dozen others could accommodate between them. But alas… only fairy tales end like that. The life we have here is real — the events and heroes are drawn from life. Archana and Per could not be happy for a long time yet, ffor the oil - remember Bulgakov? - was already bought, already spilled…

* * *

When, in September 1983, Archana flew to Calcutta for the case against Runu, it had been in court for six years and was showing no sign of coming to an end. Runu had skilfully set up barriers, and petitions were doing the rounds one after the other — he maintained that Archana's case was ludicrous. The court would suspend a session to give an audience to Runu's lawyers (the most expensive in Calcutta). When it was decided to resume proceedings, Runu would apply to a higher court. These circular tactics dragged on for several years. When he finally ran out of delaying tactics in the High Court, the second defendant started juggling with petitions, then the third, then the fourth…

Archana could never finish giving the evidence she had begun six years before. Since she had moved to Denmark the trial had become a torment of Tantalus. She flew to and fro, fraying her nerves and exhausting her funds. Runu played a skilful game, confident that another two or three gruelling years like these and his accusers would have exhausted their fighting spirit. Man is not a machine: if he overheats, he breaks down

Saumen, meanwhile, was building up knowledge, constantly in training for a fresh attack. There were no jurisprudence books left that he had not read, no cases he had not studied. Now he could conduct this kind of case himself and address the court as well as any lawyer. He reacted to every change with lightning speed, drawing up rebuttals and counterclaims so that the case did not get buried.

When a hearing that depended on Archana's presence came up, Saumen would send his sister a telegram and she would find the cheapest — but longest and most exhausting — route, probably through unheated Communist Moscow, and fly to Calcutta. Often it was only to show herself in court and to hear, after five minutes, that the session was yet again deferred for a few months.

And it happened again this time. But Archana was not too upset. The flights back and forth cost money, which meant Per was working more and more to pay for them. But even if the Guhas returned from the courtroom empty-handed, the money had not been wasted, for during these stays Archana did not leave her mother's side. And Sudharani was not getting any younger. Per had always understood this and, no matter how much he missed her, he never tried to stop Archana's visits. This time, a month after her arrival, Per joined his wife in Calcutta, and they all gathered at home for Christmas.

"Sunu," said Mother suddenly. "Why are you going back now, to the worst of the cold? Perhaps Per could leave you here another month or two?"

Per agreed, though understanding nothing. As soon as he had gone, Mother said to Archana:

"Listen… I want to die while you're here. You live a long way away. If something happens and you don't manage to get here, you'll torture yourself for the rest of your life. I want to die *now*… while you're beside me."

Startled, Archana looked at her mother — she was in her right mind — and hugged her as tightly and tenderly as she possibly could.

"What are you talking about, Ma?"

Ever since Archana had moved to Denmark, she had thought about nothing else. She was always afraid her mother would die without her there. And that thought gave her no peace, no chance to immerse herself in her new life. But why talk about it now? Does anyone really know when their time has come? Surely you can't plan these things? Mother was paralyzed on the right side, but her health was stable, and she had even learnt to write with her left hand. Her letters, written on blue paper, always ended in reassurances: "Don't be sad, Sunu dear, I'm fine, I'm not about to die. Be a good wife and make Per happy. Don't be sad, I'm fine."

Two days after expressing her wish, she suddenly lost consciousness. It looked as if she really did have a pact with death. She wouldn't allow it into her home while her children were in jail, but now she knew that Archana could walk and had a caring husband, and that Saumen and Latika were fine, and as for the lawsuit — well, clearly the real day of judgement was not on this earth, and she could go to her final rest with an easy heart. She was not being called — she was doing the calling. She herself was calling the celestial powers and allowing them to do their job.

* * *

Dear Per,

Words cannot express the depth of our sorrow at the death of Ma.

We had not realized how much this would affect us.

The whole house seems empty. Ma was our centre; our little family revolved around her. In recent years we were busy, mainly thanks to Ma. I just cannot express all our feelings…

Ma was suddenly taken ill on Sunday night. It was worrying because the local doctor had checked her and found nothing extraordinary… the usual high blood pressure and fluid in the lungs. We thought we might have time to consult Dr. Ghosal. But that night she developed a severe headache… I had to call in Dr. Ghosal. We came back to see Ma unconscious… and she stayed like that for three days.

She developed pulmonary oedema and severe bronchial congestion. The last seventy-two hours were a constant struggle for her life. I had a lot of young boys working with me and we collected money, found doctors and medicines, and went for consultations with whoever we could… day and night. On 13th December, in the afternoon, we had to give her oxygen. At 1:00 A.M. on 14th, Ma stopped breathing and started sinking. I went mad… I summoned all my stamina and all my knowledge and went into my last battle… I started giving vigorous cardiac massage and artificial respiration.

She came to life again… for another two hours and twenty minutes.

I went to Dr. Ghosal and returned with his son, to give her Coramin injections. She had two injections but had died by the third…

I saw that she was sinking.

I saw Sezdi sobbing; the room was full of people; Sathi (Latika) was standing near… I dismantled the oxygen cylinder.

I was just paralyzed. I tried to sense that empty space… for a long time I was silent, silent, travelling with Ma from my early childhood to that moment… now Ma was going far, far away, alone… If I cry, weep, shout, Ma will not come back… It is natural, that's true… But HOW CAN I BEAR THIS TRUTH, THAT MA IS LOST, MA HAS GONE FOREVER?

Ma died at 3:20 A.M. on 14th December 1983.

Now that looks like a mere statement of fact.

We three did not observe any religious rites.

Ma was taken by hearse to the crematorium and cremated.

I only took red roses… there was no wailing, no Hindu rites.

I did what I had to, mechanically, and left, to think over on my own this "undesirable freedom". I cried, wept, and sometime I tried to talk to Ma… I still feel MOTHERLESS.

At night…the ticking of the clock reminds me of Ma's last heart-beats. I felt them with my own hands…but her time was up.

A chapter of our life is complete. Ma worked for us, she was an indirect victim of torture and of those dark days. I never thought of revolution or of any work, without Ma... Ma was with me to love, to inspire, to encourage, appreciating, even without knowing the whole meaning of my work. I was bound to that OLD TREE. I cannot manage the turmoil of life unbound.

It is hard to make up my mind about any immediate work. But I know that "time is the best healer". We have refused the financial help offered for Ma's funeral. We are thinking of Sezdi: in her condition the neurological problems may increase again. I shall write to Inge and Gunhild as soon as possible. Please tell them. I hope your mother Gerda is in good health. You must look after your health.

Yours — Saumen
6.1.84."

And for a long time yet Saumen would live like a pilot whose plane has been shot from under him. He could not go into his mother's room. "I don't want to see that empty bed," he would yell, hysterical and out of control, when he went past the open door and saw the place where his mother had been lying.

"Throw that clock away! I can't bear that sound!" he would bark, seeing the alarm clock on the shelf, for it reminded him of how his mother's heart had been ticking before it stopped.

Archana was suffering no less than Saumen — she was sleeping on the bed that had been her mother's. But there were still Per and her brothers and sisters to think of.

Latika mourned silently. Only when Archana was leaving did she burst into tears and whisper:

"Sezdi, what are we going to do? Saumen won't go anywhere near his mother's room... He's lost his mind."

That evening Archana took her brother by the hand.

"Let's go into that room for a moment, shall we?"

"No!" Saumen yelled, recoiling in horror.

"Fine. Stay here. But try to think what Ma is feeling at this moment. All your memories of Ma are linked to this room, right? There's a lot that's bad in the aura here — I was ill here and Ma was ill here... But there's a lot that's good too! Ma hugged you here, stroked your head, talked to you ... do you remember how she used to call you 'my little boy'? If it's true that Ma's watching us now, then she must see... she has to see that we're cherishing her memory..."

Saumen listened to Archana, hardly even blinking, and it seemed he started to thaw... sparingly, drop by drop.

But he never thawed completely. The night when his mother chose that "undesirable freedom", he was left without the sustenance he needed, without the habitual, blind love of which only a mother is capable, without her encouragement, recognition, adoration: he thrown back on his own resources. It was as if he had, that night, passed the point of no return.

* * *

Much changed with Mother's death, though not at once. It was as if an atom had lost its nucleus, as if the sacred cow that bears the fertile dream of the whole of creation on its four slender legs had lost one vital support. The long period of mourning did not draw the family together — it pulled it apart. Old wounds were opened up — and there was no one to tend them. The Guhas retained the outer semblance of a family, but inside they were changing little by little, as if poison had been injected into their veins. Not a vat of the stuff, to get it over with, but little by little, drop by drop, so that the agony lasted longer. So that it became their destiny.

Now, when she came to Calcutta, Archana did not want to stay any longer than necessary for the legal proceedings. Previously, the waiting time had always been spent companionably with her mother. But what was she to do now, when Latika was at work all day and Saumen, even when he wasn't running about on legal matters, would take himself off to write something? When the three sat down for supper, Archana felt like an outsider: no one would even ask her how things were going in her new country. They never chatted with her about life — only about the lawsuit. Saumen and Latika found things to talk about, but they always chose esoteric subjects that were foreign to Archana.

But if Archana wanted to leave the house, go into town, and see her brothers and sisters, Saumen and Latika were unhappy, reluctant to let her go. Being the main plaintiff in the case against Runu made her a target. Thugs had even attacked a reporter recently, who was writing about the trial. And for over a month now Arun Prokash Chatterjee, the counsel acting for them, had been getting phone calls threatening to kidnap his wife — and promising his wife she'd be left a widow. Saumen and Latika were right in a way, in not wanting to let her out. But they would not let her go off to Copenhagen for long either.

Archana had missed her opportunity when, after Mother's death, Saumen had first got into his head the all-consuming conviction that now Mother was dead his sister would have no reason to come back to Calcutta when he needed her — which would have meant that their case, their joint case against Runu, brought in Archana's name, could fall apart.

Archana's departures for Denmark had begun to irritate him. He would be edgy and even fly off the handle, sometimes absolutely furious. "There was great rejoicing, an absurd amount, when her new life began," wrote Saumen in his diary. "But this new life posted a threat to the legal process. No human being in this country can conduct a criminal case while living abroad. Even a family member or a neighbour cannot follow every twist and turn when the main plaintiff is not there. The case goes most badly when Archana is in Denmark and the wheel moves only when she comes back."

The first big row was in '86, when Archana was summoned to Calcutta by telegram, only to be told in court that the hearing had been put off for another three months.

"Why go back straight away?" Saumen asked, when she started getting ready to go home. "Stay till the next hearing! Is it too much trouble to stay another three months?"

"But my husband's over there — we're a family!"

"Per'll wait! The case is more important!"

When Archana left anyway, not yet recognizing the anguish eating away at her inside, Saumen went to see Emmy, then Sibendra, and Anjali, cursing as never before: "She's got a nerve! Look what she's done now — gone running back to her life of luxury!" The family would rush to Archana's defence: "What nonsense — that's where her husband is!" And Saumen would fly into an even greater rage.

* * *

Meanwhile, life in Copenhagen was not on an even keel either. Calcutta — with all Archana's memories and its unjust, slow legal system, which, no matter how many hoops you jumped through, would never reach a conclusion — was not letting her move into her new life. And her new country was proving to be very odd — she was taking a long time to get used to it.

The hottest month in Denmark is cooler than the Bengali winter. Even right on the equator, though, there are days when you wrap up in a warm shawl and scratchy woollen socks, and the world shrinks down to letters and tea. Summer in Denmark is not the length of a pregnancy; it's just nine *days* a year — though overcast skies do also have their charm. Ideas here do not wither in the sun as they do in a southern childhood, but firm up and ripen, like mushrooms after rain.

The Danish winter is a succession of fraudulent skies. If they're clear, it means frost. If dull, it will be a bit warmer. A sari under a winter jacket looks like some absurd kind of sack. An overcoat, when you're not used to wearing one, is heavy on your chest. Feet in boots instead of light sandals feel incarcerated. Outside feels alien too. When Archana opened the street door on Christmas

Eve, she was amazed to find it silent as the grave. And when she looked from their balcony into the courtyard, it was empty. "Where are the people?" she murmured. "I can't see any people... Life has died out here..." Snowflakes landed on her cheeks and melted... And the frost traced salty lace onto her cheeks.

Dr. Genefke, who Archana thought of as a sister, explained once that:

"You need to find something nice, something that's a real pleasure to behold. The thing you like most of all... and then it'll be easier to get used to life here."

But what *did* she like most of all? Well, let's say Archana liked looking at old age in Denmark. She was happy for its old people. In India an old person's life depended on his children's circumstances. If the child was a good-for-nothing, had no work, was ill, or in prison, the parent would live out his days on the street. Here there were just as many grown-up children who could not take care of their parents but the parents lived well: they still had medicines, housing, and pensions. And they were even free to do anything they wanted.

What else did she like? The women's self-sufficiency. Their independence from men, from their husbands. And yet Archana sometimes had her doubts about that. Being dependent, just a little bit dependent... perhaps that wasn't so bad after all? It did make the family stronger.

She was also astonished by the health care. There was no probing into how much money you had. Everyone was treated the same. People didn't need to think what treatment they could afford. Sometimes she was assailed by a guilty conscience: "I'm fine, I've been helped — but how many like me are dying in Calcutta?" At times like that she wanted to rush out and do something for the world, if only to send money to a charity. But how? With what? She didn't even have a job.

When Archana was free of the wheelchair — though she would never be free of the pain in her legs and back — she went to a community college to learn Danish. She enjoyed the course, though she found it hard to study when she was thinking about Calcutta all the time, and wondering when the next telegram would arrive. Despite interruptions for her trips, Archana completed the course — though her Bengali throat never managed to re-shape itself to cope with Danish. Her hissing sibilants would emerge as hushing sibilants, not "s" but "sh". This confused the Danes, who did not always understand what she meant, and Archana, seeing their embarrassment, would falter and fall silent.

She was also troubled by thoughts of school — which, here too, remained her dream. But her bachelor's degree was not recognized. She was taken on by a nursery, where she washed the children and put them on their potties. When the pains in her back started up again, she realized she was unsuited to the job but knew she had to keep going: she must contribute to the family budget, which was continually drained by frequent trips to Calcutta for the case. But these extended absences themselves did not go down well. One day the head of the nursery told her straight:

"You've got to decide what you want to do — the trips or the job."

That day Archana came home, her face swollen. Per said:

"Do whatever's right for you. Don't worry about the money — I can manage."

Per had long since realized that the legal process in Calcutta — the reason he was left alone over and over again, in the past for two or three months at a time but now for six — was important to Archana. At heart he was often unhappy, but there was nothing he could do. He often got upset and grumbled openly, but he hoped the lawsuit would be settled in a year or two. Then they would become a normal family, and travel to other places, not just Calcutta. When it got really unbearable, he would relieve his loneliness by reading, or try to beat it watching television, but then he'd come back to books again and to the one thought that had shielded him all these years, even from his own weariness. Love endures any adversity: what else can it do? What else could it do now…?

When things didn't work out at the nursery, there was a suggestion that Archana should go to high school, to prepare to move on to teacher training college. She was young enough — by Danish standards — to start a new life. But she no longer had the strength. Archana had passed the point of no return, just like that unhappy man, the one with the still-young torso with cuts all over it, and the face of an old man. He'd looked down at her from a poster in Inge Genefke's centre, which she had attended for a long time, for the pain in her back. The poster said, in English: "I wished they had killed me instead, because they broke my dreams of becoming something in life."

Archana interpreted that vague "something" in her own way. She and Per had dreamed of having children. The day she realized that a new life had begun to glimmer inside her was the day… when she was again touched by that dream. But she lost the child. Her body, her resilient body, which looked younger than her actual age, turned out to be too damaged — too mauled, too trampled by the past — to be fit for the work of motherhood. And it was then, when Archana roared, roared uncontrollably, like a mother bear, it was then that she remembered the poster.

After that, she and Per went to various doctors, but their dreams, alas, never came true.

Chapter 22

Don't Call Me A Victim!

"**I** can't believe there's someone here *from the same town!*" cried Helga on being introduced to Archana, almost squealing with delight.

Helga appeared in Archana's life after the others. Apart from Per (who was everything to her, but could not take the place of women friends), there was Inge, who was often buried in her work for months on end, and Gunhild from Amnesty, as well as Inge's mother, Helen, who would invite her over for vanilla pastries and then ensure she left with every last one of them. These women she had known for a good while, but Helga appeared only now — holding a coffee-pot and a book.

She was a mother of four and a nurse, married to a surgeon. Now she was a housewife. Between cleaning, tidying, washing, and cooking she managed to watch television and the constant stream of putsches, bombings, and troop mobilizations that were throwing the world into turmoil. At some stage in the early days of the war in Yugoslavia, Helga couldn't take any more of it and decided to channel her devoutly Christian spirit into uses other than prayer. Someone had told her that in Copenhagen, in Nørrebro, they were opening a centre for female immigrants, to help newcomers without family or women friends. Helga signed up to help — even if only with cleaning or laying tables. She was to go once a week, to make coffee and tea, and just chat with the centre's clients. And so she met Archana.

At the time, Helga happened to be reading *City of Joy*, in which Calcutta was the epicentre of human pain and Mother

Teresa the very image of a modern-day saint. When she met Archana, Helga felt a tightening in her chest. "I can't believe there's someone here *from the same town*!" But it transpired that Archana was not the slightest bit moved by Mother Teresa's activities in Calcutta.

"Whatever was she doing? I don't get it! She didn't fight poverty; she just helped the poor to die."

"But isn't that important?" Helga would retort, and carry on arguing to the last. "Isn't it important to tell someone that he's not alone before God?"

"It's not enough to sit by suffering people and make sympathetic noises. We need to change the world."

And that, word for word, is how they became friends.

In her youth, Helga had gone as an au pair to Scotland, the land of clans and tartans, and there met students from India — all with rich families. On weekends they would cook magical meals from nose-tingling herbs in their student hostel and invite her to sing and dance with them. And through these light-hearted people Helga also grew close to India itself. She grew even closer when she married Cai.

Cai was a Dane, though born and bred in India. His grandfather had arrived there at the turn of the century. A doctor and Christian missionary, he had set up a system of tuberculosis hospitals. Cai's father was born in a provincial area of southern India, and although he was taken to Denmark at the age of five and later gained his medical diploma there, he decided to return to India. The seven-year-old Cai was also being readied for school in Denmark, but World War II broke out so he was already a teenager when he finally arrived in the land of his forefathers.

When he married Helga, Cai took her to India to meet his parents. Helga remembered how much her father-in-law had admired Indira Gandhi — and his adoration had rubbed off on her. After she befriended Archana, Helga could not, for a long time, reconcile the two worlds. Soon, however, Helga's daughter was old enough to set off for India without her parents, and there she experienced police cruelty at first hand. The daughter's horror communicated itself to her mother. Only now did she understand that India was not only the impressions of her rich father-in-law; and she now embraced Archana's story.

But for a long time, a few more years, Helga didn't even try to understand why Archana was so determined to avoid her fellow-countrymen. The cultural centre attached to the Indian Embassy was trying to forge links with the immigrant centre in Nørrebro, and Helga used to go to their parties. Each time she would urge Archana to come: "If nothing else, you can chat to people in your own language!" But Archana would stubbornly refuse. One day Helga flew off the handle:

"Why ever are you hiding from your fellow-countrymen? Have you got some guilty secret?"

"Isn't it obvious?" said Archana, upset. "There are Embassy people there — and they're supporting that regime!"

And once again Helga saw the light. Of course. How could she not have realized? At one of the parties, she'd told Archana's story to some men wearing silk ties, but they'd laughed in her face:

"That's a good one! Bit far-fetched though! Couldn't happen in real life…"

"How alone they are, people like Archana," reflected Helga that evening. She felt pangs of shame gnawing at her. When your life bills and coos like a well-fed dove and babbles like an alpine spring, when you have children, a weekend house in the country, friends, home and car, your relatives nearby, savings in the bank, and a holiday every year — it's a strange feeling when you suddenly realize that for someone else life isn't like that. Archana's life was the kind that no one dreams of. But everyone peers into it, wants to know about it. Someone said once that the true value of life can be savoured only by one who has been dying but did not die. Archana had been dying but had not died.

Where had that life force come from? Helga was too shy to ask such a personal question straight out. She decided it was to do with religion.

Once Helga invited Archana to lunch and, knowing that Hindus are not fond of meat, she bought a vegetable pie from the delicatessen. "Not a gram of meat!" she'd insisted to the shopkeeper. Happy with her choice, Helga cut and served her vegetarian delicacy:

"Here, Archana, specially for you!"

And what a shock she had, when specks of bacon were revealed in the pie. Very few — just two or three, added for their aroma — and one had stuck on Archana's tooth. Archana bent double and tensed up, as if with stomach cramp — or in anticipation of some great calamity. And then she vomited, just like that, on the floor. Helga didn't know what to do. She certainly hadn't meant her friend any harm, and couldn't understand just why that had happened. Archana had been in prison and there, as she knew, they ate all sorts of rubbish. All in all, Helga could only put Archana's reaction down to religious sensibilities, and decided that was the answer — her version of the answer — to the origins of Archana's life force. She could not have been more wrong.

* * *

In 1994, almost exactly seventeen years since they had first taken their case to court, Runu and his sidekicks had used up all their chances to lodge an appeal. They had succeeded in halting the case fifteen times, but there were no more ways for them to slow the work of the court. For the whole year Archana, Latika, and five doctors, both prison and hospital doctors (who had now retired or become professors), were being summoned for hearings, to complete testimonies begun in 1977.

Finally, in December, the court brought in indictments relating to five clauses in the penal code. By that time two of the five defendants, Arun Banerjee and Aditya Karmakar, had died of natural causes. One, Kamal Das ("Golden Hand"), was in hiding and the police insisted he was not working for them. There were only two people in the dock, Santosh Dey and, of course, Runu.

The machine whirred into action once more. While being cross-examined in court, Archana stood facing her torturer, needing the moral support of her family as never before. But it was at that very moment that a marital crisis began to fester. When a new summons to Calcutta arrived — and she had only just got back from the last — Per lost control and yelled at her.

"It's never going to end. I can't carry on like this!"

He was over fifty and had been married for fourteen years — but had never known family life. It had been constantly eroded by Archana's past, which would yank her back like a tow-rope. Per regarded his wife's sense of duty, her compulsion to seek justice, as an affliction he had to accept — and learn to live with. He had accepted. And he had learnt. And helped her. It was something else that had thrown him off course.

The time when Saumen had treated Per like a friend and family member was now long gone. The antipathy had sprung from a minor incident — an invitation to an Amnesty conference. Archana's story had created a stir. The films *Archana Can Walk* and *Free at Last* had been shown in several countries. She'd been invited to London and Tokyo on her own, but for the Chicago conference her husband was invited to come as well — if Per could pay his own fare. Saumen had taken offence at this turn of events. Why Per and not him? What had Per done for the case? Who was he? Nobody!

The hurt spread, like a Himalayan mudslide. Saumen tried to make Archana and Per feel guilty. He'd done so much for Archana, to get treatment for her! And then off she'd gone to her life of luxury — while he spent his whole life trying to get her torturers punished! He even blamed her for the attentiveness of the press, and was distraught every time the newspapers wrote more about Archana than about him.

Saumen expected some compensation from his sister, in the form of her subjugation and devotion to the case. Archana did all she could, but her marriage, the little family of Per and herself, was dear to her and she didn't want to sacrifice it. But Saumen was ratcheting up her guilt feelings. Archana was not living; she was floundering. If she got stuck in Calcutta for a long time, she would nearly die thinking about how lonely Per must be. And on her return home she would lie awake at night, knowing how furious Saumen must be over there.

Per could see that Archana was floundering but the same was now happening to him. He'd already realized long before that the case in Calcutta was unequal, that the best they could hope for was a Pyrrhic victory: their opponents had the power and that meant there'd be trickery. But he could not say "stop!" He left the choice to Archana. He was hoping that soon, very soon, she herself would understand this... and opt for the present rather than the past. When all's said and done, for goodness' sake, if you can't change the situation then you've got to change your attitude to it. That doesn't mean you've got to forgive — just to distance yourself, loose the chains. Free yourself from the situation. Have done with it. Let it go — or, rather, let yourself go. You mustn't put life off for too long... "I'll just do this, and then... then I'll start living..." Life isn't forgiving of delays — it just goes on by.

And now Per's eyes were those of a man who had lived the last fourteen years without holidays or weekends, who was tired — so tired that finally he could take it no longer. He loved his wife as much as before, but his loneliness had tripled in weight and pressed down on him like the lid of a tomb. He was like a candle flame, which can resist the wind's onslaught for a good while but then weakens and lies flat, even if the wick is still strong.

"It's never going to end. I can't carry on like this!"

He said more, too, unable to control himself and charging the air with his aggressive tones. He regretted it later, but in moments of incandescence or collapse, when our nerves are frayed, who thinks about that? Archana mumbled, distraught, that she regretted it even more, but she could not abandon the case — it was important, and not just to her. But Per seemed deaf to her explanations, just repeating over and over, "I can't, I can't, I can't…

"I can't wait any longer. You'd better leave."

Better leave? Should she?

Per stood up and went into the kitchen, not wishing to continue the conversation. Archana rushed into the bedroom and fell on to the bed, fingering the locket with her parents' portrait that she wore on her chest. The pain could not have been greater. After a moment's thought, she stood up, pulled open the cupboard doors, wheeled out her travel bag, and started dropping cholis and saris into it. Clothes were all she had accumulated, apart from her mother's letters, and a ton of documents from the newspapers and the courts.

She left her keys on the hall table, in front of the mirror. She listened for a call from Per. But Per did not call. He was chain-smoking out of the window.

By evening she was in Hellerup, ringing at Helga's door. Helga's eyebrows shot up in surprise on seeing Archana — in Denmark you don't just turn up without calling first.

"Per can't go on… living like that… it's his flat…where am I to go?"

She buried herself away at Helga's for a month, in a windowless cell in the basement, set up as a guest room. She appeared only at breakfast, having powdered the bags under her eyes, not wanting to embarrass other people.

"You mustn't think badly of Per — it's just a reaction," said Helga reassuringly.

Other people were making him out to be a monster — only Helga told her, over and over, that he was not bad, he was just tired.

Archana's new life felt like falling into a deep, endless well. She dreamed only of emptiness, of falling and falling, and never touching the bottom. She would wake thinking she must go back to Per, but could not imagine abandoning the court case. She could not have both.

For the next month, Archana spent her nights at Gunhild's, Inge's, and at Inge's mother's, before flying to Calcutta. This came as a shock for Per. He had occasionally phoned round their acquaintances to find out where his wife was. He didn't actually ask her to come home, but he was waiting. Of course he was waiting. The feeling that he couldn't — that he shouldn't — live like that was now an obsession, a constant thorn in his side. Archana's disappearance did nothing to shift it or to lessen the pain.

* * *

Saumen and Latika were not in the least upset to hear that Archana had been living apart from Per for some months — they were absolutely delighted.

"Quite right too! Well done!" Saumen was telling her approvingly for a whole week. "You're needed here!"

Latika, strangely enough, agreed with him. She did not even sympathize with Archana on being left alone at what was generally considered to be a terrible age for a woman. With the years, Latika's lips had drooped to form an iron horseshoe, her professor's spectacles now covered her face, and she had developed a habit of glowering at you, propping her resolute chin on the chiselled column of her forearm. Sometimes it seemed to Archana that Saumen was getting his strength and cruelty from Latika.

When they gathered for supper, Saumen and Latika would first sate their appetite for highbrow discussion, in which there was no place for Archana, and only then descend to down-to-earth matters, like how Per had turned out not to be as good as he'd seemed, and how he'd done nothing for Archana. "But he did, he did," Archana would insist. "That's the thing, he did!" But she said it silently, to herself. As before, no one asked how she herself was feeling about it all. The main thing was that she would be in court at the appointed time.

The longer Archana stayed in Calcutta, the stronger was the grip of that darkness. She was still falling into the well — there was no bottom, no top, and emptiness all around. When Saumen saw her unhappiness he put a gentle arm round her shoulder. "Don't eat your heart out. The important thing is the lawsuit — Per's a complete nobody…" Archana recoiled, seething. She did not want to listen.

Soon afterwards a letter from Denmark dropped into the post box. Per, stung by Archana's departure, had written to her hastily, saying he would sue for divorce unless she came home.

"There, see what I mean? You don't have to go back," Saumen urged her. "Go ahead and divorce!" He wasn't even asking — it was an order.

He had broken with the Naxalites after getting out of prison, but in his heart he was still a communist, still asserting his right to other people's property, other people's opinions — even their lives. His authoritarian nature recognized a single authority: and that was his own. Bringing, as he thought, salvation, he was also convinced he should get paid for it. Liberation did not mean liberty. He had freed Archana from one torturer — now he wanted to take the role himself.

On one occasion Archana told Saumen she had come to Calcutta only for the court case. "And it's not up to you to make decisions on anything else!" There was a massive row.

Nowadays their home constantly resounded with raised voices.

"I'm working for us all! I'm reading, preparing, going to meetings, doing the rounds of the courts… And you?? You can't even manage without your life of luxury!"

When Archana couldn't stand any more of this, she would walk out. She went to see Emmy, Sibendra, or Anjali. Saumen would follow her there, hurling insults. The family would leap to her defence: "Reading? Meetings? Courts? And you're equating that with Archana's years of paralysis?" And Saumen would parry with: "They tortured me worse than Archana!"

At moments like those all the pain in his life was focused on one thing — that one word, the second word of Saumen's rejoinder. There was no longer any need to explain, to try and understand why Saumen was living like this. If you offered him the choice between a good life, in which his torturer would escape punishment, or a poverty-stricken dog's life, in which he would see his torturer dead, Saumen, and many like him, would opt for the latter. The victim's hatred is so overwhelming that it undermines everything else. And *everyone* else.

At night Archana would sob into her pillow. How had this happened? She remembered the tilak mark, the mark of her sisterly prayers and love. And her brother had loved her too — he'd almost lost his mind when her legs were paralyzed. Which of them had changed? Was it her? Or Saumen? There was a picture she couldn't get out of her head. She was about twelve, so Saumen must have been six. He'd fallen over on the way home and sprained his wrist. Archana had picked him up and carried him the two kilometres home. Later Saumen would tell his friends, "Can you imagine, Sezdi — such a skinny little thing and me so big and strong — she wouldn't let me walk! That's my sister for you!" A few years later he asked her why she'd picked him up. "I hadn't sprained my ankle — I could have walked…" She'd just smiled and brushed it off.

But did she need to explain it even now? He'd been in pain and she'd thought she could ease the pain by carrying him.

The images from their childhood resolved into strands, and the strands wound themselves into a tight ball, which slipped out of the window, and Archana pulled at the woollen thread, trying to stop the ball falling. But the ball lay on the ground and all that was left in her hands was a tangled heap…

To untangle it, she had to cut the thread.

* * *

When there was a break in court proceedings, Archana got ready to return to Copenhagen. She wasn't sure that Per would take her back, but she'd made the firm decision to return, to find work and an apartment to rent. Only her past was in Calcutta, but she could not get back into step with that past. In Denmark were Inge, Helga, and Gunhild — they weren't her flesh and blood, but they were her family.

There were sighs of relief when Sibendra and Emmy saw Archana getting ready for home. They'd been saying all these past months that she'd been wrong to leave Per — that the case would never end and family is family after all. The past is history but the present… the present is a gift. And we mustn't betray our present for the sake of phantoms from our past.

Saumen was a pitiful sight.

"You can't walk off like that! What about the case! You're needed here! You're the victim… you're the victim, Archana!"

"Well, you know…" she said, sounding drained. "*Don't* call me a victim. Please don't… Yes, it's true, there was a time when I couldn't walk. But I learned… I was taught. And now I'm learning to stand. I need to stand on my own two feet — not on someone else's."

"You've made up your mind, then? What a nasty piece of work we've got in the family!"

And for the whole of this minutes-long eternity — while she tried to say goodbye, tried to leave decently, walked out, left, not yet knowing that she was leaving for good — Saumen was showering her with oaths, unable to forgive, unable to understand why the past was history, why the present was… the present.

Can love for one's saviour really cancel the account with one's torturer?

* * *

On her arrival at Helga's from the airport, Archana had a quick freshen-up and went straight to the phone.

"I just wanted to say I'm here," she blurted out on hearing Per's voice, "... I came back."

"Shall we meet? Talk about it?" said Per gruffly. He still sounded hurt, as if they hadn't spent a whole year apart. But his pulse was racing, beating loudly — though luckily telephone receivers don't betray the drumming of an anxious heart.

That very evening, in the corner café on City Hall Square, a waiter served a man an extra-tall latte the colour of écru linen, and served a lady a milky tea with a dash of cocoa powder. After a moment, Per managed to say:

"Come back, Archana. Please."

"Yes!!!" Archana could not hold back, and burst into tears — she'd been scared he might not offer. "Yes!!!"

"Will you be going again?"

"Yes..." she replied firmly, tensing up.

Per moved closer, put his arm round Archana's shoulder, drew her towards him and buried his nose in her hair — now cut to shoulder length and already glinting with silver threads.

They sat like that till night fell, listening to the sky, to each other, and to themselves. Only half of their fourteen-year marriage had been spent together. Even in the early years, when Per would come to Calcutta to bring Archana home, they couldn't be alone together. For some reason Archana had always stayed with Latika and Per with Saumen.

"My poor, poor husband," thought Archana, snuggling up to his shoulder and getting to know once more the warmth of his white shirt. "He hasn't had a life with me. Nothing like. He lost it the moment he married me."

And Per was thinking he couldn't be at all sure that everything would be all right. But again he followed his inner guide and felt, sensed, that with Archana's return his life was acquiring its real meaning

Chapter 23
The Justice Gene

The decrepit frame of Calcutta Metropolitan Magistrate Court No. 7 (note the lucky number) or, more simply, Bankshall Court, has a rounded façade reminiscent of the Round Tower in Copenhagen. That tower has an inclined spiral ramp, up which Peter the Great once majestically processed on horseback, his wife the Tsarina following in a carriage. There is something similar in Bankshall Court. Here, an antique spiral staircase scales the pitted external wall: magistrates, prosecution and defence counsels, court officials, and sometimes those on trial, anyone needing to hide from the all-seeing eye of the press, take this route to the top floor, climbing gingerly, wary of losing their footing on the rusty treads. The walls are sand-coloured, with spots of tar. On the ground floor, the steps to the courtroom have lost their sharp profile to concrete rot. The double doors are constructed like Venetian blinds, but the spaces between the slats are as wide as the slot in post boxes — wide enough to keep an eye on proceedings from outside.

But on a stifling, suffocating day, when the doors are wide open, you can stand on the threshold and, while the clerks in the courtroom are idly wondering what you might want, you can observe the whole sweep of the interior. The room? Trapezoid. The floor? Rough and earth-coloured. Above your head, cruciform fans, high walls, and not a single window. On a wooden platform by the right-hand wall is the magistrate's ark-shaped desk, draped in red calico. Behind that is a portrait of the murdered Mahatma Gandhi. At the other end, along the left-hand, semicircular wall, are two rows of benches for spectators. In the centre of the room, at the foot of the magistrate's platform, are two faded, extremely long table tops. Here, the defence and prosecution beaver away under a mound of files and other mouldering documents. At the rear of the room is the defendant's cage, one and a half times the height of a man, covered with finely meshed netting, its pores smeared with filth. There is no lighting — you cannot see the defendant's face, barely even a silhouette.

Even with the doors closed, the street noise penetrates inside. As does the smell of onions from the canteen. As does the clatter of typewriters, for outside, to the right, past the semicircular façade, a secretarial and typing pool toils. Two dozen girls and young men bash out bureaucratic platitudes in the open air. A word such as "justice", hemmed in on either side by intricate patterns of paragraphs, flies constantly off the keyboards, leaving a pitted trail on the paper and the grey-violet copies, which are as pale, colourless, and indistinguishable as torn and crumpled rupees worn thin by a hundred years of inflation. But those are rupees — this is justice. Can justice too be worn thin by a hundred years of inflation?

The Guhas, by the way, always said it was justice they were looking for, not revenge. Vengeance is retaliation and retaliation is a bloodthirsty instinct; and instinct, if launched at will like a boomerang, can only deepen the tragedy of societies where the legal system stands on rubbery, rickety legs. And an eye for an eye will leave the whole world blind. Justice, by contrast, does not huddle in criminal haunts but steps out, visor raised and sometimes without shield or sword, a virtue conceived by the human mind. Justice is not bloodthirsty — that is what makes it just. To seek justice is to restore lost honour. To restore what is generally accepted as *right*.

If the geneticists, neurobiologists, neuropsychologists, and all kinds of sacred writings are to be believed, man has a justice gene — some kind of inherited attraction to that which helps him distinguish between bad and good. Distinct areas of our brain control the mobilization of the moral sensibilities that can raise us up to oppose evil. They say that in ancient times the tribes best able to survive were those among whom that moral inclination, to distinguish between bad and good, was most highly developed. In those without this understanding, no one tried to rise up against evil. Everything became unstable and fell into a decline.

Contemporary scholarship has also acknowledged that time heals only the body. Only justice can heal the soul. This is why a human being chooses suffering, why he will now forego his life, because living with a damaged soul is like living without a heart — it is impossible. Even if there is little chance, it is more important for him to go on, to go on to the very end, and prove — to himself or to others — that truth is on his side. And who would dare argue that even the worst defeat cannot later be transformed into victory, if only because any struggle — equal or unequal — at least lays bare the spirit of tyranny and thus restores damaged honour. Any struggle — equal or unequal — at least lures evil out of the shadows, making it tangible and visible. And a target brought into the light is always vulnerable. If you yourself do not hit it, someone else will. So justice is simply deferred.

But even deferred justice is not bloodthirsty. Take Saumen, Latika, and Archana. Despite the length of those lost years — like the heroic distance covered by a snail, determined to inch its way to the ark — they were modest in their demands. Redress would be achieved if their torturers were imprisoned, even for twenty-four hours, even for just a day. Then they would feel able to close the file.

Even for twenty-four hours, even for just a day. Then they would be free.

* * *

This idea alone meant Saumen and Archana still had to meet, but only for the time they were in the courtroom. Saumen had not forgiven Archana for leaving — or, rather, for challenging his authority. He wanted to orchestrate everything, including her life, but she would not let him — and wounded pride is worse than any foe. Archana continued coming to court and had to stay on call in Calcutta for six months, but they only communicated via the family, and only on matters relating to the case. If Saumen had declared that talking to Archana was taboo, then he stuck to it, forgetting himself only in a fit of temper — and when he could find some pretext for yelling, for venting his spleen on her, taking his own long-endured pain out on her.

And he found the pretexts.

When Runu ran out of possibilities for lodging an appeal, the case took a new turn. The newspapers were now writing about it more and more, which was even more reassuring for the Guhas: press support was helpful. But once again it seemed to Saumen that they were unfairly ignoring him, that they were hardly mentioning him, while putting Archana in the limelight. There is no better way to understand a person's character than studying what causes him to take offence. And Saumen did not just take offence — he would blow up, rant, and rave. He was sick with suspicion that Archana was stealing his recognition, diverting it all onto herself, getting everything while he got nothing.

When his malice exceeded all bounds he would try to set the rest of the family against their sister. And when, again, he did not win their support, he would set scandalous rumours running, calling Archana a glory-seeker. When she came to Calcutta, she could not live with him and had to stay with Emmy. But Emmy was grumbling the whole time too:

"The case, the case — that's all I ever hear! How can you live like this when you've got a husband to think of?"

Eventually Archana couldn't stay with Emmy either. The Danish consulate, which was keeping a close eye on the case, found her a cheap hotel. The booking confirmation came to Saumen. When Emmy found out where her sister was staying, she was so distraught she fell ill. But then she took herself in hand, came to see Archana, and told her it really wasn't right to stay in a hotel in a town where she had family.

The sisters hugged each other and both had a good cry, Emmy because of Archana's situation, and Archana because, before Emmy's visit, Saumen had been coming to the hotel, first in the evening and then in the morning too, and yelling along the whole corridor, "Archana, you are the nastiest piece of work in our family!" People would come out of the neighbouring rooms and say she should be ashamed of herself. She should be ashamed, not Saumen.

The courtroom was the only place where he behaved himself — for the public, and Runu's lawyers, must not see the dissension raging in the family. Nor the journalists: they would certainly stop siding with the family.

The way they organized it was for Archana to take a taxi in the morning from Emmy's place to Kushtia, where Saumen and Latika would silently climb in with her. In the courtroom they would converse if absolutely necessary, but usually via other family members. Saumen no longer called her "Sezdi", Latika stopped using "sister". She was cold and formal: "Miss Archana Jensen". If you looked at the courtroom photos in the papers, where Saumen had a hand on Archana's elbow and Latika an arm round her shoulder, you might say they had held out, standing shoulder to shoulder. But together, close — no, never. In the newspaper pictures they still looked like a close-knit family, but who could know that the cement holding them together had not, for a long time, been love? It was their family drama. It was the memory those three shared, the burning, still open wound of their hatred for their torturer.

By now Archana was not the only person against whom Saumen bore a grudge. He did not trust his counsel any more, either. Arun Prokash Chatterjee had already missed a few sessions. Once he sent an assistant, who turned out to be totally unprepared. No one could convince Saumen that his lawyer was not playing a double game. Archana, however, defended him.

"Our family can't pay! It's not every lawyer who'll work pro bono all his life."

But be that as it may, in 1995 Saumen decided to conduct the case himself and fired his counsel. When people pointed out that he was no lawyer, he told them he knew the law and the law was on his side. Since colonial times, anyone had been entitled to practise the law if they could demonstrate their aptitude for the job.

They set a test for Saumen. The most senior and most respected legal experts in Calcutta gathered to watch. Saumen answered questions for an hour and a half without stumbling. At the end, the adjudicator wrote that he was satisfied with Saumen's knowledge — and that he was a simply *magnificent* lawyer.

It was the first time in state history that an ordinary citizen without a law degree had been admitted to practise the law. And in what capacity? As counsel for the prosecution in the case against Runu! So Saumen had the government cornered and was half-way towards realizing his dream. The historic metamorphosis had occurred. The prosecutor was now the accused, the accused now the prosecutor.

Archana was as delighted as he was, and wiped a tear from her eye. Her brother had undertaken a difficult mission, of a kind few could shoulder, and was endowed with the talents to carry it off. He had in him the potential for radiant victory, but he cast a dark shadow too. Like us all, no messiah but a man, he could not avoid the traps of human weakness. The brilliant and the banal tore him in two, the one pushing him towards his set goal — the other driving him away from his family. In his fanatical need to punish evil, he had stopped making the distinction between good and bad, stopped noticing that he was destroying his nearest and dearest, that he himself was the cause of their pain. Archana understood what was tormenting him and could not abandon him as he had abandoned her. She could only pity him. And support him in the courtroom, helping him move even closer to his goal. But she could not live in harmony with him. She found that even more painful than the process of getting Runu convicted.

* * *

When they knew who had been named as counsel for the prosecution, Runu's lawyers were alarmed. They immediately found people on their side who had connections in the press and tried to make Saumen a figure of fun. But the campaign quickly fell apart, withered away in the tumult of support for him and Archana from simple Calcuttans, neighbours, friends. The papers wrote and wrote, article after article. Only if you were blind and deaf could you not know, that year, that the denouement was imminent.

Meanwhile, the powers that be were following the case and sending warning signals — as they had all these years, promoting Runu to ever better jobs and garlanding him with honours. The law specified that any police officer involved in a lawsuit must be taken off police work. But this did not happen to Runu. On the contrary, from a simple Special Cell inspector he became an assistant commissioner of police. And when Saumen became the prosecution counsel, Runu was promoted to deputy commissioner, even though he was nearing retirement age.

For all these years, when he appeared in court he would always arrive twenty minutes late, saying "doesn't matter, they'll wait" and with a permanent, evil leer, which was easy to read: which of those idiots would dare cross swords with me? He had that same insolent expression in his beady, shark-like eyes when people spat after him as he clumped heavily up the external staircase — until he was lost from sight in the courthouse corridors, from where he entered the defendant's cage. While the session was in progress, he and his sidekick had to stand. The spectators in court would yell, happy to see his predicament:

"Just look at them! Two great piles of shit!"

"No, don't look at them, sister! Don't sully your eyes!"

At these times, Archana would stand up straight. If there was justice anywhere, it was no doubt there, in that human solidarity against the world's torturers. And they were legion.

Whatever mask Runu wore, the expression in those dull eyes, glimpsed through the slits of his eyelids, made you think he was, despite everything, afraid. He bent low in his car as it backed into the courthouse entrance, and waited till his bodyguards came out to him. He knew, of course, that people wanted him dead. He never walked anywhere without hired guards. His family no longer showed themselves in the street. Did they realize? Did he?

But, whether he did or not, in the courtroom Runu categorically denied everything. He and his partner in crime were charged under five clauses of the penal code. "Public servant disobeying law with intent to cause injury to any person.... wrongful confinement to extort confession... voluntarily causing hurt by dangerous weapons or means... word, gesture, or act intending to insult the modesty of a woman." They could face a minimum of seven years in prison. But Runu was paying his lawyers lavishly, shelling out thousands of rupees for each court session. And the fawning lawyers would do all they could to hack out new routes leading him away from jail.

If Runu denied the existence of the torture chamber, his lawyer would paint Archana as a fraud.

"The complainant is leading us by the nose, Sir! There was no torture chamber there! Only an annexe to Runu's office, and that annexe was the toilet!"

When the magistrate asked for an explanation of how Archana had been suspended between two armchairs, and what had happened next, the lawyer claimed the whole story was fabricated from start to finish.

"Listen carefully! Here," and he jabbed at the paper in his hand, "the complainant told us it was 'an armchair', here she said it was 'armchairs', and here it's 'the arms of the armchairs'! So what did she really mean? You yourself, Sir, have just witnessed the complainant embroidering her story as she goes along!"

The counsel now turned to science. To mathematics. X, Y, a square… Equations could, it seemed, also prove that the story about the armchairs was implausible.

"And so, Sir, you yourself have now seen that the maths proves: a body 158 centimetres long could not have hung on the arm-rests of the armchairs. No arm-rests could have withstood that. It's a premeditated lie by the complainant."

After mathematics came anatomy. Anatomy could, it seemed, prove that the positioning of the body on the arms of the armchairs was also absurd. It would be impossible to tie a person's arms and legs in that position, impossible to hang head down in that position, impossible to beat the feet of someone in that position. This was impossible, that was impossible… And even if such a thing were possible, it would be impossible to do it all in that cubicle, which was Runu's office toilet. A stick the size of a lathi needs space. That cubicle was simply too small to swing one.

And so it went on, as if following a diagram. The complainant was lying when she said the paralysis of her legs resulted from damage inflicted in the Special Cell. Excuse me, but what damage is this actually? There is no documentary evidence of any damage. A doctor was on duty round the clock, both in the custody suite and the prison. But the complainant never asked to see them. So she did not need them. So there was, in fact, no damage of any kind!

"The complainant's paralysis, Sir, resulted from traumas she must have sustained *before* her arrest."

All in all, maintained the counsel, taking this and this into account, and not forgetting that and that, you must conclude that the story about sustaining this kind of damage is a total lie, a fabrication, Sir, a foul, absurd lie.

When the defence counsel sat down, Saumen took his place and responded to his claims on behalf of the prosecution. The Danish deputy consul had, the day before, handed the magistrate the Danish doctors' conclusion. Saumen had attached photographs taken during a forensic re-enactment. They showed Archana bound and suspended as she had been in the Special Cell. To the astonishment of Runu's counsel — who had been cleverly taken in — the position of the body turned out to be entirely possible. The armchair, the armchairs, and the arm-rests did, for some reason, hold up.

It was only some of the spectators who did not hold up. And, overcome, the elderly magistrate, who had seen all sorts in his time, brought down his gavel to put an end to the proceedings, and went off to his private chambers.

Chapter 24

Judgement Day

On Wednesday, June 5 1996, at 07:00 A.M. or 12:30 Calcutta time, Magistrate Surjendu Biswas was due to deliver his verdict.

If the news agencies are to be believed, there was no other world event to overshadow the impact of that day. A few days before, an Ariane 5 rocket had exploded over French Guiana, the most expensive failure in world space exploration, burning up the money invested by European governments in a flight lasting all of 39 seconds. A month later, Dolly, the first cloned sheep, was born in Scotland. On June 5, 1996, however, nothing happened. Nothing to compare with the excitement of the day when the Bankshall Court was to deliver its verdict.

If the Guhas won, it would pave the way for others. No one had ever been convicted in any case brought by private individuals against the masters of the art of torture.

The papers had briefed the city in advance. Journalists were standing by. The public were expecting a verdict at last in the case against one of Calcutta's most influential police officers, a case that was in its nineteenth year and had been followed not only in India, but in Europe and even in Japan and the USA. Campaigners and student lawyers had been marching for two years already, bearing "Jail for Runu!" placards. The day before the verdict was due, they had been followed by children from the Calcutta slums. They jumped about as if playing hopscotch, chattering as if in competition with each other.

"We prayed for Archana today!"

"So did we!"

"And us!"

"My mum was up all night praying!"

Archana caught a cab early in the morning and went to Kushtia as usual. Saumen and Latika were waiting on the porch. In silence, they stowed their books in the boot — Saumen quoted from them in court. Usually, there were fifty or so but today, on this very last day, they had decided to take every single one along — all sixty-seven.

They rode in silence, like strangers. Archana looked out of the window the whole way. Saumen and Latika held hands and wished each other luck ... oh, and Archana too. All that year they had acted as though Archana wasn't there but they had relented a little today and seemed kinder.

Archana's temples throbbed with tension. She shrank into herself as if cold. That she had managed to get this far, had endured being harassed by Runu's lawyers for half the spring, was entirely down to Inge and Per ringing her up in the evenings. And also to the crowds of people who had gathered at the court every day. Women whose sons and husbands had died in police cellars. Men whose wives and daughters had been violated there. It was for them that she had hung on. The verdict mattered to them as well. But what would it be? Who would be allowed to triumph?

When they passed the crowded centre and turned into the legal district, they were more astonished than ever at what a lot of police officers there were. Offices, banks, shops, and kiosks with windows overlooking the road, had decided not to open that day. Aware of how people hated Runu, the authorities feared disturbances. If Runu was found guilty, the crowd would want to tear him to pieces. If he wasn't, the police would not have enough bayonets to hold the crowd back.

A solid river of people flowed along the road to the court. It became congested two hundred metres from the entrance.

A sweaty log-jam formed at the gates and in the courtyard. People perched on fences, hung from the trees, clung in wreathes to the columns. The police drove particularly persistent individuals back from the stairs Runu was due to climb but they managed not to have recourse to lathis. The whole focus was, of course, on them today.

The doors into court remained open until Archana, Saumen, and Latika arrived.

Only close family members were allowed in with the Guhas. Journalists were not admitted.

Hardly had the doors closed when the police drove the crowd further from the stairs. Shouts went up from the fences, trees and everywhere:

"Jail for Runu! Jail for Runu!"

The magistrate arrived at half past twelve. Sailing silently into his red sanctuary, as if gliding along in felt slippers, he was immediately higher up than everyone else although still lower than the portrait of Gandhi. He cleared his throat sternly in an attempt to begin (the scrape of benches and chairs came to a halt) but then looked daggers at the door. The crowd outside was as noisy as ever.

The clerk, a small woman, darted outside.

"Shush! Shush!" she shouted, threatening the crowd with a skinny fist, as sharp as an apricot stone.

With renewed strength but still not resorting to their lathis, the police sought to drive the crowd back from the door. People began to jeer, to whistle more in chorus, their stamping more and more like a drum roll. "Jail for Runu! Jail for Runu! Jail for Runu!"

Impatience was the prevailing emotion.

Latika left the courtroom.

"Please! We need quiet! The magistrate can't deliver the verdict!"

Only now did they nod their heads. The waves subsided and were calm.

* * *

"The case that led to this prosecution began on July 18, 1974, at around one thirty. In short, on that day at that time the complainant's home was raided by police officers who said they were from Lalbazar. The complainant lived in that house, at 7 Jawpur Road, Dum-Dum, Calcutta, with her brother's wife, Latika Guha, her mother, and other family members, as well as Gouri Chatterjee who was regarded as a member of the family…," the magistrate began reading the awkward phrasing in a mechanical voice.

The public in the courtroom sat back in their seats and gazed thoughtfully at the magistrate's bench. Only Archana, Saumen, and Latika opted to stand to hear him out. The two accused were not allowed to be seated.

"The police officers searched the whole house without summoning independent witnesses, and obtained signatures on empty forms from the landlords, Badal Choudhury and Panchu Gopal Choudhury. The complainant, Latika Guha, and Gouri Chatterjee were then taken to Cossipore Police Station and then, early in the morning, to Lalbazar and the Special Cell, where all three were interrogated.

"On the same day at around ten o'clock, they were taken into the office of Accused No. 1, Runu Niyogi. The Special Cell unit consisted of three rooms. The middle room was the office where Accused No. 1 worked, the back room was a torture chamber. Gouri Chatterjee was first to be taken into the torture chamber. Almost immediately, they took the complainant in to show her what the police were doing to Gouri. She saw the police officers torturing Gouri. At the same time, threats were made to the complainant that she would be tortured just like Gouri unless she confessed to what they asked her to. After that, Police Officer Kamal, on the order and in the presence of Accused No. 1 Runu Niyogi, began to beat Latika Guha. Then, on the order of Accused No.1, the complainant was taken into the torture chamber…"

The magistrate spoke a convoluted, barely comprehensible English. Without pauses, stops, or commas. It trickled out in a monotonous stream. The sluggish, mumbled burble of his speech somehow eased the intensity of the topic, dispelled the sour note of tragedy, made things simpler, made eyes close. Archana listened like one hypnotized, not missing a sound. When it came to the details—"they bound her hand and foot... and Accused No. 2 Santosh beat the complainant on the soles of her feet... and Accused No. 1 stubbed out cigarettes on the complainant's elbows and feet..." her attention wandered to focus on the ceiling.

The air was clammy. Adrenalin flowed through more than fifty bodies. Fans hung like corpses. The horror and darkness of the night that had sundered her life, then tormented her for twenty-seven days, and had now been hounding her for twenty-two years — all that horror and darkness were now set out in thirty-nine pages of officialese that failed to express either grief or pain. And yet, from the very first page, Archana's heart started thumping as she sensed that the verdict was going to go their way. As he listed the facts of the case, the magistrate constantly made reference... really did make reference to her evidence... saying over and over and over again: Archana is right... Latika is right... Saumen is right.

"Oh, my God," Archana thought, her mind a whirl, "life might have been completely different! Why did all this happen? To us? To them? To me? What was it meant to tell us or teach us, to punish us for? Why didn't I die? How did I survive? How have I lived with this? How did the pain not break my heart? Where did the strength come from?"

As a child Emmy used to read Tagore. Archana would listen and whisper the words after her. In life everything is all mixed up, just like in a junk shop: something from the Creator, something from man himself and something from other people. The question is how to tell who contributed what. That awful night — where did that come from? From the Creator? From other people? And the fact that she had been dying but did not in fact die? Whose doing was that? Other people's, her own?

In extremis, Hindus pray and ask the gods to give them strength and light to bear the pain. They never say, "Have mercy" or ask, "Preserve me". Only, "give me strength and light to bear the pain…" What is this "strength and light"? Is it something from outside? Or from within?

When Archana was little, her father used to tell her a story. He couldn't remember where he had read it himself. Seven simple men, or maybe seventy-seven, dwelled upon the earth. Hardworking family men without a penny to their name. But as for their hearts… If they heard that misfortune had befallen someone, even though they didn't know that person, if he was on their way, they would not pass by. They would share the last they had and themselves as well. Nor did they wait for approbation. They did what needed doing and went on their way. People like this hold up the world but don't know it. These are the people of whom it is said: the best are not boastful… still waters run deep… whoever saves a life saves the whole world.

If it is true that there is a little from everywhere in life — from the Creator, from man himself and from other people — then Archana had endured a great deal from other people. The horror and darkness of the night that sundered her life — that could only come from them. But the fact that she had been dying and had not in fact died… was that also from other people? However many hands had pushed her on, there was always one, and indeed not one but seventy-seven, that had kept her from falling, that had given her strength and light.

From their example, she realized how marvellous people can be.

But only after she had realized how dreadful they can be…

As he came to the final page, the magistrate's mumbling became a little more brisk. Archana emerged from her thoughts. As she waited for the final chord, she shrank down into herself to prevent her broken heart shattering should it be betrayed again.

The magistrate took a gulp of the sweat-laden air, raised an ink-stained finger to his lips, dampened it, and turned the page:

"In the light of these facts and the evidence provided, the court believes that the prosecution has proved its case ... and finds the accused...

... finds the accused...

... guilty..."

Hardly had the word "guilty" been pronounced when it became impossible for Archana, Saumen, and Latika to hear any more: the courtroom and the crowd outside burst into applause. Saumen leaped up as if stung and swept Archana into his arms. Archana huddled against his chest. Latika clung avidly to them both. For a moment, they formed a single whole. A single cry, a single tear. And so, the three of them, keeping tight hold of one another, slowly moved out of the courtroom and were immediately engulfed by the crowd.

Cameras clicked. Journalists readied their microphones. Drowned out by the roar of the crowd, the magistrate continued:

"... the court is mindful that both accused failed to admit their guilt during the investigation and maintained their innocence under oath in court ... the court does not consider it possible to order their conditional release since their crime carries a severe penalty and must not happen again ... Taking into account that the case began in 1977 and the investigation has lasted nineteen years and bearing in mind that the accused have been punished during that time... the court sentences each of the accused to one year in prison..."

"It's all down to Saumen. He did it! He did!" Archana yelled into the crowd. Saumen put an arm around her shoulder. The journalists wrote down every word.

An old man, forgetting his age, leapt like a mongoose onto a fence, cupped his hands into a narrow megaphone and thundered:

"They've won! Archana Guha has won! Latika and Saumen have won!"

He was pulled from the fence and tossed in the air. The old man's turban fell off, exposing the bald pate of an urban holy man. Tears streamed down his face and the old man clasped his hands over a blue, desiccated mouth, as toothless as a baby's.

A young activist, Tapas (for two years, he had paraded a sign reading "Runu must go to jail!") sank to the ground. Bijaya, a student lawyer, dropped down beside him. She had learned of Archana when she was only ten and had decided there and then to become a lawyer so that she could defend Archana in court. Tapas and Bijaya were rocked by paroxysms of joy.

The father of a little girl raped in police custody struggled through to the Guhas and embraced Saumen, sobbing:

"I want to have a son like you!"

An old, barefoot woman from the Calcutta slums howled like a wolf:

"My boys were killed in police custody. Perhaps they'll reopen the case?"

It took an hour for things to calm down. Thousands of pairs of eyes were fixed on the stairs. When would the convicted men be brought out? Saumen stared, unblinking. This moment, when his enemy, handcuffed and under guard, would come down those stairs, was dearer to him than anything, more precious even than the verdict. It was like standing on the summit after scrambling up a sheer cliff. Standing there at last. Standing straight and planting your flag.

But it had been an hour already and Runu hadn't appeared.

* * *

Runu could not settle his nerves. Was this the first time or the thousandth in those nineteen years? His lungs had compressed like a spring and just didn't want to expand. His hands trembled. His legs shook. So far, his armpits had never let him down but this morning they had given up as well, secreting damp patches of terror onto his shirt.

289

In court, Runu had curled up like a foetus, hardly breathing. He hid his head but not from shame or remorse. He was afraid of being photographed, that the expression in his eyes, even behind his dark glasses, would make the front pages.

Four days later the *Telegraph Look* newspaper published extracts from his autobiography: *Sada Ami, Kalo Ami (I am White, I am Black.)* It contained the following admission:

"Yes, I know, many innocent people were victimised during our operations in those turbulent times. For that, I apologize to them. But actually, we had no choice. Suppose we were suddenly tipped off about a secret meeting of the Naxalites. What would we do then? Most of the time, we didn't know them nor did we have their photos or descriptions…

"Regrettably, some people with even a passing resemblance to the wanted men or with just a similar sounding name did get arrested …

"But please don't say this is how the police harass the people. Do they do it now? We had to it then for your security…

"The police have little choice but to use force. But only as little as necessary. Nothing like the wild imaginary torture Hindi films depict. After all, youngsters who join the force come from ordinary families. They cannot turn into murderers over night because their job demands it. And the force is not where you carry out a personal vendetta. Moreover, there is no police department run by one man alone. And nobody wishes to face the human rights commission or the court.

"People who accuse policemen of torture themselves get into fights at the slightest provocation. When somebody accidentally treads on a fellow commuter's foot in a bus or tram, they flare up. The police are brought in to control the situation. And when a police officer so much as slaps a murderer, there is a furore. The consequence of this is terrible: the murderer becomes a hero and the men in charge of public welfare become khalnayaks [villains]. Such is the cruel fate of a policeman.

"It is perhaps better not to take up a job with the police. One is caught in a cleft stick. If you try doing some work you are blamed for that. Why should one risk one's life to nab murderers, robbers, and smugglers? There are people to take up the cause of beggars but there isn't anyone who would stand by a policeman. You may at most be awarded a medal or two. But that is all. So wear that medal on your chest and be kicked about for the rest of your life."

All this would appear four days later. Now, with the verdict delivered and the crowd waiting outside, eager to see him in handcuffs and under guard, Runu could not allow the crowd to humiliate him any further. He had a lawyer. That lawyer had been paid.

During the two hours the crowd spent hailing its heroes, the lawyer was filling in papers. He was constantly on the phone. He made a lot of calls. In the end, he got his way. Achieved what he wanted. Runu and Santosh were allowed home. On bail. Not for long. For a month.

In this way, they avoided being arrested in the courtroom.

Two and a half hours went by and Runu came out onto the stairs accompanied by his lawyer and five police officers. They moved in an iron wall, impenetrable by looks and shouts, separating Runu from the crowd and expressing respect not for the crowd but for Runu.

Runu smirked, narrowing his beady, shark-like eyes, as if to say, "Which of these idiots would dare cross swords with me?" The journalists could not get at him. People milled around, unaware.

Many people took the escort for guards. Runu was being taken off to jail! He was being put in a police van!

Once Runu was home, a month would be long enough to lodge an appeal against the sentence. The merry-go-round would begin again, would go round and round like the wheel of existence, deferring sentencing for years and centuries until it was time for another judgement, not of this earth, not of humanity.

The *Telegraph Look* newspaper, which published Runu's memoirs, would precede its exclusive with a single comment:

"I am the captain of my ship. I am the master of my fate."

* * *

Saumen, Latika, and Archana took a taxi and when the journalists were out of sight once again became the fragments of a broken family.

"Latika, did you hear what that journalist said?" seethed Saumen.

"But did you hear what he said about you?" said Latika, full of praise.

"You're good to say so!"

"No, you are. You're the one who's done well!"

It was as if Archana wasn't even in the car. The happiness of their joint triumph, small as it was, had not reunited the family.

They arrived in Kushtia. Archana didn't even ask whether she could go in. She simply went upstairs. It was her mother's house. And had once been hers. Here was their old bedroom. Her mother's picture over the bed. Archana fell to her knees before it.

"We won, Ma! We won!" Unable to hold back a groan any longer, she burst into barely audible sobs.

In a little while, in came Saumen. Latika followed.

They also fell to their knees. They also wept.

"We won, Ma!"

"We won, Ma!"

They knelt there, all three of them, until dusk fell. In front of the picture. In tears. Archana prayed and waited. Perhaps after all they would say: "Sezdi, don't go. This is our day. This is your home."

But Saumen didn't say that. And Latika said nothing.

They simply wept as one.

"We won, Ma…

"We won, Ma…

"We won, Ma…

The evening was as dense as plum jam when Archana arrived at Emmy's. The first newspaper reports were already out. The grapevine had trumpeted the news. Pop music blared from the many flats in the three-storey building. Somewhere there was dancing and a chorus of "They won! They won! They won!"

An old lady appeared at one of the windows. Spotting a silhouette in the dark courtyard, she waved a hand:

"Daughter, daughter! Have you heard? Archana Guha won against Runu!"

Archana raised her hands to her chin in greeting, bowed, and went her way. Power… of whatever kind …was utter evil. If there was justice somewhere, it was probably there: in that human solidarity against the torturers. And they are legion.

* * *

Forty-eight hours later Archana was in Copenhagen. Before she left, Emmy told her how Saumen had lost his temper again when he found out she was leaving:

"Off back to her life of luxury. She couldn't even be bothered to stay with us to share the family's joy."

At that time and for the next six months, Saumen became the hero of Calcutta. Journalists thronged around him, hanging on his every word. Archana decided not to stay under his feet.

As the plane came in to land and the wheels were lowered, she gazed at the furrows on the water, the vastness of the landing field, the outskirts of the town, and did not understand a thing. It was all painfully familiar… how many times had she landed in this country? But why had this marvellous sea begun to sparkle so? Why did everything seem to twinkle with festive light?

Everywhere, the colours were so dazzling it brought tears to her eyes. Nowhere is warmer or closer to your heart than where you are loved and awaited. Where your own, your only home awaits you. Even if it is in the north where the summer is only nine days long.

Heaven and hell on earth depend not on place but on other people. As they are, so is our life. As we are, so is their life. We do not build our lives in isolation. We create them together with other people. If this were not the case, we would have remained a small tribe, sparsely scattered across islands so that we could live in ignorance of our fellows. But it pleased God to nurture us as humanity so that we multiplied and crowded in on one another. So that we communicated like vessels in a body. I have an effect on your life. You have an effect on mine. Each of us is heaven or hell for someone else.

At Kastrup Airport, the luggage was delayed in the arrivals hall. Per was standing behind the glass. Through an open door, Archana managed to catch his long, searching look and whispered a "thank you".

As often happens in life we seek justice for ourselves but do not find it where we look. We open the door to justice and peer eagerly out while at that very moment it enters by the window and stands silently behind us, drops a kiss on the top of our head, and waits for us to look round. But we are still looking in the opposite direction, still gazing out across the threshold. Why is it taking so long?

In the waiting area, Archana launched herself on Per. Quiet and shy in his white shirt, he stood apart from the crowd, holding a demure bunch of flowers, not knowing how to greet the moment properly.

"I'm sorry you've had to wait again," Archana said simply.

Per embraced her, still holding his bunch of flowers, so that she sprouted wings of greenery, and pressed his lips to her hair, dusted by winter.

"Everything's fine, darling... everything..." he whispered quietly, kissing the top of her head. "We're only a hundred and ten between us... we've got a lifetime ahead of us."

Epilogue

I fear not execution, not torture and not hate,
Not death from rifle barrels, or the shadows on the gate,
I fear not restless nights with shooting stars of streaking pain,
I fear but blindness from a world, indifferent and insane.

Halfdan Rasmussen (1915–2002)

Twelve years later

Before adding my final punctuation mark (only life adds the full stop since we, mortals, who know so little of the world, can barely count on a question mark or dot-dot-dot), I decided to go and see Calcutta for myself. To shake the city's hand and pay my respects to its shadows, to look it in the eye. All the time that I was on the trail of this story, restoring its lost voice, and struggling to select words where there were none and should be none because the words to express pain do not exist, one thought kept me going. Books are not written "about" something. Books are written "for". The virtue of literature is that it can restore honour where laws are powerless. It has the power to close the gaps in justice where God has failed to keep sufficient watch. This is what I am doing when I write. And where laws are not so much powerless as amorphous and elastic, I can call upon the old formula that judgement may be in keeping with the law or in keeping with justice. Literature is the supreme judge. Society has no other moral insurance policy. And no other antidote, either.

Copenhagen, Frankfurt, Netaji, formerly Dum-Dum, Airport, and finally the city itself. It is not for the faint of heart. There were three lines queuing to make their way out into the sultry night, for locals, for foreigners, and for diplomats. I stood in the second with other foreigners like me. There were one hundred and fifty of us but an official came over and silently led me over to the third line where there were only two people. He had mistaken my sky-blue travel document for a diplomatic passport. I recalled a sentence from Lonely Planet: "Expecting the unexpected — India has an uncanny knack for throwing up surprises…"

From Netaji to the hotel — it was an apocalyptic city. I was not a tourist and I didn't need mollycoddling — just somewhere to sleep, a decent shower, and bottled drinking water.

At two in the morning, I was given the keys to a first-floor room. My first meeting was at ten o'clock. Even before daybreak I had come to realize why it is in India in particular that the quietness of meditation is cultivated.

Night plunges the guest at a cheap hotel into an orchestra pit. Everything seeps in through the window: the curses of klaxons, the roar of motorbikes, the rhino stomp of lorries, the choral warm-up of alarms, the weird whoops of men out on the town, the lure of brawling, cries for help, wailing police cars, clanging prison vans. A curs' quarrel here, a cats' chorus there. Here a rapacious crows' ruckus, there a muster of holy cows… and so on… and so on… The cosy chirrup of a hotel cricket that under other circumstances would be an endearing sound pierces the unaccustomed foreign ear like a porcupine needle. By morning, you will have regretted a hundred times not having taken the pack from the plane, which contained ear plugs along with its sealed packets of pepper and salt. Calcutta is a constant generator of noise. The earth's wild funfair. A madcap three-ring circus. Once it gets into your head, whirling and twirling and muttering expletives, you'll go crazy trying to find quiet but won't find it, not even in an ashram. Then, you'll shrug your shoulders and plunge into the maw of the cacophony.

In the morning, I jumped into my work jeans. My dictaphone and camera were in my rucksack, plus anti-diarrhoea tablets just in case, not forgetting the presents. Before going out into a world of exhaust fumes, I drew a small cross on my right hand to remind me of the local rule — left hand when you use the toilet, right hand for everything else.

Then I went to see Per and Archana. That's right. You haven't misheard. Per retired about a year ago and they rented a tiny one-bedroom flat in Calcutta, four by three metres. Since then, they have lived on two continents. They were fine, thank goodness. Finally, after everything, they were fine. It was worth crossing the globe to see this and be able to heave a sigh of relief.

We drew up my itinerary together. We marked the key points on the map. I wanted to go where I could touch the walls of this story, peer into all its cracks and into the eyes of those still alive and, where it was too late, to pay my respects to their shades.

In communist Howrah, decked out in red, I got out on Kasundia Road. This was where Archana's childhood home had stood. It was still there. Only the name of the street had changed. The residents took me trustingly into the house and I was so affected by their searing poverty that I gave them one thousand rupees. I sat down in a musty little room — evidently, what used to be the girls' bedroom. I tried to imagine just which wall the earthenware plate would have adorned. It had been a gift from Saumen to commemorate the mystery of the tilak, but was smashed during the move to Calcutta.

The road still ran to Kolorah as it did before. Bus No. 61A was well into its dotage but it limped cheerfully along Andul Road. The same sacred Oms liberally emblazoned in Devanagari script still gazed out from the dusty sides of oncoming vehicles. On the right-hand side of the road, weedy palm trees bared breasts of coconut bunches. On the left lay the botanic garden.

The school in Kolorah had been smartened up and expanded. It had a bamboo roof, an earth floor, walls with portraits garlanded in flowers. The headteacher's office (once Archana's) contained a small fan and a fireproofed safe. A little girl in a white shalwar kameez and a blue scarf gave me a coconut with the top sawn off and a straw sticking out: please, help yourself. I went to see the year nine pupils. It was an English lesson. They were reading Kipling's *If*. Defenceless necks. Clever faces. The desiccated thinness of rural labour. Smiles, eyes — an age of innocence. Something that hasn't existed in Europe for a long time now.

The Dum-Dum district stared out of the empty sockets of its windows. I walked away from the road. Saris fluttered on the balconies. There too was the two-storey hovel. There was the sunken, saturated foundation. And the window with its vertical bars. And the blue wooden door. And even the letter box, with the stencilled address: 7, Jawpur Road, Kolkata, and seven names underneath a familiar surname: Kamala Choudhury, Amit Choudhury... There were only Choudhuries at this entrance.

Inside the one flat that was of interest to me, it was neither noisy nor stuffy. Only damp. An echo lingered. It was where the bikes were kept now. The Choudhury children and grandchildren had been unable to wash the tears from these walls. Better then for no-one to live within them.

Lalbazar, Alipore Jail, the hospital, the court... Yes, I even went there, occasionally slipping inside, but the official nature of the latter meant no detailed traces were left. Just an impression: Archana was here.

I also wanted to visit the temple and say hello to Mother Durga. But I didn't. I changed my mind. Isn't she said to protect the world order from demons? She must be very busy. Why get in her way?

I did go to see people, though. Sibendra, Emmy, their children, and their children's families. They were all living witnesses, all eyewitnesses. They each sowed a precious seed in my black notebook with its four-leaved clover. There was just one thing they didn't mention, most probably out of modesty. Every other member of the family, be it Sibendra, Emmy, or Saumen, had adopted an orphan back in the times of trouble and a great many children at the Kolorah school received a grant, introduced by Archana. It was funded year after year from her pension. It would seem the family lived by *a collective promise of good.*

And Sibendra really did have thick, tufted eyebrows that jutted out like a rain shelter. When I tried to say something, he was completely transformed into a listener. He really did listen even with his eyes. Sibendra had suffered a stroke six months earlier but wanted to play the violin for me. His son, Saikat, who was a little older than me, could not hold back the tears and quietly stepped outside. When he came back, he whispered to me: "It's a long time since Dad played…" Standing in the crowded flat on a cement floor polished to a shine, I too could only weep at the majesty of the violin as it gave this affirmation of life. The sound rose and fell. The bow struck the strung like someone's fate beating against bars. The horse hair strained the nerves. Rosin dust settled at our feet like human ashes.

Eight months later and Sibendra would no longer be with us. I would take down a photograph and hear him play again. And he had played. For me. He gave me the keys to this story. I took them to pass them on. Now, I am passing them on to you. Do you hear me? To you. Now, you may pass them on again to people you trust.

I had hoped to meet Saumen and Latika but our paths did not cross. Archana, Sibendra, Emmy, and their children all objected and said I shouldn't. Not because there was anything to hide but because there was something to lose. A fragile peace.

Even when I went to Kushtia and walked around near the house where Saumen lived and he suddenly came out and headed off somewhere, tall and grey-haired, with a slight limp, a canvas backpack over his shoulder, the contours of books showing through, they wouldn't let me even then. The car under a banyan tree neighed like a panicked horse and honked its horn: keep back.

It was the same old story. Saumen was still angry with Archana and everyone who had come to love her. He had severed relations with his family because they would not sever relations with her.

When, a few years later, Latika would be diagnosed with cancer, Archana would not hold back. She would visit her in hospital with the words, "Now it's my turn to look after you!" They would embrace and weep after their long separation. Even in that situation, however, everything would happen in an inconceivable atmosphere of secrecy, with one eye anxiously on the door lest Saumen appear. He would still not want to see his sister or even hear anything about her.

And so I couldn't ask him to comment. And so I am racked with guilt. My dilemma was left hanging and there is only one consolation: Saumen has told his part of the story to the newspaper and has written about it himself, whereas I am compiling Archana's life from its pieces. It has its own skeleton and muscles but my heart and voice. Its subject matter is life and the subject matter, like a ship, is bearing us away to another place.

Saumen in his sixties had plenty of fight left, sure of himself to the last. When Runu lodged an appeal, Saumen plunged back into the fight.

He was on the alert. He monitored everything and would not let the conviction be quashed.

In 2001, Runu caved in. He couldn't take it, gave up, caved in. The national newspaper presented this event as follows: "Kolkata: Controversial former policeman Runu Guha Niyogi died on Thursday night at Calcutta Medical Research Institute. He was 66. After a severe cerebral attack on June 18 he fell into a coma and was put on ventilation in the intensive care unit of the south

Kolkata hospital. He is survived by his 92-year-old mother, his son, daughter, son-in-law and daughter-in-law…"

Runu had gone — gone where he was meant to go. But his accomplice, Santosh, was still alive. For this reason, Saumen continued his watch. His mission was not yet over.

And how was Gouri getting on? We lost sight of her after she got married.

"Gouri?" Archana brightened into a smile. "You know, she has a lovely family. Three girls — beautiful, all of them! Parimal has a good job in a bank. They've built a house, the children are in school. It's just Gouri's health that's not great… or her mood… she feels people blame her."

"For what?"

"For being in jail. She wasn't supposed to be involved. It wasn't fair. Gouri doesn't say anything herself but her mother… her mother was always telling mine that it was our fault."

Remembering her mother, Archana lifted a locket from her breast, opened her parents' picture and raised it to her forehead and lips.

I watched her and tried to understand what feelings would come to her when her life was turned into a story, when paper absorbed her pain? Would she cry? Feel more at ease? Perhaps for the first time? Would she agree with the formula? Mine though not of my making:

Judgement may be in keeping with the law or in keeping with justice.

Literature is the supreme judge.

Society has no other moral insurance policy.

And no other antidote, either.

* * *

It's good that everything is going well for Per and Archana. It's not good that everything is going wrong in the world. Everything is going wrong in the world as regards that particular issue. In 1874, Victor Hugo wrote that torture had ceased to exist. It really hasn't. Here we are in the 21st century and there is no less need for Archana's story. On the contrary, the story is getting a new lease of life, a third lease of life and another, and another, and another.

The world has somehow allowed it to happen that after the Third Reich, after all the Holocausts, and the endless succession of Kristallnachts, after all the Maos, Pinochets, and Stalins, the Lubyankas and Greek juntas, after the five Belfast methods, after Chechnya and Abu Ghraib, nearly every second person in the 19 countries where World Public Opinion conducted surveys, nearly every second person approves of violence against prisoners. Every second person favours cruelty. In India, Turkey, Thailand, Iran, Egypt, the USA, and Russia nearly every second person says: why make any bones about it? Bring on the torture, they say, if it will help to prevent terrorism.

If it will help to prevent terrorism? Oh, you bloodthirsty people, don't be naïve! Torture, help to prevent terrorism?

Not so long ago I was as close to despair as World Public Opinion when one such "peacemaker" crossed my path. I won't give the name. The lesson is what matters. It was just a writer who lives in Israel. I've even quoted her somewhere.

Our relationship began in the usual way. A curious reader wrote a letter and the author politely wrote back. Soon, I was looking for ways to organize an event for her where I live. The author came and spoke. Beforehand, my enamoured shade, charmed and delighted at our meeting, breathlessly took the writer on a guided tour of my favourite bits of her writing.

"Don't be offended if you recognize yourself in one of the heroes!" she said with a sly smile.

"Don't be silly. It would be an honour!" I said, not objecting.

Her job is to look beneath the mask, mine to study the human cosmos. A writer you have already read is interesting just as she is, apart from what she has written. I prefer questions about life to questions about the creative process.

Afterwards, we sent one another friendly letters and would have progressed a long way in that direction had it not been for an interview. A Russian magazine asked me to conduct a series of conversations. A Danish writer, an English writer, some other writer... I phoned the author: "Would you like to? The magazine's based in Russia and you're a star there!"

The author wanted to put her answers in writing and I was delighted: her turn of phrase, her intonation. The conversation was a huge success — for the author: she couldn't have come out of it better. We discussed heart-stopping topics. Why is it the fate of a great writer to be an outcast and alone? No-one is a prophet in their own country, but why not? Is the time for great writers over? Does literature need to observe the proprieties? What names will our age leave behind? Are words a means or an end?

We disagreed on the last two questions.

"Oh, come on, all these words — the 'spiritual message,' the 'idea,' — have nothing whatsoever to do with actual writing, mine at least. And I will never believe that there is any remotely serious writer who would attempt to answer these questions literally. That's what journalism's for and even then only at its most basic level. Art should not speak of things directly. To me, the most important and most natural measure of a literary work is its artistic level, its artistic merits. Do you remember Nabokov's famous contention that art is everything and big ideas are trash?

For myself, I felt closer to Solzhenitsyn's view, in which art was not everything and the word was not an aim but something akin to a knife or a scraper to clean mud off the window to gain a more honest view of the world. Or even akin to an icebreaker to cleave asunder the "frozen sea" inside us.

He believed that "literature that is not the breath of contemporary society, that dares not transmit the pains and fears of that society, that does not warn in time against threatening moral and social dangers — such literature does not deserve the name of literature; it is only a façade."

The writer disagreed. "Solzhenitsyn is not a great artist but an outstanding individual, a great social commentator, a brave man, and a very experienced political showman of immense political authority. That he received the Nobel Prize for *Literature* rather than Nabokov, for example, is evidence of the Nobel Committee's lack of competence when it comes to literature and their political bias. Nothing else."

When the conversation was almost over, I began to flick through a recent book in which the writer had set out her interviews. What had I not touched on? What had I missed? My next question was born of shock. I was like a churchgoer suddenly finding the pastor at an orgy just after making her confession to him.

"In your book," I said, "you describe a woman you know sitting on your balcony and recounting a conversation between an American journalist and a senior Israeli intelligence officer. The conversation boils down to asking whether the latter thinks the use of torture is ethical. From the way in which the answer is expressed, I conclude that you, one of my favourite authors, do indeed think that it is ethical. Please God, say you don't."

The answer came three days later so not in the heat of the moment. Here it is, full and unexpurgated:

"Alas, even at the risk of being crossed off your list of favourite authors, I can't put your mind at rest. I am very tempted just to say 'yes' and leave it at that but I think it's worth clarifying at least a little bit.

"Let's just set aside the usual terminology of the left-liberal element of Western journalists and so-called human rights defenders whose activity is in a special category. The word 'ethical', say. This word is from another conceptual category and it is an American journalist who uses it in the short essay of mine that you mentioned. So, what we're talking about is the propriety of torture, isn't it?

"Before I answer that question, I want to remind you that I am a writer, that is, a person who deals in specific subject matter, specific stories, and specific situations. I do not really like or recognize 'general questions' and can twist any one of them so that the answer is completely different depending on the point of view, but convincing every time.

"So, for a start, I'd like to say that there are several *dozen* human rights organizations in Israel, including some that are concerned with prisoners' rights — since in Israel, as in any democratic society, people are concerned about ensuring that the innocent do not suffer. And that is right and proper. I cannot give you the exact figures from their reports and, in general, I would like in my answer to distance myself from anyone in particular. My opinion is exclusively my own.

"So, do you remember the title of Ehrenburg's most popular war-time article? Let me remind you: 'Kill the German!' What a turn up for the books, eh? The horror of it: a writer, a humanist, a sophisticated intellectual, and then that. And he had no scruples about putting his views out there like that either. If only he'd called it 'Kill the Fascist!' but no, it was 'the German'. It's even rather chilling, isn't it? Nevertheless, the entire population of that vast country greeted the article with understanding and even enthusiasm. You'll say that it's obvious why. A bloody war was under way. Everyone knew what the Germans were doing in their occupied territories, and as for what they were doing to the Jews — that was just... So, yes, because of that. But not just because of that. Knowledge and understanding weren't the whole story. What mattered most was the sense of personal involvement. At that point, every resident of the Soviet Union had a relative who was fighting at the front, or had already been killed, or had been sent to Germany... In other words: the German was the *personal* enemy of every resident of the USSR.

"Can you see where I'm going with this?

"I think you can. But your *feelings* are asleep. Or rather, your imagination is asleep. Now I'm going to try and wake it up.

"Imagine that in the morning you wake your four-year-old, get him dressed, feed him, and take him to nursery school. A much loved child, with downy eyebrows, he knows his letters, is funny when he talks, still has three teeth to come through…in short at this point your imagination and mine are completely in step. The only thing is that it's important that you really imagine *your own* child. Not the next-door neighbour's, who is also very sweet but is still the next-door neighbour's, but *your own*.

"But I digress. When I was little and my grandfather wanted to catch me out in a lie or trying to avoid giving a direct answer, he would shout: 'Look me in the eye!' So, go on, look me in the eye. You've taken your child to nursery school and gone off to work without a care in the world. All of a sudden and quite by chance you find out that another 'shahid' wrapped in explosives has been caught on the very street the nursery school is in. What's more, intelligence reports say that two of them have made their way out of Gaza. The second has managed to go to ground. And since a 'shahid' is in any case prepared to blow himself up at any moment along with the bus, café, nursery, school, and since the only person to know what the second, who is still at large, looks like is the one who's been captured, every minute's delay threatens to bring — what? I'll tell you what. The death of your child. Look me in the eye. Not the next-door neighbour's although that would be an awful shame as well.

"Now, if your imagination is engaged, I suggest you imagine the state you'd be in during the hour or two before information is beaten out of that hate-filled, drug-filled thug about where the other one has gone and what he looks like. Are you going to worry that he's being badly treated? Appeal to the standards of international law?

"No, either you'll be in a deep faint or you'll be shrieking for them to do whatever they like as quickly as possible to that bastard to beat the information out of him. Come on! Get a move on!

"So it goes. I hope you've realized that I'm talking about war time, for in our region war time never stops.

"So I think *every* action by the military is permissible under these circumstances. All the more so since, unlike many other countries, Israel doesn't have the death penalty. And any one of those bastards knows that he will get however many years and then he'll be exchanged along with another thousand scumbags like him for just *one* captive Israeli soldier who, I can assure you, will come back (if he comes back) completely disabled both physically and mentally. Only recently, we received *two coffins* in exchange for the bloody murderer, Kuntar, and a couple of hundred like him. What can you do, Israel is very sensitive about the fate of its soldiers, even the dead ones.

"I cannot forget the tale of a young man who was describing the fighting in Jenin. How at night the Arabs snatched two Israeli soldiers and how it was impossible to move in the dark. And how they imagined what the enemy were doing to our soldiers. 'But everything worked out, thank God,' he said. 'They survived?!' I exclaimed. 'Of course not. They died, but luckily they were already dead when they were snatched. They didn't suffer.'…

"And I simply don't want to explain or recount what they usually do to our soldiers who are taken captive, or you won't sleep for about three weeks.

"In other words (and now I'm giving you a direct answer to your question), I accept the use of special methods for obtaining highly important information from an enemy in war time. Full stop."

End of quote.

What I read was like a ruler across my knuckles or a breath from a mouth that was unwashed and neglected… What was going on? Very tempted to say yes...? Accept special methods... torture?

It would have been fitting to grab a cigarette to reduce the adrenaline. But I don't smoke and never have and so I simply went down to the kitchen, brewed some green tea, and took a mug ("Best Mum in the World" — a present form the children) outside. It was July, the school holidays. My son was at tennis camp in Sweden, my daughter just then travelling by bus from Oxford to London, a plane and home. Much loved children, with downy eyebrows, who knew more than just their letters. And like a crazy mother I can't sleep if I don't hear from them three times a day. But does the fight against terrorism really presuppose recourse to the terrorists' methods? Does the measure of a human being not also include how we treat our enemies? Does our terror at losing our own really abolish the rights of others? By which I mean human rights. I wonder: who is the crazy one here — the world or me?

British actor Julie Christie who played Doctor Inge Genefke in the film *The Secret Life of Words* quotes Albert Camus as saying, "For every man tortured, ten terrorists are born." This quotation is the short version. In the preface to his *Algerian Chronicles*, Camus wrote that deciding to use torture "may have cost us something in the way of honour, they say, but it saved lives by leading to the discovery of 30 bombs. But it also created 50 new terrorists, who will employ different tactics in different places and cause the deaths of still more innocents."

Closer to our own day, a source from the FBI, questioned by *The New Yorker*, also adopted this position: "I don't believe these things make successful strategies — sensory deprivation and such. There is a great lack of knowledge about the mind-set of extremists. Doing these things just makes them more determined to hate us. And eventually they are going to be released. When they are, they're going to talk and exaggerate what happened to them. They're going to become heroes. So then we'll have more extremist networks and more suicide bombers."

The same source warned: "We can't lower ourselves to the level of our enemies. If we do, it will come back at us later on."

In other words, if the world continues to produce victims by these "special methods", those same victims will, at the cost of their own lives, want to change places with their torturer. Violence breeds violence. Violence only breeds violence. Terrorism is often a response to terror by the state.

I became ashamed of our friendship. A single step and the "chemistry" was over. History was repeating itself in reverse. The not unknown Einsatzgruppen were known as the cream of society: academics, professors, even a church minister and an opera star. A famous writer whose forebears made the ultimate sacrifice in the last century was now trying the executioner's axe out for size.

The question of whether to torture or not is like litmus paper. Answering other questions, it's still possible to take shelter, to wriggle out of it, by looking at the subject and at people from both sides. Not this one, though. Answering this question, you have to take a stance. Either yes or no. When you do, you show what you're like inside.

Even if we set everything human aside and leave only what belongs to the writer ("specific subject matter and story"), are writers not obliged to be humanitarians? I can only answer "yes". They have no right not to be. Because they are in control of people's minds. They have access to people's souls.

Because they are people-readers not people-eaters.

In public changing rooms in Denmark there is sometimes a sign that reads: "Do not tempt immature souls," (i.e. don't leave money in your pockets). Some people are not so much morally weak as simply immature. If no-one plays on their weaknesses, if no-one encourages them, their souls will grow without sinning.

When I went back to the computer, I knew what to do. But

who am I to be giving lessons to writers? Let the writer's own idol respond.

"Finally, let me ask you two questions that were once put to Nabokov. First: what is best in a human being? Second: what is worst in a human being?"

"The best is to pursue your calling as best you can and as fully as possible. The worst is to betray yourself by not doing so," the author wrote.

"Thank you for the interview. I expect you know how Nabokov answered these questions but I will explain it for the readers. Nabokov replied: The best thing in a human being is 'to be kind, to be proud, to be fearless.' The worst 'to stink, to cheat, to torture.'"

You would probably like to know what happened when I pressed send. Nothing I hadn't expected. The writer took offence at my comments — mine or Nabokov's, how do I know? And did not want to publish the interview. I agreed without regret. For the readers' sake not hers: there is no need to tempt immature souls.

As for me, I can agree that art is not jurisprudence and literature is not the defence of human rights. But there's another thing I'm not about to challenge either and that is that art is for people, about people, and by people. Art is people. And so the writer is held sacred of whom it can be said, "their noblest instincts I have e'er inflamed."

All told, I put this particular fish back in the water. Let it swim in its dead sea and not appear before me. The human world is much less complex when you send out a signal to which there is only one answer.

Yes or no.

* * *

While some are arguing how many innocent lives might hypothetically be saved if "special methods" are legalized in the war on terrorism, more and more Western countries are beginning to realize how many innocent lives "special methods" have already ruined.

Archana's story is example number one, Guantanamo number eight hundred. If the sources of *The NewYorker* magazine are to be believed, only a quarter of all those held in that infamous prison might have been of interest to the special services. That they "*might have been*" does not mean they "*were*". The majority posed no threat to society and could provide no valuable intelligence. Charges have been brought against barely 30 inmates.

The rest suffered innocently!

There will be no end to this tally given that this is not the first and not the only laboratoryor or prison where the authorities, in tandem with psychologists, are perfecting types of interrogation that destroy the human personality while leaving no marks on the body.

Forty-year-old Sami al-Haj from Sudan was Guantanamo prisoner No. 345. A cameraman and journalist for Al Jazeera, a popular TV channel in the Arab Middle East, he came within the sights of the US special services after Osama Bin-Laden was famously interviewed by Al Jazeera. The Americans set themselves the task of finding the person who filmed the interview.

Six and a half years in prison without charge or trial, 130 interrogations by "special methods," 480 days on hunger strike, a clutch of infections, disabled legs, and more, much more, in addition to the prison authorities' refusal to provide anti-cancer drugs. Sami had to take them after having throat cancer.

I met Sami at the International Rehabilitation Centre for Torture Victims in Copenhagen a month before Barack Obama was awarded the Nobel Prize for Peace. Sami had been released from Guantanamo eighteen months before. When I saw him, I let out a sigh of relief. As tall and poised as an Olympic runner, his legs straight and his gaze direct, Sami was a symbol of unbroken dignity. Even the cane he used to walk (his knee had been broken) was a carved, turned gentleman's cane. Nothing like a hospital crutch. Everything from his crisp shirt to his tie that went with his jacket and the badge on his lapel, everything about him said: "We are not criminals, we are former prisoners. Those who put us in jail, they're the criminals."

While three dozen journalists — from Germany's *Der Spiegel* to *The American Prospect* and Belgium's *Le Soir* — were still shell-shocked by the conference and the footage from Guantanamo, Torger from Norway and I led Sami away to talk to us. In the middle, we were joined by Elin from Sweden, Robert from Kenya, Mar Sentenera from Spain, and Iqbal from Pakistan. Torture has no international borders. *Human nature is not as good as you would like it to be…*

We sat squeezed up close, dictaphones poised. I was swinging my right foot as well. Sami's cane was on the floor and had rolled under my heel. If I put my foot on the floor, I might step on the cane. It would be like trampling on his dignity. And that's what torture's like: a direct assault on human dignity.

"Sami, many thanks for finding the strength to be here. Can you tell us how it all started?"

"Sure. In the autumn of 2001, my colleague from Al Jazeera was covering the war in Afghanistan with me as cameraman. We travelled to Afghanistan on legal work visas. We filmed everything we could. Including American troops grabbing people, killing women and children, destroying homes, mosques, and schools. When the military action became too hot for us, we left for Pakistan, sat it out for a few days, then went back to Afghanistan, to film a conference being held by the head of the Taliban, Mullah Omar. Then we set off back to Pakistan to go home.

"We were already on our way to Doha in Qatar, where Al Jazeera is based, when we heard that the Taliban had fallen and a new government had come to power. Al Jazeera's managers asked us to go back to Afghanistan to cover what was happening.

"In Islamabad I obtained a new work visa and then we went to Chaman in Pakistan, on the border with Afghanistan. From there, we planned to go to Kandahar. It was December 15. At the border post, they let my colleague through but not me.

"When I asked why I had been stopped and not the other seventy-five journalists who had crossed the border that day, the border guards showed me a letter from Pakistan's special services. It said, in English, that they were to arrest an Al Jazeera cameraman. The first name was mine but it was someone else's surname and passport number. Even so, I was arrested.

"I was held in a Pakistani special forces' jail for three days then handed over to the US military. The Americans sent me to the Bagram military base, near Kabul, where I was kept for another sixteen days. From there, I was moved to Kandahar, where I stayed for nearly five months, right up until I was sent to Guantanamo."

"Did the torture start in Pakistan?"

"Not as far as I remember, no. I was only interrogated in Pakistan. It all started in Bagram. Our clothes were taken away. We were left naked in the cold — the water there freezes in January. We weren't allowed to talk. Or to stand up and move about. We were beaten all over.

"A week later, I was taken for my first interrogation. 'You're working for Osama Bin Laden!' they said. I replied that no, I was a journalist, nothing more. They kept insisting: 'Yes, you are! You've interviewed him!' I denied it, saying that as a journalist, I wouldn't be ashamed to interview Osama Bin Ladin although I hadn't done so, that I had a colleague in Kabul and it was his interview. 'So, you're working with him,' they said. I explained that this wasn't true, that he worked in Kabul and I was in Kandahar and if they didn't believe me, there were witnesses at CNN.

"So, during the interrogations, it became clear that they were looking for the Al Jazeera cameraman who, together with a colleague from Kabul, had interviewed Osama Bin Ladin. The cameraman was called Sami but he was from Morocco, whereas I'm from Sudan. They were trying to find out who had helped them get to Osama Bin Ladin and where, geographically, the interview had taken place.

"That person had long been in Doha, thank God. The Pakistanis arrested me and I doubt it was a mistake. They knew I wasn't the right guy. But they handed me over and got money in return.

"In the end, the Americans admitted both in Bagram and Kandahar: 'You're not the one we wanted. The Pakistanis have sent us the wrong guy. But what will you say if we let you go?' I said: 'The truth. That you tortured us.' They all laughed: 'Fine, wait a few days and we'll let you go.'"

"When did you know you would be sent to Guantanamo?"

"Not until I actually went. It first became clear on June 13, at half past eleven, when we were taken to the airport. In the film you saw us put on that plane bound and gagged."

"What happened next?"

"To be really brief, there are no rights in Guantanamo. You're in the hands of the USA. They do what they want. They can beat you up. They can put you in isolation for forty days or more. In solitary, in a cell only ninety by seventy centimetres, where you sleep and eat and go to the toilet. They only let you see the sun twice a week for 20 minutes at a time. Twice a week they open the cell for barely three minutes. That's when they bring you water. They won't let you sleep. They won't let you eat. They won't let you seek legal redress. They won't even let you say your prayers. Contact with relatives is forbidden. Nine months had passed before they told my family where I was. The Red Cross helped.

"All they need is for you to agree to cooperate. They talk about it openly: 'You've got to cooperate, you've got to spy for us. Then we'll give you citizenship, we'll give you money but the amount will depend on the information you give us.' I refused, of course. But as soon as you tell them 'no', they start torturing you to get a 'yes'."

"What was the most dreadful thing?"

"Worst of all was that it's not only soldiers doing the torturing but doctors and psychologists too. Even the most heinous sexual stuff. If I start listing it all, we'll be here all night. The photos from Abu Ghraib prison in Iraq were the thin end of the wedge, barely a tenth of what goes on in Guantanamo. If ever somebody wanted to make a film, they'd have eight hundred story lines. People from fifty countries whose stories are the same as mine."

"Is it true that children are being held in Guantanamo?"

"Yes, there are more than fifty. I saw for myself. Some under the age of nine."

"Are they held in a separate camp?"

"Some are and some are with the adults. A boy of fourteen lived with me. He was tortured just like the adults. He lost an eye and became half blind in the other. And I saw an old man of around ninety. There were families too. A son and his father, but they kept them well away from one another."

"In your fifth year in the prison you went on hunger strike…"

"Yes, and it wasn't just me. There were twenty of us. No-one even noticed for a month but then… If you've lost a lot of weight during that time, they sit you down in the torture chamber and start forcing water into you. After a month on hunger strike, the stomach shrinks so much that it can't take more than a couple of small cubes of food and a small bottle of water. But they literally shove it into you. You immediately start retching but it has no effect. It just hurts. Then they start pouring it into your nose."

"At that time, your lawyer said he had seen you in prison… that you had lost the will to live. Sami, where did you get the strength to come through this?"

"Firstly, thanks to the Almighty. Secondly… When I arrived there I was sure I wouldn't be able to survive … I could see that lots of people had gone out of their minds… at that point I told myself: 'Sami, you're a journalist. You've been given the chance to see all this'… You've heard, haven't you, that there are no journalists there? Those who were allowed in from outside could only see the surroundings. They couldn't talk to the prisoners. Whereas I was living among the prisoners. I was a prisoner. I could see it all for myself. I heard more than eight hundred stories. I told myself I was a journalist even if I was in Guantanamo. We journalists believe that we tell society the truth. We believe that we help people be heard who would not be heard without us.

"And thirdly… most importantly… when I learnt that my colleagues from various countries were trying to secure my release, I realized I wasn't alone. That gave me greater strength and endurance. When we know we're not alone, we have more chance of getting through our ordeals."

"How did you know people were campaigning on your behalf?"

"From the guards. They weren't all the same. Some tormented you for no reason. They'd show me a letter from my son with every line crossed out so that I couldn't read it. There was just the name at the end so it was obvious who it was from. On days like that I could only wonder, 'What did I do today for them to behave like that?'

"But there were others who saw us as human beings. Not that they actually helped us. They just didn't torment us, didn't pick on us. If I met those guys, I wouldn't hide my respect — they showed me respect too. One of them gave me a paper that had an article about me. He believed I was a journalist. That's how I knew people were campaigning for me."

"Did you see any journalists in Guantanamo? We saw Norwegian TV's film today."

"I did. The Norwegians wore blue clothes. But do you really

not know? Journalists are always shown the 'comfort zone' — cells with blow-up mattresses, a metal toilet, a toilet roll even. There are always two people living there as a reward for 'good behaviour.' Those are the cells they are shown."

"Sami, how did you find out you were going to be released?"

"My lawyer wrote to me. He told me there were no charges against me, that I hadn't done anything, basically. And then, prisoners they were preparing to release were given clothes in a particular colour — beige instead of orange so the guards knew you weren't to be tortured any more. When I was given that kind of clothing, I knew I would be released."

"Al Jazeera has shown a military aircraft landing in Sudan and you being taken to hospital on a stretcher. What were you thinking then?"

"I was in a critical condition. By that time, I had spent 480 days on hunger strike. I'd received no medical assistance. The plane had flown twenty hours, direct from Guantanamo. In hospital, I immediately asked for my son. When I'd last seen him, he was fourteen months old. Now he had to be seven and a half but I didn't even know if he was alive. I didn't know what had happened to my family. Every time they brought me a letter with the lines crossed out I felt that my son…it was as if he had died… So when they brought him in…"

"Yes, we saw how you hugged him and couldn't let go. Can you put those feelings into words?"

"Probably not. I was trying not to lose control so that I didn't just hug him to death."

"Did the US authorities set any conditions for your release?"

"They tried to persuade the Sudanese authorities not to let me leave the country, to ban me from working as a journalist, to stop me talking about my time in Bagram, Kandahar, or Guantanamo. The Sudanese didn't accept their conditions, however. They just said that since there were no charges I was innocent and free. A week later I was given a passport. They've done the same as regards other Sudanese released from Guantanamo. They've all been given accommodation and a plot of land and offered medical treatment. But that's only in Sudan. It's been quite different in other countries. In some places people are held in isolation or in jail, some people are under surveillance, some aren't allowed to leave the country."

"Sami, after all that had happened, you went back to work and you are now head of the human rights desk. Six months ago, several ex-prisoners, yourself included, set up a humanitarian foundation in London, the Guantanamo Justice Centre. What do you plan to do?"

"We'll be working in three areas. Defending the rights of those still in Guantanamo and of those who've left and need help. And we also intend to restore justice. We're planning to initiate legal proceedings against those responsible for the torture. It's not easy to do, especially against Bush, Blair, and Musharraf, especially in the USA. But we're going to try. There's a team of lawyers working with us. We'll do everything we can. We have no grievances against Americans in general. We respect everyone. We are only accusing the administration of that country and those who carried out acts of torture or gave the orders."

I would not have brought in this story even though it is of value in itself, had not the spirit of our story shown in it too. At one time, in 1977, Saumen Guha, a prisoner in a jail in Calcutta, dreamed of getting out of prison and joining forces with other people to bring collective proceedings, to put the torturers on trial. He could find no support when he left prison. His former cellmates didn't believe in justice.

But Saumen has successors now. Sami al-Haj has never heard of, knows nothing about the Guhas, nor does he know that for nineteen years the road to justice unfairly robbed them of their lives or that, in the end, justice looked very different from the way they had imagined it at the start — the state was sufficiently cunning to come up smelling of roses even if victory, moral victory, was not on its side. I didn't tell him. Such knowledge will not stop him. Only justice heals the soul. Even deferred justice.

I would not have used this story even though it is of value in itself had it not embodied a new tendancy. As I listened to Sami's story, I asked myself: How much sleep have his torturers lost already? And how much more will they lose?

As much as Eric Fair, a young US army contractor? Unable to bear three years of nightmares, he wrote in the *The Washington Post* and made his confession in a Danish documentary, *My Brother's Keeper*.

When he was serving as an Arabic linguist in Iraq, Eric interpreted during interrogations. The commanding officer asked him for help. Eric said okay. All he did was to go into the cell every 15 minutes and wake the prisoner. If a person is prevented from sleeping for around five days, they go mad.

Back home, his contract service complete, Eric discovered he was not alone. There was somebody watching him. A man without a face would appear to him at night. He would stand in the corner of the room and beg for help. The pitiful whimper would rise to a sob and pierce Eric's brain like a spear. When the sob burst into a cry, Eric would leap up in a cold sweat. Awake, he would realize there was silence all around. There was no one in the corner. The cry was in his own head. It was a revelation, albeit a belated one. There are always two people in the "victim-torturer" relationship. First, he's your captive. Then, you are his. It doesn't matter whether you tortured him for a minute or a year. As soon as you step on to that line, you've crossed it.

* * *

"Inge… Bent… Who's all this for? Tablecloth, coffee, open sandwiches, and dessert…" I counted the delicacies on the oval table in a kitchen piled high with documents, where the main item of furniture wasn't the fat-bellied china cupboard but the bookshelves to left and right. "We agreed. I was just dropping by."

"No, no," said Bent, taking me by the shoulder in fatherly fashion. "Make yourself at home."

"Thank you but why go to so much…"

A vigorous "ha!" escaped from the utility room that contained the fridge. "Ha!" was a battle cry, typical of Inge. "Next time there won't be so much but we need to celebrate today. You're our first guest since Bent was discharged from hospital (five months earlier Bent had undergone six hours of open-heart surgery).

Inge detached herself from the fridge, holding a plate of prawns. Round her neck, in the neck of her blouse, was France's highest decoration, established by Napoleon Bonaparte, the Order of Commander of the Legion of Honour. She even wore it at home.

"Just imagine, we went swimming in the Øresund yesterday for the first time since the hospital! (The Øresund is the strait between Denmark and Sweden and just outside their flat).

"What, Bent too? But… it's the end of October! The water's not exactly bathing temperature."

"What can you do? You have to keep fit in our line of work."

That was one thing I did know. Inge and Bent are the legendary Danish doctor couple to whom this book is dedicated. They didn't know that, however, and would find out only when the book was published. Inge was 70 and Bent 84. No other couple in the world knew more than they did about the "very worst there is in mankind." They were the pioneers of this work. They were the parents of this mission. They had chosen the heaviest stone and pushed it without a break for thirty-five years.

I'd come to ask them what motivated them but let's not start with that. In fact… I didn't need to start. I was just a guest. I feasted my eyes on them and listened. The conversation flowed unaided. I tried to catch any pauses or halts. I observed the shadows of their thoughts. I was content just to be breathing the same air.

I was afraid that one day they would simply vanish and pass into the next world. I was afraid that those who came after them would not have the same degree of courage or passionate commitment, not to mention the love that is needed here more than anywhere in order to push that stone forward. I was afraid these others would just be administrators, would simply be paid for their work, but not be aflame or consumed. At least, not the way Inge and Bent were. The last mahatmas of our era.

"Inge… Bent… you've been treating and rehabilitating torture victims for thirty-five years now. Thanks to your work, the world now knows what happens to someone when they are subjected to the very worst and how such people can be helped. What matters now?"

Inge was the first to answer. "It is very important that in the end we understand that we don't only need to help the victims but to punish the torturers too. This is important for many reasons. For the victims to be better rehabilitated and to prevent future violence. Fortunately, we now have the UN Geneva Convention Against Torture. We call it *our* convention. Then there is the Istanbul Protocol, the Manual on Effective Investigation and Documentation of Torture. These two documents offer the chance to put torturers on trial."

"But there are so many of them," I said in an attempt at a challenge, bearing in mind that what might be recorded on paper and what life might ultimately concede were as different as plus and minus.

Inge smiled:

"Of course, they are legion, high and low, but I think the greatest danger to society are those who give the orders. We began with them. One of the first that I'd like to take to court is Bush, of course. The second is Rumsfeld. This work has already started in the USA. A lawsuit has been filed against Rumsfeld in Illinois. The first results weren't from there though but from Florida. Two generals were convicted there recently. One was a former defence minister of El Salvador. The court ruled that the ex-minister had to pay fifty million dollars to three of his victims. As for Bush…"

"There's news just in from Canada," Bent continued calmly. "When Bush was visiting Vancouver, a local organization brought charges against him. But in court they were told they couldn't bring charges against the president. He has immunity under the Vienna Convention. The organization didn't stop there and went to a higher court where it was told, 'Yes, you can. We'll handle the case. In addition to the Vienna Convention, there's the Convention Against Torture.' So Bush doesn't go to Vancouver any more or anywhere in British Colombia. If he does, the authorities are obliged to arrest him. It used to be the same for Pinochet. When he was being investigated, he lived under house arrest at his London flat."

"Of course, Bush can travel to other places but then, we've only just started." That was Inge again. "In exactly the same way, we initiated proceedings against Mugabe when he went to Paris. Bent himself drew up the affidavit and I told the French authorities that I would testify in person against Mugabe in court. Mugabe doesn't go to France anymore. We'll do the same to Putin and all the rest. They must not be left in peace or that scoundrel from Israel."

"What scoundrel?" I asked, not understanding.

"Haven't you heard the story?" said Inge, astonished. "Let me tell you. Eighteen months ago, an aircraft from Israel arrived in London. One of their torturers was on board. The British said… Bent, can you remember what happened?"

"Of course. They said, 'He is accused of being a party to torture. We are obliged to place him under arrest while an investigation takes place…'"

"But it was leaked. The Israeli scoundrel found out what was going on while he was still on the plane. He didn't leave the plane and flew straight home. But that was a victory for us too. We don't want any of them to be left in peace." Inge took off her glasses, wiped the lenses with a cloth, and looked at the light. "Incidentally, have you heard what a good start things have got off to in Chile? President Michelle Bachelet herself has instituted proceedings against former senior officials who ordered torture. One of them has already been sentenced to thirty years in prison. That's life, given his age. Just think. He gave orders in 1976 and went on trial in 2008. There's no statute of limitations for the crime of torture."

"And that's only the beginning," said Bent. "There are still so few trials against the masters of torture. Archana's situation was incredible. Unique, you might say. She and her family were among the first to bring a private prosecution. But they were the very first to win their case in court. And, moreover, through their own efforts. They received no financial aid, just a few crumbs from Amnesty and the IRCT. But that's nothing compared to the expenditure they sustained. They lived on bread and water for twenty years. They pulled off the most extraordinary feat but sadly not without personal losses."

"And what do you think about the sentence? Should Runu have gone to prison?"

"Of course, he should," Bent said fervently. "But a year behind bars for a scoundrel who gave orders and took part himself... The Calcutta verdict was unjustifiably lenient. I would say suspiciously so. But I don't know of any trials even since Archana's case where the sentence has been any harsher. Of course, you remember the scandal over Abu Ghraib prison in Iraq, and the photos in the press? A gang, and there's no other way to put it, of US troops, men and women, took photos of themselves against a background of tormented prisoners. One photo showed a woman. She was only very young. She was posing on naked bodies."

"Sabrina Harman from Virginia, born in 1978. She held the rank of specialist in the military police when she arrived in Iraq. In court, she was accused of sexual, physical, and psychological torture, wasn't she?" I was trying to remember what I'd read in the papers.

For the first time, Bent was a little angry although he continued to look calm.

"It's hard to believe this woman only got six months in jail. And why? You see, she hadn't been trained in how to treat prisoners. She didn't know about the Geneva Convention. But, if you had seen what she did, Dina! As well as what she was charged with, she called Muslim men 'pigs' arseholes'. And whatever gap there was in her police training, I don't think you need a degree to know that you can't treat people like that!"

"A lack of education — that's just an excuse, a ruse by the defence. I think the issue is something else…"

"And you're right to think that," Bent agreed again. "It's always the state that is behind torture. *The state*. No-one else. If it's not the state, it's not torture, it's something else — under the convention. Every time a case is brought about torture, the state is accused in the person of its representative. But what state wants to hand down a judgement on itself?"

"And what was the story with the Pope? Inge has met a lot of people: Nelson Mandela, Kofi Annan, Bill Clinton, Bill Gates, not to mention kings and princesses, and a great many prime ministers. Everyone gave her their support. It was only with the Pope that there was nearly a row."

"You see, Dina…" said Bent, his gaze moving out to the Øresund outside, "when we doctors look at Jesus Christ, we don't think of him as Christians do. In our eyes, Jesus is a typical torture victim, the most celebrated perhaps, but a victim all the same. If you look at the Bible through a doctor's eyes, everything in it suggests that Jesus responded to being tormented like a typical torture victim. At the very end even he signed — if it can be put like that — he gave in and signed. He cried out: 'My God, my God, why have you forsaken me?'"

"If you knew how many times we've heard those words from people who came to us for treatment!" Inge exclaimed.

"Everyone who has been subjected to torture has screamed it out. Our thinking was that since the church so vigorously exploits the symbolism of victimhood, why shouldn't it help us in our work? The successful rehabilitation of victims can't happen without donors.

"That was in 2001… wasn't it, Bent? The Catholic Church was holding its first meeting on human rights. I was asked to speak. Bent and I went. Bent spoke about how doctors perceive Jesus. After the meeting, we were already at the airport when we were approached by some cardinals: 'We'd like to invite you to an audience with the Pope.' 'Thank you very much,' we replied, 'but, unfortunately, we don't have much time. We need to board the plane.' 'Everyone has time for an audience with the Pope.' 'Shall we do it now then?' 'No, you'll have to cancel your flight.' 'I'm sorry but that's not possible. We have a lot of work to do and we can't afford to change the tickets.' 'Hm, right, we'll sort it out now.'

"In a nutshell, we met the Pope at the church where he's usually to be found. He was sort of…" (Inge waved her arms about helplessly). "I told him about our work, how Jesus looks to a doctor, and that the cross is a weapon of torture. I also said: 'Since you value these symbols, since you go everywhere with them, since you look on them every day or at least on Sundays, you could help rehabilitate victims.' The Pope muttered something that we couldn't make out at all. Then we left for the airport. And what do you think? Did he deign to help? Not a bit of it. His response was a great big shameless no. That's why I don't believe in the church or in church symbols. I believe only in specific people who are prepared to roll up their sleeves and work hard."

"What do you think about the recent World Public Opinion surveys, which showed that nearly one in two people, not in just one but in many countries, is in favour of torture if it helps prevent terrorism?" I asked. "It seems society's indifference to torture is increasing."

"People don't know what they are condoning. They don't

know what they are turning a blind eye to," Inge sighed crossly. "Torture can't prevent terrorism. Torture has the opposite effect. It boosts terrorism. One of our friends, the Chilean psychiatrist, Manuel Fernandez, who lives in Uppsala, Sweden, recently carried out some research. These are new studies, incidentally. A person who has been through torture experiences changes in the left cerebral hemisphere, in the regions responsible for emotions... for emotions and for mood. These changes aren't always permanent but they do always occur. You will get my meaning."

"Are there any known defence mechanisms? In countries without democracy, no-one is insured against torture. Everyone's in the at-risk zone. Is there any way of mitigating the effects?"

Inge thought for a moment:

"The first thing someone needs to know when they are taken into a torture chamber is that they cannot resist. Not on *their* territory. Anyone can be broken in there. It's simply a matter of time ... a week, a day...

"During the years of Nazi occupation, my father was a member of the resistance. He warned his family and friends in advance: 'If I'm captured, I won't say anything for the first twenty-four hours so that you've got time to look to your own safety. After that, I can't give any guarantees.' Even then, people knew that torture robs us of courage. Today, it happens even more quickly because the torturers employ doctors and psychologists.

"On several occasions I have been in a situation where I might have been imprisoned and I always asked myself how I would behave. I decided in advance that I wouldn't try to be a hero, I'd sign everything."

"And that, by the way, is one of the defence mechanisms we do know about," Bent explained. "The survival instinct. You can't just dismiss it."

"That's right. It's one way to survive under torture," Inge agreed. "I will never forget one Pakistani doctor. I've been to

Pakistan many times. Once, a colleague came up to me and said: 'They came for me at night, Inge. Took me to the police station and showed me the tortured body of a detainee and demanded that I wrote down that he'd died in a car crash. 'If you don't, we'll kill your son on his way home from school tomorrow.'

"What they did to that doctor, even though they didn't lay a finger on him, is also torture. Very serious, psychological torture. But that man didn't even know what was happening to him and I couldn't bring myself to tell him. But I tell myself and others: if something happens, sign whatever you like, otherwise you'll kill yourself and your family. Your task is to get out of there and then you can think about how to live with what happened."

"If you just sign anything and say what the investigator forces you to say, torture doesn't in fact guarantee that the information obtained is accurate. So those who attempt to justify torture from the point of view of garnering the intelligence needed to fight terrorism are not only deceiving themselves but society as well."

"Of course. Exactly that," said Inge. "Torture doesn't guarantee a thing. There is nothing more stupid and amoral than governments that rely on information obtained with the aid of torture."

"Are there any known ways of coping *afterwards*? I mean *after* the torture?

Bent looked at Inge:

"That's a big question, by the way. We give the answer in detail in a five-day seminar. But the short version… could you tell her?"

Inge looked up at a picture on the wall:

"Many years ago when we were just preparing to take on this work, I brought together scientists from various countries so that we could think where to start. One of them was called Leo Aitinger. He was a Norwegian psychiatry professor and a former inmate in Auschwitz. He was the first to come up with a formula for the initial stage of rehabilitating such people.

"The first thing that has to be done is to try and establish a daily routine and ordinary life. The person must know that when he wakes up in the morning he will be able simply to get washed, have something to eat, send the children off to school etc. just as usual. A routine has to be established.

"Secondly, it must be possible to make choices. To go or not to go, to do or not to do, to accept or not to accept. Leo Aitinger proved this using the example of Auschwitz. Every day prisoners were given their rations — a miserly piece of bread. Some ate it all there and then. Others broke it into pieces — I'll eat this bit now and that bit later. And do you know what? The ones who were able to give themselves a choice ... of now or later... they survived better than the rest."

"And it's only once a daily routine and ordinary life are established that the person can begin to look at how to deal with his feelings," Bent said. "Coping mechanisms mean, consciously and unconsciously, seeking a way out of the chaos of your feelings. A way to live despite what happened. If you don't manage to find a way on your own, and not everyone does, you need to try and do it with a psychologist. Psychotherapy aims to help a person find their own key, a personal coping mechanism.

"I do know one such mechanism. A person who has been tortured lives with a very profound feeling of humiliation. Particularly those who have been physically abused or forced to do something shameful. They are tormented by a feeling of guilt. But they must tell themselves: 'I'm not the one who's been humiliated. They are! I'm not to blame! They are!' I am forever saying this to the prisoners I meet during prison inspections. They tell me about themselves for half an hour and I leave. Leaving is always painful because I can't promise anything. To anyone. The only thing I say is: 'I will reveal how your government treats its prisoners. Perhaps the situation will improve in due course.' I always talk in such a way that people can tell I respect them. I say: 'You are not the ones to blame! The ones to blame are the ones who have done this!' It's all I can do under the circumstances.

"This is why I like the message of your book. You're saying: 'Who are the victims now? The torturers!' And it's true. Whoever abuses another person turns themselves into a victim. Because from that moment on they will be afraid. They will be afraid of vengeance. They will be afraid of the law. They will be afraid that someone will come along... someone like me... and make them a real victim."

"Why do people become torturers?" I asked the key question, not for a minute thinking there would not be an answer.

Bent looked at Inge:

"Well, our views differ on that one."

"You go first then! Ha!" said Inge, looking at him.

"Okay. I have been inspecting prisons across the world for many years now. There are countries where we discovered torture in every single police station. Can you imagine? Every single one! You have a situation where there are a hundred thousand police officers and every one of them's a torturer. Of course, not all that hundred thousand are sadists. From the psychiatric point of view, the majority are perfectly normal. Like many other men, they like women, enjoy a beer, love football. Unlike 'many others', they carry out acts of torture at work. And we are constantly asking ourselves why.

"There is one explanation. The police officers don't see the arrestees as human beings. They only see them as criminals. They're the people who put bombs in buses, sell cocaine, run prostitution, sexually abuse children. They know that kind of person is a danger to society. They think of them in advance as the enemy and they are taught to treat the enemy like enemies, in other words, like animals. A person with that attitude can quickly become a torturer. That's my opinion.

"I'll tell you a story. I was conducting a seminar for the Zimbabwean authorities. I was teaching them how to draft a report for the UN Committee Against Torture. In a break on the first day, the head of all the country's police stations came over and asked, 'But Professor, if we don't beat them, how will we extract confessions?' You see?! This commander didn't even think there were other ways of investigating a case... evidence, witnesses. He could tackle the problem only one way — by forcing a confession. When I said, 'Just remember! You have no right to inflict beatings!' he couldn't believe what he was hearing. He gasped in surprise and roared: 'What?'"

"Whereas I think," Inge finally added, "that people torture because they cannot refuse an order. Submission is a very profound phenomenon."

"There's that as well," Bent agreed.

"But what's the solution?" I said with a helpless gesture. "There's legislation in the form of the Geneva Convention. Is it the case that society's main task is still what it was one thousand years ago... to civilize people?"

"It is," said Bent with the same gesture. "A lot of countries have adopted the Convention Against Torture, but the police do the same even in those countries. So yes, civilizing, teaching, and more teaching. And explanations, explanations, explanations. From the bottom up and the top down. The prime minister has to say: 'I'm against torture.' The justice minister has to say: 'I'm against torture.' The interior minister has to say: 'I'm against torture.' They all say have to say, out loud: 'I won't stand for it. Every offender will be punished.' Then, perhaps, change will come."

"It's not just the police that must be civilized, but the politicians too," Inge elaborated. "And those who give the order for torture absolutely must be punished!"

"That's right but we mustn't forget," Bent continued, "that no-one can use being given an order as an excuse, neither a soldier nor a police officer. The Convention examines that issue in detail. If a member of the military in Iraq or somewhere in Chechnya is given an order to torture someone, their duty is to respond by saying: 'No, Captain! Under the law, I can't. If I do what you say, I'll be committing a crime and I will be punished.'"

"But they don't know about that. An order means everything to them!" said Inge, starting to get cross.

"Even so, the law exists and there is only one solution: more and more teaching. We have to keep saying over and over again: torture is not allowed. Under any circumstances. No matter what the situation in the country. Not in war time or peace time. It's not allowed. Under any circumstances. It's an easy law to learn."

"How many years do you think are still needed for this way of thinking to become the norm?" I asked.

"Unfortunately, we won't live to see the results of our work," Inge sighed with a smile. "It will take another fifty years or so. Perhaps you will see it, Dina. As for us, we're already seeing something else. People who came out of the concentration camps sixty years ago come up to us and shake our hands. They weep and I weep with them."

"I will never forget being asked to have dinner once with a man who had been in the resistance during the war." Bent again gazed out at the Øresund. "He, his grown-up daughter, and I were at the table. Suddenly, he started talking about what the Gestapo had done to him. Not about the concentration camp where he had been a prisoner. Just about what the Gestapo had done. It was sixty-two years ago. His daughter burst into tears and said, 'Papa, why did you never tell us? If we had known, if you'd breathed even a word, we would have understood you better.' He replied quietly: 'It was just too awful. Too awful to communicate. You can't talk about such things.'

"Inge, Bent, what motivates you in this work?"

Bent first looked at Inge and then at me.

"I have known Inge for thirty-five years and she is, in short, driven solely by anger. She is constantly thinking, 'This is too much. For God's sake, what are they doing! This must not be allowed! I'll fight!' So for all these years, I've been living with an angry woman. A very angry woman indeed."

"And I'm that woman! Ha!" came Inge's battle cry.

Bent went on:

"And I am Inge's opposite. I am very rarely angry. It's part of my temperament somehow. Sometimes I look at her in amazement: 'Lord, she's so irate. What on earth's going to happen next?' And the next day, I'll say to myself: 'But she was right again!'

"Life has been good to me. I had a wonderful childhood. I went through the war without serious losses. During the Nazi occupation, I wanted to join the resistance but my father wouldn't let me. I was so angry it took me a long time to recover but when the war was over I understood. It turned out my father was a leader in the resistance and couldn't let his children know. After the war, I studied to be a doctor, then became a professor. I have been a member and chair of every scientific and medical academy or group you can imagine. I have everything you could dream of. And I live with Inge. I'm eighty-four years old and I live with Inge — the very finest person in the world. Why should I be angry? Inge gets angry. She gets angry enough for us both."

As I left the flat of these people who were so dear to me, I couldn't help thinking: even if it is anger and not just the earthly name for something else, nothing drives a person more forcefully than recognition of their own involvement with the truth. There are many hands in this world that push us towards a fall and yet there are also hands that keep us from falling. Neither exists without the other, just as there is no oxidation without reduction. What is most important is that the balance not be disturbed. That, at the very least. That the hands that push us towards a fall should multiply less rapidly. That the hands that keep us from falling should not be lost. And what about in fifty years' time? Don't you think it's worth dreaming that the latter may be in the ascendant? That there may be more of them than of the former?

* * *

The integrity of the anthropologist prevents me forgetting about the question that began this story. Why does the heart not die when we think it should? Why not when something akin to death afflicts us? When the circumstances of our life are capable of cutting off our air supply and blocking out the light? When all at once life becomes a series of tribulations? Where do we find the strength to see it through? To go on living? To live at all?

A person draws energy from two sources: one inner, one outer. A great deal can be drawn from the inner source but the outer is inexhaustible. The ideal is for both to be accessible. If the external source is unattainable (it may be cut off by a prison wall), you must draw on your own resources. This skill — of drawing on your own resources — is the greatest art of all.

An art and a trial.

To see what I mean more clearly, think about mountaineers. How they move across a sheer cliff. Up and up, pull after pull, very slowly but always up. Nothing but that cliff exists for them and in order to scale it they seek out what chances of help it offers. Even the very slightest bump, even a protrusion of just a centimetre, even a gap of just a millimetre can provide a hold to support the body's weight. These chances are the external source. If there is no inner belief that the cliff can be overcome, however, there are no holds that can help.

When I sat down to write this story two years ago and asked this question, I had only Archana's answer. You can find it on one of these pages. Then came the answers of friends and later my own. The elixir of life has many flavours. The tree has many branches. If you have had to put your own to the test, please let me know. Together we will fill a book of elixirs and pass it on.

To those who most need it. And of them, there is no shortage.

Greater Copenhagen – Kolkata – Greater Copenhagen

2007–2009

ACKNOWLEDGEMENTS

I owe a debt of gratitude to many people: without them I could never have written this book.

First and foremost, I must thank the protagonists in this story and witnesses to it, who have generously and patiently shared their memories with me. A big thanks to Archana Guha and Per Jensen and the members of their Bengali family, Saikat Guha, Sibendra Guha and Padma Guha, Suranjan Maitra and Jhumu Maitra, Emmy (Smriti) Dutta, Biswajit, and Tumpa.

Thanks are due also to the pupils and staff of the Kolorah Girls' High School and many inhabitants, too many to name, of Kolorah village.

Unfortunately I was not able to meet Saumen and Latika Guha, but that in no way lessens their contribution to the story, via the collection of trial documents, entitled Battle of Archana Guha Case Against Torture in Police Custody: Arguments, Counter-arguments and Judgement at the Trial Court, edited by Saumen Guha (Calcutta, 1997), and various newspaper interviews, which also helped me reconstruct the events.

And a big thank you too to the protagonists and witnesses living in Denmark: to Doctor Inge Genefke and her husband Professor Bent Sørensen, to Professor Gudrun Boysen and her husband Doctor Troels Kardel, to Gunhild Nielsen and Helga Frimodt-Møller.

Thanks also to Yvonne Terlingen (USA), the Amnesty International representative at the UN, who also witnessed these events

Thanks to the librarian of the documentation centre of the RCT in Copenhagen, Kirsten Reimer, for making the newspaper and magazine files on the Archana Guha case available to me during the early stages of my research. Thanks also to the staff of IRCT for their support.

Thanks to Subash Ghose from Denmark and Tarit Kumar Baul from Bangladesh for volunteering their selfless contribution, translating Runu Guha Niyogi's memoirs from Bengali. Their work gave me a better understanding of many details.

Thanks are also due to Director Maxim Hodak, manager Yana Kovalskaya, editor Camilla Stein and all at Glagoslav Publications who worked on this book.

A big thank you to the Anti Torture Support Foundation in Denmark for enabling this book to be translated into English.

And thanks also to Melanie Moore and Clare Kitson for the English translation of this book.

And last, but by no means least, a big thanks to my husband, Karim, for his support and the extra hours he worked, which paid for my research expenses, including the trip to Kolkata. He was my first reader and critic.

My sincere appreciation also goes to my parents, my children and my sister, for their love and support, without which this book's journey to the reader would certainly have been longer.

Dina Yafasova

NOTES *

RCT (abbr. Rehabilitation Center for Torture Victims) — Centre based in Denmark.

IRCT (abbr. International Council for Rehabilitation of Torture Victims), head office in Copenhagen.

"You who are weary, downcast and bruised..." and "You who weep, who suffer and tremble" — These two epigraphs, before the first and second parts, are quotes from the collection *Suffering — Its Cause and Cure. Compilation from the Works of Sri Aurobindo and the Mother.*

CHAPTER 4

"I think I should drop into the story myself at this point." Quote from the novel by Dina Rubina, *On the Sunny Side of the Street.*

CHAPTER 5

I have reconstructed the story of Charu Mazumdar's arrest based on, among other sources, the memoirs of Runu Guha Niyogi, "Sada Ami Kala Ami". Extracts from his memoirs were published in, notably, the newspaper, *Telegraph Look*, in the article "How I arrested Charu Majumdar" by Runu Guha Niyogi, June 9, 1996.

---

* It is possible that I have not mentioned in this list all the materials I read while researching this book. The Archana Guha files comprise hundreds of sources from newspapers and magazines, some of which were without keywords and many of which duplicated one another or duplicated information given me in my interviews with the witnesses. I would like to apologize in advance if I have inadvertently failed to include any of the sources of information that might have been used in this work. I should be grateful to have any such lapses pointed out to me, and will be happy to add them in the next edition. — *D.Y.*

CHAPTER 6

The Secret Life of Words, 2005, dir. Isabel Coixet, film in which partially deaf Hanna is a survivor of rape and torture in the former Yugoslavia. After fleeing the war there, she received counselling from Inge Genefke.

The story of how Iron Age outwitted Bronze Age, which Archana tells her nieces, has its origin in an epic folk tale and is encountered in oral, written and dramatic variants.

"…beyond this wide earth and beyond the heavens…" —*Rigveda*, X 125.8

CHAPTER 9

"The Ogre Does What Ogres Can" — first line of W. H. Auden's poem "August 1968".

"Anyone who has experienced this desire [to sleep] knows that not even hunger or thirst are comparable with it…." — quote from the memoirs of Menachem Begin, *White Nights: The Story of a Prisoner in Russia*.

CHAPTER 12

"*All is not settled when a cause is humanly lost and hopeless…*" — *Sri Aurobindo: Thoughts and Aphorisms*. Translated by The Mother. From Volume 10 of Collected Works of the Mother Pub. Sri Aurobindo Ashram Publication Department, Pondicherry

"*There is a proverb…*" Alexander Solzhenitsyn, The Gulag Archipelago 2 trans Thomas P. Whitney Collins Harvill

"*You, (name), being an active member of the Communist (Marxist–Leninist) Party of India…*" — This quote, from the sentence of imprisonment based on MISA, appears in the collection of court documents *Battle of* Archana Guha Case *Against Torture in Police Custody*, ed. Saumen Guha.

CHAPTER 13

Seneca Letter 24.14 "Pain… you are mild if I can bear you and short-lived if I cannot." *http://www.yorku.ca/pswarney/Texts/seneca/letter_24.htm*

Includes Penguin edition the text is taken from.

CHAPTER 15

"*a collective promise of good*" — line from a poem by an anonymous 19th-century monk.

CHAPTER 16

"He felt overkeenly the social side of things." — Vladimir Nabokov, "The Stories of Vladimir Nabokov" Spring in Fialta Vladimir Nabokov, The Stories of Vladimir Nabokov (New York: Knopf, 1995) p. 375

CHAPTER 17

"*A*" — *Andersen, "B" — Bohr, "C" — Copenhagen, "D" — Dannebrog*"– The Dannebrog is Denmark's national flag.

CHAPTER 18

"Jante's law" — from the novel by the Danish-Norwegian writer Aksel Sandemose, *A Refugee Crosses His Tracks.* It is an unwritten law of Danish society, according to which a person should not think or present himself as in any way special, cleverer or better than others or with the right to teach others, that he is anything special, or that he has the right to teach others.

Suzanne Brøgger quotations taken from Deliver us from Love: pp. 123-4 Delacorte Press, Saint Lawrence, 1976. Trans. Thomas Teal

CHAPTER 19

"Poor folk, Christian discourses, and nausea" — titles of works by Dostoevsky, Kierkegaard, and Sartre.

CHAPTER 21

"The life we have here is real — the events and heroes are drawn from life. Archana and Per could not be happy for a long time yet, for the oil was already — remember Bulgakov? — bought, already spilled...This is a reference to Mikhail Bulgakov's novel *The Master and Margarita* in which a character's death is inevitable since he will slip on sunflower oil that has already been purchased and spilled.

"There was great rejoicing, an absurd amount, when her new life began…" — these words of Saumen are published in the collection of court documents *Battle of* Archana Guha Case *Against Torture in Police Custody*, ed. Saumen Guha.

CHAPTER 24

"The case that led to this prosecution began on July 18, 1974 at around 1.30 hours"– this and later quotes are from the sentencing and other court documents in the collection *Battle of* Archana Guha Case *Against Torture in Police Custody*, ed. Saumen Guha.

"Yes, I know, many innocent people were the victims of special operations in those turbulent times…"– this and later quotes are from the memoirs of Runu Guha Niyogi, *Sada Ami Kala Ami*, an extract from which was published in the newspaper *Telegraph Look* under the title "How I Arrested Charu Majumdar" by Runu Guha Niyogi, June 9, 1996

EPILOGUE

"I fear not execution, not torture and not hate." - Halfdan Rasmussen.

"Kolkata: Controversial former policeman Runu Guha Niyogi died on Thursday night at Calcutta Medical Research Institute. He was 66." *The Times of India*, "Runu Guha Niyogi is Dead". June 22, 2001

"Literature that is not the breath of contemporary society, that dares not transmit the pains and fears of that society, Open letter to the Fourth Soviet Writers' Congress (16 May 1967) "The Struggle Intensifies," Solzhenitsyn: A Documentary Record," ed. Leopold Labedz (1970). From wikipedia.

Samir Kuntar, convicted of murder in Israel, exchanged 16 July 2008

"For every man tortured, ten terrorists are born" — Julie Christie wrote that "Fifty years ago, the Nobel Laureate Albert Camus said, 'For every man tortured, ten terrorists are born'" in *New Letters. A Magazine of Writing and Art*, vol.74 no.1.

"I don't believe these things make successful strategies" and "We can't go down to the level of our enemies. If we do, it's going to come back at us later on." — quote from "The Experiment", by Jane Mayer, *The New Yorker*, July 11-18, 2005.

"The best thing in a human being is 'to be kind, to be proud, to be fearless.' The worst 'to stink, to cheat, to torture.'" Vladimir Nabokov, BBC interview 1969, quoted in *Strong Opinions*, Vintage Books, New York, 1973.

"Their noblest instincts I have e'er inflamed" Pushkin: The Memorial trans. Martha Gilbert Dickinson Bianchi *www.gutenberg.net*

Glagoslav Publications Catalogue

- *METRO 2033* (Dutch Edition) by Dmitry Glukhovsky
- *METRO 2034* (Dutch Edition) by Dmitry Glukhovsky
- *A Poet and Bin Laden* by Hamid Ismailov
- *A Russian Story* by Eugenia Kononenko
- *Kobzar* by Taras Shevchenko
- *The Stone Bridge* by Alexander Terekhov
- *King Stakh's Wild Hunt* by Uladzimir Karatkevich
- *Depeche Mode* by Serhii Zhadan
- *Wolf Messing – The True Story of Russia`s Greatest Psychic* by Tatiana Lungin
- *Herstories*, An Anthology of New Ukrainian Women Prose Writers
- *Watching The Russians* (Dutch Edition) by Maria Konyukova
- *A Book Without Photographs* by Sergei Shargunov
- *The Grand Slam and Other Stories* (Dutch Edition) by Leonid Andreev
- *The Battle of the Sexes Russian Style* by Nadezhda Ptushkina
- *Down Among The Fishes* by Natalka Babina
- *disUNITY* by Anatoly Kudryavitsky
- *Sankya* by Zakhar Prilepin
- *Andrei Tarkovsky – A Life on the Cross* by Lyudmila Boyadzhieva
- *Solar Plexus* by Rustam Ibragimbekov
- *Don't Call me a Victim!* by Dina Yafasova
- *Tsarina Alexandra's Diary* (Dutch)

More coming soon...